MHA 11-16

4-16

SECRETS SHE KEPT

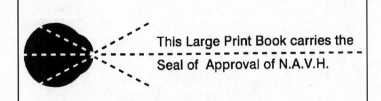

This Large Print Book carries the
Seal of Approval of N.A.V.H.

SECRETS SHE KEPT

CATHY GOHLKE

THORNDIKE PRESS
A part of Gale, Cengage Learning

GALE
CENGAGE Learning·

Farmington Hills, Mich • San Francisco • New York • Waterville, Maine
Meriden, Conn • Mason, Ohio • Chicago

GALE
CENGAGE Learning·

Thorndike Press® Large Print Christian Historical Fiction.
The text of this Large Print edition is unabridged.
Other aspects of the book may vary from the original edition.
Set in 16 pt. Plantin.

LIBRARY OF CONGRESS CATALOGING-IN-PUBLICATION DATA

Names: Gohlke, Cathy.
Title: Secrets she kept / by Cathy Gohlke.
Description: Large print edition. | Waterville, Maine : Thorndike Press, 2016. |
    © 2015 | Series: Thorndike Press large print Christian historical fiction
Identifiers: LCCN 2015041327| ISBN 9781410486967 (hardcover) | ISBN 1410486966
    (hardcover)
Subjects: LCSH: Large type books. | GSAFD: Christian fiction.
Classification: LCC PS3607.O3448 S43 2016 | DDC 813/.6—dc23
LC record available at http://lccn.loc.gov/2015041327

Published in 2016 by arrangement with Tyndale House Publishers, Inc.

Printed in Mexico
1 2 3 4 5 6 7 20 19 18 17 16

For Daniel,
My Dear Son
and
Fellow History Explorer

I delight in seeing the world
through your eyes.
All my love . . . forever.

ACKNOWLEDGMENTS

Many contributed in spirit, in prayer, and in fact to the journey of this book. I am deeply grateful to . . .

The late Corrie ten Boom and her faith-filled family for their obedience and passion in serving the Lord and His people. Their courageous story of helping and hiding Jewish people, and the consequences their family suffered at the hands of the Nazis, as told through *The Hiding Place* (book with John and Elizabeth Sherrill and film produced by Billy Graham), inspired and convicted me as a young woman, and inspires and convicts me still. Corrie's and Betsie's ability to forgive by the grace of the One who offers forgiveness freely is a magnificent reminder and a light to my path.

Rubin Sztajer, Holocaust survivor, for tirelessly sharing his experiences before and during WWII — as a prisoner at Dachau and, later, as one who overcame great odds to build a new life in America. His moving memories of determination, human compassion, and resiliency of spirit inspired part of this story.

Two other Holocaust survivors — one Gentile woman now in America and one Jewish man in Germany — who graciously shared their amazing survival stories, but who for family reasons wish to remain unnamed. One of those was truly a miracle child born from a heap of corpses at Dachau — her mother survived with barely a pulse when rescued by American liberators. The other realizes that anti-Semitism is on the rise throughout the world and, although we say and pray "never again," knows that the world has too short a memory.

WWII veterans in the US and in Germany who shared their stories. History is said to be written by the victors, but I've learned that we each embrace our own story and our own view of history.

Jamie Dow Suplee, son of one of the Nuremberg trial lawyers, who years after the war met with some of the Nazi officers his father helped prosecute. Thank you for sharing your insights into the Nazi psyche.

My son, Daniel, who joined me for WWII walking tours of Berlin and the Sachsenhausen and Natzweiler concentration camps, and who interpreted the stories of museum guides in France. My husband, Dan, who joined me in visiting the Ravensbruk and Natzweiler concentration camps and interpreted German stories of Wehrmacht veterans and Holocaust survivors in Germany. My daughter, Elisabeth, who explored Berlin with me and shares my passion for stories. That we four made this journey together was an amazing gift and a blessing I'll treasure always.

Museums and their curators and guides in Berlin and at Ravensbruk.

Meticulous records kept by the Holocaust Museum in Washington, DC, and their wonderful list of speakers, who faithfully share their stories.

Writing colleagues and friends Terri Gillespie and Carrie Turansky, who brainstormed portions of this book with me, read and critiqued early versions, and continually raised prayers and offered encouragement during its writing. You are dear sisters in Christ.

My family — husband, son, daughter, son-in-law, granddaughter, mother, sister, brothers, nieces, nephews, all their spouses, and the generations fast on their heels. Your love and laughter, constant prayers, brainstorming, and encouragement are the wind beneath my wings. You're also the best word-of-mouth marketing team an author could imagine.

Natasha Kern, agent extraordinaire, who encourages my tough questions, champions my stories, and blesses me with her friendship and guidance.

My amazing team at Tyndale House Publishers who've helped to shape this story, design a wonderful cover, and bring my heart to readers: Stephanie Broene, Sarah Mason, Shaina Turner, Christy Stroud, Alyssa McNally, and Stephen Vosloo.

Elkton United Methodist Church — my church family in Maryland for many years — for your love, prayers, and encouragement, and McLean Bible Church Loudon Campus — my new church family in Virginia, for welcoming me into your fold and challenging me with new ideas, new questions to pursue in story form.

My uncle Wilbur, who reminded me once that a sure way to know if I'm working in the will of God is to ask, "Do I have joy? Is this yoke easy? Is this burden light?"

And above all, my heavenly Father and Lord Jesus Christ, for forgiveness, for life, for love, for hope and a future. You are my everything.

1

Hannah Sterling
November 1972

A summons to the principal's office had the same effect on me at twenty-seven as it did when I was seven, and seventeen. Giant bass drums struck and rumbled my insides. Crashing cymbals raced my heart — all as loud and out of step as our high school marching band's rehearsals for the Christmas parade.

I'd grabbed my bag of sophomore essays to grade over the Thanksgiving weekend, desperately hoping to get an early start up the mountain to Aunt Lavinia's, when the order to report to the office crackled over the loudspeaker.

Buses pulled from the school parking lot, the long hand of the clock ticked past four, and all the while the school secretary drummed her nails, eager to leave. At last the principal's door opened. Out strode a grim-faced Mrs. Whitmeyer, mother of Trudy Whitmeyer, the latest tenth-grade student crushed by my short-tempered venom, and the one I especially regretted humiliating. Mrs. Whitmeyer swept past, ignoring my half smile. I swallowed cardboard.

"Miss Sterling, come in." Mr. Stone, six feet two inches tall, with broad, linebacker shoulders that filled his office doorway, dwarfed me as I squeezed past. "Take a seat."

Grown women should not be terrified by school principals. . . . Grown women should not be terrified by school principals. . . . Grown women should —

"You saw Mrs. Whitmeyer."

"Yes. Mr. Stone, I'll apologize —"

"She's not the first." He sat on the front of his desk, two feet from me, arms crossed. "We've talked about this before. You assured me you'd get it under control. This isn't working, Hannah."

At least he's still calling me Hannah. "I'm sorry, Mr. Stone. I know I shouldn't have snapped at Trudy —"

"Or Susan Perry or Mark Granger — all Advanced Placement students, none of whom are traditionally discipline problems. And that's just this week — this short week."

14

"I know," I acknowledged.

"If it had happened once, I'd say forget it. Twice? Apologize. But this snapping and ridiculing has gotten to be an ugly habit, not good for the students — not the ones on the receiving end and not those who witness it. I don't know what's going on, but it's got to stop."

I bit my lip. *I'm turning into my mother — the last thing on God's green earth I want.* "I'm sorry. It won't happen again. I promise."

"I'm not convinced that's a promise you can keep."

"I can. I —"

"Hannah, stop." He walked around his desk and took a seat, then leaned back, considering. "Last year you were voted Forsyth County's most innovative teacher."

I moistened my lips. "That meant a great deal to me — truly." I'd poured out my heart for the kids and parents, and they'd responded. I felt wanted, appreciated.

"I know it did." He softened. "To all of us. But you've got to see that something's changed."

"I'll get past it," I promised, trying to assert confidence I didn't feel. "By Monday I'll —"

"Not by Monday. Take some time."

"I don't need time. I don't want time."
The drums in my stomach began to rumble
again.

"The day after your mother's death, you
walked back into the classroom."

"Her funeral wasn't until the weekend. I
didn't need —"

"Everybody needs time when they lose a
parent."

How could I lose a parent I never had? "We
weren't close." How many times did I have
to explain that?

"You've not dealt with it."

"I don't —"

"Go home, Hannah. Take some time and
figure this out. Grieve. Grief is nothing to
be ashamed of. It takes time to process, to
figure out how to move on. Life goes on —
in a different way."

*I'm not grieving because she died. If I'm
grieving at all, it's because of what never was
— what can never be changed now, what
wouldn't have changed if she'd lived another
fifty years.*

"I'll arrange for a long-term substitute."

"A long-term — No, please, Mr. Stone,
I'll be fine by Monday."

"Take until the first of the year, then
contact me. We'll talk."

"The first of the year?" The cymbals

16

crashed and fell to the floor three seconds before my frustration and voice rose. "I don't need a month —"

"I don't know what you need, Hannah, but find out. And when you do — when you find again the Hannah Sterling, teacher extraordinaire, who taught here last year — we'll be glad to have you back."

It was well past midnight when Aunt Lavinia put the teakettle on for the third time and wrapped her favorite burnt-orange and earth-brown afghan around my shoulders. "Maybe he's right. Maybe you do need some time away. That doesn't mean you have to take it here, sweetie. A trip, somewhere completely different — a vacation, a fresh view — might be just what the doctor ordered."

"A fresh view." I pulled the afghan closer, battling irritability. "How can I see anything new if I can't sort my past?"

"There's nothing to sort. She's gone. She made your life — and Joe's — miserable. You did everything you could to please her from the time you could walk, but it was never enough. Let her go, Hannah, and move on. Don't let her demons wreck your life."

"Daddy always said it was the war. Something happened to her and her family during the war, but he'd never tell me what."

"I don't know that he knew."

"He married her in Germany. He must have known something."

Aunt Lavinia stiffened, as she always did when talking about Mama.

"You were his favorite sister," I accused. "If he'd told anybody, he'd have —"

"As much as it may surprise you, he didn't confide everything to me. I doubt he knew all of your mother's past. She certainly never told me." She poured the steaming water over fresh tea bags. "Ward Beecham's still trying to get in touch with you. He said you didn't return his phone call. He's got to read the will, you know."

"You're changing the subject."

She raised her brows.

"I know. I'll call him. I just couldn't stay here after the funeral. And I already know what it says. There's nothing but the house and land."

"Well, you'll have to go see him. It's his obligation to finalize things, and you need to do that before you can sell the house."

"Next week."

"Why your mother used him and not Red Skylar, I'll never know. Red's family's been part of Spring Mountain forever."

18

"She probably just liked breaking the mold — or not having an attorney so eager to share his clients' business."

Aunt Lavinia ignored me. "Did I tell you that Ernest Ford agreed to take the house on multiple listing? He said he might be able to sell it without you fixing anything up, but you'll have to clear it out. I talked to Clyde about that. He's between jobs now. If you let him sell the contents, that would cover his labor. There's not much there worth anything."

"I don't want anything."

She pushed the cream pitcher my way. "Do you want me to confirm it with Clyde? It's the quickest way."

"Sure." I dropped my spoon to the saucer, startling us both with the clatter.

"We can tell him at dinner tomorrow. He's got no family, so I invited him and Norma. You don't mind, do you?"

"Of course not, as long as they don't ask me how I'm doing since Mama died or how my job's going or anything personal." Aunt Lavinia regularly invited her best friend, Norma Mosely, and half the kinless in her church for holiday meals. By tomorrow there would be at least seven more. There was nothing I could do to change that, but I didn't have to like it.

19

Aunt Lavinia ignored my sarcasm. "I think Clyde might be a little sweet on you."

"You've been saying that since I was ten."

"It's still true. It wouldn't take much encouragement on your part to light that fire."

I rolled my eyes. "Please, Aunt Lavinia."

Aunt Lavinia ignored me and pried the teacup from my fingers. "Now, you'd best get to bed. I'd like to keep my good china in one piece, and I've got a date with a turkey at half past five."

I'd hidden the windup alarm clock in a bureau drawer between bed linens so I couldn't hear it tick, but that meant the alarm was just as useless. Still, the aromas of rosemary-stuffed turkey in the oven and cranberries and apples simmering in cinnamon and cloves made their way up the stairs, tickling my nose beneath a mountain of quilts, drawing my feet to the bedside rag rug. *I should have been downstairs and helping two hours ago.*

The back porch door slammed, the kitchen door opened, and a "Yoo-hoo!" rang through the house. *Norma, with three pies and a bridal congealed salad. Aunt Lavinia won't miss me.*

Still, I raced through my hair and makeup,

20

zipped my favorite gray wool skirt, and pulled on a rose knit sweater set and the pearls Daddy'd given me for my sixteenth birthday — the only thing I'd kept to remember him by. Aunt Lavinia believed in dressing for Thanksgiving dinner. It was one of the things I'd always groaned over as a child, but had secretly appreciated. It made the day seem more special.

Another favorite pastime was spying on my aunt whenever she let me sleep over. Anytime things got too tense or loud or silent at home, Aunt Lavinia gave me sanctuary. I must have been five or six when I discovered I could peek through the coarsely cut circle in the floor, the one the black stovepipe shot through to reach the roof. It heated the upstairs bedroom just enough to keep icicles at bay. If I caught the right angle, I could watch Aunt Lavinia working in the kitchen and learn more than my share of gossip.

Twenty-seven was too old to be eavesdropping, but when Norma hissed, "Why don't you tell her? She's a right to know," my ears perked. I sat cross-legged on the floor and squinted until I saw Aunt Lavinia shushing her. But Norma protested, "She can't hear me; she's not even up yet. I'm just saying —"

"I know what you're saying, but it would only bring her more grief. She's had a lifetime of that woman's cold heart. No matter how bad things were between Joe and Lieselotte, he was a good provider and a good father and I'm not about to shame him now."

"He's been dead eleven years. There's no shame for him — only credit due. I don't know another man who'd do what he did for that woman."

"It would break her heart. I won't do it."

"What if she finds something telling in the house? There's bound to be something from Lieselotte's past." Norma snapped a dish towel open and plucked a pot from the drainer. "That could open up a whole new can of worms, and when she finds out you knew and never told her . . ."

"Clyde Dillard's going to clean out the house, burn everything he can't sell. That'll be the end of it."

"She's not going through it herself? Not even curious?" Norma sniffed. "I don't know. It seems like an awfully big gamble. All it takes is a little math."

Thirteen squeezed around Aunt Lavinia's table built for eight. Despite the cheerful banter, I barely touched her lavish Thanksgiving dinner. Norma teased that I seemed off my feed. I stared back, doing my best to bite my tongue. She flushed and turned away. I wouldn't confess that I'd eavesdropped, but I couldn't pretend what they'd said made no difference.

After the meal, Aunt Lavinia sliced the pumpkin pies. I cut the mincemeat and apple. Clyde grabbed two half gallons of ice cream from the freezer, and Norma carried trays into the dining room.

"I haven't eaten this much since last Thanksgiving at your table, Mrs. Mayfield." Clyde heaped dollops of vanilla ice cream over too-big slices of pie. "I'm much obliged."

"We love having you, Clyde. You and that strong arm just keep dipping that vanilla."

"Yes, ma'am. And I'll get busy over to the house first thing tomorrow. I know you want to get it on the market before Christmas." He glanced at me, his face as red as the cranberry chutney.

"That'll be wonderful." Aunt Lavinia patted his shoulder. "The sooner the better."

"About that . . ." I wiped the stickiness of the last pie slice on a tea towel. "Let's hold off on clearing out the house. I want to think about it some more."

Aunt Lavinia straightened, and from the

corner of my eye I caught Norma's sideways glance as she set down the empty pie tray.

"But, honey, we settled that last night. Clyde has some free time now. And just think, if you could sell the house before the end of the year, you'd have all that money to do whatever you want. There's no need to wait." Aunt Lavinia spoke a little too brightly.

"You mean, in case the school won't take me back?"

"I didn't mean that. Of course they'll take you back. They're lucky to have you. But, Hannah, honey, you don't want that old house. It's best to let it go."

"Whose best? Yours? Mine? My dead parents'?"

Aunt Lavinia's color rose and she smiled, flustered, at Clyde, who glanced uncertainly between the two of us.

Aunt Lavinia didn't deserve that after how good she'd been to me, all my life. But I couldn't get past the idea that she knew something about Mama and Daddy and hadn't told me — something that even Norma knew and thought might be important. If there was something in the house that might help me reconcile my relationship with my dead mother or at least help me understand her and move forward, that would be worth any amount of embarrassment.

I picked up Norma's second tray and headed for the dining room. "I want to go through the house on my own, Clyde. I'll let you know soon what I want to do about the contents — but it won't be tomorrow."

The company gone and the dishes finished, Aunt Lavinia shoved the clean turkey roaster to the back of the pantry for another year and turned on me. "I don't understand you. You wanted nothing to do with that old house. You couldn't wait to get away after high school, and you hated coming back last summer to nurse your mother. Have you forgotten?"

"It was just after she died in her room — right there — that I didn't want to go back." I spread the fourth wet tea towel on the rack to dry. "I couldn't go back. But now, before I leave it forever, I'm thinking I should sort through things — things Mama never let me see. No telling what I'll find."

"Wallowing in that old house will just make you miserable."

Couldn't Aunt Lavinia understand that I needed Mama — no matter that she hadn't needed, maybe hadn't even wanted, me? "You sound like one of your soap operas."

"I'd arranged everything — just like you asked me to, let me remind you. You —"

"I need some time, Aunt Lavinia. My career as a teacher is over if I don't get my act together. And I can't get on with my future if I don't settle things with Mama — once and for all. Running away from home resolved nothing. Coming back to nurse her last summer didn't redeem our years of misery. She barely spoke to me the whole time, except to say things out of her head. Crazy, raving things as if she was fighting someone, and other times whispering and then pleading, begging for something not to happen. Once she screamed, and I had no idea what any of it meant. All things that made absolutely no sense, at least as far as anything I ever knew about her. But that's it. I never knew her, not really. Going through her things is the only thing I haven't tried. I'm going to live in the house — alone."

"Please don't do this to yourself. Let God close that door."

"God never opened the door, Aunt Lavinia. I don't see what reason He'd have to close it."

"Leave it alone, Hannah. You don't want to dig up things that can hurt you."

"What, you believe in ghosts now?"

"There are ghosts and then there are ghosts." She peered at me over her glasses.

"What's that supposed to mean?"

"It means leave the past alone. What you don't know can't haunt you."

"Then tell me. What is it you and Norma were talking about this morning — 'do the math,' or whatever?"

Aunt Lavinia paled and turned grim in one go. "Still listening at keyholes?" she quipped defensively. "I'd have thought you'd outgrown that."

I stared her down.

Aunt Lavinia pulled off her dirty bib apron and tossed it toward the washer, then pushed her fists into her hips. "I will say that I did not always treat your mother as kindly as I could have — as I should have. But she didn't do right by you or your daddy from the get-go. Joe would tell you to leave sleeping dogs lie and get on with your life. Even Lieselotte would have wanted that."

"What 'math'?"

But Aunt Lavinia simply closed her eyes, threw up her hand, and headed for the door.

"Why did they move to the mountain in the first place?"

She stopped, shook her head, as if I'd asked a wearisome question, but turned to

27

face me. "You know that Henry and I settled here because his family was here. What you probably don't know is that he'd joined up in Oklahoma because he was going to college out there. That's why he and Joe ended up in the same unit once the war started. Henry and I met through Joe — you know that. When Joe came back from Germany, there was just no reason for him to stay in Oklahoma."

"But all your family was there — all Daddy's. I never understood why Mama and Daddy followed you out here."

Aunt Lavinia wouldn't meet my eye. "Joe and I always got along — the closest of the siblings — and I guess he thought your mama might be more accepted here than out there, where so many families had lost boys from their unit."

"Why wouldn't people accept Mama in Oklahoma?"

Aunt Lavinia sighed again, this time exasperated. "The war changed the way people treated foreigners. The war changed everything."

"I know about the US internment camps during the war. But the war was over by the time she got here, and it's not like she was German or Japanese. She was Austrian. They were victims of the war — people we

28

fought to liberate."

"So she said."

"What? You think Mama wasn't Austrian? C'mon, Aunt Lavinia. She'd have no reason to lie about that. And she certainly sounded Austrian."

But Aunt Lavinia had turned again and taken off, down the hallway for her favorite fireside chair and footstool.

"This isn't about me." She pulled off her shoes, rubbed her arches, and lifted her feet to the ottoman. "It was a different time, and you're too young to understand." She massaged her temples, as if to relieve an ache lodged there. "Leave sleeping dogs lie, Hannah. That's all I'm going to say."

"But what if I find something that tells me who my mother was — I mean, who she was really?"

"I don't believe anything or anyone could explain that woman."

"Nobody's born so closed off, Aunt Lavinia. I need to know if that was her own warped nature or if something happened to her . . . or if it was because of me." That confession cost me everything, though I turned away, fussing with the afghan on the sofa, so Aunt Lavinia could not read my face.

"It wasn't you, sweetie." She shook her

head. "What if you find it was because of something she did? Something neither she nor you can ever reconcile? A lot of bad things went on in the war. You just never know. Besides, she couldn't love herself; how could she love another person?"

I sat heavily on the sofa, swinging my legs up to lie down and stare at the ceiling. "She never loved Daddy; that's for certain. I hated that — for both of them. I think part of him wanted to love her, but he wasn't good at it. He could be soft with me but awfully hard on her. But she must have felt something for him, sometime. They married. They had me." I couldn't keep the hope from my voice, or my glance from her eyes, just in case she knew something, anything.

But Aunt Lavinia closed her eyes and turned away. "I don't believe your mother ever loved another soul."

2

Lieselotte Sommer
November 1938

I'd loved Lukas Kirchmann all my life — from the time I was old enough to breathe, or at least to bat my eyelashes. Lukas was my older brother's friend — both two years older than me. But unlike Rudy, Lukas took the time to smile and talk with me, to ask the names of my dolls as I set out their china plates and cups and metal spoons, or to mention that his mother and sister were very fond of tea parties too.

When I was old enough to walk to school, Rudy ignored Mutti's instructions to walk beside me, determined to run ahead. But Lukas insisted they keep a step behind to watch over me and his sister, Marta. No one dared tease or torment us with two big boys on patrol. In all those years I never saw Lukas afraid of anyone — not until *Kristallnacht,* the Night of Broken Glass.

31

I'd just turned thirteen and was long past playing with dolls. My father had warned me to stay home that night and keep the door locked, no matter what I heard or saw from our windows. He and Rudy — so full of himself in his Hitler Youth uniform — would be out late. Our housekeeper had long gone home to her family for the evening, and of course Mutti lay upstairs, sound asleep from the laudanum drops taken to ease her pain.

I'd finished my school lessons and the dishes, then hung the dripping tea towel to dry. It was half past ten, and still no sign of Rudy or Vater. Only when I stepped outside to stuff rubbish into the bin did I catch the faint, far-off whiff of wood burning and a faded light painted across the sky. No one dared openly burn brush or wood with the current rationing, certainly not at night and not in Berlin — unless a house was burning. I'd followed my nose to the street when a roughened hand clamped over my mouth and a strong arm yanked me back into the shadows. Scratching, kicking, clawing, biting — I did it all — but he dragged me into the bushes.

"Lieselotte! Lieselotte, it's me, Lukas!" he hissed in my ear. "Stop biting me, for pity's sake!"

"Lukas!" He relaxed his grip and I jerked away. "You scared me to death. What are you doing?"

"Is Rudy home? Your father?"

"*Nein.* Lukas, what — ?"

"Let us come in, just for a bit."

"Let who?" And that is when I glimpsed another shape in the dark, one I couldn't make out, hunched and lurking behind the courtyard door.

"Please," Lukas begged. In that moment I sensed his fear — a thing so foreign in Lukas Kirchmann that I immediately shoved open the door and pulled him through, the hulking form on his heels. "Bolt it." Lukas had never ordered me to do anything before, but I turned the lock without thinking. He put out the kitchen light and peered around the edge of the curtain. "Your father's not home?" he repeated, as if he'd not quite believed me.

"*Nein.* He said he'd be late. Your arm is bleeding — and your face! What's happened?"

"Nothing. It's nothing."

The other man, more than twice Lukas's age, moaned toward the pale light cast from the street, nursing a crumpled arm.

"Herr Weiss?" I recognized him as the butcher from the market three streets over.

The Jewish market, where I was no longer permitted to shop, no matter that we'd shopped there ever since I could remember and it was so very close and had always carried the best cuts of meat — at least, Mutti claimed that once it did. According to Vater, good Aryan girls didn't buy from Jews — not meat, not anything. The Führer had made that clear for a long time.

Herr Weiss nodded miserably.

"Lieselotte, do you have some cloth? A strip I can make into a sling for Herr Weiss?"

"Sit down, Lukas. You're bleeding all over the place! Let me get you a face flannel."

"Never mind me." But he sat and grabbed my arm, warming me through despite the shock of seeing him roughened up. "Help us."

"Anything," I swore.

"I've got to get Herr Weiss and his family away."

"His family? Where — ?"

"That doesn't matter. Can you help us? Can you help me — without telling your father or Rudy?"

He wants me to do something secret and dangerous — he wants me, without Rudy. I didn't know exactly what Lukas needed or had planned, but I knew that helping Jews was forbidden and that I ran the risk of my father's wrath, Rudy's wrath, and of being denounced by our neighbors. It was frightening, and thrilling. "What do you need? What can I do?"

"We need bandages, coats, some food. And we need a place to hide Herr Weiss and his family until tomorrow night."

"Tomorrow night?" Bandages and food and even coats were one thing, but hiding them . . . Where could I hide them? Did I dare?

"Others will be able to get him away from Berlin by then."

My heart raced. This was more than I knew how to do.

But Lukas stepped near, so near I could feel his whispered breath on my face. "The brownshirts smashed his shop. They threw all his meats and goods into the street. They've set fire to the synagogue and to a whole string of Jewish houses. No one's trying to stop the fires, unless they endanger Aryan houses. There's a good chance every Jewish shop and house nearby will burn, including the Weisses'. His son's been beaten senseless and arrested for trying to protect his parents. Herr Weiss and his wife need to get their daughters away before . . . before something worse happens to them. Help them. Please. Help me help them."

*How can I refuse? But not in the house —
there's no place safe.* "The garden shed in
the courtyard. No one goes there now.
There's room for all of them in the cellar
just beneath, where you and Rudy made
your clubhouse when I was little — when
you wouldn't let me in." I remembered the
long-ago slight, even in that moment.

He kissed my cheek. "You're an angel,
Lieselotte! I'll take them there now. The key
— I need the key."

I pulled it from the hook by the back door.
"I'll cut some sandwiches."

"And cloth — something we can fashion a
sling from."

"Yes, I'll find something."

"And coats or blankets — anything you
—"

"Yes, yes, you'd better go. Vater and Rudy
might return any moment. I'll get them to
you."

"*Danke schön,* Fräulein Sommer." Herr
Weiss took my hands in his, then seemed to
think that too forward and stepped back,
bowing his head twice. "There is no way for
me to thank you."

"There is no need, Herr Weiss. I can't
imagine who would do such a thing." But
the reserve in Herr Weiss's eyes and the pain
in Lukas's told me I should know, and

36

without being absolutely certain, I'm afraid I did.

They slipped through the door and into the night. As I pulled bread and cheese from the pantry, I remembered the chest of woolen steamer blankets in the attic above Mutti's room. I ran there first, pulling out three of the heaviest, and two coats Rudy and I had each outgrown. I couldn't remember the Weiss girls, how old or tall they were, but it was all I could carry.

"Lieselotte," Mutti called faintly as I passed her room. I froze outside her doorway, realizing I must have woken her with my rummaging through the attic.

"I'll be back in a moment, Mutti. Just give me a minute."

"Lieselotte," she called more urgently. "Lieselotte, come now!"

I hadn't heard her so strong in weeks, but it could mean her pain had returned. I dropped the coats and blankets in the hallway and stepped into the dimly lit room. "What is it, Mutti? Do you need more laudanum? It isn't quite time yet."

"My coat." She lifted her hand toward her wardrobe. "Take my coat."

"We're not going anywhere. It's the middle of the night. You must have been dreaming."

Her voice was frail, as was everything about her, and I knew it took great effort for her to speak. "I heard them . . . Herr Weiss. Take my coat for Frau Weiss, my warm fur. It will keep her warm."

"*Nein.* That's your best. You'll need that." I pulled the duvet above her shoulders, horrified to realize that she'd heard us, fearful of what she thought, if she knew and would tell Vater. He would never approve, and the trouble it would mean for Lukas . . .

"I won't need it. I won't be going out again. Frau Weiss was always so friendly and kind to me. Herr Weiss gave generous cuts whenever I shop —" But Mutti gasped, her back arching and her face contorting as she cried out in pain.

Quickly I repositioned the small pillow beneath her back to better support her. It was so little to do and did so little good. "I'm not sure Vater will think it a good idea. I'm afraid —"

A crash came from the street, followed by raucous shouts and the broken rhythm of a poorly beaten drum.

"Take it. Go quickly." Mutti closed her eyes.

I stood beside her bed, uncertain. But there was no more time. I grabbed Mutti's rich brown fur coat from her *Kleiderschrank,* inhaling her sweet scent from days when she was well enough to walk down the stairs and out into the world. I knew Mutti was right that she would not wear it again, that she was past those days forever. But I couldn't let myself think about that now.

I grabbed the pile of blankets from the hallway and a sheet and pair of sewing scissors from the linen shelf, balancing the load on my hip as I made my way down the stairs and carefully crept out the back kitchen door before I lost my nerve.

More shouts and drunken laughter erupted from the street in startling bursts. Smoke hung in the air and the odor of something pungent that I couldn't identify, couldn't separate from the smell of wood burning.

A furtive knock on the shed door, and I passed the load through, into Lukas's arms. He squeezed mine in gratitude, and I raced back to the kitchen. My knife had just cut through the loaf of bread when Vater and Rudy burst through the kitchen door in high spirits, Rudy recounting some exploit and Vater laughing too loudly in hearty approval. My stomach flipped.

"Lieselotte, what are you doing up at this hour?" Vater's tone suddenly changed.

"Why is this door not locked? You've been out?"

"Nein," I lied, something I never remembered doing to my father. "But you were both so late. I was worried."

"Did the noises in the street worry dear little Lieselotte?" Rudy teased. "You'd best get used to it. It's only the beginning!" He rose up on his toes and stretched his arms above my head, menacing like a gremlin.

"Enough, Rudy," Vater admonished. "You're making sandwiches at this hour?"

"I thought you'd be hungry." To lie again came more easily.

"That's good of you," Vater approved, pulling off his overcoat and muffler. "It was cold out tonight."

"I'm famished!" Rudy tore off his coat and threw his cap to the table. "Make me two! Is there any coffee?"

"Ja, a little ersatz. I'll heat it up." I turned to the stove, praying my face would not betray me. But Rudy was too full of himself to notice, and Vater had other things on his mind.

"How's your mother? Did she wake while we were out?"

"I don't think so. She's sleeping now. The laudanum . . ."

"Ja, das ist gut. She didn't need to hear

40

this night."

"Mutti wouldn't understand." Rudy sounded so offhanded.

"What were you doing that Mutti wouldn't understand?" It was a bold question, but I wanted them to tell me they'd been drinking or playing cards or anything but beating up young boys and burning synagogues. For the first time in my life I wanted Lukas Kirchmann to be a liar.

"It's retribution for the murder by that Bolshevik Jew in France. Haven't you listened to the radio? You must keep up with these things. You're not a baby anymore, you know."

"Rudy, that's enough. Lower your voice. Don't wake your mother. She needs her sleep." Vater plucked a sandwich from my board. "Bring the coffee when it's ready. I'm going to check on Mutti, then to bed." He stopped. "Ah, I have a gift for you, Daughter." He pulled a book from his coat and handed it to me. "Take good care of it."

"*A Christmas Carol?* And in English! Vater, where did you ever find such a thing?"

"A first edition, so mind how you keep it."

"*Ja, ja,* I will. *Danke schön.*" It was not like my father to bring me gifts. And this

41

book — my favorite!

He was through the door when Rudy whispered, "There's more where that came from." He winked. "And what he meant is that he doesn't want Mutti to know about tonight. She's been giving him grief about the 'growing militancy' of the Hitler Youth. She doesn't understand. The Führer has plans we've not dreamed of — mark my words! He'll call us to arms before long. The world will see what the New Germany is made of, and I'm part of it!"

"That's a boy's bravado. You're all about rowing and exercising and camping and —"

"Not anymore, little sister — not after tonight. The Hitler Youth of today will become the army of tomorrow."

"What did you do tonight? You still haven't answered."

"Poor little Lieselotte." He stroked my cheek, uncharacteristically kind — or was he being sarcastic? "Your world is about to change and you don't even know it. You've been too much at home with Mutti and her old-fashioned ways. You've missed more meetings of the Young Girls League than you've attended. Next year you must join the other girls in the Bund Deutscher Mädel. You won't be excused, even if Mutti's still alive."

42

"Don't say such a thing!"

He shook his head. "It's a mercy for her if she's not. She's draining our finances and her life is no longer productive. You must see that. You need to take your place in the New Germany. Because Mutti's dying, she's excused. But you're not. Your laxness looks bad for me and for Vater. The Führer says —"

"You're talking crazy, Rudy, and I won't listen to any more. Go to bed." I wrapped the remainder of the loaf of bread in a cheesecloth, as if I planned to return it to the pantry. As soon as he and Vater were snoring I would slip what food I could to Herr Weiss in the shed.

Rudy grabbed two sandwiches from the board and headed for the stairs. "Don't mock me. It's a dangerous pastime. You don't want me to report you, do you?" He turned and raised his brows in mock surprise. I wasn't entirely sure he was teasing. "Next time you do something Vater's forbidden, best wipe your shoes."

He pointed to the caked mud on my socks and school shoes. "I don't know what you've been up to and I don't care. I have my own life apart from Mutti and Vater now, so why shouldn't you? It's time you grow up, little sister."

3

Hannah Sterling
November–December 1972

Old houses creak in the day; at night they moan as if their bones crack and separate. Sleeping in my old room felt just as creepy as when I was a kid. Shadows from the tree limbs outside my windows still loomed with outstretched arms, still danced on the wallpaper opposite my bed. There was still a family of hoot owls — generations old — calling to one another after midnight, unnerving my feeble attempts at slumber. And the safest place was still buried beneath my mountain of patchwork quilts, head and all.

By 2 a.m. I gave up and pulled on jeans and one of my old high school sweaters still hanging in my closet.

Thankfully, the electrician had come out to reconnect the line the day before, so I flooded the house with light, top to bottom. It didn't seem so spooky then, just old and a bit decrepit, in serious need of care — care someone else would give. The telephone couldn't be reconnected until midweek, but Aunt Lavinia was the only one I'd call, and a little space from her was in order.

Tea, good and strong, would surely keep me awake, but might make me think more clearly. Tea had always annoyed Mama. She'd liked her coffee, strong and sweet with cream, as if she couldn't get enough, as if somebody'd take it from her if she didn't hold on with two hands. Maybe that's why I liked tea — plain — just to spite her, just to be different.

The kettle whistled. I poured steaming water into the pot, stirring the leaves. Tea leaves constituted my solitary return to nature — rejecting tea bags in the modern era. Real leaves redeemed time. I pulled my sweater closer and cradled the mug in my hands. So many things I did, so much of my life felt in response — or more in reaction — to my mother. *Which is crazy. This has to stop.*

A list. The first thing I ever did to focus on a new project for my classes was to make a list. I ripped a sheet of notebook paper from my school binder and scribbled at the top: *Understanding Mama. Moving Forward.*

Those two things encompassed my goal. Everything else fell between.

The first step was to go through the house, top to bottom, and search for clues. I'd no idea what kind of clues. Mama and Daddy were both dead, after all.

But what if Mama kept a diary, or what if Daddy did? Hard to imagine, but I wrote it down: *Look for diaries, family pictures.* I listed the rooms, determined to remain objective: kitchen — the easiest to tackle. After having spent the summer cooking there, I felt pretty sure there wasn't anything I hadn't seen, but I'd tear apart every cupboard and cookie tin. In the process I'd see if there were things I wanted to keep. Everything else, Clyde could deal with.

Most of Mama's kitchen pans and utensils had come from rummage sales and yard sales. She didn't believe in spending money on herself, and truth be told, there wasn't much to spend. Clipping coupons and saving string and a ball of rubber bands and using tinfoil twice or three times was a way of life. All of that I'd toss in the trash, and feel guilty in the process.

Next, I'd tackle the bathroom, then the living room. The cellar and attic stored little. Mama hadn't been in those in years, as far as I knew, but I added them to the list. My

46

old bedroom was as familiar as the back of my hand. I only needed to go through boxes of high school stuff and see if I really wanted to keep anything. I'd leave Mama and Daddy's room for last. It conjured too many memories of last summer and Mama dying. I couldn't think about that, couldn't get sidetracked by memories or misplaced emotion.

I flicked the power switch on Mama's old electric radio on the kitchen counter. Cat Stevens belted out "Morning Has Broken," then The Main Ingredient came on the air and we vied for the right to sing "Everybody Plays the Fool." The line "But there's no guarantee that the one you love is gonna love you" surely seemed to fit. It didn't have to be a man, a boyfriend — as if I'd ever get to that point. All that about loving yourself before you could love someone else might have something to it. And what about God's love for me? I believed in that, but where were the arms to hold me? How could I love myself if my own mother couldn't love me? How could I believe Aunt Lavinia's assertion that Mama's attitudes had nothing to do with me? How could they not? Neither set of lyrics helped.

At half past noon I finished the kitchen. I'd found a couple of old wooden spoons —

ones Daddy had carved from a fallen maple the summer he took up whittling, thinking it might be a nice sideline. But Mama had frowned when he'd given her the spoons and stuffed them in the catchall drawer. He never carved another thing. My mind ran through the year's hit parade, and I wondered if there were lyrics for spurned love. I tossed the wooden spoons on the countertop in my Save pile. I should have a song too.

Mama wasn't one to hide money in canisters or Ball canning jars on the backs of shelves like Aunt Lavinia. Unlike so many Depression-era parents, Mama never hoarded cash for a rainy day, even though she saved tinfoil and rubber bands. She'd lived simply, as though everything important was inside her rather than outside, though she never showed what that was. Though grim and frugal, she was generous to a fault, which made no sense to me. Generous people are known to be happy people, but not Mama.

I pulled a can of tuna fish from the pantry and grabbed a loaf of brown bread I'd picked up from the local grocer. That bread — that grocer — reminded me of a day years back . . . I couldn't have been more than five or six. Mama, Aunt Lavinia, and I had stopped in the grocer's to do our weekly shopping, which for Mama generally amounted to a small sack of flour, salt, half a pound of sugar, one paper sack of staples, and a pound and a half of red meat she'd spread through the week to add to Daddy's butchered hog and chickens and occasional fish from the creek beyond the house. Anything else we grew in the garden.

A tramp came through the door and asked the clerk if he could work — maybe sweep up out front and empty the trash, unpack boxes, whatever needed doing — for food. He asked the clerk if he knew of anybody needing an extra hand in exchange for a place to sleep and board. But he talked funny — a lot like Mama.

The clerk turned him out straightaway, saying they didn't need his kind. Aunt Lavinia whispered that nobody'd let a stranger sleep in their barn. No telling where he'd been or what he'd been up to, let alone where he was from, dirty as he was. His faded brown suit jacket was ripped in the sleeve as if he'd been in a fight, and even the top of one of his shoes had come away from its sole.

When the man left by the front door, the grocer called the sheriff. Just as we were leaving the store, the sheriff came over and ran the man off the town bus bench for loitering.

Mama stood stock-still, staring after the sheriff. I couldn't tell if she was angry or frightened or if she approved of what she'd seen. Her face was blank. But she took me by the hand and marched me back into the grocery, shoving our purchases in my arms and leaving Aunt Lavinia standing outside.

Mama pulled a loaf of white bread from the shelf — something we never store bought — along with two bottles of soda pop. She ordered the grocer to cut a half pound of bologna, sliced thick, and a quarter pound of American cheese, sliced thicker — a veritable feast of riches. She plunked down money I knew Daddy would prohibit and marched me back outside with this largesse. Whisking past Aunt Lavinia, who'd waited impatiently in the late-September sun, Mama searched the street both ways, then nearly ran the tramp down chasing after him, me breathless on her heels.

My visions of a lakeside picnic high up the mountain vanished as Mama caught up to the man and laid a firm hand on his shoulder — a thing I instinctively knew no well-bred Southern woman would do and that every woman in town would gasp over and some did. When the tramp turned,

50

almost fearful, she thrust the grocery sack into his hands, then pulled half the apples from our bag and added them to his. She squeezed the man's arms and searched his eyes, her chin quivering, as if offering a silent benediction.

That thin, wearied man looked so sad and startled and half frightened that I thought he might fall over. He never even looked in the sack, but his eyes grew big as saucers till the tears overflowed.

He stared at Mama the longest time, as if he meant never to forget her face, then looked down at me. He smiled and leaned down, stroking my hair till I wanted to turn away. But he lifted my chin with his finger and his thumb gently stroked my cheek. Neither he nor Mama ever said a word, which I thought strange even for her. At last she shuddered, then just spun on her heels and headed for home.

I remember looking back at Aunt Lavinia, worried that she'd tell Daddy and he'd be mad at all the money spent on a stranger. But Aunt Lavinia just stood there with her mouth open, then shut it, turned, and walked the other way by herself.

I followed Mama home, trailing her at a clip. Halfway she seemed to lose her steam and grow suddenly weary. When we reached the house, she walked straight to her room and locked the door. Two hours I heard Mama cry — the only time I ever heard her cry. She didn't shed one tear at Daddy's funeral a good ten years later, but she bawled two hours of heart-wrenching sobs for a tramp she didn't know.

I hadn't thought of that day in a long time. It had seemed so out of character for Mama and yet so like her at the same time. *Who were you, Mama? How could you treat a perfect stranger better than you treated me or Daddy and have that seem natural?*

What Aunt Lavinia had said about Mama being foreign was the first I'd thought about Mama's accent in years. Once, a cluster of mean boys in grade school had tormented me on the playground, shouting, "Your mama's nothing but a Nazi spy! You should hightail it back to Krautland!"

Daddy'd said that simply wasn't true, that they were just ignorant young mountain children and not to pay them any mind. Daddy's comfort had been enough for me then, had enabled me to stick my nose in the air at school, even though I'd felt stabbed inside.

But now I wondered. *Was Mama's accent why she'd connected so strongly — so strangely — to the tramp, or was it the puzzle*

of some great emotion, foreign even to her?
Was her accent why the other women in the
church and community kept their distance, or
was it her standoffish nature?

Three more days I spent rummaging through the house, attic to cellar, turning cupboards and dressers and closets and drawers inside out, even tapping for hidden walls and loose floorboards, as foolish as I knew that to be. I sorted for donations and trash and packed the few odds and ends I wanted to keep. That felt like progress, better than leaving it all for Clyde to handle.

By Friday I felt sick of the house and its contents. I'd given up looking for diaries and mysterious family photo albums. There simply were none. The only room left was Mama and Daddy's.

Going through Mama's personal things was a love/hate pilgrimage. I found the Bible I'd been given in second grade at Sunday school in the bottom of her bedside stand. Mama had learned to read English with my Bible. But if she knew I saw her reading, she'd close it and push it away, like she didn't want me to see. I never understood that.

Every drawer held the scent of her home-made lilac sachets, alternately making my stomach ache and filling my heart with a longing I knew I'd never satisfy. Seeing strands of her faded gold hair in her hairbrush made me grip my stomach and throw the brush in the wastebasket.

Not a thing was out of place. Five dresses hung in the closet — one for church, one for shopping, three for the house. She'd owned a pair of black pumps for Sunday sitting beside a polished pair of brown tie shoes, heels worn down, for every day. When other mothers had donned open-toe sandals and patent-leather heels, my mother had ignored the fashion and continued to wear the plainest clothes and "sensible shoes," as if she didn't deserve better, as if dressing like a pauper helped her martyrdom. And yet I knew part of her had looked down on those women who'd dressed to the nines, as if they'd missed the point of living entirely.

In a last attempt I pulled the dresser from the wall and searched its back. I turned the oval dressing table mirror over. . . . Nothing.

I lay on her bed, the bed she'd died in, and waited the longest time to see if I felt something, anything, wondering if I might be given a sign. *Please . . . please, God. Help me understand.* Nothing . . . nothing . . . nothing. It was that nothingness that felt like suffocation — like all the air was gradually being sucked from the room. *Who were you, Mama? Did you feel anything at all for me?* Finally, I cried a good long cry and fell hard asleep. I didn't dream, and never woke until the phone rang.

My first call on the newly reconnected phone. It had to be Aunt Lavinia. I couldn't bear talking to her now.

The phone finally stopped ringing for the space of thirty seconds and started up again. I groaned and dragged myself from the bed because I knew she wouldn't give up until I answered.

"Hello?"

"Miss Sterling? Hannah Sterling?"

"This is she." A lump rose in my throat. *No, please don't let something have happened to Aunt Lavinia. Dear God, I'm sorry I was so mean to her! Please . . .*

"Miss Sterling, this is Ward Beecham, your mother's attorney. Allow me to offer my condolences on her passing. I'm sorry I've not done so sooner."

My heart nearly stopped. *Thank You, God!* "It's all right, Mr. Beecham. I never gave you a chance. It's just been —"

"These things are always hard."

The lump rose higher in my throat. He had no idea.

"Your mother left a will — a simple will, but I do need to give that to you, as well as the key."

"The key?"

"To her safe-deposit box. She was explicit that I place it directly into your hands, privately. Would you be able to stop by my office tomorrow sometime? It shouldn't take more than thirty, forty minutes for us to finalize things."

Mama left me a key to a safe-deposit box? She owned nothing of monetary value. What could — ?

"Miss Sterling? Are you there?"

"Yes . . . yes, Mr. Beecham, I am. I'm just stunned. I didn't expect anything from my mother."

"I understand. Shall we say ten o'clock tomorrow?"

"Yes, of course. I'll be there."

4

Lieselotte Sommer
December 1938

It seemed that growing up was all I did, but never fast enough. My fantasies about Lukas and me — the new, adrenaline-pumping ones where we fought jackbooted SS tooth and nail or risked our lives sneaking terrified Jews below the Gestapo's brutal searchlights by night — were short-lived. And try as I might, I could not seriously conjure the fantasy I craved most — the moment, after our all-important night's work, when we would gaze lovingly and longingly into each other's eyes while the sun rose over the dark roofs of Berlin.

In fact, I walked nowhere but school, and Lukas didn't come to the house for weeks, not even when Rudy invited him for supper or to join him for Saturday hikes. He and Rudy no longer walked behind Marta and me weekday mornings. It seemed that Lukas had evaporated like a morning fog from my life, as though our late-night adventure had never happened, as if it were the fantasy.

But Mutti's fur coat was missing from her closet, and that told me truly something had happened, that I wasn't losing my mind.

It was nearly Christmas when Frau Kirchmann began her daily visits with Mutti. They'd always been friends, but now they grew inseparable, like sisters, laughing, sharing secrets, whispering. Frau Kirchmann read aloud until Mutti, drifting in and out of pain, fell asleep midsentence. Her visits helped pass Mutti's lonely hours while Vater worked and Rudy and I attended school. Frau Kirchmann left just before Vater returned home, but always stayed long enough after school to share ersatz and bread with jam or sometimes a little *Apfelkuchen* she'd baked for Mutti and me.

For those few moments I was one of the women — a friend and equal. They were both interested in me, interested in what I was learning and thinking — at least Frau Kirchmann was, and Mutti when she could stay awake. It was all I could do not to inquire about Lukas, about the Jews we hid that night, about anything at all that might concern him. But I would not betray Lukas's trust or the fury of my feelings for him.

If Frau Kirchmann hadn't drawn me into their circle, I don't know what might have become of me that autumn. With Mutti's illness and Rudy's wild life and Vater's ill temper, all my ends had frayed.

Christmas crept painfully upon us. Vater worked long hours at his municipal office, sat by Mutti for a few minutes in the evenings, then fled to the library for his pipe and schnapps. Rudy stayed out all hours, marching and drilling and carousing with his Hitler Youth. I had no heart for Christmas, and Mutti barely knew one day from the next. But the afternoon before Christmas Eve, there came a pounding at our front door.

I opened it. Herr Kirchmann and Lukas pushed through, dragging a fulsome fir, Frau Kirchmann and Marta laughing in their wake.

"*Guten Tag,* Lieselotte! Where shall we set it? By the front window?" Herr Kirchmann did not wait for an answer, but led his merry band into the front room. "Marta, bring the pail. Lukas, the bricks."

"Shh," Frau Kirchmann hissed. "Don't wake Elsa; surprise her when we're finished!"

"Lieselotte, the ornaments! Hurry!" Herr Kirchmann stage-whispered to me, blue eyes winking in conspiracy.

I nodded, blinking, backing from the room. What would Vater say? How could we celebrate Christmas while Mutti lay dying? How could we not?

Frau Kirchmann must have anticipated my dilemma, for she was beside me in a moment, her arms wrapped around me. "Do you remember how your mother decorated your house last year with evergreen boughs and so many candles that your father feared she might burn it down? How she baked the sweetest *Kuchen* in the church for Christmas breakfast? That her voice was the sweetest and the highest — the only one able to reach those first soprano notes as we all sang *Weihnachtslieder* two years ago? Your mother loves Christmas. Let us give her one more — one more with cheer and music."

"I don't know if I can. I can't pretend. And Vater is not —"

"Your father is confused and hurting. But he will see this is right. He loves your mother."

"How? How can we — ?"

"Courage. You must be brave, my darling girl. Let her see you — see all of us — sing and smile. She needs to know that our lives will go on, that you will remember all she's

60

given you . . . that you will not forget to live."

The scorched lump in my throat threatened to suffocate me, the pressure in my chest to crush me. I pulled from her arms, though I wanted to remain.

"Do this for your Mutti."

"I don't know . . ."

"You do not do it alone. We'll be here, every step. I promise."

It sounded right; it sounded impossible.

"Do you want Lukas to help you with the ornaments?"

"Nein." I felt the heat rise up my face.

"Of course she does," Marta broke in, teasing. "But she's too shy to ask. So I'll go. Come on, race you to the attic."

Relief — that's what it felt like for someone to take the lead. Relief for anything, even something so normal as Christmas ornaments pulled from beneath the eaves.

Two hours later we hung the last ornaments. Marta steadied the chair as I pinned the star to the top of the tree. Frau Kirchmann went to wake Mutti, and Herr Kirchmann to carry her down the stairs.

They'd not reached the bottom stair when Vater and Rudy in his Hitler Youth uniform stomped from the kitchen. I'd not heard them come through the back door. Vater

61

took in the tree before he saw Mutti. Color drained from his face — hurt, sudden anger, betrayal written in his eyes. But in the next moment he caught sight of Mutti's face — a face lit as I hadn't seen it for months. She clasped her hands to her chest in joyous surprise, her eyes as bright as the *Tannenbaum* with candles that Lukas quickly lit. Tears spilled, making those blue orbs shine.

To think I nearly forbade this! To think Mutti almost missed her Christmas — that we all almost missed it!

Even Vater thawed in that moment, and Rudy straightened, taken as I was by the surprise of Mutti's pleasure and the surge of life in her form.

"A surprise — a Christmas surprise for our dear friends!" Frau Kirchmann cried, pulling Vater in by the arm as if it were any other year. She ushered him to the sofa, next to Mutti, where Herr Kirchmann had gently placed her.

Mutti reached for Vater's hand. "Oh, Wolfgang! It is wonderful!"

But Vater had been out drinking again. I could smell his schnapps from across the room. "It wasn't Vater," I protested. "It was —"

Lukas grabbed my hand, helping me — pulling me — from the chair. "It's a surprise from all of us — everyone." He didn't meet my eyes, but the electricity of his touch shot up my arm.

Vater's glassy eyes registered a moment of gratitude, but only a moment.

Dr. Peterson, my father's colleague and our family doctor — I'd not heard him enter through the kitchen, either — spoke from the hallway. "A party? Wolfgang, we have work. You did not say —"

"A small party, Herr Doktor," Frau Kirchmann insisted. "Please join us."

It was clear — at least to me — that Dr. Peterson wanted no party, that he was annoyed at the gathering in our home. Why, I don't know, but he shouldn't have taken it out on Lukas.

"Lukas Kirchmann, isn't it?"

"Ja." Lukas extended his hand. "And you are Dr. Peterson."

Dr. Peterson ignored the gesture. "You're not in uniform? Surely you are of age."

Lukas set his mouth. "I have not joined."

"Lukas helps his father with work on Saturdays and Sundays — essential work," Frau Kirchmann insisted. "His duties conflict with the youth program."

"Essential work," Dr. Peterson repeated. "Tell me, what is — ?"

"Please," Mutti begged, "no talk of politics

63

today. Rudy, please change from that uniform. I want no reminder of things outside these walls today. This is our Christmas celebration, and the Kirchmanns have been so kind to provide everything. Isn't it wonderful, Wolfgang?"

Vater could not resist Mutti or the good angels of her nature. "We are most grateful to you both. We did not expect . . ."

Frau Kirchmann hugged Mutti. "It's what good friends do. You would help us celebrate if things were different."

Vater nodded, but I wondered. I could not imagine him carrying a tree in for anyone.

Dr. Peterson spoke again. "It will become mandatory soon, you realize."

"Celebrating Christmas?" Mutti teased. "I should hope so!"

"The youth programs. Compulsory in the new year." Rudy thumped Lukas in the chest. "You won't be out of uniform for long!"

"Rudy, I asked you to change your clothes — today, for me," Mutti half pleaded, but Rudy ignored her again and Vater did not speak up for her.

"Is that certain?" asked Herr Kirchmann. "That would prove most inconvenient for our work."

"Your work? The Führer's work comes

first, or do you not agree, Herr Kirch-mann?" Dr. Peterson challenged.

"You've brought presents!" Marta squealed, pushing between them, pointing to the velvet sack Dr. Peterson carried. "Just like *der Nikolaus!*"

"*Ja!* Presents — *der Nikolaus!*" Rudy laughed and clapped Dr. Peterson on the back. "Perhaps this is the first time you've been called that, eh, my good doctor?"

"Rudy," Vater admonished. "Respect. Show respect."

Rudy bowed before the doctor. "*Ja,* sure. You must forgive me." He didn't sound sorry at all. "Why don't you show us what you have in your sack, Herr Doktor."

I didn't understand. They all acted as if we performed a play upon the stage, spouting lines that held no meaning, or that meant something quite different from the words spoken.

"Leave it alone, Rudy," Vater warned.

Mutti's smile faltered. Frau Kirchmann looked confused. Dr. Peterson glanced at Rudy and Vater once again. Rudy gave a mock salute. The doctor hesitated only a moment. "Why not?"

"Peterson, do not . . ." Vater cautioned, rising from the sofa. But he still held Mut-ti's hand.

She gently pulled him back. "Wolfgang? What is it?" she whispered.

"It is cause for celebration, I think." The doctor plunked the heavy bag on the table, pulling open its drawstring. "Why not share our good fortune with your friends?"

Vater's face reddened. "Another time. Not today — not —"

Two ornate silver candlesticks were pulled from the sack — each a good eighteen inches and weighing enough to make Dr. Peterson heft them, one in each hand. "Quite a prize — perfect for the holidays, don't you think?"

"They're exquisite!" Mutti agreed. "You bought them today? For Christmas?"

"Bought them?" Dr. Peterson all but smirked. "Did we buy them, Wolfgang? What would you say?"

Rudy grunted with pleasure.

"Wolfgang?" Mutti squeezed Papa's hand.

"It was . . . a complicated transaction."

"Yes," Dr. Peterson coughed, barely suppressing his grin. "Yes, Frau Sommer, it was 'complicated.' "

I was still thinking that Lukas had taken my hand, that he'd not immediately let it go. I didn't care about candlesticks.

But Marta cared very much. "They're magnificent. May I hold one?"

Dr. Peterson shrugged, taking pleasure in her interest.

"Oh," she said in approval, "it weighs a ton. Are they real silver — through and through?"

"Through and through." Rudy pushed in, taking up the other, flirting with Marta. "Worth a fortune."

"They're heavier than yours, Mama. But look, they have almond buds engraved on each of the branches — just like yours."

"You have such candlesticks, Frau Kirchmann?" Dr. Peterson took new interest in her. "I should like to see them."

"They're not for sale!" Marta exclaimed. "They're to come to me one day — they were Grandmama's, from Austria, and her mother's before."

"Indeed?"

"Oh, they are nothing so grand," Frau Kirchmann said quickly. "We have so many things of Mama's and Papa's — sentimental value, I suppose." She made light, but I could see the questions unnerved her.

"Engraved with almond blossoms?" Dr. Peterson probed.

But Frau Kirchmann had turned away.

"Hyacinths," Herr Kirchmann offered. "They are hyacinths."

"But —" Marta objected.

"You've forgotten, my dear. Hyacinths were your grandmother's favorite flower. They're on everything."

Now Marta looked uncertain.

Herr Kirchmann hefted one of the candlesticks. "But these are certainly lovely. A bargain at any price."

Dr. Peterson pulled it from his hand, returning both candlesticks to the velvet bag. "I'm glad you think so."

"Where did you get them?" Mutti asked quietly. No one answered. She insisted, "Wolfgang, where did you and Dr. Peterson find them?"

"I'll leave that to you, my friend." Dr. Peterson lit a cigarette.

But Vater only moistened his lips and would not meet Mutti's eyes.

"It's nothing," Rudy scoffed. "We got them off some Jews near Pankow. They were moving out." He emphasized the last, smiling wickedly.

A pall fell over our company. Mutti slipped her hand from Vater's. Her eyes lost their light and all the room dimmed, no matter that the late-December sun streamed through the windows. A minute passed, or two.

Frau Kirchmann — always Frau Kirchmann — came to the rescue. "Marta, Lieselotte — help me with the *Weihnachtsgebäck* and finger sandwiches," she ordered. "Lukas, come, carry the punch bowl. We've a party to get under way!"

Rudy plugged in the phonograph and set a record on the turntable, placing the needle carefully into the groove. Soft Christmas music poured through the rooms. But the day was ruined. Even I knew what Rudy had meant. More property "Aryanized." More Jews sent into the streets or to the community house — a ghetto forming. The knowledge that Vater took advantage, that Rudy gloated, that Dr. Peterson egged them on, eager to share the spoils, would send Mutti into a dark place.

And yet, gradually, the others pretended otherwise, forcing more levity than before the intrusion. In that moment I couldn't care about the Jews who'd been forced to move — at least not so much as I cared about Mutti. Her last Christmas — for surely it was — had just been stolen by that hateful Dr. Peterson. And by Vater . . . and by Rudy. I hated them . . . and yet, Lukas had held my hand. Why did I care more about that?

By the time we returned with platters of food, Mutti had recovered some of her color, which surprised me. She was engaged in a conversation with Herr Kirchmann, doing her best to draw Vater in. It was Dr. Peterson who intervened yet again.

"I understand you have not been able to keep up with these things, Frau Sommer, but you must realize that these Confessing Churches have challenged the authority of the Führer. It can't be wise to send your children into their midst — and most unwise for Wolfgang's future in the Party. Impossible for him or Rudy to attend."

"Herr Kirchmann has asked me my Christmas wish, and this is it: that my children attend church — with the Kirchmanns, if no one else will take them. But I would prefer they go with you, Wolfgang, if you will."

"I won't go, Mother," Rudy asserted. "I'm sorry to disappoint you, but I'll have none of it."

"You must realize you are asking political suicide of your husband, Frau Sommer. You do not want that, surely," Dr. Peterson insisted. "At least the National Reich Church has pledged allegiance to the Führer. Let them go there if they must. Even that —"

"The church's allegiance is to our Lord Jesus Christ. The National Reich Church seems to have forgotten this." Mutti's blush

70

deepened.

"It is not that simple, Frau —"

"It is as simple as a child born of the Holy Spirit, as simple as His perfect life offered in place of our sinful ones. You are a guest in my home, Dr. Peterson, and entitled to your opinion, which you have stated clearly." Mutti was her old self, for the first time in months. What had happened while I was out of the room? "I am disappointed, Rudy — very — but you are old enough to decide. However, I want your promise — all of you — that Lieselotte will be allowed and encouraged, provided a way to attend church."

Vater looked at Mutti, drawn by forces stronger than his own.

"Wolfgang, do not —"

"Dr. Peterson," Herr Kirchmann intervened, "do you not think this is between Frau Sommer and her husband?"

"I want to go. I want to go to church with the Kirchmanns." It was my voice, but from where the courage came to use it, I don't know.

"Wolfgang?" Mutti pushed. "Promise me."

Vater glanced at Dr. Peterson, at Rudy, at me, but would not look at Mutti. When he shrugged in defeat, Mutti's mouth set, but she nodded.

"It's settled, then. Lieselotte goes with the Kirchmanns on Sunday — every Sunday."

"We'll be so glad to have you, my dear," Frau Kirchmann soothed as though there had been no displeasure.

I glanced at Lukas, who eyed me, surprised. A taste of triumph surged through my chest. *Could freedom be so easy?*

And then the party changed again. Rudy switched the record and swept Marta into a waltz, delighting Mutti. It was his gift to her — no matter that he'd not changed his uniform — and Mutti accepted it graciously.

Lukas became in that moment the same old Lukas — full of life and joking with Rudy, kind to Mutti, reserved and respectful toward Vater. He even watched playfully over Marta when the dance ended, catching his sister as Rudy spun her out. Nothing had changed in him. But everything had changed in me these last months. Could he not see this?

"Stop mooning," Marta whispered as we poured new cups of punch together.

"What?"

"You know what. Stop mooning over Lukas. It's obvious to everybody. You'll never capture his attention that way. You look silly, like a child."

I turned away, biting my lip to keep from

crying. Why must she spoil it yet again? And how could a person keep love and longing from her face? Was I really pushing Lukas away? I hadn't said anything to him!

Perhaps Frau Kirchmann overheard, perhaps not, but she called me. "Lieselotte, help me find the knife for the *Rumkuchen*."

"*Ja,* certainly." I was only too glad to escape Marta and the others.

Frau Kirchmann whispered, as we set the tray in the kitchen, "Don't mind Marta, dearest. She's only a child. She does not think about what she says."

That one small bit of sympathy sent me over the edge, and tears spilled, running down my face. It was silly to cry. I was allowed to attend church with the Kirchmanns. I'd see Lukas every week. Mutti had her Christmas and her Christmas wish. I should be thrilled, and all I could do was pour salt tears onto Frau Kirchmann's shoulder.

Gently she drew me to the sink, took out her handkerchief, and wet it, dabbing my face and eyes. "It's a big day — a great accomplishment — and so much tension in the air. There is every reason to cry for joy and sorrow and confusion. If it helps any, we're all confused. We're simply doing the best we can."

The best we can . . . and I must too. I pulled away, sniffing.

Lukas appeared in the doorway, and my heart sank. My eyes must have looked like swollen fish bellies, my cheeks stained and splotched. What would he think of me now?

"Take the knife and matches, Lukas. The brandy for the cake is in my purse. We'll be there in a moment," his mother ordered.

But he waited a moment longer, concern written in his face. *"Ja — ja,"* he stammered. "But what is — ?"

Why shouldn't he be embarrassed? I was embarrassed too. But we women pulled apart and stared at him, as if he were the one caught in that awkward moment.

When he left, Frau Kirchmann clucked her tongue. "Ach, men. Don't they know that tears shed are never wasted? What would they do without women to keep their lives interesting?" And we both laughed.

5

Hannah Sterling
December 1972

The brass bell over the door of Ward Beecham's downtown office tinkled. There was no secretary in the lobby. No secretary and no desk for one. Just an orange vinyl sofa with walnut-veneer legs and a matching chair that might have come off the floor of the five-and-dime, or been left over from my principal's office.

But the paintings on the walls could have been set in any upscale attorney's office in Charlotte. Instead of the printed portraits of the founding fathers, Franklin D. Roosevelt, and John F. Kennedy sported in black plastic frames by every judicial and political office in town, Mr. Beecham's walls held cityscapes of Paris and London, and the ruins of two castles set somewhere in Scotland — places the locals had probably never dreamed of, let alone visited. The paintings — original oils in carved gilt frames — drew me and gave me a tingling sense of freedom, that perhaps the world held more possibilities than I'd imagined, that maybe one day I'd sit in a Parisian café or walk the paths of the Highlands. And then I pinched myself. *Who am I kidding? At the rate I'm going I'll be lucky to pay my weekly boardinghouse room rate and hold on to my ancient Royal typewriter.*

The inner office door opened. I wouldn't have guessed that the bespectacled, brown-eyed man with curly dark hair and sporting the first signs of a midlife paunch was the owner of the paintings — the vinyl sofa, maybe.

"Miss Sterling, I'm pleased to meet you." Ward Beecham, with loosened tie and shirtsleeves rolled above his wrists, extended his hand. "Please come in."

His office was as mismatched as his lobby. He offered me the single wine-colored leather wingback chair, taking a seat behind a gunmetal-gray desk — Army surplus, by the looks of it.

"I appreciate you calling me, Mr. Bee-cham."

"Call me Ward, Miss Sterling." He smiled, brown eyes creasing at the corners.

"Then call me Hannah."

"Hannah."

The way he said it warmed my face, which was just silly and further proof that I needed a life. "You mentioned that my mother left a key, as well as her will."

"To her safe-deposit box. She was very particular that I see you privately and place it in your hand."

"Yes, you said. I had no idea my parents rented a safe-deposit box, or that they owned anything to put in it."

He nodded, but shifted forward and, all business, clasped his hands on top of the desk. "Let me go through the will with you. Then we'll talk about the box. I'll share with you everything she told me."

There was nothing in the will but the house and land — the title free and clear, just as I'd expected. "Won't I need a deed to sell the house?"

"Your mother opened the box at the bank when she learned her cancer was terminal. I advised her to place the deed and any other documents, some extra cash, whatever she thought pertinent, there."

The vise in my chest tightened. *That's it? You made it sound so important, like there was something . . . something special from my mother, just for me.* But I nodded, as if that were what I'd expected, and stood to

77

go. I wouldn't cry in front of this man.

He stood too. "Miss Sterling, I don't know how to say this."

I bit my lower lip and straightened my shoulders, waiting.

"Your mother was an unusual woman."

You're telling me this as if it's news? As if I need a perfect stranger to point out my family's strangeness?

"That came out wrong. What I mean to say is that I admired her very much. She endured a great deal."

"The cancer," I conceded.

"I didn't mean that. Yes, certainly, she did endure that with grace, but she was a kind woman, a brave woman . . . in a none-too-friendly community."

It was the nicest thing I'd ever heard anyone say about my mother. *But how do you know this? Why did she come to you in the first place? "A none-too-friendly community"* . . . "I guess you know something about that."

He half grunted and sighed. "It's not easy being the newcomer on the block."

"But my mother wasn't a newcomer. She lived here for over twenty-five years."

"It could have been a hundred and I don't think it would have mattered, do you?"

"Or a hundred and fifty. No, I don't. But

I never fully understood why, unless it was her accent. She was Austrian, you know."

He looked away. *He knows something.*

"Mr. Beecham —"

"Ward."

"If you know something about my mother, I beg you to tell me. We were not close, but I need to understand . . . to . . ." But I couldn't finish. I didn't know how.

"To put the puzzle pieces together."

"Yes. But I don't even understand how you know that. What did she tell you?"

He shook his head. "Only that there are things she couldn't explain, that she'd never been able to talk about. But she said you are bright; you would figure it out. She was fiercely proud of you."

He's lying.

"She said only that the things she left in the box would create more questions than answers for you. She hoped you'd be satisfied with what you find there. But if you need help or legal advice, she asked me to assist you in any way I can."

I nodded my thanks, still uncertain, and turned to go.

"Your mother paid for a year."

"Excuse me?"

"Retainer . . . for me to handle anything you need."

■ ■ ■ ■

I couldn't leave his office fast enough, couldn't walk to the bank quickly enough. I shook as I showed the clerk my mother's key and signed the registry. My knees wobbled as I followed the bank manager into the small vault and watched him insert my key and the bank's key into the slots on a metal box. He handed me the box, which for some reason I'd expected to be heavier, and showed me into a private room, then closed the door.

Please, God. Let there be something here . . . something that explains, that helps me understand her. I drew a deep breath and opened the box. Papers — nothing but papers. My heart sank. My parents' marriage certificate, Mama's naturalization papers, the deed to the house, Daddy's Army discharge papers. A couple of pictures of me as a baby — one was an old sepia-toned snapshot of Mama holding me. And an array of empty, faded envelopes with foreign stamps. I'd expected something personal — a diary, a letter written to me, an heirloom ring or brooch — something to link us, to explain.

Stop being so juvenile. You knew she owned

*no such thing, would write no such thing. Then
why all the cloak-and-dagger, Mama?*

I turned over the envelopes, all addressed
to Mama, all in the same handwriting but
one. I could barely make out the addresses
and dates on some of them. The words were
certainly foreign to me, but all the stamps
were German.

Aunt Lavinia phoned two nights later, the
first time since Thanksgiving weekend.
"Norma mentioned that she saw you in
town today. I'm glad you're getting out,
Hannah. Working in that old house day after
day must be depressing."

*Did she mention that she saw me coming
out of Ward Beecham's? Or the bank?*

"It's not so bad. I'm nearly finished." I
traced the letters and numbers on Mama
and Daddy's marriage certificate — the
certificate I'd read two hundred times since
pulling it from the safe-deposit box. But no
amount of tracing or rubbing the paper
changed the date.

"Oh?" Aunt Lavinia waited. "Everything
all right?"

"Sure, why wouldn't it be?"

"I'm just concerned about you, that's all.
You haven't been by for over a week. I miss
you. I don't want all this to come between

us, sweetheart."

"I don't want that either, Aunt Lavinia, but I don't really see much way around it. You know something about Mama and Daddy and refuse to tell me, even though you know what this means to me — even though you know I'm apt to lose my job if I don't get some closure, some resolution. Sooner or later I'm going to figure it out. I'd much rather hear it from you."

"Did you talk with Ward Beecham?"

"Didn't Norma tell you that I did — twice this week?"

"Don't get so defensive. Did you settle everything? Can you go ahead and sell the house?"

"The death certificate was issued and the deed is free and clear. I can sell whenever I want — when I'm ready, when I find a buyer. Why are you in such a hurry for me to do that? You know if I don't own the house, I'll never move back here."

"And you know you're always welcome to stay with me. But you deserve a life of your own, Hannah. You have a good job and —"

"I'm not sure I'll go back after Christmas, at least not right away."

"You're staying here?" Aunt Lavinia paused. "Does this have something to do with Clyde?" She sounded so hopeful.

"No! I might take a trip is all. I don't know yet." I couldn't keep the snap from my voice.

"Oh, honey, that vacation we talked about? That's just what you need. It will do you a world of good."

"I certainly hope so."

"Where are you going?"

I knew that telling Aunt Lavinia might start a new war, a war I didn't want or need. But maybe it would inspire her to tell me what she knew before I traveled halfway around the world.

"Germany."

The silence on the other end of the line was deafening.

"Why do you want to go to Germany? I'd have thought Myrtle Beach or Nags Head, maybe even Hawaii if the house sells."

"I think Mama might not have been Austrian after all. I think she might — I might — even have family still living in Germany."

"You're not serious."

"I've been busy, Aunt Lavinia. I contacted one of Daddy's old war buddies. He was in Italy, with the 45th, until the month before his unit helped liberate Dachau, and that was just a month before he was shipped back to the States."

83

"What difference does that make?"

But I knew from Aunt Lavinia's voice — strained and quiet — that she knew very well. "Mama was pregnant before she married Daddy."

"Well, you know, soldiers during the war. Your daddy —"

"Daddy couldn't have been my father, not my real father. They didn't even meet until a few weeks before I was born." Saying it aloud made me sick, sick at heart and sick to my stomach. *Why did you never tell me, Daddy? How could you and Mama keep that from me all my life, pretend I was yours?*

"Hannah, how can you say such a thing? He loved you. He raised you from a baby."

"I saw his discharge papers. I tracked his war record. I have their marriage certificate and I know my own birthday." It was all a statement of fact, but it sounded so cold.

"Oh, Hannah."

"All it takes is a little math."

6

Lieselotte Sommer
April 1939

When Mutti closed her eyes for the last time at the end of April, just as the fragrance of purple and white lilacs filled the air, Rudy and Lukas helped to carry her coffin to the grave site, both dressed in their Hitler Youth uniforms — mandatory since March. That made me sick — sick for Mutti's memory and sick for me.

I didn't understand Lukas, and that is what I thought of as I sat on the hard wooden chair at Mutti's graveside, half listening as the pastor droned on.

Lukas attended a Confessing Church with his family each week that he could — when no marches were scheduled or mandatory camping trips with the Youth kept him away. He sang and prayed, his eyes lit with the fire of purpose as the pastor talked about allegiance to Christ as the head of the church, as the head of our lives. How could he sing praises to Jesus Christ one moment and pledge his undying allegiance to Hitler the next?

The pastor lifted a handful of dirt above Mutti's coffin and let it fall, plunking, across the lid. I looked away. Mutti was not there. I didn't know where she was, but she wasn't in that box.

She'd been gone in spirit since Christmas, in and out of consciousness since the last of March. When she'd stopped eating and drinking, we'd all just waited, kept a death-watch. When at last her chest stopped rising and falling, we sighed in collective relief. I could take no more, and I knew Vater could not. He'd stopped coming to her room the moment she lost consciousness the first time. Only Frau Kirchmann had been faithful to the end, staying through the night those last weeks and sleeping on a cot in Mutti's room.

I didn't expect anything of Rudy. He'd left our lives on *Kristallnacht.* All he cared about was rising in rank in the Hitler Youth, longing for the day he could enlist in the Wehrmacht. He even tried to catch the eye of the SS — thank heaven Mutti never knew. He'd become brash, bordering on cruel at times. But Vater boasted of him, proud of his fervor for the Führer.

It was as though they'd both found purpose in their lives — patriotism, obedience, a passion for the New Germany. They were not the only ones swept up in it, despite the cost. In fact, I hardly knew anyone other than the Kirchmanns who'd not caught and spread the flame.

Did Lukas still help Jews in need? Was his appearance at our door on *Kristallnacht* a one-time abnormality in his life — because he was a friend to the butcher and his family, because he believed in the rightness of the thing at the time? Had the uniform turned him into another Rudy? I closed my eyes, not wanting to believe that.

Frau Kirchmann wrapped her arm around my shoulder. I straightened, realizing I should be thinking of Mutti, not Lukas, at such a time. But I'd grieved so long for Mutti, had begged God to heal her. I'd even bargained with Him, to no avail. Now that her ordeal was over, I wanted peace. I wanted to close my eyes and sleep for a month.

Everyone stood. A last hymn was sung and the coffin lowered. Vater threw one handful of dirt into the grave and walked away, Dr. Peterson by his side.

Rudy nudged me forward. "Wake up,

Lieselotte. This is the last. You can go home to your dolls after this."

He pressed dirt into my hand and nudged my arm forward yet again. I didn't want to drop it on Mutti's box. It was like throwing dirt in her face, but that made no sense since she wasn't there. My fingers clutched the soil all the tighter, until it formed a clod. Frau Kirchmann wrapped her arm around me again and led me away. I heard Rudy's clod thunk the lid of the coffin behind me.

Ten feet away I heard Dr. Peterson's wheedling. "It will do you good, Wolfgang. Best to get away from this. You endured it to the end, but now it's over. A new chapter. A new beginning is in order. There's nothing to stop you now."

Rudy swept past me, headed for the street, but Herr Kirchmann stopped him. "Do you want to come to our house for luncheon and coffee, Rudy? You and your father and Lieselotte? We'd be honored to have you."

"*Nein, danke.* I think my father has other plans, as do I. I need something stronger than coffee."

"You should not be alone now, son."

But Rudy pulled away. "I'm meeting friends. Are you coming, Lukas?"

I saw the *no* in Herr Kirchmann's eyes, and am certain Rudy caught it too.

"Go on then." Lukas sounded casual. "I'll catch up later if I can."

Rudy snorted and took off. Marta ran to catch up to him — to pay her condolences, no doubt.

The Kirchmanns pulled Vater to them, expressing sympathies and extending their invitation, which I knew he would refuse.

"Lieselotte." Lukas stood close behind — close enough to make me jump. "I'm so very sorry about your mother. She was a fine woman, a great lady."

The pressure in my chest expanded, making it hard to breathe.

"You'll miss her very much, I know. I wish there was something I could do to . . ."

"To what?"

"To ease the pain."

"Her coat, then."

His eyes widened.

"Mutti gave her most prized possession — the fur coat her mother and father gave her when she married Vater. Was it too much for you to tell us if they made it to safety? Or has this uniform changed you so much that you no longer care, that you want to forget what we did that night?" I did not realize my voice rose with each phrase until Lukas pressed my arm.

"Lieselotte, not now. Not —"

I slapped him. I don't know where it came from, but I slapped him hard across the face, biting back tears. I would not cry — not in front of Lukas, who'd betrayed me, betrayed Mutti with his hateful uniform and forgetting of everything important.

Frau Kirchmann stood beside me in a moment, drawing me away from Lukas. I glimpsed my father, far off, pain in his eyes and resignation in the slump of his shoulders.

Dr. Peterson pulled him along, ordering Frau Kirchmann to bring me. "Take her home. I will order a sedative."

"Nein." I pulled away. "I don't want a sedative. I want . . . I want . . ." I didn't know what I wanted. But I hadn't meant to strike Lukas. "I'm sorry. I'm sorry, Lukas . . ."

"Pull yourself together; you're making a scene," Dr. Peterson ordered.

Frau Kirchmann helped me to the car. "Perhaps Lieselotte could come home with us, for a time."

But Vater shook his head. "You've done enough, Frau Kirchmann. I am grateful. But we must find our own way now. Lieselotte must come home."

She started to protest, but something pulled her back. She squeezed my hand. "Your father is right. Go home and rest. Be together as a family now. It is the best thing. I'll check on you tomorrow."

I was barely aware of the ride home, only that the rain started — at first a trickle down the windshield, then in gusty torrents across the windows of the black car. It seemed a fitting end until the downpour slammed wild sheets against the sides of the automobile, shaking its heavy frame. Thunder boomed and lightning cracked the sky. I wondered if Mutti's coffin sat drenched in a pool or if the grave diggers had done their work quickly.

When we pulled into the drive before our house, Vater made no move to get out. I'd paid no attention to what they'd said, but now Dr. Peterson shook me. "Lieselotte, do you hear me?"

"What? Yes, yes, I hear you. What did you say?"

"I said I am taking your father for a drink. Do you need someone to stay with you?"

I could only stare at him. "Vater needs a drink."

"*Ja,* it's been a hard day for him. It will do him good to get out."

I wanted to scream, *"What about me? What will do me good?"* But of course I didn't. If Vater cared so little, why should I ask him? I didn't want to go into the house alone, though it was hardly different than before. Except that Frau Kirchmann was gone and Mutti's shell was no longer there. Vater had let the housekeeper go when Frau Kirchmann came to help, saying there were too many coming and going from our house, so now there was no one.

"You are all right, then," Dr. Peterson insisted.

I stared at him until he blinked and looked away. "I am all right."

The driver opened my door, holding a gigantic black umbrella for us both, and we rushed up the walkway. I didn't realize I'd forgotten my key until the driver produced one, quickly unlocking the front door. "Where did you find that — the key?"

"It is Dr. Peterson's, of course."

I stepped inside as he closed the door, his footsteps splashing back through puddles to the car. "Of course," I said to no one. *Why does Dr. Peterson have a key to our house?* But the question was too hard for me, and why should I care? What did it matter?

It was not late, but the storm, pounding and pounding against the windows and door, darkened the house as if already dusk. I stood in the foyer listening to the sounds of the empty house. I tried to conjure memories of days before Mutti's illness, before Herr Hitler came to power and he, along with Dr. Peterson's Jewish "purchases" and work schemes involving Vater, divided our house. But I couldn't remember . . . couldn't even remember last Christmas, as much as I tried.

The clock in the sitting room struck three, as if giving me permission to leave off my wet things. So I did, and lit the sitting room lamp. The puddle of light helped. So I lit the hallway, and the kitchen. It was the only thing I could do to chase away the darkness — the darkness so heavy I could barely breathe. I tore through the house, lighting every lamp in every room — except Mutti's. I would not go there, but pressed my back against the wall next to her door.

And that's when the storm inside broke loose. The tears, the sobs that rivaled the downpour outside, racked my body, racked every nerve until I slid to the floor, my back still pressed against the wall and my head buried in my hands. I cried and moaned and screamed until I thought I might throw up — all the tears I'd held in through Mutti's illness, through Lukas's indifference. I cried in the bright hallway with no one to hear me as I'd never cried in the dark.

When my storm finally spent itself, I curled in a ball and slept on the floor. One hour . . . two hours . . . I didn't know until the clock struck seven how many had passed. The house remained silent. No Vater, no Rudy . . . certainly no Mutti. The storm no longer raged — inside or out.

I pulled myself to my feet, splashed my face with cold water in the bathroom sink, and leaned my hot forehead against the cool tile. My temples and neck ached. My stomach rumbled. A cup of coffee . . . or at least a cup of sweet and creamy ersatz might help. Who cared about rationing today?

The kitchen stove had gone cold. I lit the pilot and set the kettle to boil. I'd just taken the pot from the shelf and spooned the coffee substitute into the pot when a soft knock came at the back door. Who could it be at this hour? With Rudy and Vater gone . . .

The knock came again, this time more insistent. "Lieselotte!" A whisper loud enough to be heard through the door.

"Lukas?"

"*Ja,* it's me — open the door!"

Greater heat than that from my aching head crept up my neck to my cheeks. How could I face him after what I'd done?

"Lukas, it's late. Please —" I pushed my hair from my eyes, combing it back with my fingers. *I must look a fright!*

"Mother sent some refreshment. Open the

door, Lieselotte — please."

I pulled my cardigan tight across my chest, drew a deep breath, and turned the lock.

He pushed in with a platter of sandwiches and a kettle of something that smelled like heaven, making my stomach rumble again.

"Mother's cod stew." He set the platter and warm kettle on the kitchen table. "You know she cooks enough to feed armies. She wanted you all to have some."

"They're not here. There's no one here but me." I didn't know what else to say — was afraid to say more lest the tears shoot up and spill out again. So I shook my head, just shook my head, but it wouldn't stop.

"Lieselotte, my little Lieselotte." Lukas pulled me into his arms. "It's all right. It will be all right."

"I'm sorry. I'm so sorry I slapped you. I don't know —"

"It's all right. I'm still here, you see? If you're going to slap someone, let it be me. I'm a safe person to wallop — but only for you." And he tweaked my fallen braid.

I laughed. I couldn't help but laugh, and pulled away, wiping my eyes. "Same old Lukas."

"Better, and no harm done." He smiled, pulling off his coat.

"No uniform? Aren't you all marching in

some parade tonight?"

"*Nein* — well, yes, our unit. Rudy is there. I told them I have essential work tonight."

"With your father?"

"Eating this good soup with you."

"Lukas, they won't like — You'll get into trouble. You'll —"

"It will be all right. I saw your father with a group from the Party. He and Dr. Peterson are not likely to be home before the parade. I thought this would give us a chance to talk."

"With me?" Mutti had just been buried, but the knowledge that Lukas wanted to talk with me made my heart beat faster, made the blood that had seemed so still in my veins an hour before rush through them.

He pulled me to a seat at the table, holding both my hands. "I should have told you what happened. I should have found a way to thank you and your mother for your help that night."

"Why didn't you?"

"I thought I was protecting you, protecting her. The less you know about . . . anything, the safer it is for you."

"You're a Hitler Youth member now. You do what Rudy does. He hurt —"

"*Nein,* Lieselotte. I wear the uniform because I must. I am not one of them. You must know this."

I had known, at least had begged in my heart that he was not one of them, but I'd needed to hear him say it. How I'd needed to hear him say it! "What happened to Herr Weiss and his family?"

"We got them across the border."

" 'We'?"

"Who doesn't matter."

"It matters to me."

But he ignored me. "Your mother's coat saved their lives. The nights turned bitter. They slept in your shed one night, then in ditches two more. Had it not been for the fur, the children might have frozen. Your mother saved them. You saved them."

The wonder of having helped to save a life — several lives — stole my breath. It gave meaning to Mutti's sacrifice, to the danger of lying to Vater and to Rudy. "Have you saved more? More Jews?"

Lukas sat back. He pulled his hands from mine and the warmth was gone. I wanted him to take them up again, but I wanted even more to know. "It's not something I can talk about."

"Are you afraid I will report you? I would never!"

Very quietly he said, "You almost gave me away today. You almost gave all of us away."

He was right, so very right. "I'm sorry. It will not happen again, if you'll only —"

"It is not a game to play. It is not —"

"Not for children? Is that what you think, that I am a child not to be trusted?"

"I didn't say that. Of course I trust you. It's just not so simple. There are other lives — not only my own — at risk. I cannot talk about anything, for their sakes."

"I could help. I could help again."

"*Nein*. It is too dangerous."

"No one would suspect me. I can —"

"*Nein*. Lieselotte, your father is a ranking member of the Nazi Party and, with the help of Dr. Peterson, rising every day. Your brother is more eager to please the Gestapo than Müller is to lead it. One mistake — one word spoken in anger or in your sleep — and you could be arrested. There would be nothing I could do to stop that. And I won't have it on my conscience. I won't have you in danger."

I would have protested more loudly, vehemently, but for the first time Lukas did not look at me as he had before. I did not see a child reflected in his eyes. And suddenly he was embarrassed, reaching for his coat.

He cares for me.

"I thought you were staying to eat with me."

"Perhaps it's better if I —"

"I'll heat the soup. You find the bowls — in the cupboard, there."

I wouldn't look at him, but busied myself at the stove, stirring the fragrant stew. This was something new, something different with Lukas. And if this had changed, what more might change?

I heard him rummage in the cupboard, pull the spoons from their holder.

"Tumblers are on the shelf by the sink."

Less than five minutes later we sat at the table, like two members of a family. Lukas searched my face, and whispered, "I'll pray, then?"

"Ja." I bowed my head, certain my heart sang. "You pray." With Mutti and all the angels in heaven, my heart sang.

7

Hannah Sterling
December 1972–January 1973

Three anxious and excruciating weeks passed while I waited for Ward Beecham's call. He'd felt certain he could track the two addresses in Germany. Whatever he discovered might close the door on my past with Mama or open it wide. Either way, there was so much I wanted to know. Why had Mama and Daddy both lied to me — never told me Daddy wasn't my father? And since he wasn't, who was? I couldn't see myself closing the door on the past without knowing. What would that search mean for my teaching position in Winston-Salem? And what about my future relationship with Aunt Lavinia? Was there anything else she wasn't telling me? All my life I'd trusted her implicitly. Now there was no one to trust.

Ward and I had agreed that all correspondence to and from Germany would go through him. It felt safer that way, he was still on Mama's retainer, and I needed a confidant and ally. I certainly didn't have one in Aunt Lavinia, despite our tentative truce.

Clyde emptied the house of everything I didn't want and sold what he could to a secondhand shop and the local junk man. The boxes and few pieces of furniture I'd saved were stored in Aunt Lavinia's attic. I closed up the house and turned the key over to Ernest Ford and multiple listing two days before Christmas Eve. Ernest posted a For Sale sign on the property before the ink was dry. It felt like the beginning of the end.

The day after Christmas, Ward Beecham phoned me at Aunt Lavinia's. "I've received a reply. You'd best come by the office."

Ward reached across his desk, handing me a sheet of embossed ivory letterhead, the name and return address in German, the body of the letter in English. "I was only able to track the address on one of the envelopes. I couldn't get a return on the others." The furrow creased between his brows. "I'm not sure if you'll think this is a belated Christmas present or a lure through a dark tunnel."

I smiled tentatively, eager and afraid at once.

Dear Esquire Beecham,

I write on behalf of my client Herr Wolfgang Sommer, who is naturally distraught to learn that his daughter, Lieselotte Sterling, is now deceased.

Herr Sommer searched many years for his daughter to no avail and believes now that she must also have assumed he perished during the war. Though he deeply regrets this lonely passage of time, he would be most happy to make the acquaintance of his granddaughter, Hannah Sterling.

Herr Sommer invites Fräulein Sterling to his home in Berlin at her earliest convenience and trusts that she will consider his home as her own. He has instructed me to transfer the amount of five hundred American dollars to your account for her travel expenses.

I must convey to you that Herr Sommer is elderly and infirm. Unable to provide the hospitality he would like, Herr Sommer requires his physician, Dr. Gunther Peterson, or myself to act in his stead.

Sincerely,
Heinrich Eberhardt
Attorney at Law

"Hannah?" Ward Beecham asked. "Are you all right?"

All right? "This says I have a grandfather . . . a grandfather I never knew existed. And he's German . . . Wolfgang *Sommer* . . . That's not even the name on Mama's marriage certificate."

"Apparently. Yes, that's right, on both counts."

"Everything my mother told me about her past was a lie."

"We don't know anything about the man, other than he appears to have money sufficient to buy you a ticket."

"If he was a bad man, why would she have left me this address to reach him? She never told me about him, but she opened this door for me to walk through — after her death. I don't understand."

"Maybe she regretted not telling you, not letting you know about him." He hesitated. "But she might have been ashamed of him too. She might have had good reason not to use his name or respond to his letter. We don't know."

"Aunt Lavinia said people did crazy things during the war. She suspects Mama took advantage of Daddy, that she got him to marry her so she could get away from something bad she'd done."

"I find that hard to believe."

"Do you? She let me believe my whole life that Daddy — Joe Sterling — was my father, and that she had no family at all. That she was Austrian, for pete's sake."

"Maybe your father — Joe — wanted it that way. Maybe she thought she needed to protect you from her family or from the American community. We weren't known for treating Germans — even German Americans — very well, you know."

"But after Daddy died, she could have —"

"Honored his memory."

"She didn't love him! She wouldn't have put a headstone over his grave if Aunt Lavinia hadn't shamed her into it. He wasn't a good husband, any more than she was a good wife. I know that, but he was good to me — as good as he knew how." *Why are you taking up for them? Why am I taking up for him?* "She lied to me, and she didn't exactly make it easy for me to figure out all that we've learned." That truth kept a tornado spinning in my head, and hurt like a rock crushing my chest. *It's like she's playing games with me from the other side of the grave!*

"I'm just saying that your mother must have had her reasons. I don't know what those were, but I'm willing to give her the benefit of the doubt and caution you to be careful with this man who claims to be your grandfather. Just because he invites you to Germany doesn't mean you should go." He shook his head. "We don't know anything about him or this lawyer. I need to think how best to proceed."

But this was the first clue I'd found to my mother's past and possibly to my own. If I had a grandfather in Germany, might I also have a father there? Could the other envelopes from Germany, the one Ward was unable to trace, lead me to him? Understanding my past might give me a clue to my future. I wasn't about to let Ward Beecham talk me out of it. "There's one way to find out, isn't there? Book my plane ticket."

Aunt Lavinia fought me every step of the way, begged me not to go, and cried as the taxicab pulled from her drive. Broken-hearted and trying not to be angry with her, I set my jaw, refusing to look back. I wasn't leaving forever, just for now, for me. I promised to write.

The plane — my first plane ride ever — bumped all the way to New York. Courage waned as my breakfast came very close to revisiting my teeth. But I couldn't go home or back to Aunt Lavinia, not until I found some answers.

For two hours I wandered JFK's eclectic airport stores, discovering scarves and sweatshirts and coffee mugs all touting the Big Apple — a world as surely foreign to a Southern girl as Berlin. Boarding took another hour, but at last we pulled to the runway. I sat back, closed my eyes, chewed my Doublemint, and felt the world fall away.

I changed planes in Munich. It was late morning when my plane taxied to the gate in Berlin's Tempelhof Airport. The little German I'd gleaned from an English-German dictionary on the plane through the night did not help much through customs. Weary and bleary-eyed, I finally stood in the middle of a terminal aisle, doing my best to read signs and thumbing through the book for inspiration.

"Fräulein Sterling?" A silver-haired gentleman of perhaps fifty-five spoke softly.

"Mr. — Herr Eberhardt?"

"*Ja,* very good, Fräulein." He smiled.

"Oh, I'm so glad to meet you. How did you know who I was?"

He gestured toward my dictionary, then glanced around the terminal.

No one else looks so green or lost. I didn't know whether I should be miffed that he'd pointed out my inability to blend in or show my relief at being rescued. I felt very much like Alice having fallen down a rabbit hole. "Thank you for meeting me."

"You must be greatly fatigued from your journey. Allow me." He lifted my carry-on from my shoulder — a weight gladly released — and grasped the heavy suitcase whose contents had been rummaged through and turned upside down in customs. Gratefully, I trailed him through a maze of corridors, out the door, into a frigid German morning, and to a waiting Mercedes.

"If it is convenient, Fräulein, we will go directly to your grandfather's home. I spoke with him last night and he is most anxious to make your acquaintance. Certainly, you are ready for a hot meal and some uninterrupted sleep."

"They fed us every little bit on the plane, but a hot bath and a bed would be fabulous."

Herr Eberhardt's eyes widened, as if I'd said something too personal and entirely inappropriate. I turned away, feigning interest in the passing landscape, realizing that I had a great deal to learn about German men and their culture.

I must have dozed, despite my embarrassment, for the next thing I knew the driver stood by my open door, coughing discreetly. Herr Eberhardt waited on the cobbled walkway with my luggage at his feet. The driver offered his hand, and it was all I could do to let him pull me up from the deep leather seat and the lethargy of plane fatigue.

A low stone fence bordered every front yard or garden on the street — just enough to keep trespassers out and small children in. Or to mark boundaries, territories. The house, of matching gray stone, loomed three stories high and ran narrow for its shape. Daddy would have called it an efficient roofline — *"lots of living below, minimal expense above."*

Herr Eberhardt introduced the stocky older woman who answered the front door as Frau Winkler, Grandfather's cook and housekeeper. Frau Winkler eyed me with more suspicion than welcome, but hefted my bags up the stairs with a grunt.

"Will you meet your grandfather now, Fräulein?" Herr Eberhardt took on a more kindly, almost fatherly, tone — perhaps to make up for Frau Winkler's frost.

"Yes — please." It was what I'd traveled thousands of miles to do, hopeful and glad that someone wanted to meet me — perhaps wanted to claim me as his family. That

108

meant as much as — maybe more than — discovering Mama's secrets. But now that it was time, my feet dragged like somebody'd stuffed pie weights in the toes of my pumps. *What if he doesn't like me? What if I remind him of Mama?* I knew I looked very little like her, though we'd at least shared a resemblance before the cancer. *Will he think that's a good thing or bad? Whatever happened between them that Mama never answered his letter?*

Herr Eberhardt knocked softly and pushed open the heavy wooden door, revealing a dimly lit room. "Herr Sommer? *Hier ist Eberhardt mit deine Enkeltochter, Fräulein Sterling. Können wir eintreten?*"

The form in the bed did not move or speak or snore. Herr Eberhardt guided me to the bedside, then crossed the room to pull back the curtains, allowing the late-morning sun to pour in. The white-haired and bewhiskered man in the bed moaned softly, turning his head from the light, though his eyes never opened. There was nothing of Mama in his face, not that I could tell.

"That woman! She has not even roused him for the day," Herr Eberhardt hissed.

A tray of cold, half-eaten food sat on the

bedside table. "It looks as if he's eaten," I offered.

Herr Eberhardt picked up the plate and sniffed. "Stew, I think, from last night. This is no way to treat an employer. He should be shaved and dressed by now. She knew you were coming. Dr. Peterson must be informed." Herr Eberhardt set the plate quietly on the tray and motioned me toward the door, pulling me into the hallway. "He will not want you to meet him like this."

"I don't mind, really. I took care of Mama in her last weeks. I know what sick old people are like."

"Herr Sommer does not think of himself as a sick old man. He wishes to welcome you to his home — your home — as your grandfather. We will do him the honor of granting that wish. I will make certain Frau Winkler has your room ready. You may rest and refresh yourself, enjoy a meal, which I trust she has prepared. I'll return later today and make proper introductions. Herr Sommer's use of English is . . . limited."

Eager as I was to meet my grandfather, I wasn't sorry to see him as a pitiable old man without his knowing. It quieted some of the percussion in my stomach, made me feel even more kindly toward him. I nodded. At that moment anything leading to a hot bath

110

and a warm bed suited me just fine. But at the door I turned and took one last look at the sunken man beneath the eiderdown. I hoped I could make up to him whatever Mama had done.

Frau Winkler, in her broken English, told me that Grandfather had insisted I stay in Mama's girlhood room on the third floor, that he was certain I'd want that. I wasn't sure I did. But I was curious, just the same.

To sleep in my mother's bed from a time when she was younger than me, to see the pictures she'd hung on her walls and set on her dresser and even the German scrapbook on her closet shelf gave me a glimpse of Lieselotte as a girl. Still, it seemed more eerie than wonderful. The only thing familiar was an old copy — on closer look, an 1843 first edition — of *A Christmas Carol,* by Charles Dickens. In English, of all things. I'd always loved that story. Inside, it was inscribed, *Zu meine Lieselotte, mit Liebe, Vater, November 1938.* I thumbed through my dictionary to translate each word, then sat back in wonder. Such an inscription, such a gift! He surely sounded like a man who loved his daughter.

It was as though Grandfather had kept Mama's room as a shrine — or he expected her to return at any moment, just as she'd gone and at just the same age. The styles and fabric of the dresses hanging in Mama's closet all looked like they'd stepped out of an old Humphrey Bogart and Ingrid Bergman movie — *Casablanca,* maybe — only for a younger woman. I'd have loved to try one on, especially a rich teal satin, surely a party dress, but it seemed too much like walking over a person's grave. I shuddered and closed the closet door.

Something inside me stirred, unsettled. Surreal. Everything, surreal. Snare drums from the marching band rolled, but no cymbals this time. I ran a hot bath, much to Frau Winkler's dismay at my American extravagance in the middle of the day, and nearly fell asleep in the tub. When I finally climbed between the bottom sheet and eiderdown, I blocked out everything before me and fell fast asleep.

8

Lieselotte Sommer
September 1939–April 1940

The Führer swept Poland in less than a month. People in the street stood in shock and uncertainty while others reveled, drunk with victory. The Führer claimed it was our right, that Germany had been provoked.

My father drank more and stayed out late at political meetings with Dr. Peterson and their friends. Rudy, sixteen, begged to enlist, but Vater ordered that he wait for his eighteenth birthday. The row that followed beggared description.

I wanted only to remain invisible. I kept up my schoolwork, but lived for Sundays — Sundays, when I attended church with the Kirchmanns. Sundays, when I glimpsed Lukas at the far end of the pew.

I turned fourteen in October, and Vater ordered me to join the League of German Girls — the Bund Deutscher Mädel. I didn't want to join, couldn't imagine myself running races and hiking and camping with the other girls. I felt so much older — as old as the Alps — since Mutti passed.

But Marta joined, and that was something. At least we trooped together. Walking to and from the meetings gave us good opportunities to talk about our brothers. Marta appeared nearly as smitten with Rudy as I was with Lukas. But Marta appeared smitten with so many boys, it didn't seem serious.

BDM meetings were held weeknight evenings. For that, I was grateful. Nights alone at home loomed long, especially as winter set in.

And I believed it was just a matter of time before Lukas asked me to walk out with him. Surely he'd been waiting for my birthday so I'd seem older, so my father would allow it. I waited, as patiently as I could, through Christmas. And then the New Year celebration arrived and my hopes soared again. But Rudy and Lukas ran out on the town, carousing with their Hitler Youth, never mind the curfew. I told myself Lukas must keep up the ruse, though it was hard to see in him the same person who sat slurping soup with me the night after burying Mutti.

By the late spring of 1940, just after the

114

invasion of France and the one-year anniversary of Mutti's passing, concern for Lukas waned as worry increased regarding the new woman Vater courted about Berlin.

When Vater shrugged on a new suit coat and announced that he would be out late one evening, I grew bold, asking him where he was going.

"To a dinner party, that's all."

"With her? With that woman you saw last week?"

" 'That woman' is a friend of Dr. Peterson, sister of an important SS officer, and an influential woman in her own right. He wants her to have a pleasant time, and I'm honored to help." Vater lit his pipe.

"Then why doesn't Dr. Peterson show her the town? Why doesn't he take her to the party?"

"Peterson is helping to host the affair, Lieselotte, though that has nothing to do with you. If you've finished your schoolwork, you might take up more duties with the BDM. You should spend more time —"

"I've plenty to do, Vater. I just think it's too soon for you —"

"You think? You have no right to think of what I do." His face reddened.

"But — Mutti. Have you forgotten Mutti?" As soon as the words were out of

115

my mouth I wished them back.

Vater's shoulders sagged, but nothing compared to the slack in his face. "I will never forget your mother, Lieselotte. She was the best part of me. But she is gone. That part of my life is gone too — over. Peterson encourages me to —"

"Dr. Peterson again! He runs your life, Vater! You don't have to do what —"

"That's enough, Lieselotte," he ordered, uncharacteristically harsh. "I will hear no more. Dr. Peterson has been kind enough to point out my potential within the Party and see that I meet the right people. We're colleagues working for the Reich. We must all think of the future. You most of all."

"What do you mean?"

"You will be fifteen this year."

"Yes? And sixteen the year after, and seventeen —"

"It is not too soon to consider your future."

I didn't want to think what he meant.

"You come from good stock. Your mother's family line is impeccable, and my —"

"Breeding? You're grooming me for breeding?" I'd heard the Führer's talk of the responsibility of German women to increase the population — inside marriage and out. Lebensborn — the Nazi program encouraging young, racially pure women to produce Aryan children fathered by SS officers. There were even breeding playgrounds for the convenience of the SS and Wehrmacht.

"Don't be impertinent."

"It's a question. Can you answer the question, Vater, or should I ask Dr. Peterson? Is this his idea?" I tempted him to slap me.

"Lieselotte, there is no conspiracy afoot. It's simply . . . expedient. You're of an age to begin thinking about marriage."

"I'm fourteen! I've two years of school and then university before I think of such things."

Vater drew back as if I'd hit a sore spot.

I hated and feared the red flags that rose in my brain. "We've always talked of this. Mutti, you, me — we knew, always, that I would attend university."

"Times have changed. You must see that. In the New Germany, strong young women must contribute as —"

"As breeding sows?" My voice climbed.

"It is a privilege — a duty — to increase good Aryan families. If your mother and I could have had more children, we would."

"So, it's that you want more children? With this woman?"

"If not this woman, then perhaps another. I am not too old. It would be best if you . . .

You're nearly fifteen . . . It would be expedient if . . ."

"If I were not here." The truth dawned. Why had it taken me so long to grasp? A nearly grown child from a first marriage would not be wanted . . . would interfere with a new wife . . . would be in the way . . .

Vater did not answer. "Perhaps Dr. Peterson can arrange a meeting in the near future — a dinner, an opportunity for you to meet a suitable officer or two."

"You will auction me off to the highest-ranking Party member?"

"You speak nonsense!" But I saw in his eyes that that was exactly what would happen.

"I won't do it. I'll spit in his face. Do you hear me? I'll drool across the table and pick pretend nits from my hair. That will show them my wonderful Aryan breeding." Now I nearly begged him to strike me.

"We'll speak of this another time. It's enough now that you think of it." Angry, he stepped closer. I did my best to stand my ground though I shrank inside. I wanted a fight and I feared a fight. "Lieselotte," he said, softening. "You look so like your Mutter, but these sudden tantrums are not becoming. Your temper —"

"Is becoming fierce."

"You must learn to control your emotions, to use them for good. A strong nature will serve you well, or it can ruin your life." He looked as if he might say more, but turned, pulling his topcoat from the rack. "Do not wait up."

I never waited up, not intentionally. But I lay awake, staring at the ceiling of my room, each night until the key turned in the front lock, until the massive oak door swung in, creaking on its hinges. Once for Rudy, and once for Vater. It was a guessing game who might come home first.

Neither called my name. Neither checked on me. If I'd not been in my bed, they'd never have known. I could have been anywhere, doing anything, and neither the wiser. And though that was not a noble reason to change my life, it was what gave me the idea.

I waited until after church on Sunday, until we'd finished the delicious *Schmorbraten* Frau Kirchmann had stewed, until Marta and I had washed and shelved the dishes. Vater knew I spent Sunday afternoons with the Kirchmanns. He would not expect me home — which was good; it would likely be a long conversation. But I never expected such an explosion.

"You cannot be serious!" Lukas looked as if he might burst a blood vessel. Even his mother could not calm him. "There is nothing you can do to help, Lieselotte. I've already told you, it is out of the question!"

I would have pledged my life to honor Lukas, but to obey him in this? "I know what you're doing — what you're all doing. Do you think I sit beside you in church each Sunday and don't see the looks exchanged between you? Do you think I do not see the pastor pass the hat after services at the back of the room, do not see the ration books dropped in or the forged identity papers, all while someone stands watch for the Gestapo? I know those collections are not going for the running of the church — not like the weekly collection. You're hiding Jews, feeding Jews, helping them move from place to place . . . or someone. You're all helping someone, and I want to help too. There must be something I can do."

"You're mistaken. There is nothing!"

"Then why are you shouting, Lukas?" I shouted back.

Herr Kirchmann placed a heavy hand on both our shoulders. "This is not a football match. Stop it, both of you."

"I think Lieselotte has a right to know." Frau Kirchmann spoke softly to her husband. "She is right. She could help. She has helped before."

Herr Kirchmann considered. My heart swelled with Frau Kirchmann's affirmation, with the knowledge that Lukas had told his parents about me, and about Mutti.

"*Nein!* There is no need, and we operate on the basis of only those adults who need to know," Lukas insisted.

"I know," Marta took up my defense. "Since when have you considered me an adult?"

"No one suspects you. You're a child!" Lukas spat.

"Then why would they suspect me? I'm the same age as Marta."

"You are not a child. You don't even look like a child!" Lukas declared the words before he thought — it was written on his face.

His father smiled. His mother turned away, also smiling. My heart soared.

"It is too dangerous."

"It's dangerous for all of us," Herr Kirchmann reminded him. "If Lieselotte believes the Lord has called her to help, who are we to turn her away?"

"She could run courier — with me." Marta leaned closer, her arms crossed over her chest. "Or we could both run in different directions at once and confuse them utterly!"

"I like the idea of both girls going together," Frau Kirchmann intervened. "I worry each time Marta goes out, but with two — there is comfort in numbers, if not safety," she urged her husband.

"Ja," I agreed, hardly knowing what I agreed to.

"Has the Lord called you, Lieselotte?" Lukas pushed.

"Has He called you?" I countered.

"Yes, I think so. I've believed it for a long while now. . . . Well? And you?"

They all stared at me. If I said yes, I would be lying. If I said no, would they let me help? I could not lie to Lukas or his parents . . . nor could I tell him — explain to him — that if I did nothing, I would die inside. I would burst and die of loneliness, of anger, of frustration, of helplessness. "I only know I must do something that helps someone. Everything I see frightens me nearly to death. If I am caught, I would rather die for something than live for nothing."

Lukas understood. I saw in his eyes that he understood, though he didn't want to. I saw that the consequence was not what he'd hoped, that he felt defeated despite his understanding. I could not stop him as he grabbed his hat and slammed the back door on his way out, or tell his parents to wait for me to run after him as they drew me into the parlor to explain their work. But I knew there would be another day. At least I'd earned the right to fight — to get up and breathe — another day.

9

Hannah Sterling
January 1973

I must have slept the day away. Frau Winkler's pounding on the door at half past six roused me.

"Dinner is served at seven, Fräulein Sterling." It was a pronouncement brooking no decline.

My head felt like somebody'd plopped an anvil there. But as the fog faded, excitement stirred. *I'm going to meet my grandfather, at last — my grandfather!*

After believing that all my mother's family was dead and that I'd been entirely orphaned, except for Aunt Lavinia, I'd now gained a grandfather, my mother's own father. I repeated the words over and over in my head, just as I had during the plane trip; it still seemed impossible.

Sconces in the dimly lit hallway cast gloomy shadows the length of the walls, reminding me that during the war even electricity had been rationed — or so I'd heard. I suspected the house had never been updated for stronger wattage.

Feeling eerily as if I'd stepped back in time, I rubbed my hand over the banister as I took the staircase down to the second floor and then to the first in search of the dining room. *Mama must have run up and down these stairs hundreds of times as a girl.* Herr Eberhardt had mentioned that Grandfather Sommer's family had lived in the same house since the early 1900s.

I reached the dining room five minutes early, but Grandfather was already seated at the head of the table, Herr Eberhardt at the foot. "I'm so sorry if I've kept you waiting. I didn't realize the time."

"We are simply early, Fräulein. I had business matters to discuss with my client." Herr Eberhardt rose from his chair and came to meet me. At the far end, Grandfather rose too, though more feebly.

"Please, don't get up." I walked quickly toward him, but was at a loss. *What's appropriate? At home I'd hug his neck. Do Germans even do that?*

Herr Eberhardt came to my rescue, his hand on my elbow. *"Herr Sommer, mai präsentieren Ihnen Ihre Enkelin, Fräulein Han-*

125

nah Sterling."

"Oh, please, call me Hannah."

"Fräulein Sterling, allow me to present your grandfather, Herr Wolfgang Sommer, my client and my friend."

"Hannah." Grandfather clasped my hand and repeated my name warmly, with an accent so similar to Mama's that my breath caught. He looked pleased to see me — almost triumphant in his pleasure — and so very frail that I couldn't help myself. I hugged his neck and kissed him on the cheek, just as I would have done to Mama if she'd not held me at bay.

"I'm so pleased to meet you, Grandfather. Thank you for inviting me, for the plane fare, and . . . for everything. It's just amazing to me to be here in the house my mother grew up in and —"

"One moment, Fräulein; allow me to translate," Herr Eberhardt interrupted.

"Oh, I'm so sorry. I forgot he doesn't speak English."

"Much English."

"Yes, much."

Herr Eberhardt translated, though I didn't think he did it with enough enthusiasm. Then he pulled out my chair and I sat. Frau Winkler served dinner.

It should have been a party — a celebra-

126

tion, a homecoming. But the minutes ticked by and Grandfather said nothing. He stole glances at me each time I turned to Herr Eberhardt. I could feel his eyes searching my face. I wondered if he was looking for some trace of Mama in my features. It felt like sacrilege to break the silence.

After a time I wondered if chewing troubled him too much to speak. I didn't know if all German food tasted like this or if Frau Winkler preferred to cook her meat dry and tough. And there was absolutely nothing green on the plate.

"You are not hungry, Fräulein?" Herr Eberhardt asked when Frau Winkler took away my plate of half-eaten sausages and potatoes.

"It's just been a long day for me. I think my body clock hasn't quite adjusted to the time yet." I smiled and straightened, dabbing my napkin to my mouth. Even my smile felt a bit out of place.

I thought there was an upward lift at the corner of Grandfather's lips but was uncertain he could have caught what I'd said.

"Perhaps tomorrow."

"Yes, I'm sure of it." The silence lasted through dessert — dry cake covered in whipped cream and coffee so strong I expected my spoon to stand up straight.

Good thing I got that nap. There'll be no sleep tonight.

Grandfather said something to Herr Eberhardt in German, and the exchange went on for a minute or so.

"Your grandfather wishes for you to ask Frau Winkler for anything you need and offers to provide a tour of Berlin. Are you prepared to begin tomorrow?"

"Yes, I'd love it. Will you go with us to translate?"

Herr Eberhardt looked surprised and a bit offended all at once. "Your grandfather has bid me hire a tour guide for you — a guide who speaks enough English to accommodate your lack of languages."

"Grandfather won't be going?" I did my best to ignore the slight on my "lack of languages."

"Surely you can see that is unwise, Fräulein Sterling. There will be a great deal of walking."

"Oh, I'm sorry. I didn't realize it was a walking tour. I thought perhaps he meant we'd drive. It's just that I was hoping to spend the day with Grandfather." But Herr Eberhardt's expression gave no quarter. "Please tell Grandfather I'm most grateful and I'll surely enjoy getting to know Berlin."

Herr Eberhardt nodded and stood. I realized he signaled the end of the meal but didn't realize I was being dismissed.

"You will be so kind as to excuse us, Fräulein Sterling. I have further business with Herr Sommer. Either I or your grandfather's longtime physician, Dr. Peterson, will join you for dinner tomorrow evening. Dr. Peterson's English is quite good, and you will find him a tremendous help in communicating with your grandfather."

"Thank you; that sounds very nice. Well, good night, and thank you again. Good night, Grandfather."

"Gute Nacht," Herr Eberhardt corrected.

"Gute Nacht," I repeated to him and again to Grandfather. Grandfather nodded, barely looking at me, as though I'd been privileged to address the king of England.

I passed Frau Winkler in the hallway. She raised her eyebrows significantly but I looked away. I had no idea what her expression implied or if I was to take particular meaning from Herr Eberhardt's comments.

My family — it felt less like a family than I'd hoped or imagined. *Maybe it's just the language barrier, and that I'm tired. I need to communicate directly with Grandfather, not go through a translator, to ask him questions about Mama. Well, I'm not stupid. I can learn German, and I can learn it as quickly*

129

as I need to.

"Everything looks brighter in the morning" —
that's what Aunt Lavinia would say. And she
would have been right. I woke early, my
sleep patterns thoroughly confused by the
time change, and enjoyed watching the sun
rise above Berlin's dark rooftops, drenching
the frosted tiles in diamonds.

Frau Winkler stirred down the hallway
about half past six. At seven she descended
the stairs. By the time I'd finished in the
bathroom and put my room to rights, the
clock hands approached eight and still no
summons. So I made my way downstairs to
the dining room . . . dark and silent.

But the kitchen hummed — egg water
bubbled and a load of clothes spun in a
primitive electric washing machine. A loaf
of dark, dense bread stood on the counter
with a long knife and a crock of butter.
Steaming-hot coffee beckoned from the
stove. I'd just about decided to help myself
when Frau Winkler stepped into the kitchen
behind me.

"Good morning, Frau Winkler." I tried to
sound bright and cheerful.

"Guten Morgen," she responded, reserved.

I smiled.

"It means 'good morning.' "

130

"Yes, I understand. *Guten Morgen.*"

"*Ja. Das ist gut.* You need to learn the language. You need to learn it quickly."

As if I don't know. "I don't expect to be here long, but I would like to learn."

"We will see."

This woman gives me the creeps! But I simply smiled, stepping back to give more space. "May I help myself to breakfast?"

"*Ja, ja.* Here is bread and the butter. Americans like a little sweet, so here is the marmalade. The *Kaffee* is ready."

"Thank you so much."

"*Danke schön.*"

"Excuse me?"

"Thank you — *Danke schön.*"

"Oh. *Danke schön.*"

"*Bitte schön.*" She waited, but I must've looked blank. "You're welcome."

"Oh." I nodded. "Thank you."

She looked as if I'd tried her patience beyond endurance. I was saved by a knock on the back kitchen door, and while she answered it, I cut and buttered my bread. I'd have preferred toast smothered in apple butter or preserves, but didn't dare ask, grateful for the "sweet" we Americans craved, even though I'd say their marmalade was mush and slightly bitter compared to the preserves made from Aunt Lavinia's

131

mountain blackberries. The strong coffee that had curled my toes last night unfurled them with the morning sun's rays.

"Your driver is waiting in the street."

"My driver?"

"*Ja.* Your tour guide."

"He's here? Now?"

"In New York they say, 'the meter is running' — *ja*?" She raised her brows significantly toward me.

I swallowed one last steaming gulp of the bitter brew and bolted for the stairs, dark rye bread in hand. "I'll be down in five minutes!"

I had no idea where we were going or what I'd see but was certain I'd at least need my Brownie camera and a couple rolls of film, a notepad and pen, my English-German dictionary and shoulder bag, and some of the deutsche marks I'd exchanged at the airport yesterday. A sturdy pair of walking shoes and layers beneath my coat and scarf must be in order.

Fifteen minutes had passed by the time I emerged, breathless and frozen stiff by the outside temperature. My driver stood nonchalantly by the car, reading the morning newspaper. Wrapped against the cold, he didn't seem to mind it or me until I coughed two feet from his ear.

"Ach, pardon me, Fräulein. I was lost in the events of the day."

"Your English is perfect!"

He smiled, his teeth gleaming like a Colgate commercial. Then he sobered. "Is that not what you require?" He sounded as British as Prince Charles.

"Yes, I mean, no — I just expected you to be altogether German. I'm glad you're not." *That doesn't sound right! Will I never stop slapping egg on my face with these people?*

Now he raised his eyebrows — thick, arched brows over brown, smiling eyes that twinkled at my expense. *What is it with Europeans and their eyebrows?* "*Ja,* I am German, born and raised in Berlin — except, of course, the years I spent in one of England's finest boarding schools."

Where you surely knocked the local girls dead. The man stood at least six feet and his curly blond hair hung over his eye in the most appealing schoolboy fashion. He must have been several years my senior, but his broad shoulders and athletic build looked that of a younger man. "I'm so sorry. I meant no offense."

He really did look sympathetic, as if pitying tourists was an everyday affair. "None taken, I assure you. Americans often say exactly what they're thinking, even if it's

133

not quite what they mean."

I smiled, nodding to agree, then stopped, nonplussed.

"Carl Schmidt." He tipped his cap.

"Hannah Sterling." I extended my hand.

He took it, smiling, then opened the car door. "Shall we?"

I slid into the backseat, doing my best to regain my composure.

Carl glanced into his rearview mirror. "Where to, Fräulein? Anywhere in particular, or would you like the general Berlin tour?"

"Are you on a clock? I mean, is there a certain length of time we have, or should I choose from specific options?"

"We have all the time you want. Herr Eberhardt has hired me to be completely at your disposal, both for driving and for translation purposes."

"For the entire day?"

"For as long as you're in Berlin, as often as you like."

"Just like that. I can't believe it. This must be costing Grandfather a fortune."

"I believe he can afford it."

Why do I hear ulterior motives behind every statement? I've got to stop this. I leaned back against the soft leather seat and breathed. "The general tour sounds wonderful."

■ ■ ■ ■

Unter den Linden, Humboldt University, the Brandenburg Gate, the Reichstag, and Charlottenburg Palace topped Carl's choices for the day — a long and exhausting day that focused on the accomplishments of the German people. I wanted to ask about the Berlin Wall, but there was no time or space, and I didn't want to interrupt his obviously prepared tour.

By midafternoon I was weary, but grateful for my companionable guide. "I must say it's so good to speak comfortably in English. I haven't needed my dictionary once today."

Carl laughed. He didn't look tired in the least. "You give me good practice, Fräulein. Most of my clients are German, of course. It's a pleasure to use my English."

"I hope you don't mind my asking . . ." I hesitated.

"Ask."

"You mentioned having attended a fine boarding school in Britain, and therefore I assume university."

"So, why am I driving for hire? Is that your question?"

"Yes, not that it's any of my business."

"It's not so bad a job, and it gives me flexibility to do other things, to research other projects of interest to me. It's temporary, until I find something better here . . . or elsewhere."

"Elsewhere? You're thinking of emigrating — to England?"

He smiled indulgently, but without condescension, and winked. "I think of many things."

He bantered as flirtatiously as I could have wished, but explained no further. At the coffee hour Carl introduced me to the most amazing apple strudel smothered in custard sauce I'd ever eaten. We laughed and talked as we sat in a cafe, and part of me wanted the day to wear into evening right there. But it brought me no closer to understanding my mother or learning who my father was, the purpose of my trip.

I can't ask Herr Eberhardt to translate my questions. They're entirely too personal, for me and surely for Grandfather. Grandfather must be so anxious to know what became of his daughter, and I need to understand why she left Germany, why she left him.

"Carl," I interrupted our banter once we'd settled into the car, "I need to learn to speak German."

He smiled into the rearview mirror. "On

your first day? Americans are so . . . indus-
trious."

"My grandfather speaks no English, and I
really want to get to know him. Learning
German is the only way I can imagine doing that."

I couldn't see Carl's mouth in the rearview
mirror, but the creases in his forehead deepened.

*Does he think I'm incapable of learning a
language?* "I took French in school and
picked it up quite easily. I'm sure I can
learn; I just need to find a teacher. Can you
help me?"

"You expect to stay, then?"

"For a while. I've taken a leave of absence
to come here, but I'll have to get back to
my job at home soon. My grandfather is all
the family I have on my mother's side now,
you see — at least I think he is. I need to be
able to talk with him."

"You are certain he speaks no English,
Fräulein?"

"Practically none. Why?"

He hesitated, shifting in his seat. "It is
common for Germans to study English."

"Well, now, perhaps." I hoped I sounded
knowledgeable. "But Grandfather's an old
man — old school. I doubt he would have
had that opportunity."

Carl's glance into the rearview mirror undermined my confidence.

"Perhaps your grandfather could hire a tutor for you."

"Yes, I suppose that's possible. But I'd really like to work more independently, to do this on my own."

He glanced into the mirror again, taking my measure. His shoulders squared as he stared at the road ahead. I was certain he was about to say something but stopped, and we drove into the lowering dusk in silence.

10

Lieselotte Sommer
June 1940–July 1941
Mein Vater courted Fräulein Hilde all that summer and into the fall. I made certain to keep from sight as much as possible — and, I prayed, from their minds.

I turned fifteen; only the Kirchmanns noticed. By then — October of 1940 — there was no sugar to be had for anything so frivolous as cakes. It always puzzled me why they demanded our sugar to win the war. Couldn't soldiers have spared a little for a Fräulein's birthday *Kuchen?*

Sugar was not the only, or most important, thing gone. Simplicity and innocence had disappeared — in our culture and in our church. I questioned everything — the state's insistence that we blindly obey the Führer, the Confessing Church's insistence that we give our allegiance first and only to Jesus Christ, and my moral obligations to my family, who seemed as fiery and radical as the brownshirts on the street.

I wanted the assurance that enveloped Frau Kirchmann, that radiated peace in her soul and through her eyes, her smile. But I knew that came from her relationship with Jesus, and I was still uncertain about giving my life to Him. I'd learned that I must rely on myself, trust only myself.

With Vater swooning like a teenager and Rudy blustering his manhood and Lukas pretending to be half-crazy for the Führer through the weekdays and carrying out his furtive exploits to help Jews by night, I felt my world stood in limbo — inside out and upside down.

Marta and I ran or bicycled as couriers, black market ration cards and forged identity papers wrapped in our school satchels or slipped into our kneesocks after evening BDM meetings. Sometimes I bicycled outside the city in the dark to fetch milk or butter or potatoes from a farmer, then dropped them in a ditch for the next runner to pick up and deliver to a household hiding Jews in their attic or cellar or in a secret room behind the false wall of a kitchen pantry.

How many people helped in similar work, I've no idea, but the missions gave me purpose, and the danger raced my blood.

Late at night, I slipped through our kitchen window, left unlocked. I don't think Rudy or Vater even knew I was not asleep in my bed.

Vater believed I spent long afternoons and evenings with the BDM, helping with the choirs that sang for wounded soldiers or assisting nurses in the hospitals. He believed that in the interim I absorbed all the appropriate and needful things to become a good German *Hausfrau,* and mother to lots of little Aryan babies for the Reich. Let him think that. I learned those housewifely skills from Frau Kirchmann with pleasure, but did not expect to need them for years. As far as I was concerned, life could go on like this forever . . . at least until the war ended.

But in April, our troops marched into Yugoslavia and Greece; in June, the Soviet Union. Lukas turned eighteen. I held my breath. He'd soon be sent for compulsory military training — there was no avoiding that. By all rights he should join the Wehrmacht.

By some miracle — or miraculous connection — his father convinced the authorities that Lukas assisted him in essential war work. But his birthday party — a picnic luncheon held in the Kirchmanns' back garden with Rudy and me — should not have been the place to make that announcement.

"You're not signing up?" Rudy said in disbelief. "All our unit is signing — this summer. I will next month. The day I turn eighteen you'll find me on the doorstep of —"

"There are more things to do for Germany besides marching and crowing." I shoved the plate of cold cuts toward my brother. I would not stand for Rudy's condescension toward Lukas.

"Lieselotte —" Frau Kirchmann reached for my arm.

"So, now you hide behind my sister's skirts?"

"I hide behind no one," Lukas countered. "But Lieselotte is right — there are many spokes required to turn the wheel. Supplier contracts are essential to the war effort. I've been trained to help my father in this as much as I've been trained to march in the Hitler Youth."

"Old men, like your father and mine, do those jobs — desk jobs, talking jobs. Young men, strong and in their prime — you, me — we're needed at the front. You will be branded a coward!"

"Is that what you think of me, Rudy? That

142

I am a coward?" Now Lukas condescended, but it was clear Rudy's words cut him.

We all looked to Rudy. I felt my brother's turmoil. Lukas had been his friend since childhood. His family was our family now.

"It's a question of bravery — and obeying orders. We are trained to obey orders. You know this. There is honor in —"

Herr Kirchmann interrupted quietly, "There is honor in work well done. Remember that Lukas's work has been approved by authorities with a broader view of the war effort than yours or mine."

"And who are these 'authorities'?" Rudy challenged.

I cringed inside but kept my spine straight. Herr Kirchmann was a gentleman and a gentle man, but he brooked no disrespect.

He waited, perhaps half a minute, until all eyes were on him and Rudy shifted in his seat, a slight squirm beneath Herr Kirchmann's stare. "I do not believe I need explain that to you, Rudy. As you know, questioning orders that come from above is *verboten*. Obedience, as you say, is a noble thing."

It was a soft reprimand, but a reprimand. Something Rudy never took kindly to.

Frau Kirchmann tried to lighten the brooding. "Marta, pass the bread. Rudy, won't you have some? Take two slices! I bought it fresh, this morning — the last loaf the baker pulled from his oven, saved especially for me, for our party."

But the day had gone sour. I was not so much angry at Rudy as afraid of him. He was crazy for fighting — ready to fight and die for his beloved Führer — and could not understand anyone who thought otherwise. Even more than not understanding, he'd grown suspicious of almost everyone. The Hitler Youth taught him that — as the BDM tried to teach me.

Rudy had already reported our neighbors, the Stoltzfus couple, for helping a beggar who came to their door — a man they knew from before the time all Jewish businesses were liquidated. Thousands had lost everything.

The man had only come for a meal, but Rudy reported it as if the Stoltzfuses were harboring fugitives — criminals. And the man was just that, according to the new laws of the Reich. He should have come forward for not paying the exorbitant taxes placed upon Jews — taxes he couldn't pay — not gone into hiding and begging. But that didn't matter. Both he and the Stoltzfuses were taken away.

Rudy expressed great pride for his part in

the witch hunt. And he searched for witches everywhere. What might that mean for Lukas? For the Kirchmanns? What might it mean for me if he even suspected what I was doing for the "war effort"?

The next morning a white feather appeared on the Kirchmanns' doormat. The next week Marta told me the family had woken to whispering, arguing, in their front garden in the dead of night. With lights *verboten* because of the blackouts, they saw no one. In the morning they discovered a white feather painted across their front door, initials of the perpetrators proudly scribbled in ink across its feathers. The "R. S." in the lower left corner fit only one young man I knew.

But it was the ever-present Dr. Peterson who frightened me most. In July, just after Rudy's eighteenth birthday, he hosted a dinner in his home, in Rudy's honor. Vater and Fräulein Hilde attended. I was ordered to be there, dressed well and on my best behavior. Rudy had enlisted that morning and appeared, resplendent, in his new uniform.

No one mentioned that Dr. Peterson had also invited two young Nazi officers, or that they would be seated across from me, each vying for my attention. Both handsome and well mannered, one I privately dubbed Mustache and the other Green Eyes.

Dr. Peterson rose. "A toast to Private Rudolph Sommer: may he serve long and well in the Führer's army — for the Führer and the Fatherland!"

Glasses raised all round. "For the Führer and the Fatherland!" We drank, though the champagne burned my throat. As much as I wanted Rudy gone, he was my brother. I didn't want him at the front, fighting, perhaps dying — for the Führer or the Fatherland or anyone.

"Pardon me, Fräulein, but your enthusiasm seems lacking," Mustache whispered conspiratorially across the table. "You must not be concerned for your brother's safety. He is fighting with the strongest army in the world. His training will serve him well."

I considered picking nits from my scalp, if only I had some.

Green Eyes refused to be outdone. "You will certainly miss your brother's companionship and protection. I hope you will allow me to call upon you on occasion, to accompany you, perhaps to dinner or the theatre, to brighten these first weeks of his absence."

I thought I might throw up, at least say something sarcastic, but I glimpsed Vater's head turn in my direction and Dr. Peterson's piercing gaze.

"You are most kind — both of you. I know you intend to comfort me. But you misunderstand. I'm very proud of Rudy. I know he will do well at anything he undertakes, and so must I. You all depend on the girls and women of Germany to stand strong. I promise you I will do so."

They both looked taken aback by my bold assertion and newfound confidence. Dr. Peterson drew a breath. Father suppressed a scowl. But the dinner proceeded and I busied myself making small talk with the half-deaf uncle of Fräulein Hilde on my right.

After the fruit and cheese, once the compotes of candy and nuts were passed, the ladies prepared to retire to a separate drawing room for demitasse. Dr. Peterson pulled me aside. "I commend you, Lieselotte. You comported yourself well this evening. Perhaps we can interest you in someone of higher rank next time."

"I was simply being polite, Herr Doktor. I'm not interested in —"

"Lieselotte is besotted with a childhood flame," Vater interrupted. I'd not seen him approach. "It dims her view of the better opportunities before her."

"Then perhaps it's time to leave the things of childhood behind."

The hairs rose on the back of my neck. "I don't know what you mean."

"No? Then let me help you understand. Lukas Kirchmann is a nobody, a nothing. Even his 'work' is suspect. In order for your father to continue to rise within the Party, in order for him to find favor with such a woman as Hilde von Loewe, he must be favorably noticed. His family must be noticed, must be seen as strong supporters of the Führer and the Reich.

"Now, Rudy has done his part. He has performed admirably within the Hitler Youth and enlisted at first opportunity. He is officer material, and that will soon be made clear. But you, Lieselotte, have a different field of battle."

"I'm a member of the BDM — as befits my age." I felt I might drown. "I'm not even sixteen."

"But nearly, and the last year has served you well." I hated how his eyes roved over my chest. "Rather than enter a program you might not naturally choose, you have the opportunity to catch the eye of an officer of rank. If you prefer someone older than those you've seen tonight, I know of several —"

"*Nein!* I mean, I'm not ready." But I was

ready to burst into tears. *Oh, Lukas, where are you?*

"Then it is time to prepare yourself."

"Lukas and I have — we have an under-standing." It wasn't true, but I wanted it to be true. More time. I needed more time to make Lukas see — see me.

"An understanding is not a marriage," Vater broke in.

"He works for the war effort," I begged. "His mother took care of Mutti — to the end."

"His family's part of that Confessing Church," Dr. Peterson persisted, directing his speech to Vater, as if I no longer stood there. "A number of their pastors have already been arrested. No matter. It won't be long before the whole thing is disbanded — blows up. You want no connection with them, Wolfgang."

11

Hannah Sterling
January 1973

It was nearly five when Carl returned me to Grandfather's. He stood, cordial, as he waited for Frau Winkler to open the door — as cordial as he'd been all day, but preoccupied. He spoke briefly in German to Frau Winkler, who looked over her shoulder and into the hallway, nodding with understanding. Carl tipped his hat to me before leaving.

I followed Frau Winkler toward the kitchen.

"Dinner is at seven."

"Thank you. I just wondered if I might make a cup of tea, please. I'm frozen to the bone."

She filled the kettle and set it on the burner, then pulled a canister from a high shelf and measured out a teaspoon of leaves.

I perched on the stool beside her counter,

understanding I was not welcome to "make myself at home." "I'm so glad you use real leaves. I don't much care for tea bags."

She raised her brows, this time in mock amusement.

"Have you worked for Grandfather long, Frau Winkler?"

She visibly stiffened, as if I'd questioned her regarding something personal, but after a moment's hesitation answered, "Five years, nearly six."

"You must know him very well." Hope rose. I'd no idea she'd been there so long the way Herr Eberhardt had spoken. "I want to get to know him too, but the language is such a barrier. Perhaps you could help me."

"Help you? What do you mean?"

"Tell me what you know about him, what he likes, what he's done in life, anything you know about his family — my family, really. Does he ever speak of my mother? Did she have siblings — does she? What happened to Grandmother? I saw her picture — at least I suppose it was her picture — in Mama's room."

They seemed like such normal questions, but Frau Winkler fumbled her spooning of the tea into the pot and looked as if I'd asked her to steal across the Berlin Wall. She didn't look at me, but busied herself

151

scooping up the spilled tea.

"Perhaps Grandfather told you. My mother recently passed — the middle of September, actually. I'm sorry to say that I didn't know Mama very well, never understood her. I didn't even know until recently that I have a grandfather, let alone one who lives in Germany. So, you see, I really know nothing about my own family. I'm anxious to learn all I can."

Frau Winkler continued to fuss with the teapot, pour the tea, and finally pushed me a cup with a spoon and a sugar bowl. She opened her mouth to speak but, looking up and over my shoulder, froze, clamping her lips into a grim line.

"Good afternoon, Frau Winkler. Fräulein Sterling, I presume." A man who looked to be nearly as old as Grandfather, but taller and with a full shock of thick white hair, filled the doorway to the hall.

Startled by his bigger-than-life presence, I didn't speak, but caught the sudden fade and rise of color in Frau Winkler's cheek.

"I am Dr. Peterson, your Grossvater's physician."

"Dr. Peterson." I rose, extending my hand, but he stood at attention and bowed his head slightly. I half expected him to click his heels.

"Herr Eberhardt told me you had arrived. I am honored to meet you." He nodded again.

"Thank you for taking such good care of my grandfather." What else could I say?

He looked slightly amused. "Herr Sommer has been my patient — and colleague — for many years."

"Then you know him well."

"I have attended the Sommer family since 1930."

"And you're still practicing, over forty years? That's amazing." Immediately I realized what I'd said might offend. "I mean, it's wonderful to maintain relationships with clients so long. I'm sure he counts you his friend as well, from everything Herr Eberhardt told me."

"We have a long history."

This was more like it.

He gave a half bow, charming. "I will go to Herr Sommer now and see you this evening at dinner."

"I look forward to it." I smiled my best Southern smile.

The moment he left I turned back to my tea, but started when he spoke again, having reappeared in the doorway.

"Any questions — concerning your Grossvater — you may ask me. My long and

153

intimate acquaintance with the Sommer family should qualify me to explain all you might need to know. I am also able to translate any particular questions you might have." He smiled ingratiatingly toward me, but his eyes frosted over Frau Winkler, who'd busied herself washing a pot that didn't need washing.

I had the distinct feeling I was being reprimanded, or warned. "Thank you, Doctor. I'll keep that in mind."

His departure sucked the warmth from the kitchen. Frau Winkler refused to look my way, did not open her mouth, even when I attempted to resume our conversation.

What a long and wearisome — and confusing — day since Carl had picked me up, even if a mostly pleasant one. The sights and sounds of Berlin intrigued me, but the people and their expressions, verbal and nonverbal, made my head swim. I didn't know if I'd imagined apprehension lurking around every lamppost. I carried my cup of tea upstairs and sank into the wingback chair by my window, closing my eyes, trying to fit together the pieces of the day's puzzle.

Nobody in this household seems happy. They avoid one another like the plague, and every time I open my mouth it feels like I'm pirouetting on eggshells. I just want to know about Mama. Why did she leave? Why did she never come back or tell me about Grandfather? Why hasn't he asked about her? Why hasn't he asked about me?

Dinner with Dr. Peterson felt just as strained as dinner with Herr Eberhardt the night before.

"You enjoyed seeing Berlin today, Fräulein?"

"Yes, very much. Please thank Grandfather for me. I appreciate all the arrangements he's made for my well-being."

Dr. Peterson nodded but didn't say a word to Grandfather.

After Frau Winkler served the meat and root vegetables, I tried again. "I'm very interested in my family, Dr. Peterson. Can you tell me something about them, or ask Grandfather if there are family albums I might look through?"

Both men shifted in their seats, and Grandfather's face clouded as he first addressed Dr. Peterson. Dr. Peterson replied at some length to Grandfather in German. It seemed he questioned him, that they disagreed, perhaps negotiated, but that finally Grandfather gave an order — almost an ultimatum.

"Fräulein Sterling, your Grossvater realizes that it is natural you would like to know more about your family, but the loss of those dearest is a very painful subject for him. It has been the cause of much heartache in his life, the reason for the serious decline in his health."

He sounds like Daddy talking about Mama.

"Nevertheless, he does not intend to disappoint you. After dinner he wishes me to show you his library and the family album. They will reveal happier days, before your Grossmutter's death, before the war. Perhaps then you will understand your Mutter's family better, and all that my friend has lost."

"Thank you; I truly appreciate that. And thank you, Grandfather — *danke schön.* I can't tell you what this means to me." *Picture albums aren't answers, but they're a beginning.*

Grandfather nodded, his brow creased as if he understood at least part of what I'd said.

The rest of the meal passed in silence. The moment I set my dessert spoon down, Grandfather stood and spoke softly. *"Schlaf gut, Hannah."*

"He is wishing you a good sleep."

"*Schlaf gut,* Grandfather," I returned, so pleased to communicate with him directly.

"Grossvater," Dr. Peterson corrected.

"Danke, Doctor. *Schlaf gut, Grossvater."* I smiled at Grandfather.

He nodded his tentative approval, picked up a cane from the floor beside his chair — a cane I'd not noticed before — and made his way through the door and up the stairs.

Sitting alone with the intimidating Dr. Peterson had clearly been Grandfather's design, but I forged ahead. "Dr. Peterson, what caused the rift between my mother and grandfather?"

"You have no idea?"

"None. Before December I didn't even know that I had a grandfather. Mama claimed all her family had died in the war. She never spoke of them — not one of them."

Dr. Peterson sighed. "It's a long story, and I'm afraid it does not cast your mother in a pleasant light."

"My mother and I were not close. I'd say . . . she kept a part of herself shut off from Daddy and me."

"Your father was an American soldier, I understand."

Now I was uncomfortable and looked away. "Yes." I forced a smile, wondering if Dr. Peterson might have any idea as to the identity of my real father, wondering if I dared ask.

"Your mother was an unusual young woman. I admit that I was surprised to learn she had married an American. It must have been soon after the war ended."

Was he quizzing me? "Yes, I believe it was. But my parents never really shared that part of their lives with me."

"As though she had something to hide?"

I thought about that. "Maybe. I don't know. She certainly hid her father from me. I don't think Daddy knew anything about him either."

He nodded. "Your Grossvater commissioned an attorney, you know — Herr Eberhardt's predecessor — to locate your mother some years after the war. He found her in America and wrote to her. She never answered."

"That was the envelope that led me to Grandfather. I just don't understand why she didn't respond, why she cut off communication like that. I'd have thought she'd have been glad to hear from her father."

"Perhaps your mother was afraid."

"Afraid of Grandfather? That's hard to imagine. He's so . . ."

"So . . . ?"

"So feeble, and kind." I spread my hands.

"This is true."

158

"Then?"

"I am not certain Wolfgang will appreciate all that I am going to tell you, but it is clear to me that you are a determined young woman."

I straightened my shoulders, relieved that someone at last took me seriously and glad that I'd given the impression I wanted.

"Come, let us see what we can find in the library."

The library door opened to a smallish, fairly dark room, more like a study. Floor-to-ceiling bookcases lined two walls. In the center of the room stood a mahogany desk polished to a high sheen, covered by a blotter holding an ornate gold pen and inkstand. Two large wingback chairs in black leather flanked a fireplace. Everything in the room spoke of order and sobriety and looked as if it had not been used in a very long time. Not that there were dust mites floating — nothing of the sort. But it looked more like a museum — a place to see rather than to work in.

"What did Grandfather do for a living — before he retired?"

"Your Grossvater has not needed to work for many years."

Grandfather — wealthy? "But . . ."

159

"He worked for the government in younger days — a well-positioned clerk. He has not squandered his finances through lavish living. Sadly, since your mother left him, he has had no one with whom to share his life."

"But that had to be at least twenty-seven years ago."

"A long time to live alone." He ran his fingers over a shelf of thick books, stopped, and pulled a slim volume from the case. "Here you will see your family, Fräulein."

For the next hour Dr. Peterson pointed out the people in photographs — many of them stilted and posed, but a few more candid snapshots taken at odd moments or family events.

"This is your Grossvater when he was a young man, and your Grossmutter, when they married. She died in the late thirties — of cancer."

"Like Mama." Grandmother looked like Mama, but smiling — in all the pictures, smiling. How I wished I'd known her.

"The cancer tends to run in families. You do not resemble her so much — a little, maybe."

"No. But I don't look much like my daddy, either." I held my breath.

"No?" He studied me. "Your name . . .

Hannah. It is an interesting name. A family name from your father's side?"

"No, I don't think so. Mama just said it was a name she'd always liked."

Dr. Peterson's brow creased, but he pressed on. "And here is Rudy — Rudolph, your Mutter's older brother." He sighed. "A fine young man. Such a loss to Herr Sommer. Rudy's death stole the wind from Wolfgang."

"How did he die?"

"Killed in the war, as were thousands upon thousands of good men."

The next picture showed the same young man in a uniform, proud, even arrogant. "Was he a Nazi?"

"A Nazi?" Dr. Peterson adjusted his glasses. "Why do all Americans think that every German was a Nazi?"

"Excuse me, but I didn't say that. I just asked —"

"He was a soldier in the Wehrmacht. Every young man served, doing his duty for the Führer and the Fatherland."

"Boys in America were drafted too."

"Drafted?"

"Conscripted."

"Rudy was not conscripted. He joined eagerly, to help create a New Germany."

Dr. Peterson sounded so proud of Rudy. I

161

didn't want to be rude, but that gave me the creeps. "What about Mama? What was it like for girls in Germany then?"

"They joined the Young Girls League, then the BDM — the Bund Deutscher Mädel, a female division of the Hitler Youth for girls ages fourteen through eighteen. A very important part of a girl's education at that time." He closed the album. "The organizations provided excellent training for the physical and mental growth of young people. Sorely missing today."

And provided brainwashing, from everything I've read. "So, Mama was part of the BDM?"

"At first. But she was not regular in her attendance."

"Is that because she took care of Grandmother — Grossmutter?"

"Perhaps . . . at first. Sadly, after Elsa's death, your mother spent a great deal of time unsupervised. Rudy was diligent in his studies and training, and your Grossvater worked very hard in those days."

"What di—"

"Your Mutter became involved with a fanatical group, much to the embarrassment of her parents and to the detriment of her Vater's reputation. I'm sorry to say that she was not concerned with the shame she

162

brought upon her family." Dr. Peterson's tone spoke as much disapproval as his words.

Shame? Mama? "Mama was always very strict with me. As poor as our relationship was, it's hard to imagine her bringing shame on anyone."

Dr. Peterson removed his glasses. Rubbing the bridge of his nose, he sighed again. "Perhaps her strictness with you was how she reconciled her behavior in later years. It was, in some ways, a relief when she ran away."

"She ran away?"

He closed the album. "I have no wish to destroy whatever fond memories you may have of your Mutter, Fräulein Sterling. I only wish to protect the fragile health of my patient. Your Grossvater and I have been business partners since before the war; did you know that?" He gave a benevolent half smile. "That must seem like a very long time to you."

"Longer than my lifetime." *But my lifetime is shrouded in confusion, in absolute mystery. What did Mama's relationship with this fanatical group have to do with her running away? And who is my real father? Did she become pregnant — not married, and pregnant? Is that the shame she brought on her family? Am I*

163

the shame? But I couldn't ask Dr. Peterson. It was too personal . . . and too humiliating that I didn't know.

I took the album with me and pored over its pages for hours, tracing Mama's and Grandmother's faces and forms, searching for some link to them, until I heard Frau Winkler turn off the lights in the hallway and lock her door. The hall clock struck eleven. *Why does she lock her door at night? It's not like Grandfather's going to climb the stairs and attack her.*

I turned back to the album. *I look so little like you, Mama, or like Grandmother or Grandfather either. Not even Uncle Rudy — at least not much. Only enough to see that I'm related. Did Grandfather know my father? Did you run off with some boy you hardly knew — some political dissident who shamed Grandfather? Was that boy a Nazi or some-thing else?* The possibility that my mother was a Nazi swept over me like the flu, and I thought I might vomit. *If my father was a Nazi, what did he do?* But I shouldn't have to ask. I knew what Nazis did.

12

Lieselotte Sommer
September–December 1941

I pled chronic trouble with my monthlies until Vater agreed to wait until my sixteenth birthday before parading me in front of more officers. He said Fräulein Hilde had offered to help him throw me a party the likes of which I'd never seen, never enjoyed. I doubted very much that I would enjoy it at all.

Lukas left for compulsory military training in late September — there was no avoiding it now that he'd turned eighteen. We hoped against hope that his ranking for "essential war work" might even yet keep him from the Wehrmacht. Marta and I did our best to cover the routes he'd developed in delivering food to those in hiding, adding them to our own.

The same month, Jews were forbidden to use public transportation, which complicated everything. How could people get to work? How would they buy food? Helping older members of the Jewish community find food and fuel became a full-time occupation.

I attended the BDM as usual, volunteering whenever possible for projects across the city. I prayed I'd not be reported for not showing up each time. Too often I made the excuse that the bus did not run on schedule, or that my bicycle tire punctured and I couldn't find a rubber patch in time. Meanwhile, I pedaled furiously through the countryside collecting whatever I could and lied freely when stopped for identity papers. I prayed those on patrol never compared notes. There was no plausible explanation for one schoolgirl having so many sick relatives on the outskirts of Berlin.

My favorite customer was old Frau Bernstein, very much alone since her husband died the year before. Each time I brought her a thermos of Frau Kirchmann's soup you'd have thought I'd stolen all the crown jewels of Europe and laid them on her doorstep. Long white hair braided into a high bun and smile wrinkles wreathing her cheeks, Frau Bernstein greeted me warmly. Effervescent despite her poverty, she was everything I imagined a Grossmutter to be.

My next stop for her came on a Tuesday afternoon near the end of September. Sunshine dappled between the changing leaves as I pedaled through the streets beside Marta. We kept pace, laughing and joking, until we passed Unter den Linden, then winked and swerved our separate ways. Frau Kirchmann had been given a little bit of sugar, and I carried a thimbleful tightly wrapped in my sewing kit for Frau Bernstein's tea. She'd clap her hands in surprise, so pleased. I pedaled faster to have extra time to visit with her.

Had I not been so intent on envisioning Frau Bernstein's pleasure and our happy scene to come, I might have sooner seen the crowd gathered, or the blockade and the black cars at the end of the street. I nearly ran into a curly-haired toddler escaped from his mother's arms.

"Watch where you're going, stupid girl!" the mother yelled, scooping him into the air. "You could have killed him! *Dummkopf!*"

"Bitte," I pleaded, thankful the screaming child was only frightened. "What's going on?" I pulled my bike to the side of the road, along the edge of the crowd.

A girl not much older than me jostled through the onlookers, rising onto her toes to see beyond the shoulders in front of her.

167

"Who did they take? Who's going now?"

"What is it?" I said again.

"Don't you know? It's the rehousing," she whispered. "Transporting those Jews to settlement houses. Everybody's been waiting, wondering when they'd be taken. It will be a rush for the best things — wait and see."

"They won't take them all, will they? The old — they'll leave them?"

"A clean sweep of the block is what we've heard. They're supposed to catalog everything — take it all for the Reich. But you know they can't do it all at once. Everybody's hoping for a chance to go through. Some of those Jews have gold hidden beneath their floorboards. They just pretend to be poor, you know. Hoarders — it's bad for the war effort. Well, this will be the end of that."

I strained my neck, my eyes, but could barely see past the crowd pressed to the blockade. A car horn blared from behind, an official car with swastika flags flying. I pulled my bike onto the curb, ducking my head. The crowd parted and the driver pushed through. I lifted my eyes just in time to catch the profile of a man against the back window — *Dr. Peterson, surely!*

Brownshirts patrolling the blockade

shouted for the crowd to disperse as groups of people were pushed and dragged from their houses. Two shots fired into the air told us they meant business. People fell back upon people.

Please, I prayed, *not Frau Bernstein. Let them leave her. Let her hide. Let me take care of her.*

The crowd had not complied with the order, at least not quickly enough to please those in charge. Gasps and cries rose from the front of the crowd as brownshirts pushed them, roughing them up. I pulled my bicycle back and turned the wheel as quickly as I could. I didn't want to go. I wanted to see Frau Bernstein one last time, to give her sugar and soup. I wanted to pull her aside, reassure her that she could stay, that I would come in two days and help her find a new place to live and hide. That everything would remain the same between us. But I couldn't risk being seen by Dr. Peterson, couldn't risk having my bicycle confiscated, couldn't risk identification by begging for the life and freedom of one old Jewish woman.

The moment I turned the corner I pedaled — faster and faster — to the Kirchmanns', abandoning the rest of my route and my supposed identity, tears of fear and frustration, of futility, streaming down my face, sure there were Gestapo at my heels. I broke every courier's rule so carefully planned and rehearsed. Fear is a formidable enemy, as real as the foe that openly threatens.

I threw my bike against the wall and burst into the Kirchmanns' kitchen.

"Lieselotte! What in the world?" Frau Kirchmann needn't have pulled me into her arms; I nearly bowled her over. "What is it? What's happened? Where is Marta?"

"Frau Bernstein — they're emptying her street. Rehousing — I don't know where." I blubbered and blubbered, not even sure she'd understand me.

"It's started, then." She held me close. "We've heard rumors."

"You knew? You knew they would take her away? Why didn't you tell me?" I all but screamed.

"Calm yourself, be quiet! They'll hear you in the street."

I moaned, swallowing my grief, still crying — afraid for dear Frau Bernstein, ashamed of the terrible fear for myself.

"We'll find out if she's taken — where she's taken. We won't abandon her, not if we can help it. Did you see her go?"

"*Nein, nein.* I couldn't see anything. The girl beside me said there would be a clean

170

sweep of the block — even the elderly."

"Those who cannot work do not eat," Frau Kirchmann mumbled.

"What?"

"That's our New Germany's view of the elderly — Jewish or not, but Jewish most of all." Frau Kirchmann sat down at the kitchen table and put her head in her hands.

I'd thought only of my own grief, my pain for Frau Bernstein. But there were so many more in our network. I'd supped with the Kirchmanns often enough to know they ate little of the huge pots of soup Frau Kirchmann made, delivered enough jars and thermoses of soup to be aware. So many friends, so many dear ones, so many strangers. Where were they headed now?

In this topsy-turvy world, things changed daily. Within days every German Jewish person had been required to wear a yellow star — pointing them out as objects for ridicule and harassment on the street by day, prohibited from every advantage of citizenry at a glance, and making them subjects of persecution by night.

I'd believed the worst that could happen to Frau Bernstein was that she'd be sent to the Jew house in Berlin. But I was wrong. In late October, she and the Jews from her street were deported — to Poland, as essential workers, promised better food and housing. I did not believe this. Frau Bernstein could barely walk with her arthritic and swollen legs. What work could they send her to do? If she was not worthy of public transportation or medical assistance or adequate rations in Berlin, what would make her deserving of these things in defeated Poland?

I had just turned sixteen, and I was not stupid. I worked and prayed with the Kirchmanns. At least, I worked. Sometimes I prayed, though I doubted my prayers were heard.

By day I participated in school and BDM meetings, and heiled Hitler. On Sundays, during church services, I wanted to believe in God, the author of love and mercy. I bowed my head when the pastor prayed. But outside, in the dead of night or on my bicycle runs into the countryside, even though I prayed then too, I believed nothing and no one. I trusted no one.

Deportations stepped up in November. I couldn't count the cattle cars or the hundreds of Jews that left from the stockyard. I don't know where they went, only that they never came back, that no one expected them to come back. Their property, too, was

172

confiscated for the Reich and "Aryanized."
Yellow stars, which had bloomed across Berlin overnight, now shrank as the weeks passed. Jews, who'd believed things would surely calm down, surely work out, now sold everything to obtain passports, to have their names added to lists for admission to countries anywhere outside German rule.

Most could not afford that luxury. Every day, more went into hiding. We could not feed the ones we knew, and that felt like murder. I longed for the nights I used to lie awake, waiting for Rudy or Vater to come in. I counted myself lucky if I made it through the kitchen window, legs muddied and scraped from cycling madly, before Vater stumbled through the front door in his drunken stupor.

I could not understand Vater. Fräulein Hilde kept him dangling, like a fish lured by luscious bait. One moment he appeared a broken old man, lamenting that she tormented him by demanding he establish himself first, only to declare the next that the hunt was on, that her teasing energized him, as though he'd all the passion of a seventeen-year-old boy in love. He kept away long hours, saying his business had increased thanks to new connections. He authorized builders to modernize and improve our house, and told me to keep out of their way and let them work in peace. All I cared was that he and Fräulein Hilde both seemed to have completely forgotten me and birthday parties and Nazi officers.

I didn't realize I should have kept closer watch, that I should not have been so naive.

The announcement crackled through the parlor radio. Germany had declared war on the United States, days after the Japanese attacked Pearl Harbor — some Pacific port of the Americans'. I'd no idea what this meant for the weeks ahead, except that the Kirchmanns believed it would draw the war out longer, and that Japan and Germany had foolishly roused a sleeping dragon — an opinion no one dared utter in public. One more worry to add to those that abounded.

Perhaps it wasn't right or reasonable, but I pushed those worries aside as best I could and pinned my hopes on Lukas's coming home before Christmas. Home to his family, home to me. Would he have changed in these three long months?

Herr Kirchmann received reaffirmation that Lukas's work was essential to the war effort. *He won't be going to the front! Thank You, God!*

13

Hannah Sterling
January 1973

Carl Schmidt waited by his car for me the next morning, ready to renew our tour. But I bore no stomach for touring Berlin, no matter his insistence and unadulterated enthusiasm for "the city's world-renowned Tiergarten, boasting animals in as near their natural habitats as possible."

A respectful audience, I nodded at the loveliness of the pond he pointed to, listening only with my face. All the while my brain conjured pictures of concentration camps and Jews being shamed and beaten, worked to death and gassed — by someone who might have been my father.

"And the hip bone is connected to the leg bone, and the leg bone is connected to the ankle bone, and they're all connected to the eye socket. Wouldn't you agree?"

"What? Oh, yes, yes, of course."

Carl stopped in the middle of the Tiergarten path. "You've not heard a thing I've said."

"Of course I have. I've heard . . ." I stopped too. Those raised eyebrows again.

"I don't usually have such a poor effect on my clients, especially my feminine clients." His smile disarmed me.

"I'm sorry. I'm really not very good company today, Carl. Maybe you should take me back to my grandfather's."

"And lose my employment? I'm under strict orders to help you discover Berlin as the most fascinating city on earth."

"You've done a splendid job. But I just can't stop thinking about the reason I came here in the first place, and it wasn't to see the sights."

"Ah, your family."

"Yes." I picked up a stone and cast it into the pond, nearly skimming the ear off a little boy. "Oh, dear."

"Those are lethal weapons in the hands of a distracted woman."

I closed my eyes. Why couldn't the world just go away?

"Do you want to talk about it? Would that help?"

"It's too humiliating."

"You're talking to a man who's grown up

with humiliation ground into him."

"I don't believe it."

"It's true of every German. We're tainted. The 'sins of our fathers,' you know."

I knew precisely what he meant. *What about the sins of my father?* But he'd offered to help, and there was no one else. "I came here because I thought my mother had no family. My mother always claimed to be Austrian, and that all her family died during the war. When I learned I had a grandfather living, I couldn't believe it, and I couldn't wait to come, to meet him."

"Yes?"

"Yes."

"So?"

"So, last night I learned that my mother ran away from home."

He waited. I turned away, bit my lip, testing the waters to see if I could speak without crying. I tried again. My breath caught. It was no use.

"Many young people run away from home," he offered.

"This was during the war. She got caught up with some radical group."

"Your Grossvater told you this?"

"Dr. Peterson. He's been the physician of the family forever — Grandfather's friend and colleague since before the war."

"Ah. There were many political groups dur—"

"He said she ran off, that she shamed the family and hurt Grandfather so he never recovered." I turned away again, unable to look at him, to guess what he, a modern German who'd come of age after the war, must think of me, of my mother. "I think my mother was a Nazi — probably an extreme Nazi."

"Did this Dr. Peterson tell you so?"

"Yes — well, no, not word for word. But what else could such shame connected with a radical group mean at that time?"

"You forget that in Germany during the war there was no shame in being a Nazi. There was, in fact, great pressure to join the Nazi Party. Those who didn't were blacklisted and, if they were vocal in their opposition, sometimes sent away — arrested, taken to camps. If your Mutter — your mother — was part of a radical group, that meant she was in all probability not a Nazi, but opposed to the Nazis. And Herr Sommer, of all people . . ." Carl had become quite animated, almost indignant, but stopped.

"What do you mean, 'of all people'?" But I could see that he was struggling with what to say, or maybe how much. "Carl, what do

178

you mean?"

"This is a family matter. You should ask your Grossvater."

"But I can't talk with him. He speaks no English!"

"Herr Wolfgang Sommer speaks English. Do not say I told you this, but I know he does. Everyone who knows him admires his ability to speak excellent English. They are playing you for a fool, Hannah Sterling. Shame on you if you let them get away with it."

I couldn't stop thinking of Carl's words: *"They are playing you for a fool, Hannah Sterling." Why? Why would Grandfather pretend he can't speak English? So he can study me without committing to me — easier to send me packing when he feels he's done his duty by me? So I won't ask questions he doesn't want to answer? And if Grandfather was ashamed of Mama because she spoke or worked against the Nazis, does that mean he was for them?*

If only I could turn back the clock and see what happened, witness the events that shaped them all. I'd been in Berlin three days and was no closer to solving the mystery of my mother — only compounding the issues.

And then I thought of Aunt Lavinia and what she'd say: *"There's more than one way to skin a cat."*

The next morning I listened for Frau Winkler's steps on the stairs. She'd just put on the coffee and was slicing brown bread from the loaf when I startled her in the kitchen.

"I'd like to take Grandfather his breakfast when it's ready, Frau Winkler."

Her eyes widened. "*Nein,* I must help him shave and lay out his clothes."

"Is that something you do before or after he eats?"

"After he eats, of course —"

"Then I'll let you know when I've finished talking with him."

"You know German already," she mocked. "So soon?"

"I think we both know that isn't necessary," I said softly. "Is it?"

She turned her back to me, intent on the breadboard.

"The first night I thought it odd that Herr Eberhardt didn't translate everything Grandfather seemed to comprehend. And last night Dr. Peterson didn't even ask him before Grandfather ordered him to show me the library. I came here to learn about my mother, and it seems everyone is playing games with me . . . even you, Frau Winkler. But for the life of me, I don't understand why."

"Old houses don't give up their secrets easily, Fräulein Hannah. The things that happened during the war — even years before the war — still haunt all of us. The world condemns every man, woman, and child in Germany."

She sounded like Carl, but I really couldn't grasp that in light of people like them. And that didn't explain the rift in my family. Could there be two different sides to Mama's story? "You said you were only here for five or six years. How do you know anything about my family before that?"

"I've lived in this neighborhood all my life."

"You knew my mother?"

"*Nein.* But I remember seeing her. As a child. My family lived in the next block. I was younger." Frau Winkler wrapped the loaf in a tea towel and set it in the cupboard. "She was very beautiful, with her golden hair and smile . . . turning the boys' heads as she walked to school."

"Did she have a boyfriend?"

"She paid them no mind. Not until I saw her walk out with her beau . . . her older brother's friend, I think."

181

My heart pounded against the walls of my chest. "Do you remember the boy's name?"

"*Nein,* I did not know him."

"Did he live in this street, or yours?"

"*Nein.* I don't know anything." She glanced at me, then looked away. "Perhaps your Grossvater knows."

I swallowed. To be this close . . . possibly . . . I smoothed my hands over my skirt. "I'll carry Grandfather's tray."

Frau Winkler raised her brows and poured the coffee.

I knocked three times on the door.

"Eintreten." Grandfather did not sound at all frail, more the authoritarian.

I pushed open the door. "I asked Frau Winkler to let me bring up your breakfast, Grossvater. The coffee smells wonderful this morning."

"Hannah." His eyes registered surprise as I set the tray on his bedside table.

"It's time I started earning my keep, don't you think?" I smiled.

He frowned. *"Ich verstehe nicht."*

"Oh, Grossvater, that's not entirely true, now is it? You do understand. We both know your English is excellent." My heart pounded, but I stood my ground. He didn't answer. Momentary confusion, then indignation, flashed through his eyes.

I took his hand gently in my own. "I don't know why you've not trusted me. I want only to know you, to have you know me. You're all the blood family I have now, Grossvater. Please don't push me away."

Hesitation flickered through his blue orbs, but they bored into mine, weighing me in the balance, searching my temper, my mettle. "You are not like your mother."

"No? Who am I like?"

He ignored my question. "She would not be so direct."

"Fearful? Shy?" I remembered that about her.

"Deceptive." He pulled his hand away. "I do not wish to misplace my trust, not again."

"I hope you'll always have reason to trust me, Grossvater. I want very much to have a good relationship with you. There are so many things I want to know — about you and Grossmutter, about my own mother, my father."

He visibly winced. "No good comes from dredging up the past. Even the good cannot be relied upon."

"And the bad? Don't we sometimes need to understand what went wrong so we don't repeat it?"

"We learn from experience, this is true. But if the pain is beyond endurance, we cannot — must not — be asked to take it out and examine it. Your Mutter is gone, Hannah. Let her and her deeds rest in peace."

"But I —"

"If your intentions toward me are honorable, if you truly want to reunite our family, you will prove yourself trustworthy and do as I wish."

"I do want that, but —"

"Lieselotte broke the law — the laws of Germany and the laws of my house. I never expected to say her name aloud again. I did not know for years that she moved to America, or until recently that she bore a child. I can only go forward in this life, not back. If this is enough for you, you are welcome to stay here, with me. You will be to me the child I lost."

"Grandfather, I —"

"If this is not enough for you, then you will return to America. I cannot bear another great loss. Do not ask this of me." His eyes filled and I realized that this man, this German patriarch of my family, had humbled himself to make such a speech. But the promise he required of me was more than I could give.

"I want to please you, Grandfather — Grossvater. I want to know you and love you and want you to know and love me."

"Then it is settled. We move forward." He squeezed my hand and gave a gruff smile.

It wasn't all I wanted, but it was something I craved. I couldn't resist a tease. "*Ja,* we move forward — in English."

He hesitated; then the sparkle in his eye warmed me.

When Dr. Peterson joined us for dinner that night, it was an entirely different affair. Grossvater spoke in English, except for an occasional lapse into German. He was more comfortable, free in his speech, almost jovial at times. But the tension emanating from Dr. Peterson was palpable.

"You must rejoice, my friend," Grandfather egged him on. "The lost lamb is found."

But Dr. Peterson would not be cajoled, and at one point he let loose a torrent in German of which I understood nothing. Grandfather reacted strangely, raising his head as if considering his friend's words, glancing at me almost suspiciously, then responding in German. When Dr. Peterson seemed to insist, Grandfather finally pounded his palm on the table, exclaiming,

"Enough." Both men sat back, and the meal continued in silence until Grandfather spoke to me again.

"You will continue your tours of Berlin, Hannah? You like all that you have seen and learned?"

"I've enjoyed them very much. But I'd rather spend time with you, Grossvater. It's you I came to see, remember?" I smiled.

He smiled in return. "There will be much time for that, my child. I think it is well for you to learn your new city."

The telephone rang in the hallway. Frau Winkler answered it, speaking quietly, then insistently in German. Grandfather's hearing seemed to vastly improve and he called out to her. She opened the dining room door, explaining . . . something else in German I could not understand.

Grandfather stood, reaching for his cane. "Excuse me, Hannah; I must talk with this man."

The dining room door closed and it seemed the light went out along with Grandfather. Dr. Peterson's dislike of me shut off the air.

"You realize the fragility of your Grossvater's health, Fräulein Sterling." It wasn't a question.

"Not entirely, Dr. Peterson. He seems

much relieved and stronger since we've come to a better understanding. Since I no longer need you to translate for me," I said pointedly.

"Then it is important that you should know, that you should understand why your presence is of the greatest concern."

"And what is it I should understand?" The man was beginning to unnerve me.

"That Herr Sommer is dying. He has three months to live . . . at most. I will not have you upsetting him."

I didn't care that Frau Winkler was off duty. As soon as I bid Grandfather and Dr. Peterson good night I tiptoed to her room, knocked softly on her door. She'd already changed into her dressing gown.

"There is something you need, Fräulein Hannah?"

"Why didn't you tell me Grandfather's dying — that talking to him and bringing up the past would endanger his heart? Did you think I'd do it anyway — that I wouldn't care about hurting him?"

"You wanted answers to your questions, what your mother did to be cast out, perhaps even to know your father. Please to remember that you asked me. I simply told you what I'd heard."

"My mother was cast out? I thought you didn't know her."

"I heard them talking — Dr. Peterson and Herr Sommer. It is why I encouraged you to learn to speak German, to understand the language. You will not know the truth by what they tell you. They perform for you."

"What do you mean?" But I'd had the same feeling.

"Herr Sommer was known during the war, for the things he did during the war."

"That was thirty years ago! I don't understand why it matters so much now, or what it had to do with my mother running away." I needed explanations, but I desperately wanted them to be ones I could live with.

"Running away?"

"Dr. Peterson said she ran away, that it hurt her father deeply."

"She disappeared, it is true. I never saw her after . . ."

"After what?"

"Her engagement was announced in the newspaper."

"Engagement? To who — whom?"

We both tensed at the sound of Grand-father's cane upon the stairs. I knew it as well as I understood the sudden fear in Frau Winkler's eyes.

"I remember nothing. Please do not ask me any more."

"But —"

"I need this job, Fräulein Hannah," she hissed and gently but firmly pushed me out the door, locking it.

The gentle click of Grandfather's cane made its way back down the stairs until I heard his own door softly close.

14

Lieselotte Sommer
December 1941–October 1942

Lukas did not come home for Christmas, nor for New Year's, nor for Easter. Summer came and still his parents could not tell me where he was stationed. They claimed he did essential war work; that was all they knew. But one night, when her parents believed she slept, Marta overheard them talking about Lukas's work.

"They said Lukas is in and out of Munich on a regular basis, working with the Abwehr," she reported to me the next day.

"But that's military intelligence. How can that be?"

Marta shrugged, hugging herself as if to ward off a chill. "That's all I heard. I don't understand it either."

"Did you ask them?"

"*Nein.* I'd have to admit eavesdropping. In my house that's like treason."

"Ja, schön." I understood that. But I didn't understand Lukas. The Abwehr was aligned with the government — the military. We were all knee-deep in breaking the law. Had he turned against us? Could he betray us? I wouldn't believe it.

I waited a few days. Just after Sunday dinner, as I dried the last plate, I asked Frau Kirchmann, "I heard Lukas is in Munich. Have you heard from him?"

Frau Kirchmann was not a good actress. She nearly dropped her fish platter. *"Nein,* not for a time."

"I suppose working for the Abwehr, everything is hush-hush. He's probably not allowed to talk about it much."

"The Abwehr? What makes you think he's — ?"

"I'm so sorry, Frau Kirchmann! I thought you knew! Please don't tell Lukas I said anything. He'd never forgive me."

"He'd never — I . . . Did Lukas write you? How?"

"Never mind. I shouldn't have said anything." I made as if to go, then turned. "But I confess, I don't understand. How can he be working for . . . for them, and still be working with us?"

She looked at me skeptically, but I kept up the ruse.

"You don't think our work here is in danger, do you?"

Frau Kirchmann straightened. "Lieselotte, you do not bluff well. I don't know how you learned this, but I beg you — trust you — not to share what you know with anyone. You could endanger Lukas — his very life."

"You know I would never do that. I only want to hear that he's safe." But that wasn't all I wanted, and I didn't know if begging might help, or if I could do it without tears. "I want to understand. You've trusted me with so much; why can't — ?"

"And you've proven yourself trustworthy in every way, but some things are not easy to understand, not what they seem."

"I'm sick of that, sick of hearing that things are not what they seem! What does that mean?"

She held out her arms to me, and though I meant to stand aloof, I walked into them. She pulled my head to her chest just as she'd done so many times when Mutti lay dying. "You must trust me, dear one. Trust Lukas."

I did not see Lukas again until October — my seventeenth birthday, and the party that Vater and Fräulein Hilde had expected to throw the year before. Fewer Wehrmacht officers remained in Berlin to invite; so many had been deployed. But a never-ending stream of Gestapo and SS officers paraded in and out of our newly renovated house — particularly Vater's library — all of whom received invitations.

More free with money than I'd ever known him, Vater hired a hall for the party, and caterers besides.

With so many coming and going, it was no longer easy or safe for me to slip through the kitchen window at night undetected, so I often sought permission to sleep over with Marta. Miracle of miracles, Vater thought that a splendid idea, as long as I kept up with my studies and BDM meetings. It made our work for those in hiding so much easier. And that was good, for the pressure increased, greater than ever.

Jews discovered in hiding were arrested and deported, sent to camps, sometimes shot on sight. Any German caught helping Jews hide or so much as storing their belongings might be arrested. News of the wretched and brutal prison camp conditions filtered into our lives, the fear of them daily in our minds.

Stealing food or ration books, delivering forged identity papers, inventing a different story each time I was stopped, getting home in one piece and making sure Marta did the same — these were the things that goaded me, that gave me purpose to get out of bed each day.

I'd almost forgotten that I was to be paraded before officers seeking a young and fertile wife, or that I should be soliciting a prime Aryan husband, until Fräulein Hilde took me in hand.

Dance lessons came first — ones I'd never needed and would certainly never use again. The dance master omitted all the wonderful jazz and swing dances made popular in American films we used to see — steps Marta and I still practiced every night in her parlor. Those — the films and the dances — were forbidden by our Führer. But my Viennese waltz was perfected.

Fräulein Hilde and I toured the fabric stores, attended fittings for my dress — a shimmering teal satin, its square neckline cut lower than anything I'd ever worn and one that I was certain the Führer would not publicly approve, despite the contradictory high fashions of the wives of the SS. We bought shoes dyed to match with two-inch heels — all but *verboten* in broad daylight for the new German ideal woman. My fingernails were manicured and polished, my toenails pedicured. I was powdered and puffed and squeezed, my hair swept high and piled onto my head.

By the night of the party I didn't look anything like myself, though Fräulein Hilde declared it a vast improvement as she fastened a string of stunning pearls — a birthday gift from her and my father — round my neck.

"What is it the Americans say? 'You'll knock them dead.'" She winked at me, which took me as much by surprise as that she knew what Americans said.

One look in the mirror nearly knocked *me* dead. When Fräulein Hilde turned to touch up her own makeup I pulled my neckline as high as I could — which wasn't high enough. *Seventeen, and I look like a trollop.* I turned one way and then the other. *Well, that's not exactly true. But I no longer look like a schoolgirl, and could not pass for one. Mutti, if only you were here.*

At my insistence and much to Dr. Peterson's displeasure, Vater had allowed me to invite the Kirchmanns. I could not imagine facing the evening without them — more my family than friends. With any luck, I could maneuver myself to spend more time with Marta than with those searching the reproductive meat market.

Greta, the lady's maid Fräulein Hilde kept

at her beck and call, tapped softly and slipped in the door. "Herr Sommer said to say the car is waiting, that guests will be arriving at the hall any moment. He sent me to ask how long the ladies will be."

"And what did you tell him?" Fräulein Hilde quipped.

Greta did not suppress her smile. " 'As long as it takes to take your breath away' — just as you've always told me to say. And then I curtsied."

Fräulein Hilde smiled and turned to me. "Take note, my dear."

I couldn't imagine speaking to Vater in such a way, but I smiled in return.

Fräulein Hilde looked me over critically and tucked a loosened curl into my coiffure. "You'll be the toast of the ball, as well you should be. You'll have your pick of officers and gentlemen this evening, Lieselotte. Choose wisely."

I swallowed, wanting desperately to protest, knowing it would do no good.

Three hours later, the agonizing multicourse banquet had ended and I'd danced with every officer in attendance. My wit had held through Green Eyes's rhetoric and parlay of words, though my pasted smile faltered after twenty minutes of listening to

Mustache's military prowess.

Older officers stood back in mock amusement, as if waiting their turn for the children to finish their play before moving in. Their lurid, roving eyes sent cold chills up my spine. Vater kept back, observing from across the room, nodding in approval when I smiled and kept up my end of conversations, lifting his chin in warning when I faltered or apparent boredom crept in.

The clock struck eleven. My toes pinched and my arches ached. The three-tiered cake was wheeled into the ballroom, candles lit, and the company broke into song. I was about to blow out the seventeen candles — I'd puffed my cheeks with air — when a movement at the back of the hall caught my eye.

Behind a woman with a ludicrously high coiffure, and to her side again — barely a glimpse — stepped a man in uniform. *Lukas!* Lukas, in Abwehr uniform, just as tall, but older, and more handsome than ever. I gasped and one candle went out. Not enough for wishes.

"Ach! Try again, Fräulein!" the chorus rang. "Deep breath!"

Vater followed my eyes, and frowned. But thanksgiving at seeing Lukas alive and well — and simply here — stole my heart and

197

smile from their hiding places.

Two officers stepped forward to assist me, but I wasn't about to need their help. I ignored the pulsing in my brain and drew a deep breath. In one long sweep of the cake every candle extinguished and the room cheered. Through happy tears I saw Lukas's unbroken stare; then he cheered with the rest.

"Congratulations, Fräulein! Well done!"

"A good set of lungs!"

"All your wishes will come true!"

"And tell me —" Green Eyes leaned closer — "what are your wishes tonight, my lovely Fräulein?"

That you will disappear. That you will all disappear and leave Lukas standing here alone with me. But I said, "That peace will come soon. That all our brothers and fathers and sons will come home safely."

The festive mood shattered. Women nodded, their faces registering the burden we all carried in our hearts.

"Peace will come with glorious victory," Dr. Peterson shouted, breaking the solemnity.

"With glorious victory! *Sieg Heil!*" Arms shot high in salute. *"Heil Hitler!"*

I lost sight of Lukas in the flash of raised arms and the sudden swarm of his family around him. I cut the first slice of iced cake, buttery and dense with raisins — from where such unrationed luxury had come, I couldn't imagine — then handed the knife to Greta, who helped with everything, everywhere. I smiled and nodded, accepting congratulations as I moved through the room toward Lukas. Nothing would deter me.

Nothing but my father, who tucked my arm through his and whispered in my ear, "You have many guests tonight, Lieselotte. You will entertain them."

"Yes, of course, but I must greet Lukas. He's only just come — and from a long distance, surely." But I felt the pinch of Vater's arm wrapped too tightly around mine, the pressure of his elbow against my breast, and I stopped walking.

"Please, Vater, it's Lukas." I lifted my eyes to implore him but they were drawn to Lukas, who glimpsed Vater and me through his mother's hugs, and frowned at what he saw.

"Nod to him, Lieselotte, but turn around and accept the attentions of Standartenführer Gruder. He, too, has come a long way to see you, to celebrate your birthday. Do him the honor he deserves."

For what? For his fat hands traveling the

199

length of my back as we danced? Or for throwing German boys as cannon fodder before the Russians? For ensuring the transport of Polish Jews to concentration camps? Do you think I do not know what your great men do? But as always, I did not say this. I replied, "I will greet him as your guest. I will thank him for coming."

Vater's eyes probed mine, and his teeth clamped behind tight lips, but I did not falter. If he wanted more than that, he would have to beat me.

The party went on forever — at least another hour, but it seemed like forever. I was not able to find release from the officers long enough to make my way to Lukas, until I saw Frau Kirchmann gesture for her coat. It was after midnight, and surely they were weary, eager to go home and welcome Lukas in earnest before tucking themselves — their family — into beds and peaceful slumber. But I could not let Lukas go without seeing him, without speaking to him, without thanking him for coming all this way. I excused myself a moment and walked quickly toward the hall stairs. Surely my father would imagine I'd gone to powder my nose.

I crept down the back stairs and to the kitchen, threw a coat around my shoulders, and slipped out the alley door. I rounded the building just as the Kirchmanns left by the front door.

"Lukas!" I hissed. "Lukas!"

Marta heard me first. "I think someone is wanting you to wish her a happy birthday, *mein Bruder.*" I heard the purring wink in her voice.

He turned. "Lieselotte." My name on his lips was a song.

"I couldn't let you go without thanking you — for coming." I stumbled through my words.

"You had many admirers tonight. I did not expect to be noticed."

"I don't care anything for them." *Does he understand?*

"Happy birthday, little Lieselotte." I heard the sad smile in his voice. "Not so little anymore, I think. I hardly knew you. Womanhood and all its charms become you."

"You're teasing me."

He laughed. "Ask any man here. He will vouch for what I say." And then he grew serious and said more quietly, "Be careful, Fräulein. Your charms are not a game."

Does he think I don't know this? Does he think I wanted — ? "And I am not a child, Lukas."

201

"No. Obviously not."

"I did not ask for this party or this dress or —"

He pressed his fingers to my lips. "They will hear you." He stepped nearer, guiding me deeper into the shadows of the building. "Your father is planning for you — for your future."

"My future is not in his house. It's not in his hands."

"And which of tonight's suitors wins that pleasure — the dashing young officers or the grand old Standartenführer?" I heard the glint of accusation, the shred of uncertainty in his voice. But he should have known better, should have known *me* better.

"How can you ask that?"

"I've been away a long time, Lieselotte. More has changed than I realized."

Was he being sarcastic, or sincere? "You? Have you changed so much?"

"We all change. . . . You've only to look in the mirror to know." His eyes left mine and his fingertips caressed my cheek and stroked my neck.

I stepped back, out of his reach. What did he mean? Innuendos and liberties were not what I'd envisioned, not what I'd dreamed of our first meeting. It should have been simple and wonderful and warm. *He* should have been simple and wonderful — and warm. But he'd turned suddenly old and superior. He stepped toward me, but I stepped back again, and again. "Welcome home, Lukas." There was no welcome in my voice as I rounded the corner of the hall.

"Lieselotte —"

I could take no more from him or anyone else, and though I bit my cheek, I barely held back the tears. I heard Lukas come after me, but the front door opened then and he stepped into the shadows as light spilled across the hall's entrance and into the street. The next couple left the party, and two came behind them. They would all go soon.

Vater would have my head on a platter were I not there to thank them for coming, to accept their good wishes. How could I do that with a broken smile, with smeared eyes? I slipped through the dark to the kitchen door, wiped beneath my eyes with the hem of my slip, and smoothed my hair. I straightened the shoulder straps of my dress and then my spine, despite my aching arches, and lifted the latch.

No, I was not a child. And this new Lukas in Abwehr uniform was not my dream.

15

Hannah Sterling
January 1973
Anxious for Grandfather's failing health, confused that Frau Winkler seemed so frightened of him, frustrated that Grandfather thought he needed to spy on me, and pensive because I was no closer to understanding my mother, it took hours before I finally closed my eyes.

When I opened them, sunshine flooded my room, all the more blinding because it sparkled off a dusting of late-night snow. I stretched and rolled over, realizing I'd overslept by two hours and surprised that no sound in the house below had caused me to stir earlier. Still, it felt a relief to have slept beyond my questions. *Maybe there's a simple explanation for everything. Maybe we all need to calm down a little.* I checked the bedside clock again and reality dawned. *Carl will be here in thirty minutes!*

By the time I'd raced through my hair and makeup and thrown on the warmest skirt and sweater I owned, I had five minutes to eat. But every sign of breakfast in the kitchen had been cleared away. The stove sat cold, the room unlit. There weren't even dishes in the sink.

I set the coffee on the burner. The pot was cold, as though it had never even been heated. *That seems unlike her. . . .* I took the stairs to the second floor, stopping outside Grandfather's room, wondering if Frau Winkler was there, if all was well. Muffled voices came from beyond the door. I recognized one as Dr. Peterson's. *He's here early.* A small worry niggled at the back of my mind, one I didn't want to entertain.

A knock came from below. *Carl — right on time.* But I couldn't go — not yet. I took the stairs two at a time to the third floor. Frau Winkler's bedroom door stood ajar, the bed unmade. The closet and bureau drawers stood open and empty, as though she'd left in a great hurry. The worry in the back of my mind formed a knot in my neck.

By the time I reached the stairs, the knock from below came again. I couldn't leave Carl standing in the cold. I grabbed my coat and purse and camera from my room and hurried down, pausing on the second floor.

Grandfather's door was still closed, the voices still audible.

The knock came again, more insistent. I raced down the stairs and through the kitchen. When I yanked open the door, it jarred the overhang and dumped snow on Carl's head. I laughed despite myself. "You look like a snowman!"

"I'm a frozen man, to be certain!" He brushed the snow shower from his head and shoulders. "Where is Frau Winkler? She usually greets me with a sweet and a cup of coffee — not an avalanche."

"I wish I knew. I overslept, and when I came down . . . she was gone."

"Gone to market?"

"No, *gone* gone. Her room's empty — bag and baggage."

"Did she tell you where she was going? When she'd be back?"

"No. I'm sure she wasn't planning on leaving. Last night she said . . ."

"She said?"

"That she needed this job. She was worried about . . ." But I wasn't certain what. *Grandfather? Talking about the past, about my mother? What could that have to do with leaving?* "Wait here. I need to see my grandfather."

"No coffee, then." He pouted.

206

"Yes, there is — help yourself. It's on the stove. But let's go somewhere to eat. I'm starving and there's no breakfast here. I won't be but a couple of minutes. I just want to make sure Frau Winkler's okay, and that Grandfather's okay." I left Carl standing on the doormat and, before I could lose my nerve or rationalize what I was doing, knocked on Grandfather's door. The voices stopped immediately. A moment passed. I knocked again.

"Eintreten." Grandfather was fully dressed and shaved, sitting in an armchair by his broad picture window. Dr. Peterson sat opposite him, writing in a notebook.

"Good morning, Hannah." Grandfather's voice came weaker than it had last night. Dr. Peterson glared at me as if I were evil incarnate. "You slept well."

"*Ja,* in fact I overslept, Grossvater." I tried to make light, wasn't quite sure how to go about asking all I wanted. "I'm wondering where Frau Winkler is, if you've seen her this morning."

Dr. Peterson answered for Grandfather. "Frau Winkler's been dismissed — finally."

"Not dismissed," Grandfather corrected. "She simply had family matters to attend to — an older brother's illness. She does not know when she will be able to return."

207

He's lying. "I see. Why did you say she's been dismissed, Dr. Peterson?"

He shifted his feet. There was no mistaking the warning glare Grandfather sent his way. "I beg your pardon, Fräulein Sterling. I spoke out of turn. It has been my wish that your Grossvater employ a more responsible cook and housekeeper. I have not been pleased with her thoughtless care for my patient, let alone my friend. It was a rash thing to say. Please forgive me."

"Yes, of course." But I didn't believe him. "I'd planned to go touring again today, Grandfather, but I'd be glad to stay and prepare something for you to eat. Have you had breakfast or anything at all?"

"*Nein,* Hannah. Do not change your plans, my dear. Go and see our fair Berlin."

"You will need to hire someone right away, Wolfgang. You cannot manage without help here."

"We shall see; we shall see." Grandfather seemed suddenly weary beyond his years and illness.

"Let me at least cut you a sandwich before I go," I insisted. "And I'll bring some coffee."

"A sandwich!" Dr. Peterson scoffed.

"Well then —"

"A sandwich will be fine, and most wel-

208

come. And then I insist that you go. Perhaps this evening we can have something more."

"I'll be right back. It won't take a minute." I closed the door behind me, uncertain what had just happened. I'd barely opened the door again, to ask Grandfather which meat he preferred for his sandwich — pork or beef — when I heard Dr. Peterson.

"You should have told her it was her fault your housekeeper was sent away — all this prying and digging up a past best forgotten. You must not shield her from the truth; she's persistent and will simply cause trouble. Send her home now, Wolfgang, before it is too late."

"Peterson, Peterson." Grandfather sounded exhausted, but pleased at the same time. "You must not fret so. Nothing need change between us — that is surely your greatest concern. But I will not send her away — not now. It pleases me to have her here. I have been too long alone. What she is able to learn cannot hurt us. Yet, if we should decide to confide in her —"

"*Nein!* Wolfgang, you promised!"

"I only say *if* we change our minds, it will be for good reason. She will do what is needed. She is my granddaughter, after all."

I found Carl waiting patiently by the kitchen

door. "Ready?"

"Not yet." I was still trying to absorb what I'd heard, to understand what Grandfather meant.

"What's wrong?"

"I don't know." I pulled Frau Winkler's worn apron from the hook behind the door. "I just need to make Grandfather a sandwich before we go, and take him some coffee."

"Turned chief cook and bottle washer, have we?" One brown eye winked.

I half smiled, pleased by his flirtation while still confused by what had transpired upstairs. "Maybe."

Carl set his cap on the table and turned serious. "How can I help?"

"Pour the coffee." I pulled the breadboard to the counter and cut two sandwiches, one for Grandfather and one for Dr. Peterson. It was a gesture of goodwill, and perhaps, after all, the doctor was hungry too. *He must have been here since early this morning. Is Grandfather worse? What did he mean that it's my fault Frau Winkler was sent away? Because of last night? Because of what she told me about Mama? But she knew nothing. Why did Grandfather make up that tale about her brother being ill if it isn't true?* My head ached and it was barely ten thirty. I couldn't wait to get out the door and talk with Carl — the only normal person I'd met since coming to Berlin.

It felt so good to sit across from Carl in a warm café, to have someone wait on me without Grandfather and Dr. Peterson or Herr Eberhardt sitting across the table, frowning in stony silence or critical observation, to eat food without complex emotions or guilt attached to it. When the young waiter smiled at me, I was reminded that Frau Winkler had never really smiled, reminded of how very much she'd been on edge. "Such a house of gloom and tension!"

"What did you expect?" Carl sipped coffee so dark it looked like North Carolina tar.

"I expected life here to be pretty much like life at home, only everybody'd speak German. That maybe I'd learn some German, that I'd get to know my grandfather, that I'd learn something about my mother. He wanted me to come, after all. He invited me, even paid for me to come. But it's as if he doesn't want to acknowledge that my mother lived, as if there was something vile about her and her associations that he refuses to speak of. And there's something else, something I haven't told you."

Carl's forehead creased.

I pulled the envelopes from Mama's safe-deposit box from my purse and pushed them across the table to him. "These are all I have. These are the only clues Mama left me."

"Envelopes?"

"German envelopes. Look at the date stamps. It looks like a series of letters sent over a period of time . . . and then they just stopped. I can't read the address in each case, but they're mostly in the same handwriting. The one that doesn't fit is the one from Herr Eberhardt's law firm, though I think that might have been from a time before he worked there."

Carl squinted at the address. "I don't recognize this street name. That is not surprising."

"Why? I thought as a driver you'd know every street in Berlin."

"*Nein* — not from this long ago. Names of streets and entire sections have changed. Conquerors claim the privilege of renaming their territories."

I searched his face to see if he was teasing me, but he wasn't. I stuffed the envelopes back into my purse and sighed. "None of it adds up — not the envelopes, not Frau Winkler, not Grandfather. Frau Winkler said she didn't know Mama personally, but that she seemed a nice girl. She said she was engaged, but didn't know who to. I need to know who that was."

"It matters?"

I set my cup carefully in its saucer, toying with the handle. "Yes, it matters."

"That had to be before she married her American soldier."

I needed to confide in someone. I sighed again, shaking my head, so uncertain. "That American soldier, the one I loved and called Daddy, the one who loved me and raised me from the time I was a baby, was not my father." I looked up, sure I'd shocked him. "I want to know who my real father was. If he was this man she was engaged to, then —"

"Then perhaps I can help you."

"You?"

Carl stared into his coffee cup.

"You can help me? Carl?"

He sat back. "There are stories and secrets from the war. Everyone has them. Someone knows them. We must find that someone."

"But how? What do you mean?"

He set down his fork. "See that old woman over there?" He nodded toward a white-haired woman, head bent, arthritic fingers awkwardly clutching a soup spoon. She sat across from her middle-aged daughter — the resemblance between the two strong. "She has a story from the war, surely. That balding man in the corner, the one with the newspaper and the thin mustache?"

I nodded.

"He has a story. Every person in this room — every older person you see — has a story they've probably kept hidden since the war. What they did, what they didn't do, what they failed or refused to do. Who their actions impacted, who lived because of something they did, who they allowed to die because of what they did not do . . . What happened to them because of what others failed to do, what happened to their families . . . who they shielded . . . who they betrayed."

I held my breath.

"Just because you see them sitting here, eating soup, sipping coffee, buttering bread, it doesn't mean they have changed inside — in their thinking. Their outward circumstances have certainly changed since then, yes. But what they think about life, how they viewed the Reich and Hitler's accomplishments or even his executions . . . I would be very surprised if much of that has changed in their minds."

"But Germany lost the war. They've

repented for what they did to the Jews, the Poles, everybody. I see museums in progress everywhere here to recount the horrors, to remember so history's not repeated. I've read that they bus schoolchildren to museums to drill in the horrors so it never happens again. I know that doesn't erase Nazi cruelty, doesn't make up for it, but —"

"Just because we lost the war and were forced to stop doing what we did, just because the status quo openly acknowledges the immorality of inane cruelty, doesn't mean each person's thinking has reformed. The younger generation, maybe they see things differently. But the ones who lived through that time, who were already adults, making decisions . . ." Carl shook his head.

"But how could they — ?"

"They saw their Führer as a savior for years. They were willing to go along for their own sakes. Anti-Semitism was rife — we embraced those prejudices before Hitler ever came to power. He simply ran with them. Some were seduced, and some were afraid, it is true, but most supported the Third Reich. They saw it, lived it — it was their life, and they saw themselves stepping up, a cut above their 'lesser' neighbors. *Nein,* what most Germans believed didn't go away because we lost the war."

I searched the face of the man in the corner and the woman across from her daughter. "But that's crazy."

"Is it?" He sat staring at me.

"You're saying there's still anti-Semitism here, a belief that Germans are better than others, like Jews — not that they want to reopen concentration camps, surely."

"Anti-Semitism is more than believing they're better than Jews. Why do you think Germans tolerated the elimination of Jews — some openly calling for the elimination — and a hundred other things unleashed during that time? Some of those sins were exposed and punished through tribunals; many were swept under the rug, for they weren't really embraced as sins by the people. They'd simply been caught in something so heinous the world could not explain it.

"After the war, people across Germany reinvented themselves. They rewrote their own history — they had to in order to survive — no matter what they'd done. Like Herr Sommer."

"I don't understand what any of that has to do with my mother — or my real father. My mother left for America." My head hurt from trying to follow his reasoning. But then it dawned on me. "You think Grandfather's

hiding something he did during the war —
something awful, something that might
explain about my mother and father. But
what?"

Carl waited while I processed his words.

"You said that everyone here has a story
— what they did or didn't do. How would
anything Grandfather did be different from
the things hundreds — you said thousands
— of people did? Even if he did something
shameful he regrets now, why do you think
that's connected to my parents? And why
do you think if he did things then that he
hasn't changed — that he's not sorry? This
is 1973." Even as I said it, I prayed my
grandfather had not been a member of the
Nazi Party. I didn't want to believe that.
Surely he would have had the moral fiber to
stand against them.

"My parents were members of a radical
— many considered heretical — church
during the war. It was called the Confessing
Church."

"A Catholic church, with confession?"

"*Nein,* Protestant. They were a schismatic
portion of the Evangelical church.
'Confessing' simply meant that they confessed Jesus Christ as their Lord and Savior,
not giving that allegiance to the Führer or
any other leader, but to Jesus only. They op-

posed Hitler's attempts to control the church."

"Okay. That makes sense." *But as a Christian, I would have thought that was the norm for Christians, not considered radical or heretical.*

"They opposed the expulsion of Jewish Christians from the clergy, opposed the rejection of Jewish Christians from their congregations and the Reich's attempts to break up marriages between Jews and Aryans, at least those of professing Christians."

"So what happened to them?"

Carl shrugged. "Some were arrested, sent to concentration camps, if they became a nuisance to the Reich. If they became a perceived threat, they might be shot; some more prominent members — especially clergy, or those determined to throw a spoke in the political wheel — were hanged."

"And your parents?" I held my breath, almost afraid to ask.

"Did not do much." Carl all but winced. "I am ashamed to say they did not do enough. I did not do enough."

I almost laughed. "You had to have been a child!"

"I was ten years old when the war ended."

"Hardly old enough to be held morally accountable." I tried to lighten the mood.

But the pain in his eyes told me he didn't agree.

"There were some who risked much . . . speaking publicly, protesting. And then there were those who worked behind the scenes: buying food on the black market, forging identity cards, stealing ration books to feed Jews, concealing them in their attics or secret rooms or basements or barns, moving them from hiding place to hiding place or smuggling them across the borders into Switzerland or Belgium or France or the Netherlands — at least early on."

"I can't imagine such a life."

"Then there were Germans who turned them in — not always card-carrying Nazis, either. Sure, there was the Gestapo, the brownshirts, the SS to worry about, but there were also everyday people who turned others over to the Nazis — neighbors, relatives, people you worked with. Even children reported their parents. And then there were people like your Grossvater."

"You remember Grandfather from the war?"

"*Nein,* but I heard the stories."

"What stories?"

"You won't like what I say."

That's what Frau Winkler said and she disappeared — but this isn't Nazi Germany! "I want the truth, if it is the truth. Though how you would know after all this time . . ."

"He sold Jews to the Reich."

I felt slapped. "He what?"

"He claimed that he would help them, get them out of Germany. He created false paperwork and passports, pretended they'd been accepted within the quota of a country willing to take Jews. He demanded exorbitant prices in cash and jewels, fine art — whatever they owned to sell or barter."

"No — wait. You're saying it cost them, extravagantly, but in the end he got them out. So, in the Germany of that time, my grandfather was a sort of hero — a mercenary, maybe, but a hero."

"He sold them to the Reich. He turned them in."

My head filled with cotton I couldn't shake out. "I don't understand." *I don't want to understand.*

"It was an arrangement. He worked for the Gestapo. He convinced the Jews to trust him, to give him their valuables, then reported them to the Reich. The Gestapo demanded that he turn over the valuables he'd collected — currency for the great Nazi war machine — but they gave him a cut after they arrested those who'd trusted Herr Sommer with their lives. They were sent to camps or hard labor in Poland." Carl leaned closer, across the table, inches from my face, and whispered vehemently, "While men and women starved and were sent to camps and beaten and raped and experimented upon and murdered, Herr Sommer grew fat and rich because he'd tricked them."

My meal heaved to my throat. *He's lying — he must be lying! How does he know this?* I knew if I didn't leave that café, I would vomit on the table.

I nearly turned over chairs in my rush out the door. I left my coat, my scarf, even my purse. Standing in the bitter January cold, I heaved against a metal lamppost.

Carl must not have been far behind, for he wrapped my coat around me. "I'm sorry to tell you this, but you deserve to know. You must not let him deceive you as he deceived them."

I came searching for my parents, for the family I want so desperately — have wanted all my life — and this is what I get? Dear God, what have I done in life that I deserve this? This is not the family I want! "It's a horrid accusation! You have no proof!"

"My parents remember Herr Sommer." He pulled my coat sleeves over my arms, but all the life had gone out of me. My arms hung like a rag doll's — like my Raggedy

221

Ann from childhood.

"I don't believe it. I won't believe it."

"Ask him, Hannah. You came here to learn the truth."

How can I ask such a thing?

"Ask him about the Confessing Church. Make him tell you what happened to your mother."

Carl must have driven me back to Grandfather's, but I didn't remember it. I didn't remember unlocking the door or walking up the stairs to my room. I only remembered curling into a ball on my bed — my mother's bed — still dressed in my wool coat and boots, shutting tight my eyes and willing the world to stop, to close down until it had righted itself and I could wake from this wretched dream.

When I opened my eyes the sun had stretched across the sky, and late-afternoon rays filtered through Mama's white organza curtains, dancing in patches over my coat. Against all reason my stomach growled. I was famished. And then I remembered Carl and his accusations. Hunger fled as quickly as it had come.

There was no way I could ask such questions of Grandfather, demand such answers or make those accusations. *But what if it's true? What if he sold people? What did Carl mean about my mother? Was she opposed to Grandfather or did she play a role in selling Jews — is that what he thinks? Impossible! That doesn't fit — she could be irritable and disagreeable, but would never . . . Please, God, don't let that fit.*

I sat up on the side of the bed and unbuttoned my coat, pulled off my boots. Whatever the truth, I was alone in the house with Grandfather now. Neither he nor Dr. Peterson could have found a housekeeper in a day. The thought of preparing dinner for us both and serving Grandfather with Carl's accusations ringing in my ears made me nauseous and dizzy.

I pulled on an extra sweater — as much for an imaginary shield as for warmth — and combed my hair. I ran the tap water until it came out scalding, then bathed my eyes and face with a damp cloth, holding it until the flannel chilled. *If Grandfather were guilty of such a thing, he wouldn't have invited me here. Knowing that I'm looking for answers about Mama . . . Carl's wrong. It can't be. It can't be.*

16

Lieselotte Sommer
December 1942–October 1943

Once again, the misfortunes of others gave me reprieve. Deportations of Berlin's Jews stepped up. Vater's secretive work kept him so busy with Dr. Peterson and even Fräulein Hilde — something I feared was connected with the Aryanization of Jewish property — that I seldom saw any of them.

Increased deployments sent Green Eyes and Mustache to the east, and though it would surely be seen as unforgivable, I failed to return phone calls or acknowledge the flowers and candy delivered by the Standartenführer's driver.

I was only sorry the special dinners had stopped. Smuggled pounds of leftovers had been such help in feeding those in hiding. It was getting harder and harder to obtain extra ration cards. Sometimes I feared Marta and I might be reduced to begging.

Rudy had not written for my birthday — a thing neither Vater nor I understood. We supposed at first that the mail had gone awry, as it often did from war zones. We received one postcard at the beginning of November, but it had been mailed in September.

By the middle of December Vater began making inquiries, to no avail. We kept busy. Still, it did not seem right to put up a Christmas tree. We placed holly and a candle beside Rudy's uniformed photograph on the mantel in the parlor. But neither of us wanted to sit in that room.

I remembered Mutti's last Christmas, and how the Kirchmanns had saved us all in so many ways. Marta asked if I'd like them to come to our home this year, to help us celebrate, or if we would come to Christmas dinner at their house.

"Thank you, sweet Marta, but no," I answered. "We've heard nothing from Rudy. Vater will not want to celebrate, and I'm not sure it would be right. It doesn't feel right." I could not say it to Marta, but I didn't want to go to their house for Christmas, didn't want to see Lukas, who would surely try to come home for the holiday if he could. I couldn't bear to have him look at me the way he'd looked at me the night of my party.

And I knew that Vater would not welcome any of the Kirchmanns. He'd made it clear he wished to distance himself from them and their connections to the church, no matter that Lukas worked for the Abwehr. Even allowing me to remain connected bordered for him, as Dr. Peterson insisted, on political suicide. But he did not forbid me, for the sake of Mutti's memory, I think, and because the Abwehr was respected.

Perhaps he also thought time with the Kirchmanns kept me busy and out of trouble until he could deal properly with me. Little did he know.

In May of 1943, Marta and I finished our secondary schooling. The Kirchmanns celebrated Marta's graduation with a picnic in their garden, and Vater allowed me to plan a dinner for all I wished.

But two days before the dinner we finally received a telegram that Rudy's unit had been taken prisoner somewhere in Russia — that they'd been imprisoned through the long winter. We didn't know the names of those who'd lived or died in battle, let alone languished or slaved in a Russian prison.

The news and the long winter of waiting had grayed Vater's hair and made him hesitant in ways uncharacteristic. But now, with such fear at our door, he threw himself into his work with greater zeal, spending each evening with Fräulein Hilde and Dr. Peterson, sometimes at our house and sometimes away with them. I didn't know where.

It was as though he could not allow the silence of our house to catch up with him. I think he did not force me to choose a husband because he didn't want the house empty at night. I was glad of that, and if that was what it took to keep the wolves at bay, then I would gladly become a prisoner in my home.

Soon after, the Nazis reported a great victory — that Germany was *Judenrein* — free of Jews — though I knew that was not true.

Around the same time, Vater hired a cook and spent more evenings at home. Though Fräulein Hilde had not committed to him — a thing I didn't understand — Vater began hosting more lavish dinners, inviting every dignitary he could wheedle into attending. I deemed it all calculated to impress Fräulein Hilde, and to keep noise in the house.

Vater's social calendar, his comings and goings, became my barometer for safety — to know when I dared run food routes or risk the curfew. Despite my care, I was stopped and searched one night in mid-June, returning to the city by a different route than usual.

The guard stood uncomfortably close. "Do you not know these streets are not safe at night for a young girl?"

"*Ja.*" I stepped back. "This is what my father, Herr Wolfgang Sommer, tells me all the time."

"Herr Sommer, the Party —"

"*Ja.*" I nodded vigorously, pointing to my full name on my papers. "He'll have my head for being so late. I was stupid — not watching the time. Listening to records with my schoolmate." I made good use of my eyelashes.

He smiled. "You're lucky it's me who stopped you."

"*Ja, danke schön.* I will tell my father what a good and careful man you are."

He handed me back my papers. With a stern warning and a wink I was sent on my way.

But it meant removing my muddied shoes and slipping through the kitchen door after the dinner had already started — Vater's dinner alone with Dr. Peterson that night. I crept through the kitchen and up the stairs as Sophia, our latest cook, carried platters to the dining room. But the intensity of Dr. Peterson's and Vater's voices drew me to the banister, and I leaned over.

"Our work is not over. The Führer might have declared Germany *Judenrein,* but we know there are Jews still in hiding — wealthy Jews, perhaps the wealthiest with their treasure troves. Wolfgang, we cannot stop now — do you not see this? Fräulein Hilde would not understand your hesitancy to grasp this opportunity."

"I am not hesitant; I am tired. I'm hoarding what we cannot sell — dare not sell until after the war. We've been successful, but we must wait until things settle down."

"He who slumbers —"

"I do not slumber!" Vater's fist slammed the table; I heard the silver and crystal jump. "But I'm prudent. I'm careful. I did not get this far by —"

"You're home, Fräulein!" Sophia gawked at me from the landing below. I jumped, dropping my satchel. I'd not even heard her soft shoes leave the dining room.

"Lieselotte?" Vater called. I closed my eyes and swallowed. "Sophia, is Lieselotte there?"

"I'm just home, Vater! Let me change and I'll be right down." Without waiting for a response I took the stairs two at a time to my room, hastily threw off my muddied socks, ran a brush through my hair, and pinned it back. I changed into my Sunday dress and flat dress shoes. I knew that would please Vater — if anything could please him. In less than five minutes I slipped into my seat at the table.

"You're late again, Lieselotte," he accused. "What kept you?"

"Another flattened bicycle tire?" Dr. Peterson mused.

"Ach, nein." I swept my napkin across my lap. "I stopped to talk to . . . to a young man." The lie heated my face, but perhaps created an appropriate blush. "I'm sorry to be late, Vater. Please forgive me."

My innocence and my respect before Dr. Peterson stroked Vater's ego. He would have dismissed my errant ways, but Dr. Peterson did not.

"And who is this most fortunate young man?"

"I didn't ask his name." Sophia placed a steaming bowl of soup before me. "Thank you, Sophia."

Dr. Peterson tipped his head, waiting.

"One of the guards near the train station. I thought I recognized him as one of Rudy's old friends and thought, if he was back, he might know something."

Vater's eyes flashed with hope. Immediately I regretted misleading him.

"But I was mistaken. He was not with Rudy's unit. He knew nothing."

"You assumed a guard had been at the front? You cannot possibly be so ignorant of our country's military structure," Dr. Peterson all but scoffed.

I swallowed. Even a child should know that. "Sometimes, if a man had been wounded, I thought they were reassigned to work in the city until they could return to the front."

"He was wounded?" The doctor's sarcasm grated my nerves.

"Not that I could see. But why else would a strong young man be on guard duty now, when all are needed in the field?"

He ignored me. "I find it fascinating that you did not find time within your busy schedule to reply to the Standartenführer's gracious gesture of goodwill, and yet you willingly miss your father's dinner table to converse with a guard for — what — nearly an hour? A guard who knew absolutely nothing?"

Dr. Peterson dabbed the corners of his mouth with his napkin. Without looking at Vater, he said, "Wolfgang, I suggest you instruct your daughter in both the structure and etiquette of the Reich, and influence

231

her ability to choose her companions wisely."

I lifted my eyes and chin to challenge Dr. Peterson but detected Vater's stiffening. Submissively, I lowered my eyes, rethinking my demeanor. "It will not happen again, Vater. I'm so very sorry."

"About being late, Lieselotte, or about ignoring and insulting the Standartenführer's attentions?" Dr. Peterson pressed. "Do you not realize the opportunities such a liaison could provide you? Could provide your father?"

I was sick of his meddling and could stand no more. "And you?" I asked, feigning innocence. "In what way would such an arrangement benefit you, Herr Doktor?"

"Lieselotte!" Vater brooked no disrespect toward guests at his table. "That's enough. Apologize this instant."

"I apologize," I said, smiling through gritted teeth.

"Lieselotte," Dr. Peterson crooned, "I have known you since you were a little child — since you were born. Your father and I have been friends since boyhood. I desire only the marriage that is best for you. You have grown into a beautiful young woman with impeccable bloodlines.

"You've no doubt read Herr Goebbels's

words — words that should be inscribed on every German woman's heart: 'The mission of women is to be beautiful and to bring children into the world.' As Herr Goebbels says, this is not so 'unmodern' as it sounds. 'The female bird pretties herself for her mate and hatches eggs for him. In exchange, the male takes care of gathering food, and stands guard and wards off the enemy.' " He shrugged. "It is natural — the natural order of things. Do you not see?"

I could not answer him respectfully. He would twist my words. The tension increased and the silence prolonged. My temples pounded. I could not eat with this man, could not sit across the table from him. Finally, I folded my napkin, placing it on the table. "You must both forgive me. I'm afraid I'm not feeling well and must excuse myself."

"You have not eaten."

"Truly, I cannot, Vater. I'm sorry. I'll see you in the morning." I looked directly at Dr. Peterson as I rose and saw that in some way he believed he'd won this round. "Good night, Dr. Peterson."

"Lieselotte." He smiled. "I trust you'll soon recover."

"*Danke schön.*" I walked as quickly as I dared from the room and up the stairs. As I reached the landing above, I heard Dr. Peterson below.

"She's lying. She bears watching, Wolfgang. The girl has far too much liberty now that she's finished school. It's bad enough she's not made a useful match. You don't want her to become a liability. If she won't comply, I urge you to reconsider Lebensborn."

Except for BDM meetings, Vater insisted I remain at home and help Sophia through the summer. Sophia was only too glad to let me carry the market basket and stand in the long lines, waiting for food, while she visited with friends. That was the one opportunity that allowed me to buy more food with the ration cards Marta slipped to me whenever she could.

Sundays, Vater insisted I accompany him to Party lectures, so that my attendance at the Confessing Church fell off to one Sunday a month — if I were fortunate enough to go at all. Even then, dinners with the Kirchmanns were *verboten.* I dared not reproach Vater about the unfairness of it all, let alone confide to him that I missed the church sermons or the Kirchmanns. Tensions ran too high and Dr. Peterson remained too much a presence in our house.

I couldn't understand his hold over Vater, or Vater's continued tolerance of the man's overbearing demeanor.

And still, no word came from Rudy. That was worrisome, but not surprising. For some time, casualties had not been listed in the newspapers, and telegrams reporting deaths were long delayed. The Führer claimed such reports demoralized the German people and that we must all remain strong, must all sacrifice for the good of the Fatherland. But that decision lacked popularity. Every mother waited for news of her son, every wife for word from her husband.

Despite Dr. Peterson's urging, Vater did not force me to marry that year. I wanted to believe that he had changed toward me, that there was some part of him that loved me especially, that would miss me too much if I left his house. In truth, I'm sure that if Fräulein Hilde had married him — as he asked time and again — he would have sent me out with pleasure. Until then, I continued to be a semblance of life in a dead house.

My eighteenth birthday approached with no talk of parties. Vater, Fräulein Hilde, and Dr. Peterson made a trip to Munich the day before. I didn't know why — only that their absence gave me a blessed opportunity to visit the Kirchmanns. I'd missed them so.

Over ersatz coffee and sugarless *Apfelkuchen* in her warm kitchen, Frau Kirchmann shook her head and sympathized with my plight. She pitied me, poured a second cup, and appeared to listen as I lamented. But I sensed she was distracted, that her eyes strayed to the clock above the stove and that she started at every small sound outside the door.

"What is it, Frau Kirchmann? Is something the matter?"

"What? *Nein,* of course not. I'm so glad to see you. It's been so long; that's all."

It didn't look as if that was all. "How are the Levys? Have you seen them? Has Anna birthed her baby? Are they still —"

Frau Kirchmann paled and pressed her fingers to my lips, shaking her head. "*Nein.* I've not seen them for months. They all went away with the transport in June. I don't know where — somewhere east, I think. I hope they're happy in their new home."

I didn't know what to say. She spoke nonsense. The Levys were hiding in the Weisses' old attic — at least they had been last month, and Anna should certainly have birthed her baby by now.

236

Frau Kirchmann closed her eyes. Her lips formed a straight line and she zipped her thumb and forefinger across. *Silence* — I understood. Why, I didn't know. When she opened her eyes she opened them wide, more frightened than I'd ever seen her. I saw the pinch in her cheek. She'd just opened her mouth to speak when Marta burst through the kitchen door, face flushed and braids thrown askew from running.

"They've stopped them. They're going to arr—"

Frau Kirchmann was on her feet in a moment, pushing Marta out the door. They whispered and gestured in the back garden, Frau Kirchmann growing frantic. It was not my business, but they were my family. I couldn't sit inside eating *Kuchen*.

Marta was nearly crying when I stepped behind them. "What's happened? Tell me."

"It's Lukas. They're going to arrest him, I know."

"What? He's part of the Ab—"

"That's just a cover! He's really —"

"Marta!" Frau Kirchmann grabbed her arm and shook her. "Stop! Stop now!"

"A cover?" I said. "You mean — ?"

Marta ignored her mother. "He's moving the Levys. The baby made too much noise — crying — in the Weisses' attic, and they

237

must be moved to a safer place. Frau Braun carried the baby away an hour ago, as if it were her own. Lukas is moving Anna — and now they've been stopped. He's pretending they're lovers, that she's Aryan, but —"

"Show me!"

"Stay here, both of you. Wait till your father comes. He'll know what to —"

"That will be too late, Mutti!"

"At least we can see where they take them. Show me!" I shook Marta until she pulled away from her frantic mother.

And then we were running through the streets, cutting through back alleys, breathless. "I didn't know Lukas was in Berlin," I huffed, accusing, doing my best to keep up with Marta.

"He made me promise not to tell you." She tore through the next alley.

Her confession stabbed my heart. "He hates me that much?" I didn't know I'd said it aloud.

Marta stopped as we neared the entrance to the street and I ran smack into her back. She pulled me behind the building. "There! There they are! They haven't taken them. Maybe . . . He doesn't hate you, *Dummkopf,* he loves you. He didn't want you to know because he loves you — to protect you as he protects me — so that you will have nothing to do with him. What he does is so dangerous, Lieselotte, so very dangerous. He'll be furious when he finds I've told you."

He loves me! "He'll be arrested if we don't do something."

"But what can we — ?"

"Stay here. Stay here and do not come out. If we're taken, tell your parents."

"Lieselotte! No!"

I heard no more of Marta's words, for with every step toward Lukas and Anna I schemed a story and raised a fury. Two steps from the confrontation between the brown-shirts and Lukas and the frightened Anna, I stopped and screamed, "You Nazi cow! How dare you!" I pushed between the startled bullies with truncheons raised and shoved Anna, hard enough to make her stumble backward into the building. "I told you to stay away from him. My own cousin, and you would betray me?"

"You know this woman?"

"Know her? The ungrateful daughter of my father's sister? The poor, dear cousin who needed a home while her father fights for Führer and Fatherland?" I turned again to Anna. "To think we took you in. To think I shared my home — my room! Well, that does not include sharing my fiancé! Wait,

239

just *wait* till *mein Vater* hears of this."

Then I turned my venom on Lukas. "And you — you think because you are a respected Nazi Party member, you can do whatever you wish. If *mein Vater* did not insist I marry you, I would spit in your face."

"This man is your fiancé?"

"Lieselotte, let me explain . . ." Lukas's eyes widened, but he took up the ruse while poor Anna cowered against the building.

"And what are you doing about it?" I insisted to the brownshirt. "What is it about men that gives them the right to think they can marry one woman and bed another — even before they're married? Is there some unwritten code that makes men immune to marriage vows? Eh? You tell me!"

Before he could answer I turned again and thumped Lukas in the chest. "And you tell me which you prefer. You tell me if my stupid cousin can kiss like this." I pulled his face down to mine and gave him the first kiss of my life . . . long and full and warm and one he would never forget. I heard Anna gasp and felt Lukas's rigid frame relax in shock, then surge with heat as I kept on. Finally, I pulled away, gratified that Lukas's eyes had glazed over and his breath caught. "Now, Lukas Kirchmann . . . you tell me who you'd rather spend the rest of your life with, because the decision must be made here, this instant."

The first brownshirt raised his arms in playful surrender. "All right. All right. A lovers' quarrel. Come on, Heyden, I don't think we need take this to headquarters."

But the other was not so easily put off. "Let me see your papers."

I pulled my papers from my inside coat pocket and slapped them into his hand, daring him to give me trouble.

"Lieselotte Sommer."

"*Ja,* daughter of Herr Wolfgang Sommer, Party member."

"*Ja,* I know the name." He looked away.

And that's when I recognized him but couldn't recall his name.

"Fulstrom," he offered.

"Heyden? Heyden Fulstrom?"

"I remember you as a little girl with pigtails."

"That was a long time ago. You were friends with *mein Bruder,* Rudy."

"*Ja,* and this sorry piece of work, Lukas Kirchmann. But no more, not if he's hurt you. I'm sorry about Rudy."

"*Danke.* We haven't heard from him in months. No word. The waiting is hard — hard for *mein Vater.*"

"You haven't seen the lists? They were

241

finally posted this morning."

I felt the world fall away. "The lists?"

"I . . . I thought you knew." Heyden pulled the newspaper from his coat pocket. It was folded open to the casualty lists.

I grabbed it, trembling, running my finger down the death list. *Scheitzer, Schwarz, Seiler, Sommer . . . Bruno, Heinrich, Max, Rudolph . . . Rudolph Sommer.*

"No," I whispered. "No, not Rudy." I'd have fallen backward if Lukas had not caught me.

"Lieselotte, Lieselotte." It was the old Lukas, the one I knew before the war. He steadied me, wrapped his arms around me, held me up. "Let me take her home."

The brownshirts stood back. The one called Heyden tipped his hat and looked away. "Treat her well."

Lukas all but carried me back to his home, Anna trailing behind. Marta met us there and Frau Kirchmann took me in, put me to bed, still clutching the paper. But I could not stay there. I had to get home to Vater, find a way to tell him, to show him the lists. I feared and sometimes abhorred *mein Vater.* I'd feared and sometimes abhorred Rudy. But I did not want this, could not imagine what this would do to Vater, or to me.

Even then, I wanted to think of Lukas's

warm lips on mine, to believe Marta's words — that he loved me. But what good would that do either of us now? Rudy was dead. *Mein Bruder* was dead. Vater would need me more than ever.

17

Hannah Sterling
January 1973

The kitchen stood empty, as cold and barren and clean as it had been this morning — a lifetime ago.

Regardless of how bad things are, we've all got to eat. That's what Aunt Lavinia would say, and that's what I'd think about, count on, now. I rummaged through the pantry and the tiny icebox to see what I could conjure for dinner. What I wouldn't give for Aunt Lavinia's comfort food: fried chicken, mashed potatoes, peas piled in a swimming pool of chicken gravy, and sweet tea. In the mountains, every quandary began its sorting over a heavily laden table.

But nothing resembled the ingredients I'd need for such a meal. The only thing I recognized was the loaf of bread and a rectangle of day-old strudel. The German labels on cans were a complete mystery to me. *They aren't big on pictures.*

I wonder if there's such a thing as German take-out — or delivery? German pizza? Aunt Lavinia would roll her eyes in horror at the very suggestion.

I took the stairs slowly to Grandfather's room and pressed my ear against the door, not sure I wanted to see him. No snoring from within, no light from the keyhole. "Grandfather?" I called softly. "Are you awake?"

"Come in, Hannah." He sounded relieved and looked even more so in the dim light. But I stayed by the door.

"It's been a long day. Can I get you anything?"

He set aside the book he'd been reading and pulled his wire-rimmed glasses from his nose. "I didn't hear you return. I feared that you'd left me too. I wasn't sure what I would do if that happened."

In that moment I recognized a vulnerable soul, a feeble old man in need of my help and attention. Carl had to be wrong. "No, I just came back and took a nap — longer than I realized."

"It must be the time change from your North Carolina. It takes time for our body clocks to catch up to changes in a changing universe."

245

I closed my eyes for a moment and nodded. *"Changing universe" — he has no idea.*
"I'm thinking I should do something about
dinner, but I'm not very familiar with the
foods in your kitchen."

"Do you cook, as well as teach the schoolchildren?"

I laughed nervously. *He doesn't sound like
a seller of souls.* "Don't look so astonished.
Every Southern girl grows up learning how
to cook, but I'm afraid there's nothing here
that resembles the foods I know."

"Ah, the labels are not in your language."

"No."

"Then perhaps I can help you." He bright-
ened.

"You cook?"

"*Nein, nein* — not unless you want a sleep-
less night. But I could read the labels and
tell you what is in the cans. There must be
something we can eat tonight. Perhaps we
could make a market list and tomorrow hire
someone to do a little shopping for us." He
looked so hopeful, so entirely at my whim.

"There's no need to hire someone. You
can tell me where the stores are and I can
walk if they're close."

"It's a long walk in the cold. Perhaps you
could telephone your tour driver —"

"No, I think I'd rather walk or ride the

246

bicycle I saw in the attic."

He hesitated. "You were in the attic?"

"Frau Winkler sent me up for extra comforters the other day." That part was true. I didn't think I needed to mention that I'd also gone exploring.

"You must see if the tires are still good. I would feel better if we had it worked on before you ride it, Hannah."

"It's a girl's bike."

"Yes, there is just the one."

"Was it my mother's?"

He looked suddenly older, closing his eyes, his chest working its way into a sigh. "*Ja,* it was my Lieselotte's." He opened his eyes and considered me. "It is good that it will be used again . . . by her daughter."

I gave a half smile and crossed the room to his chair. *My grandfather. My very own grandfather, and he's glad I'm here. It's what I've wanted so long — family that wants me, needs me . . .* "Are you ready to try those stairs?"

He stood, leaning on my shoulder until he grew steady. "I was born ready!"

I laughed out loud and kissed him on the cheek. *Carl Schmidt is crazy. He's either cruel or misinformed. Sell Jews to Hitler's minions? This man could no more do that than I could.*

We spent the next half hour taking inven-

247

tory of the kitchen. Frau Winkler hadn't kept a large stock of food. Shopping regularly was part of her workweek. And if I didn't miss my guess, she'd been glad to get out of the house day by day. Despite my sympathy for Grandfather, I'd have done the same.

He set two cans on the table and handed me a can opener. "I'm afraid my old fingers have become too arthritic."

"Sauerkraut?" At least I knew that German word. I couldn't imagine eating sauerkraut, though I knew Mama had lived and breathed the stuff. Maybe that's why I couldn't stomach it. "There must be something else in that pantry."

"It is good for the digestion. You will see."

"I believe I'll stick to coleslaw. That's cabbage too."

"Cold what?"

"Not *cold . . . coleslaw*. Grated cabbage stirred in mayonnaise. Oh, I forgot. You don't have mayonnaise. Do you have salad dressing? Did Frau Winkler make salad dressing?"

"*Nein.* You must mean 'salad cream.' Frau Winkler made nothing like that. She was a terrible cook."

My mouth fell open at his blatancy now that she was gone. I think he was as sur-

prised as I was, and we both laughed — a
real laugh, not the timid or cautious smiles
we'd passed since I'd arrived.

"I suppose we do not need to eat in the
dining room. We could eat here." Grandfather spread his hands across the old
kitchen table. "It would be . . . less formal."

I nodded, my heart too full to speak. *At
last, at last I'm getting to know my real grandfather. Thank You, God, that the others have
gone away, that it can just be us.*

I set the utensils on the table and Grandfather set the plates while I stirred the
miserable sauerkraut that I absolutely would
not complain about and pan-fried the cut
of pork I'd found in the icebox. It felt so
companionable, even sweet — so entirely
out of character for the man I'd barely
begun to know and nothing like the man
Frau Winkler or Carl had warned me
against. *Maybe now I'll get real answers to
my questions.* But a little voice within
cautioned, *Bide your time, Hannah Sterling.
Bide your time.*

Grandfather telephoned a mechanic that
very evening to come pick up the bicycle
and make sure it was in top-notch working
order, including new tires. He said the tires
on the bike must be circa 1940s — thread-

bare rubber from wartime. It sounded almost like a prompt to open conversation about Mama, but I didn't want to break the spell. I wanted this little bit of light to go on longer, to strengthen and sweeten. Then it would surely be easier to ask.

But two weeks went by in this vein. I pedaled to market every couple of days with a string bag over the handlebars and a woven basket I found in the pantry tied to the back of my bike.

Grandfather gave me a coin purse that he'd stuffed with cash and told me to buy all that I needed or wanted. His only caution was that I not hold back. He wanted me to buy everything I dreamed of to introduce him to my wonderful American cooking.

Never had anyone prompted me to extravagance. With Mama we'd had to scrimp and save every penny — especially after Daddy passed. And when I'd taught school . . . well, a teacher's salary simply didn't go far, what with room and board, school loans, and trying to keep a car on the road.

It was like we were playing house, and both so happy to do it. We ate each night in the kitchen and the second week we shared coffee in his library. He urged me to take extra cash and stop at the dressmaker's in town, to buy something special and pretty for myself.

"You must try our Berlin fashions. They may not be the latest from Paris or New York . . ."

"Well, I never had the latest from Paris or New York anyway. Are you sure? I mean, clothes cost an awful lot, and I know things are expensive here."

"You are *meine Enkelin* — my grand-daughter, Hannah. There is no one else in this world as important to me as you. I want you to feel at home here, to have everything you need."

"You're not just angling for me to stay on as your housekeeper, are you?" I teased. "Because if you are, it will require shoes and stockings as well!" I laughed, but he didn't.

"There is nothing I would like more than to have you stay with me always, Hannah. Everything I have can be yours one day, should be yours."

"I was joking, Grossvater. I'm so sorry; I was simply trying to be clever."

"I am not joking." I could see him swallow, as if what he said was difficult for him. "It is true I need a housekeeper, but that is something I can pay for — a service I can buy. So many people are searching for employment now. But companionship I cannot buy, nor loyalty."

"I love being with you, Grossvater, but you know I have a job I need to get back to in North Carolina — a teaching career. If I don't return soon or let them know when I'm coming back, I may not have that job." That was truer than I wanted to admit.

"But your school will close for the summer, yes? Stay here, at least through the summer, and then decide."

"I'm afraid it's not that simple."

"Simple?" He shrugged. "It can be so very simple. I can provide all that you need — whatever you ask. Here, you see this purse?" He pointed to the men's pocketbook on the bookshelf behind his desk. "Take whatever you need."

"But —"

"Only search your heart . . . think about it. Perhaps the summer will be long enough." He took a wad of deutsche marks from the bag and pressed them into my hands. "I am going to lie down now. You do not need to hurry back. Go to the café for lunch and enjoy yourself. Dr. Peterson will be coming to see me soon and will bring our lunch."

"Are you feeling worse today?"

"Just the same. He comes as my doctor,

252

but also as my friend and business colleague. We've grown old together and must keep an eye to see which one goes first." His eyes narrowed in jest. "I'm betting that I outlive him by at least twenty minutes. Ten would be nothing, but twenty — ah, that would be victory."

I couldn't help but smile as he climbed the stairs to his room. He was elderly, somewhat frail with terrible heart problems, but he'd not given up, and I so admired that. Daddy had been a worn-out shell of a man, and Mama so tightly wound I never knew if she'd snap, even at the end. But it was more than his attitude. He'd gained a new purpose, a light and a little bounce in his step since Frau Winkler had gone — as though my caregiving had given him reason to get up each morning. That he needed me — wanted me — meant everything. That he thought the summer would "be enough" worried me, though Dr. Peterson's prognosis that Grandfather would live no more than three months worried me more.

But I needed to go home, didn't I? I wasn't sure I wanted to go home, but this wasn't my real life. It was more like living in the twilight zone — time out of time. And yet, for all the improvement in our relationship, I'd not really accomplished what I'd come for. I was living — sleeping, waking — in my mother's old bedroom every night and riding her old bicycle each day. I laughed and joked with Grandfather and cooked and cleaned as if I'd been living here all my life and would go on living here forever. But I hadn't found the opportune moment, or the courage, to ask more about Mama, much less about his role during the war.

If Grandfather truly believes he's not got long, then neither do I. Maybe I should stay. What will a few more months matter? Mr. Stone can certainly keep the long-term substitute through the school year. I could return, fresh, in September. He promised he'd be glad to have me back. That would give me another six or seven months, easily — plenty of time, no matter what happens.

Rationalizations buzzed round and round my brain while I sat in the warm café eating luscious apple strudel smothered in hot custard sauce — the one food in Berlin that made my mouth water. I hadn't been in the café — hadn't been out to eat — since the day Carl had astonished me with his tales about Grandfather. Even though I'd not completely forgiven him, I missed our talks and bantering, and the offhand way he would nudge my elbow to share a special tourist site or secret about Berlin or insight into German culture or families — not mine. I half hoped he'd walk in and warm me through with his smile and half hoped he'd never darken my doorway again.

"Pennies for your thoughts," Carl whispered from behind, very near my ear.

"Carl Schmidt!" I nearly jumped out of my skin. "You startled me. I was just thinking of . . . of what I need to buy at the greengrocer's."

"Ah, you're now doing the shopping for Herr Sommer."

I hated the knowing insinuation in his tone and lifted my chin. "I enjoy going to market, and cooking is something I've always wanted to have time and an appreciative audience for."

"And I suppose you have strict instructions regarding which shops to patronize and which to avoid?"

Grandfather had specified not going to Goldman's for bread or Rosenbaum's for meat. *"They are not trustworthy — they will cheat you."*

"Grandfather's lived here all his life. He knows which carry the best food for the best value; that's all." But my defense of his insistence was pitiful, even in my own ears. I could not deny his anti-Semitism.

"I see. . . . May I join you? Or do you wait for someone?"

"No — yes — I mean, no, I'm not waiting for anyone. Please join me. I'll be glad of some younger company."

He grinned. "Thank you for not linking me with the geriatric set — not yet. Though I realize that ten years makes quite a difference."

"Not so much." I blushed, astonished at my boldness, but it only set a light off in his brown eyes. I moistened my lips and swallowed.

"Ah, good. Then I will be bold. Would you like to go to dinner some evening this week?"

"Dinner?"

"Yes, something more substantial than — though not necessarily as delicious as — your apple strudel." He grinned, helping himself to a bite. "And a film, perhaps."

"Oh, well, I don't know. I mean, I'd like that very much, but I'm not certain about leaving Grandfather alone in the evening."

"He is not well?"

"He has a heart condition, and he depends on me, you see."

"He depends on you so much that an evening out with a friend is not possible? Has he not hired another housekeeper?"

"No." I stirred my coffee, realizing how strange that must sound. "Not yet."

Carl waited.

"While I'm here there's no reason I can't do those things. I'm just on my way now to pick up an order at the greengrocer's."

"Yes, I see."

This was the half that I wished might never darken my door.

"Have you asked him about your mother?"

"No," I admitted. "We're getting along really well right now, just getting to know each other for the first time."

"And you fear that talking about his daughter would upset him so very much."

"He's made it clear that the past is very painful for him; he doesn't want to talk about it."

"I imagine not."

"You're quick to jump to conclusions."

"And you refuse to accept that there are conclusions to be made after considering relevant facts. But if you do not examine those facts, Hannah, if you do not investigate to find out if they *are* facts, you avoid having to form any conclusion."

"You have no proof."

"That doesn't mean there is no proof. Germans are known for keeping meticulous records. There may be —"

"Just because I don't believe my family hunted Jews and sold them for blood money doesn't mean —"

"I never said that your family hunted Jews — not all your family. You should listen more carefully."

I yanked my coat and scarf from the chair and threw down the marks for my bill. "Good-bye, Carl." This time I made my dramatic exit on my own terms.

Who does he think he is?

"He convinced the Jews to trust him, to give him their valuables, then reported them to the Reich. . . . They gave him a cut, after they arrested those who'd trusted Herr Sommer with their lives. . . . While men and women starved and were sent to camps . . . Herr Sommer grew fat and rich because he'd tricked them."

No matter how many days passed, Carl's words echoed in my brain. I jerked my bicycle from the rack and sped off, pedaling faster and faster, skidding on icy patches, nearly losing my brake blocks as I tore down the hill. I just wanted to get home, to forget Carl and all he implied.

I must ask Grandfather, must summon the courage to tell him what Carl said — how else can he deny it? Surely he could explain the source of such a vile rumor and how we might set it straight. I'd grown to love

258

Grandfather, was sure he loved me. I'd stay in Berlin until we had set it right, even if that meant all summer. The community at home had ostracized my mother because of her accent. Here Grandfather's accent was perfect, natural, but still the community ostracized him, if Carl's words or Frau Winkler's attitude was any indication. Certainly no friendly neighbors had popped in during my stay. Next it would be me. I wouldn't take it — not anymore, not again.

Someone called to me as I raced round the bend, but I refused to slow. I swerved into the narrow drive only to find Dr. Peterson's automobile blocking the path. I guided my bike to the outside kitchen wall, let myself in through the back door, and leaned against it, willing my heart to still. Voices rose and fell from up the stairs, intense, argumentative.

I set the kettle on the stove. A cup of tea might warm me through, might stop my hands from shaking.

The door behind me rattled with a sharp pounding and I jumped, clapping a hand over my heart. I pulled it open, half expecting to see Carl, ready to give him another piece of my mind. But it was the greengrocer's son.

"I have your order, Fräulein Sterling." The

boy, fourteen or so, removed his cap. "I saw you race by, and *mein Vater* thought you may have forgotten."

"Oh, I'm so sorry. I did forget — completely. Thank you." I took the box, heavier by half than what I'd imagined, grateful for his kindness and help.

"Do you want me to put it on Herr Sommer's bill?"

"No, I have the money — just a sec. How much?" I set the box on the table.

"Five marks should cover it."

"Five marks. Here." I pulled the change purse from my coat pocket. "One, two, three, four . . . I'm a little short." I remembered the purse Grandfather had shown me on the library shelf. *I shouldn't interrupt him and the doctor upstairs.* "Please come in and have a seat; it's too cold to wait outside. I'll get the rest."

The library door stood ajar. It felt like prowling to walk in without Grandfather there. *That's silly. He said his house is my house. I'm just taking him at his word.* I'd switched on the desk lamp to better see when I noticed he'd left a small brass key in the lock of his desk drawer — unlike him. He was always very particular about his desk.

For all the frustration and even humilia-

260

tion I'd felt about Carl's accusation, a tiny doubt lingered at the corner of my mind. Grandfather's desk was the one thing I knew he kept locked, the only place I could imagine there might be secrets hiding.

It took but a moment. Before I could rationalize the impropriety or think myself out of it, I turned the key and pulled open the narrow drawer. Inside was a single object — a long, gray-bound book, frayed at its browned edges, worn round at its corners. Carl's words flashed through my mind. *"That doesn't mean there is no proof. Germans are known for keeping meticulous records."*

I took a deep breath and pulled it out, opened the cover. The front page had one word, *Rechnung,* with dates penned below: *15 November 1938–1944.* The second page was divided into columns. The first entry gave the date again — 15 November 1938, under the word *Verhaftung* — then a surname, Goldstein, with four Christian names indented beneath. *Or are they "Christian" names?* There was an address in Berlin, and then a list — perhaps an inventory of some kind. I tried to read the German words, but I wasn't sure what they all meant. One heading was *Geld.* I knew that meant money — like the word *gold* in English. I didn't know what the next word, *Juwelen,* meant, nor *Ausgabe* nor *Gemälde,* and under that, *Renoir.*

My pulse beat loudest in my ears, my brain.

"Fräulein?" It was the greengrocer's son calling through the hallway. I'd completely forgotten him.

The rumble of voices upstairs stopped. Footfalls down the stairs and a sharp tirade in German — *Dr. Peterson!*

I slid the ledger back into the drawer and had barely turned the key when the library door flew open.

"What are you doing in this room?" Dr. Peterson thundered at me, his grip on the boy's arm formidable. His eyes flew round the room, then back to the desk and me. "Answer me! What are you doing here?"

Stop shaking . . . stop shaking . . . stop shaking. "I just came in to get the purse for market money. I need to pay the greengrocer, and I respectfully suggest that you stop manhandling his son."

"He is not a thief?"

"He is most definitely not a thief. He was kind enough to bring over a delivery too heavy for me to carry on the bike." I summoned all the indignation I could muster. "Now, if you'll excuse me, I will pay this kind young man, whom you've most certainly traumatized, and send him on his way." I pried Dr. Peterson's fingers from the boy's arm and gently pushed the frightened young man through the door, intending to brush past Dr. Peterson. I willed my steps even, tried to appear in control of my pounding heart and racing pulse.

But Dr. Peterson stepped between the boy and me. "You will forgive me, Fräulein Sterling. I am most concerned with Herr Sommer's privacy in his vulnerable state. I am his lifelong friend, and there is nothing I would not do to protect him. Do I make myself clear?"

"Perfectly, Dr. Peterson. But I must remind you that I'm his granddaughter, and he does not need protecting from me — or the greengrocer's son. And as far as I know, Grandfather and I do not have secrets from one another." I waited, perhaps a heartbeat too long. "So you really have nothing to worry about." I straightened my spine, glaring.

He stepped aside. "Did you not forget something?"

He caught me off guard.

"The purse you require . . . the reason you came into this room."

"Yes, of course." I brushed my forehead,

263

doing my best to look as though forgetting my head were an everyday occurrence, and retrieved the purse from the shelf behind Grandfather's desk.

I paid the pale, wide-eyed grocer's son, who would surely never deliver another thing to this house and would warn every other merchant against doing so. I closed the back door, chilled to the bone — and not because of the northeast January wind that whipped through the kitchen.

18

Lieselotte Sommer
October 1943

Lukas did not evaporate into thin air this time. He and the entire Kirchmann family attended Rudy's memorial service, a quiet and simple event with close friends and our dwindling family. Once the lists were published, there were so many funerals, so many memorial services, and too few bodies returned to families. The Führer ordered private affairs for the most part. It was too demoralizing for the people, just as he'd predicted.

Rudy's body was not returned. Still, Vater erected a stone for him next to Mutti's. Because we did not know his death date, Vater had it inscribed as July 18, 1943. Rudy would have been twenty years old on that day. So young. That was the hardest of all.

After the service, just as after Mutti's

funeral, Dr. Peterson took Vater out drinking, as if that would make him forget the death of his only son. Fräulein Hilde cast me a pitying glance, but joined them.

Sophia had gone to visit her mother, so that night I put the kettle on alone in the kitchen. Was that to be my funeral ritual?

The days had grown short, and it was dark before seven. I opened the door to the larder but had neither heart nor stomach to eat. I brewed the ersatz strong and dark and dumped a week's worth of sugar rations into the pot. Sophia would be furious.

I lit one small lamp and sat at the kitchen table, sipping the too-sweet brew and scalding my throat. At least I felt something.

Three light taps at the window made me jump.

"Lieselotte! Let me in!"

I opened the door and there stood Lukas, a platter of sandwiches in one hand and a kettle of something hot emanating an amazing fragrance in the other. I blinked. I'd played this role before.

He held up his offerings with a conciliatory smile, recognizing the sad irony.

I stepped back, glad that he brushed my shoulder, glad not to be alone, glad it was Lukas bearing gifts. "Your mother's soup?" I inhaled.

"You know Mutti. She means well."

"Thank her. But I can't eat. Not now."

"Ah, ah." He wagged his finger. "Mutti says you must or she will come over here herself and spoon it into your mouth." He set the pot on the stove. "I begged her to let me do it."

"Lukas." I couldn't hold back the tears.

He said nothing but pulled my head to his chest, wrapping me in his arms, stroking my hair as he would comfort a child. "I'm sorry, my little Lieselotte. I'm so very sorry."

No more words between us. Only soft kisses in my hair and a gentle drying of my tearstained face before he slipped through the door and into the night an hour later.

I slept that night as I hadn't slept in months.

The next morning I left before Vater came downstairs, to return the platter and pot to Frau Kirchmann, in hope of seeing Lukas once more. But he had already gone.

"A message came last night, and he packed his bag right away. He said it was urgent and didn't know when he could come again."

I nodded, as if that were the most natural thing in the world; inside, my heart was breaking.

Frau Kirchmann motioned me into the back garden and closed the kitchen door behind her. "Lukas thinks our house might have — what do they call it? — a listening device of some kind. That they might be suspicious of our work, or of his work."

"Have you seen this?" I'd heard of such things in novels and films, but not in real life.

"*Nein,* but our house was searched. Things . . . were taken. We cannot be too careful. His life — all our lives and those we help — might depend on it."

"That's why you talked so strangely about Anna the other day. Now I understand."

She nodded. "I didn't mean to frighten you, but I dared not let our conversation steer them to Anna. Marta told me what you did for Lukas and Anna. It was a terrible risk, but I thank you. From the bottom of my heart, I thank you, Lieselotte. If Lukas had been taken —"

"Shh, shh — it did not happen. We'll all work to make certain it does not happen."

She pulled her cardigan tight around her, as if the threat of arrest chilled her through. "I don't know exactly what he does. But it's dangerous, so very dangerous. We must pray hard for him."

"Gathering intelligence? This is dangerous?" Of course it was; I knew this. What was it but spying, and what could be more dangerous except standing in front of a firing squad? But I wanted to talk to her, to anyone, about Lukas. To say his name. Despite the terrible loss of Rudy, I could not stop thinking of Lukas as I'd boldly kissed him that day in the street, as he'd tenderly held me last night. It could mean nothing for our future, or everything. It was my lifeline.

Frau Kirchmann must have understood — when had she not? She caressed my arm. "He can't make commitments now, you know. The work he does is uncertain and depends so much on his having no ties, no inhibitions about anything — not even protecting his own life for the sake of another's heart. You understand that, don't you?"

"Yes, yes of course, I understand."

She nodded, as if she believed me. "Good. That's good. You must plan your future apart from Lukas, Lieselotte. You must protect your heart."

I didn't want to think about what she'd said, refused to think about it. "I must get back. Vater does not know I've gone out. He — he came in late, and will need something for his headache."

"*Ja, ja* — you go, my dear. But come anytime — anytime at all. Only remember: be very careful what you say in our house or on the phone. *Ja?*"

"*Ja,* I will. Thank you again for the soup and sandwiches, Frau Kirchmann." I forced a smile and she hugged me in return.

The door closed behind her, and I was left in the cold. I'd come with such warmth and hope — and now, nothing. It was only October and the sun shone brilliantly, the sky a startling blue, but all the world felt gray, and the numbness of an early winter seeped into my bones.

I was halfway down the street, lost in my own world, when Marta, breathless, caught up to me, shook my arm. "Did you not hear me calling? Are you deaf?"

"*Nein,* I did not hear." I stared at her. Her nose, her forehead resembled Lukas's. I didn't even want to think about that. "What do you want, Marta?"

"Lukas," she panted.

"Your mother already told me he left." I turned to walk away.

"He gave me this — to give you. He said not to tell anyone and that if something happens to him, you must ignore this. He said it breaks every rule he's bound to." She shoved a folded paper into my hand. "Don't tell Mutti."

"Did you read it?"

She laughed, "Yes, of course!" and was gone.

I unfolded the paper. Three words scribbled in the hand I had memorized since childhood: *Wait for me.*

19

Hannah Sterling
January–February 1973

Grandfather was quiet at dinner that night, picking at his food, not enjoying his beef or beer or even his after-dinner coffee as usual. I knew he suspected I'd pried in his office. No telling what spin Dr. Peterson had cast on my words or actions. I didn't trust the man as far as I could throw him, but dared not bring up the subject for fear I'd look as guilty as I felt.

We sat across from each other, both restless. I excused myself early, claiming I was worn out from my shopping trip. I hoped that a good night's sleep would calm his nerves and mine, that we could begin again tomorrow.

But I feared him, this old and feeble man — so silly on my part. At the same time I'd grown angry, hurt, uncertain after seeing the ledger. Despite all of that, I craved his good opinion and grandfatherly affection.

I wasn't ready to submit to Carl's accusation. *There must be another explanation for the ledger. But I need to know, need proof. How can I get that proof? How can I tell him — ask him? He'd be heartbroken to know I doubted him. There's just one way, the only way.*

It was after midnight before Grandfather stopped rummaging through his library and pacing his bedroom floor. I held my breath, waiting to hear his even breathing. Creeping downstairs with a flashlight to snoop through someone's personal papers was not something I'd been raised to do, but I was desperate to better understand what I'd seen that afternoon.

The floorboard creaked as I stepped onto the first-floor landing. I stopped, switched off my light, and held my breath, straining my ears. It's hard to tell how long a person stands in the dark, waiting. But after a time, I switched on the flashlight, minimizing its glow with my other hand, and made my way to the library door. Locked.

I closed my eyes and silently sighed. *Back to square one. He doesn't trust me now. Which means — which may mean — he has something to hide.*

■ ■ ■ ■

Three days passed. The library door remained locked. Gradually Grandfather grew
less reserved — not at all playful in his
banter as before, but at least we ate together
more companionably. I dared not ask about
the library; I knew not asking could make
me look guilty but still hesitated to reveal
that I'd tried the door.

We'd just finished luncheon and I was
washing the dishes when Grandfather
stopped in the kitchen. "Dr. Peterson will
be coming by tomorrow morning, and Herr
Eberhardt. Could you serve us some luncheon?"

*How can I not after Grandfather invited me,
took me in?* But the idea of serving Dr.
Peterson anything — of being in the same
room with him — both frightened me and
set the whole marching band playing inside
my stomach. *Hannah Sterling, you're turning
into mincemeat. Buck up!* "No, I'm sorry,
Grandfather — Grossvater — I can't. I'm
going out tomorrow and won't be back until
late in the day."

The silence stretched so long I was
tempted to turn around to see if he'd gone.

"What I can do is prepare something cold

and leave it on the dining room sideboard just before I leave. You can help yourselves." I kept washing the same dish. It was my last one, but I wouldn't turn, couldn't look at his face.

Half a minute passed. "I see, Hannah, that it is too much to ask. Do not trouble yourself." He walked out.

I couldn't stop the first tear that spilled, nor the second, nor the many that followed.

I waited that night until Grandfather's soft snores came steady and even, then crept downstairs to the hallway telephone. I pulled the card from my robe pocket and dialed the number. A sleepy, weary male voice answered.

"Are you there?"

"Hannah. Hannah Sterling."

"How did you know it was me?"

Carl's chuckle came warm through the phone. "What do you want, Hannah?"

I swallowed, humiliated and needy and eager to see him. "I need to talk with you. I'd like to invite you to lunch tomorrow — early."

"Early?"

"Ten thirty?" I whispered.

"That is early for lunch." I could hear his smile. "Why are we whispering?"

"Well, yes," I whispered again, ignoring his question. "The café?"

"Let's meet there, and then let me take you somewhere new. I'll have the car."

"That would be wonderful," I sighed.

"Until tomorrow."

"Tomorrow." I replaced the receiver, relief flowing through my bones until I heard the closing click of Grandfather's bedroom door.

The four-star Parisian bistro surely ran well beyond Carl's budget.

"You are in Europe, and yet not planning a trip to France. So you must experience the closest thing possible." His smile held all the light of a spring sunrise over North Carolina mountains.

I was homesick.

"You are not happy, Hannah?" His hand covered mine, twining our fingers. I should have pulled back. But I didn't. I needed a connection to someone.

"I'm confused." I laughed softly, self-consciously. "That's an awkward confession."

"Tell me."

It was so hard to formulate my thoughts, so hard to articulate what I knew with my heart but desperately hated to acknowledge with my brain, my mouth.

"Herr Sommer?"

I nodded. "The day we talked in the café . . . When I got back to the house, the greengrocer's son had followed me with a delivery. I didn't have the right money, so I went to the library to get the purse Grandfather said I should use. Grandfather was upstairs with his doctor."

"Peterson — his cohort."

"Yes. You know him?"

"I know of him — that he and Herr Sommer have long been colleagues. Go on."

"Ah," I said, not really understanding what or how he knew. But that didn't matter now. "The key to Grandfather's desk drawer was in the lock. He never leaves it unlocked." I searched his eyes, praying I could trust him. "Inside, I found a ledger — a ledger that began in late 1938." I hated to say what came next. "There're lists — names, addresses, and dates. I think they were family names, and some sort of inventory of things. Cash, possessions — I don't know what exactly. I could read so little of the German."

"How many pages were filled?"

"I don't know. I'd barely read the first page, or tried to, when the greengrocer's son came looking for me and the noise brought Dr. Peterson thundering down the stairs. He went ballistic when he found me in the library."

"He caught you with the ledger?"

"No — I shoved it back in the drawer before he came in. I claimed I was looking for the purse Grandfather told me to use."

Carl sat back and massaged his chin, considering, and shook his head. "You were very lucky."

"I don't believe in luck."

"God is watching over you."

I nodded. "Yes, I think perhaps He was. But I was scared," I whispered. "I don't know what's up with that man, but he's a total creep. Obsessed with Grandfather's 'privacy,' as he calls it. He as much as threatened me."

"Can you get another look at the ledger?"

"No. Grandfather locked the library door. Everything's changed. You could cut the tension in that house with a knife."

"Has Herr Sommer asked you to leave?"

"No, he still seems to want me to stay. He asked me to prepare and serve lunch today for him and Dr. Peterson and Herr Eberhardt."

"Herr Eberhardt meets with them?" Carl seemed surprised.

I shrugged. "I don't know why they're

278

meeting."

"He's a much younger man — midfifties at most. I don't know if he's a native of Berlin. It's possible he might not know of Herr Sommer's past."

I waited.

"After the war, when Germans were arrested and ostensibly held accountable for their crimes, they were not able to find proof that Herr Sommer broke any laws, no matter that Jew after Jew testified against him. Dr. Peterson spoke in his defense."

"They tried to send Grandfather to prison?"

"If my parents and their friends were correct, your grandfather sent dozens of families — men, women, children — to their deaths. Do you not think he deserves prison?"

"Of course he deserves prison — at least, if that's true. But he's an old man, and what if you're wrong? Arresting him now — if that's what you're suggesting — won't bring them back. And I didn't see enough of the ledger to know. I couldn't read what I saw."

"The irony is that if he did that — no matter how heinous his crimes against humanity — he was not breaking the law of his time. He was simply ferreting out 'lawbreakers.' Taking a cut of the plunder was normal practice."

"The whole thing is immoral, criminal."

"Today, we would say that. It's criminal because we look at it with the justice of God. The goal of the Reich was to rid Germany of Jews and confiscate — Aryanize — their wealth." Carl pushed his hand through his hair. "Those things might be returned to their owners — if they still exist, if he hasn't sold them. But a ledger . . . You remember nothing? A name? An address — anything?"

I closed my eyes, sitting back, breathing in and breathing out.

"Hannah?"

"I'm trying to remember." The music in the bistro played on and on. I summoned the words in the ledger in the same way I remembered answers from textbooks for school tests as a child. "Goldstein . . . Martin, Roseanne, and two more — I don't remember them. But there were four names. The last one crossed out."

"A date? An address?"

The figures, scrawled in German, broke apart in my mind and reassembled themselves. "Rochstrasse; Wohnhaus — I don't remember the numbers. Something about *Geld* — I think that's money."

"*Ja,* very good. What else?"

"There were other columns — I think one said *Juwelen,* and something that said *Ausgabe.* Another . . . I can't remember the word, but it might have had to do with artwork. At least there was a painter's name — Renoir. I don't remember what else."

"You said there were dates on the pages?"

"The first said November 1938. I don't remember the exact date on that page. *Verhaftung.* It said *Verhaftung* at the top of that column."

"*Verhaftung* means 'arrest.' "

I opened my eyes. "I'm afraid . . . I'm afraid you were right. But what I saw isn't enough. What if there's some other explanation? I want there to be some other explanation."

"You need to get that ledger."

"He keeps the door locked, and the drawer in his desk. I have no idea where he keeps the key. And even if I did, Grandfather never leaves the house. He listens at keyholes. I think he even listened to me talking to you last night."

"He was on the line? He knew who you called?"

"I think he only heard me talking. I didn't say your name. I was afraid to."

"You're right to be afraid."

"I don't believe Grandfather would hurt

me for anything. He loves me. But that Dr. Peterson . . . I don't know. I don't trust him."

"Open your eyes, Hannah. You must understand that that ledger may stand between your Grossvater and the public assassination of his character by Nazi hunters in and outside of Germany, between life as he knows it and the end of that life. It could mean the confiscation of his wealth — and probably Dr. Peterson's wealth — to be restored to its rightful owners. Maybe the loss of Eberhardt's license to practice law, if he knows too."

"I can't believe Grandfather would do anything to hurt me, even to save his own skin. He might send me home; that's all." I prayed that was all.

"Send you home?" Carl straightened the knife by his plate. "If he believes you're connected with Nazi hunters —"

"I'm not a Nazi hunter! I just want to know about my mother and father. That's the only reason I came to Germany."

"We will find out about your mother. It may take time, but I will help you. And I'll look into the street you saw — who lived there, what happened to them. So many of the streets were renamed after the war. If this was in the eastern sector, we might have more difficulty, but we'll find it. You must be careful. Be very careful."

20

Lieselotte Sommer
December 1943–July 1944

Weeks passed with no word from Lukas. But I'd known it would be this way. That's what *Wait for me* meant. . . .

As Christmas neared, I dared hope he might come home, at least for a few days. I dreamed of our meeting. Then I struggled with how it would happen — where we could meet in private, what his parents might say considering the danger of his mission, how Vater would react once he knew our relationship had grown serious. *Serious about what? The future . . . planning a future together in this uncertain world?*

Vater would object to Lukas's lowly Abwehr status and lack of impressive connections with the SS, but he could not object to Lukas's bloodline — "impeccable," as Dr. Peterson would say. Lukas's father descended from Prussian noblemen.

His mother was Austrian. Together, we'd produce lots of lovely Aryan babies. That should please him. I could fulfill my "duty" to the Reich.

But Lukas did not come home for Christmas. The Kirchmanns either did not know where he was or would not say.

By March my hope began to wane and Vater began speaking again of my marriage. "We have put it off too long, Lieselotte."

"I told you, Vater, Lukas and I have an understanding. It's just not time yet. The war . . . and everything."

"In wartime most couples marry quickly, start their families quickly. I've seen no sign of such intentions. In any case, it is a marriage I do not approve. You will choose by August or I will choose for you."

"With Lukas's work —"

"Yes, Lukas's work. You know, I suppose, that there have been numerous arrests in the Abwehr."

"That has nothing to do with Lukas."

"That is the only reason I haven't forbidden all association with the Kirchmanns, though Peterson urges me to do so."

"They've been great friends to us, Vater — always. Remember how Frau Kirchmann cared for Mutti, day and night, like a sister."

"*Ja,* I remember. But your association

285

with them will not please your husband. You should expect to —"

"My hus—"

"By August, Lieselotte. It will be a year since Rudy's death. It's time. And once you are married, I believe Fräulein Hilde will accept my proposal. I intend an October wedding. I'll wait no longer."

"We conjured Rudy's death date to match his birthday, Vater. It doesn't mean —"

"August. That is final."

"And if I don't —"

"Then Dr. Peterson will make arrangements for Lebensborn."

"Vater!"

"You have five months to lure a husband, Lieselotte. Do it."

If Vater watched me like a hawk, Dr. Peterson tracked me with the beady eyes of a vulture. Their scrutiny made it all but impossible — and too dangerous for everyone — for me to run my circuit of food procurements and deliveries to those in hiding.

That, in turn, placed more pressure on Marta and Frau Kirchmann. Each time I saw them, they appeared thinner and more worried. Gray had begun to streak Frau Kirchmann's beautiful auburn hair. The lines in Herr Kirchmann's forehead deepened, and Marta had long since lost her buoyant step, her winsome wit.

Fear grated our nerves raw, and severe rationing took its toll on the strongest. We could not adequately feed those in our care, and week by week we saw them waste away until their lives sometimes seemed too great a burden — for them and for us.

I shared my fears and agony about Vater's demands with Marta, but what could she say? What could she do? I would never marry another than Lukas. Lebensborn crept into my nightmares.

June arrived and the white and crimson roses in our front garden bloomed as they hadn't done in years. Why that was, when they received the least amount of attention, I don't know.

Fräulein Hilde claimed it was because we were both planning weddings and portended a brilliant fall blooming just in time for her wedding with *mein Vater*.

That's how she told me she'd accepted Vater at last. Vater's delight in the prospect was nearly contagious. I was glad for him to be happy, and I think Mutti would not have minded his remarrying. She would have cautioned against marrying someone barely ten years older than her daughter, but in the New Germany that was no longer surprising. Mutti would have been appalled at his threat to me, or that I should be ejected from our home in time for Vater's nuptials.

At least, those were the things I told myself as I lay awake at night. I wanted — needed — someone to champion me . . . even if it was Mutti from beyond the grave.

Fräulein Hilde insisted I walk as her maid or — as she said she prayed — *matron* of honor. I protested, but it did no good, and I dared not make an enemy of the neck that turned my father's head.

It was the last day of June. We'd just finished a first fitting of her beaded ivory wedding gown and my attendant dress — fitted apricot with a sheer overlay — and stopped for luncheon at an outdoor café near the Tiergarten. Fräulein Hilde knew everyone of consequence, and everyone — of consequence or not — knew her. Each course was interrupted by well-wishers and curious admirers, especially when she told them I was to be her new daughter.

"I love being told I'm entirely too young to be your mother."

I smiled, confessing in silence that I was glad she was not my mother at all.

We'd finished consommé and were awaiting the next course when I looked up. Across the street stood Lukas, in uniform, staring at me as though he'd never seen me. And then he broke into a smile that would shame the sun, and my heart soared higher than the towering linden trees.

"Lieselotte?" Fräulein Hilde whispered. "Who is that young man?"

"Lukas — my Lukas." I stood and my napkin fell to the pavement. Before I could step away from the table he was running across the street, laughing, heedless of the traffic. Two horns honked angrily and he threw up his hand in apology but kept running.

Tears that I didn't know had been pent up burst through my eyes, with gulping sobs to match. "Lukas!"

He swept me into his arms and spun me around — not once, but twice — and hugged me to his chest. I looked up, laughing, barely able to catch my breath. He bathed my cheek, my lips, my forehead with kisses.

"Lieselotte." Fräulein Hilde tugged the hem of my skirt. "Heads are turning."

Lukas pulled away. "I beg your pardon, Fräulein." But he couldn't stop grinning and neither could I.

"Won't you join us?" Fräulein Hilde's curiosity and amusement laced her question.

"I would love to, Fräulein —"

"Hilde von Loewe — soon to be Frau Hilde Sommer, Lieselotte's new mother." She smiled, as if sharing the season's best-kept secret, to good effect on Lukas.

He gaped, appropriately flabbergasted. "The wedding? It is soon?"

"October 12. Lieselotte will walk the aisle with me. Lovely, don't you think?"

Lukas sat back and did not hide his astonishment. "Indeed." Lifting my glass, he said, "I raise a toast to the two most beautiful women in Berlin. May all others weep for the honor that is taken."

Fräulein Hilde laughed delightedly. "Quite the charmer, your young man, Lieselotte."

"Quite the charmer," I repeated joyfully, as astonished as she.

Lukas smiled and lifted my hand to his lips. If only we'd been alone.

"This is the mysterious young suitor your father told me about?"

"This is my Lukas." I squeezed his hand.

"You were at Rudy's memorial service," she remembered.

"This is correct," he said, growing serious. "A very sad day. Rudy was my friend

— all our growing-up years."

"Then I don't understand. Why haven't the two of you married? You're quite obviously head over heels. What are you waiting for?"

Lukas's eyes grew wide and I felt the heat creep up my neck. He moistened his lips, as if that gave him time to think of how to respond. I held my breath. What had Vater told Fräulein Hilde — that I'd claimed we had an understanding? That wasn't exactly true, and now it would out. Then what?

Lukas looked from Fräulein Hilde to me, and back again. He nodded his head, as if considering an important proposition. "You make a very good point, Fräulein Hilde. Why have we waited? Why should we wait longer?"

"Lukas!" I gasped, not believing the conversation. Was he toying with me?

He turned to me, then left his seat and, bending one knee, clasped my hands. "Lieselotte Sommer, would you do me the honor of becoming my wife?"

Fräulein Hilde clapped her hands, delighted again, and heads swiveled to take in the scene.

"Lukas! I can't believe you're asking me this —"

"But I am, and I need your answer, my

Lieselotte." He squeezed my hands, communicating something more, something urgent. "Will you marry me?"

My head moved up and down before my mouth caught up. "Yes, yes, I will."

He broke into a relieved smile — a glow — and stood, cheering, "She said yes!"

The entire café broke into applause, Fräulein Hilde most of all.

I felt — not for the first time — that I stood at the center of a stage, played a role that might or might not be real. But this time I chose to play it to the hilt, to revel in the spotlight. I wrapped my arms around his neck and kissed him until I knew he'd caught the fire in my heart. I didn't hear the cheering stop, didn't know when Lukas returned to his seat or returned me to mine.

"That was the most spectacular proposal I have ever seen," Fräulein Hilde enthused. "Your father will be so pleased." And then, as if suddenly inspired, "I'll help you plan your wedding."

"Oh, that's not nec—" I began.

But Lukas broke in with, "So kind. That is so very kind of you. With your knowledge of weddings, Fräulein Hilde, it will make things run so much more smoothly."

"And quickly?" She raised her brows in conspiracy.

"And quickly." Lukas grinned in return. "If that's all right with you, Lieselotte. I'm here only for today and must return to Munich, but I can return in September and we can marry. I've already cleared it with my superiors."

My head spun and my breath — my breath was completely stolen. "You've — Yes." I stumbled over the word. "Yes!"

He sighed in pleasure, relief evident on his face. And then a shadow crossed it. "I should speak to your Vater. I should ask his permission. But my train leaves in half an hour."

"Half an hour?" Panic set into my chest.

"I think I can grant that permission, Herr Kirchmann." Fräulein Hilde smiled. "I believe on this matter I can speak for my future husband. Herr Sommer and I will be delighted to welcome you to our family, and for one so gallant to spirit our Lieselotte away. We could not otherwise let her go so easily."

The pit of my stomach rumbled. Nothing she said was true. They would not miss me. Vater would not approve of my marrying Lukas. But if Fräulein Hilde pushed him . . . would that work? Would that convince Vater? Would a marriage to Lukas prove a suitable alternative to sending me to

293

Lebensborn?

Fräulein Hilde did her best to convince my father. Dr. Peterson was another matter. They all seemed to have forgotten I sat on the sofa in the library, in the middle of their argument.

"A celebrated wedding of a beloved daughter to an Abwehr agent is preferable to dragging her kicking and screaming to Lebensborn, Wolfgang." Fräulein Hilde lit a second cigarette and threw her lighter to the table.

"You shouldn't be smoking, Hilde." Dr. Peterson spoke with the patience of a tried saint, holding out his hand for the offending cigarette. "You know it is *verboten* for women to smoke."

She smiled through narrowed eyes and flicked ash on his palm. "I'm telling you, the boy's in love with her and she with him. Why not let her have her way in this? What harm can it do?"

"What good can it do?" Dr. Peterson answered for Father. "The Abwehr is under intense scrutiny since Canaris and his men were arrested for attempting to assassinate the Führer last week. Do you not understand what this connection means?"

"Was Lukas Kirchmann part of that plan?"

Fräulein Hilde challenged.

My heart stopped.

Dr. Peterson ground his own cigarette into the ashtray on Father's desk. "Apparently not. At least no connection has been established. But if that should change, it would put Wolfgang in a most detrimental light — and by association, I might add, Fräulein Hilde —"

"If there was a connection, it would have been found. You said yourself the Gestapo searched —" She glanced at me and stopped. "They are thorough. He'd have been arrested if there was something — anything. I say let her marry him." Fräulein Hilde walked behind my chair and tucked a curl behind my ear, momentarily clasping my shoulders. "You should have seen them today, Wolfgang. Young, beautiful — both of them — in love." She smiled. "I believe Lieselotte will be happy to do her duty for the Fatherland with her Lukas."

My face and neck burned, even my arms, down to my fingertips. I felt them all looking at me, imagining the process by which Lukas and I might meet the Führer's expectations.

"Perhaps," Vater began.

"There is something not right," Dr. Peterson objected. He frowned, concentrating, as if trying to remember something.

"What is that supposed to mean?" Fräulein Hilde insisted, hands on hips.

"I can't place my finger on it at the moment, but I remember something . . . something. Could it be about the bloodline?"

"It's been researched. Herr Kirchmann is the descendant of Prussian nobility. I suppose we cannot ask for better than that," Vater conceded.

"But the mother . . ."

"Austrian," I offered quickly. "Frau Kirchmann came from Austria as a child with her parents."

"Yes." Dr. Peterson hesitated. "So she said. Although I think we —"

"It's settled, then." Fräulein Hilde clapped her hands. "Wolfgang, my darling?"

Vater shrugged, hinting at defeat.

Fräulein Hilde smiled at me — a genuine, victorious smile. "I think, my dear, that it's time we planned a party."

My heart dared to swell. But just as we linked arms to walk from the room, I heard Dr. Peterson speak softly to my father. "I'll check. I'm not sure what it is, but there's something, and I'll find it."

21

Hannah Sterling
February 1973

The clock struck five thirty as I returned to the house. Grandfather was out, unusual in itself. I waited until six thirty, set places for both of us at the table, then heated soup left from the day before. He still hadn't returned. Perhaps Grandfather had decided to dine out on the town in the company of Dr. Peterson or Herr Eberhardt. Who else might he know? Rarely had anyone else telephoned since I'd been here, and no others had visited. I waited until seven, ate, washed the dishes and cleared the kitchen, then checked the library door. Still locked.

Mentally exhausted, I slipped into bed at nine thirty. *What if something's happened to him? What if he's had a heart episode and gone to the hospital? How would I know? Who would know to telephone me?*

An hour later I heard a car stop outside

the house and the front door unlock. I held my breath, waiting for Grandfather's footsteps on the stairs. They came to the second floor, the tap of his cane helping him climb. But they didn't stop. They continued up the stairs to the third floor and down the hallway. He stopped outside my room and waited.

The doorknob turned in the moonlight and the door opened slowly. My bed was in a darkened portion of the room. I knew he couldn't see my face, but he peered in, glancing round, and strained to see me. I turned on my pillow, as if something had disturbed me, and he pulled back, softly closing the door.

Maybe he wanted to see that I was safely home. Still, I lay awake until dawn.

I rose early and prepared breakfast at the accustomed time as on any ordinary day. I carried a tray with boiled eggs, toast, and coffee, knocking gently on his bedroom door. Whatever happened, it was better to get it over with than to cower in my room.

"Enter." Grandfather struggled to a sitting position. "Hannah. Good morning. I am glad to see you."

The uncertain relief I felt surely flowed through my voice. "I'm glad to see you, too, Grandfather." *Should I be glad to see him? I* wanted my grandfather to be my grandfather, not a bounty hunter, and not someone who drove my mother away. Who was he?

I shook the fog from my brain. Now it was about playing the part, keeping the conversation going. Aunt Lavinia's old adage tiptoed through my brain: *"You catch more bees with honey than with vinegar."*

"Did you enjoy your day yesterday?"

"Yes, I did. It was nice to get out for a bit. How about you? You were gone when I got home. Everything all right?"

"*Ja,* certainly. Why not?"

"No reason." I shrugged. "I've just not known you to go out at night." *It was the first time you've left the house since I've been here.*

"I met with some friends — friends I've not seen in some time." He eyed me suspiciously, which unnerved me.

"That's nice." I set the tray across his legs but wouldn't meet his eye. "It's nice to get together with friends."

"I suppose you miss your friends since you've been here."

"A little. I think about my students mostly — wonder how they're doing, how the substitute teacher is managing." I smoothed my skirt and opened the drapes, lifting the

299

shade. The morning sun poured in.

"You boil the eggs precisely as I like them."

"Good." I smiled but continued to stare out the window, summoning my courage.

"Hannah?"

"Yes?" Still I didn't turn.

"I think we should have a talk today."

"Oh?"

"When I've dressed and shaved, I will meet you downstairs. Herr Eberhardt will come at ten and join us for this discussion."

"Herr Eberhardt?" Dealing with Grandfather was one thing. He was older and frail enough that I felt certain I could hold my own physically and probably intellectually. But Herr Eberhardt was a different matter. He was a lawyer, for pity's sake. *What do they want with me?*

"We have matters to discuss with you. I believe you will not be displeased." He sounded so confident, so self-assured. "We will speak in the library."

The library? But you've kept me out of that room for days. Breathe, breathe, breathe . . .

"I'll show him in."

"Very good, and bring coffee, if you do not mind."

"Of course I don't mind." I closed the door behind me. *"Coffee" doesn't sound like anything dangerous is likely to happen. Carl, have we let our imaginations run wild? Please, God, help me. Help me understand what's going on. Help me find out about Mama. We keep getting further and further from the point and the truth.*

Herr Eberhardt arrived at ten. I showed him into the library, where Grandfather sat as if he did so every day, as if every day I'd been welcomed there and not locked out.

I assembled a tray with a steaming pot of coffee and thick, fragrant slices of an apple nut cake, warm from the oven, that Mama had taught me to make — some Americanized version of a cake she'd grown up with. When I walked in, both men stood, as if I were a lady and not a servant granddaughter. I didn't know what to make of it, but lifted my head and smiled, nodding, doing my best to remain poised.

"Ah, you made this yourself, Fräulein Sterling? No wonder Wolfgang wants to keep you with him. You will grow fat on such luxury, my friend."

"That I should live long enough to grow fat. There is no better way to do it." Grandfather watched me with what looked like a mixture of pride and some amount of ownership. I tried not to rattle the cups and saucers.

"Well, neither of you have tasted it yet, so you'd best reserve judgment." My teasing was lost on them.

"*Ja,* well, sit yourself, please, Hannah. Herr Eberhardt will explain our meeting."

Definitely not a social call. I sat across the desk from Grandfather, in the chair beside Herr Eberhardt, and sipped my coffee.

"Your Grossvater has asked me to create a new deed for him, one in which he makes you co-owner of his property and its contents."

I nearly dropped my cup.

"As you know, neither of his children are living, and you are the only child of your mother. This is correct, is it not?"

I could barely speak, but stumbled, "I am. Mama never had another. But I didn't expect this — truly."

"Nein?" Herr Eberhardt's skepticism cut me.

"No." I glanced from man to man. Not even Grandfather looked convinced. "This is most certainly not why I came to Germany."

"Why did you come now, after all these years, Fräulein Sterling?" Eberhardt pressed.

"You know why. Because I only learned that my grandfather existed after my mother

302

passed. I wanted to meet him, to learn about my mother and her family — my family." I turned to Grandfather. "Is that what you think? That I came for your money?"

Grandfather raised his brows. "I did not say this. Only Herr Eberhardt is concerned. I told him you have agreed to stay, to care for me in return."

"What?"

"That arrangement is not agreeable to you?" Herr Eberhardt prodded.

"It's not that; it's that I have a job waiting for me at home — my home in North Carolina. I never intended this visit to go on as long as it has." I felt like I'd been turned on my head. "Grandfather, we talked about this."

"You promised to consider my request that you stay."

"Consider, yes, but I didn't promise to stay indefinitely."

"I see." Herr Eberhardt set his cup and saucer on the desk and reached for his attaché case. He pulled a sheaf of papers from the top folder. "Do you understand the nature of your Grossvater's illness? That he has less than a year to live?"

"He's been doing so much better."

"Since you arrived," Grandfather interrupted. "I feel stronger, more sure with you here, Hannah. I want you to stay. You can see that I need someone."

"You said that Frau Winkler will return as soon as her family is stable."

A tiny spark of caution and perhaps anger flashed through Grandfather's eyes.

"We can all appreciate that the begrudging service of an employed housekeeper is not the same as the loving attention of a family member, particularly an appreciative heiress." Herr Eberhardt pulled a sheaf of papers from his case. "Because your Grossvater lives simply and responsibly, you may not realize that he is also extremely wealthy."

"No, I don't know anything about his financial affairs and don't need to. It's not a question of wealth."

"Perhaps more of family loyalty." Herr Eberhardt was not a lawyer for nothing.

"If I agreed to stay, it would not be because of inheriting money," I challenged. "And it wouldn't be because I felt a need to prove my loyalty, but because I chose it."

"I told you, my friend. My granddaughter knows her own mind and will not be purchased."

"Thank you, Grandfather. I'm glad someone understands."

"That is why I told him to make you coowner. It is not a binding agreement to coerce you to stay. I am sharing my worldly goods with you, Hannah — even now. They are yours to do with as you will. Only I will live in this house as long as I live — as long as I am able — and maintain a staff necessary for my comfort and well-being. All of the remainder is yours — should be yours, now rather than later."

"Grandfather, I don't know what to say. I appreciate your generosity more than I can tell you, but I'm extremely uncomfortable with this. I don't know if —"

"If you wish to stay?" Herr Eberhardt broke in.

"Heinrich, Heinrich, do not push so. Hannah will decide in her time. You have the papers?"

"I did as you required, Wolfgang, but I must urge you once more to reconsider. By all means, rewrite your will to make Fräulein Sterling your heiress, but do not make her a co-owner. You could end up homeless and ultimately penniless if Fräulein Sterling decides to liquidate your assets now."

Grandfather motioned for him to hand over the papers. "You forget that the needs of the old and dying are not great. I have confidence that Hannah will not see me neglected. Will you, my granddaughter?"

The walls closed in. "Grandfather, we

must talk about this — about all of it, about —"

"Talking is done."

"Rushing into this before talking it through is foolishness, Wolfgang. I beg of you —"

"Where are my witnesses? You brought them?"

"Peterson refused to come, refused to be a part of it. I brought two clerks from my law office."

"Call them in."

Herr Eberhardt walked to the window and rapped on the pane. He motioned to someone, pointing round to the front of the house. "I'll let them in."

When he left the room I took my only chance. "Grandfather, really, we must talk things through. I don't want you to do this against your lawyer's better judgment. There's no hurry — no reason to do this now."

"I am an old man, Hannah."

"Then if you want to leave me something, leave me something that meant a great deal to you personally — something about Mama. That's what —"

Herr Eberhardt and his two associates walked in at that moment.

"Talking is finished." Grandfather pulled

a pen from his middle desk drawer and signed the last page of the contract with a flourish. "I have set my seal. It is done. My witnesses?"

The two men came forward, signed their names, and Herr Eberhardt, his mouth in a grim line, set his seal.

My stomach dropped to the floor. I could barely comprehend what had just happened. *Have I been gifted or bought?*

Herr Eberhardt motioned for his minions to leave. He folded the papers.

Grandfather sat back, smiling. "You will keep them on file for us?"

"Of course. But I fear you have done foolishly this day, my friend."

"But we are still friends."

"Friends, *ja,* but you have flouted my advice as your attorney. That makes me angry."

Grandfather shrugged. "That is unfortunate. Please close the door on your way out."

Herr Eberhardt purpled like he might explode, cast me a scathing glance, and shoved his hat onto his head. He grabbed his coat and attaché case and left the room without another word.

I rose to see him out.

"Let him go, Hannah. He knows his way,

and we have much to talk about, to plan."

"He believes I'll abscond with your property."

The front door closed with force, sending a gush of cold air down the hallway and into the library.

"He is . . . protective. That is all. He has guarded my privacy and finances for several years. He does not understand that your coming to Berlin is the most wonderful turn of events in my life. I believed I had no family, and you have come — as one from the dead."

It would be so easy to melt into this welcome, to let it swallow me up.

"You do not need to work — not for the rest of your life, unless you choose to do so."

The thought took me by surprise — financial freedom. What might that mean? Travel? A home of my own here in Germany or, if I sold the house, perhaps a home in Winston-Salem? I looked around me. Even the fine things in this room — the mahogany desk, the marble-edged fireplace, the shelves of books, some first editions if I guessed right — could not keep me in sneaker tread the rest of my natural life. Either he was exaggerating or delusional or there was something I couldn't see . . . something more than a man of his means and life experience as a government employee should have — and that was what worried me.

"When I am gone — I only ask that you stay until then — you will be free to travel, to study anything you wish wherever you wish, to marry anyone you wish and live in any country of the world."

"That sounds so lavish, too fantastic to be real, Grossvater."

He smiled. "I like it best when you call me that, Hannah. It means a great deal to me."

I smiled in return, hesitantly.

"Now, it is nearly time for luncheon. I propose we dress and go to town. I will call a driver and we will dine in the best restaurant Berlin has to offer. It is time we celebrated."

"Please, Grandfa— Grossvater. Please, there are questions I need to ask you, things I've put off entirely too long."

He sat back. "Ask me anything, my granddaughter, as long as it is not about the past. I choose not to remember darker days, but to go forward. . . . We must go forward together."

"I don't wish to bring any sadness to you, but I must know two things. The first is, how did you come by such wealth? Dr. Peterson told me you worked as a government employee until you retired."

He breathed deeply, and I'm sure his chest trembled. "This is true. But I have worked hard and invested wisely. And you must remember that for many years I have lived alone. I had no son to set up in business after my Rudy was killed, no daughter to marry to another after she ran away. My wife died years before."

"You never remarried. Was there never anyone else?"

He looked away and his eyes filmed, as if I'd plucked hairs from his head.

"Grossvater?"

"There was someone." He swallowed. "But she was above my station. I was not so well established at that time, and she accepted the attentions of another after . . ."

"After what?"

"After Lieselotte disgraced our family. I do not wish to discuss this."

"I'm sorry. It must have been very lonely for you."

He tensed.

"And you missed Uncle Rudy."

"My handsome boy — my warrior son — rotted and starved in a Russian prison." I could see Grandfather age before my eyes.

"Why do you bring these things to mind again?"

"Not because I wish to hurt you, but I need to know, to understand. Most of all, I need to understand what happened to Mama."

"Peterson told you that she ran away — though it was not his to tell." His voice rose. "She ran away and left me — alone — with nothing and no one."

"Where did she go? It must have been in the middle or near the end of the war. Where could she have gone all alone? Was she alone?"

"How would I know this? If I knew where she had gone, would I not have brought her home?" He turned away.

"You searched for her?"

"She made her choice — she was disloyal."

"Disloyal to you?"

"*Ja,* disloyal to me, to the Fatherland, to her brother who was fighting for the Führer!"

"How was she disloyal? In what way?"

He shook his head. "Stop interrogating me!" But he looked less certain, and I knew this might be my only chance, his most vulnerable moment.

"What was Mama's connection to the Confessing Church?"

311

He paled. "How do you know of this?"

"I've heard of it. I heard something from Mama about having been a member, an advocate." That part was a lie, but the fear in his eyes showed me that I'd hit the nail on the head.

"Heretics, traitors disloyal to the Führer and the Reich, saboteurs. A shame to the national church and the German *Volk.* Lieselotte might just as well have stabbed a knife into her brother's chest as taken up with them."

"Because she was part of a church?"

"A church that was nothing but a front for breaking the law — a pretense at holiness to thwart the Reich and all the hopes of the German people."

"How could Mama do that?"

"She was a sneak — a thief, a liar!" He stood, enraged. "She is dead. She has been dead to me since the day she ran away with —" He stopped abruptly.

"With who? Who did she run away with?" My heart beat faster. *Who would she run away with but my father?*

"It does not matter now."

"It matters to me. Did she run away or did you drive her away?"

"Drive my daughter away? *Nein!* Why would I do this?"

"She was young and ran away at a terribly uncertain time. There must have been a reason. Was it because she discovered you had tricked Jews and were selling them to the Reich?"

Grandfather swayed, as if I'd punched him in the stomach. "This is a lie! Who told you such things? I demand to know! Frau Winkler, yes? Always sympathy for *die* poor *Juden*! Why is it you Americans always want to dredge up the past? To accuse us?"

"I'm not accusing you, Grandfather; I'm trying to understand what happened to my mother, why she did what she did — what it was that she did."

"Grossvater. You must call me Grossvater!"

"Grossvater. Please, tell me about Mama — did you argue?"

"*Nein!* Lieselotte — foolish girl — ran after that boy. She was besotted from the time she was a child. If I had known that his whorish Mutter was *der Juden* I would not have allowed them in my house! She would not have nursed — never touched — my Elsa."

"A Jewish boy? I don't know what you're talking about. Who was the boy?"

"I forbade her to see him. I should have known when his father refused to join the

313

Party. She shamed me! Criminals. His family — all of them!"

"Because they were Jews? Because they were part of the Confessing Church?"

"Because they were vermin! Because they hid criminals from the authorities. They turned against the Führer and dragged my daughter with them! They broke the law. They broke the law!" He pounded the table, veins throbbing in his temples.

I sat down. "Resistance? Mama was part of the resistance." I could barely comprehend it. But it fit — perfectly — all the odd things I knew about her. The time she'd helped the tramp despite the sheriff, despite the offense she created and the ridicule she knew she'd endure at the hands of women in the community.

"The shame she brought cost me everything. I was ostracized by my peers, questioned by the authorities, dismissed from my position in the Party. Dismissed!"

Drums pounded in my stomach. *Mama stood up for the weakest of the weak. She stood against her own father.*

"And when the shame came, the woman I had intended to marry, to take as my wife, turned against me."

"She turned against you because your daughter helped people?"

"You make it all sound so . . . so . . . You do not understand. You are young and foolish." He groped for his cane, his hands shaking. "I no longer wish to celebrate this day."

At the door, he turned. "Do not delve so deeply into the past, Hannah. It is over, forgotten. It cannot be changed. And your future depends on it."

22

Lieselotte Sommer
July–September 1944

The very next day, Fräulein Hilde invited Frau Kirchmann and me to her home and private parlor for afternoon coffee, to plan my engagement party. Now that Vater had capitulated, despite Dr. Peterson's protestations, Fräulein Hilde could not move fast enough. I didn't care; never had I been so happy.

Neither Fräulein Hilde nor I counted on Frau Kirchmann's hesitation.

"I simply do not understand the rush. Why not wait until the war is over? The Führer says we are so near. What a glorious celebration that would be!" Frau Kirchmann sat on the edge of the chintz sofa, did not touch her honey cake, wouldn't look at me. All her conversation was directed to Fräulein Hilde, as if she knew my life's cards lay in her hands. "Lieselotte can certainly stay with us while you and Herr Sommer honeymoon. She's welcome to live with us, in fact."

"Wolfgang and I want to be certain Lieselotte's future is secured before we marry."

"But in these times so little is certain. Lukas's work, you understand, is so very —"

"Let me be plain, Frau Kirchmann." Fräulein Hilde placed her cup firmly in its saucer on the low table between us. "Wolfgang and I will not marry until Lieselotte has married . . . or until she is . . . settled. We marry in October. Our plans are made. If this marriage is not an option, then I'm afraid Wolfgang will take matters into his own hands. She will not live with your family unless she is married — that's simply too temporary a solution."

"I see." Frau Kirchmann replaced her cup as well.

"Do you not wish me to marry Lukas?" I held my breath, realizing that for whatever reason she might not want me either. "Do you not wish me for your family?"

"Oh no." Frau Kirchmann instantly clasped my hand. "No, my dear Lieselotte. Of course I want you! I think of you as my daughter already! I am delighted that you love my son and that he loves you. It's just,

I'm afraid for his work, and your future, that —"

"As you said, Frau Kirchmann, these are uncertain times. Is it not better for the young to marry and have one another to hold through challenging times? I daresay you and Herr Kirchmann have enjoyed that pleasure." Fräulein Hilde sat back in her deep chair, the pose of one victorious.

Frau Kirchmann stared at her, taking Fräulein Hilde's measure. It seemed to me she took too long to respond. Finally she nodded. "Yes, of course. I understand." She took only a moment more before smiling at me. "Then it's settled, isn't it? We'll plan an engagement party together. And a wedding. But I'm afraid if you're intent on marrying in September, the party and the wedding will be nearly back to back. Lukas said he can only get two weeks away."

"It needn't be big at all," I offered, nearly pleading. "I want only my family — our family."

"Nonsense," Fräulein Hilde intervened. "You can have your intimate engagement party if that is what you wish, but the wedding must be worthy of your father's station in life."

"I don't think Vater will want a big —"

"Leave it to me. As long as it doesn't rival

our own, Wolfgang will be pleased with my arrangements." She purred like a cat who'd eaten two canaries. "We'll put on quite a show for those Party members who've hesitated to promote your father through their ranks. It will be a good investment — for everyone."

Frau Kirchmann gave my hand a warning squeeze, so I smiled at Fräulein Hilde and squeezed the hand of my dear mother-to-be in return.

August sped by. Arrests among our network of Jews increased. No one could understand why — how it was our hiding places were revealed. Helping became more dangerous — at least it felt more dangerous, and I found myself nervous, forever looking over my shoulder. Being loved and loving Lukas, planning our wedding — suddenly my life meant more. I had so much more to lose if caught.

By mid-September Fräulein Hilde was in and out of our house at all hours, as were caterers, florists, wine merchants, and others whose function I'd no idea of. She kept the house abuzz and food flowing freely. It was not hard to steal away with small bundles at odd times — bundles I knew might save our starving fugitives.

No one seemed the least bit concerned about my coming and going. I supposed there was greater freedom afforded a young woman about to wed, and I took good advantage of that freedom.

My satin wedding dress and lace-edged veil hung outside my wardrobe door. My case for our honeymoon sat on a chair nearby, half packed. Everything else could wait until Lukas and I returned from our three-day wedding trip — two precious nights in the country home of a colleague of Fräulein Hilde. Before Lukas returned to duty I'd move in with his family, until we could secure a house — a home of our own, perhaps in the spring if the war truly ended by then. How good that sounded — how impossibly wonderful!

Fräulein Hilde promised a simple dinner for our engagement party — herself, Vater, the Kirchmanns, and a few Party members Fräulein Hilde insisted could not be omitted from "family affairs." Now that she and Vater had announced their own plans, she played me as a pawn — a convenient Aryan daughter to show off, a daughter preparing to take her place among the ranks of good German wives, for Führer and Fatherland. My "simple dinner" grew and grew.

Frau Kirchmann counseled me to acquiesce, to maintain a sweet and low profile and pray that we'd all be forgotten in the wake of Fräulein Hilde and Vater's far more lavish wedding soon to come — what Fräulein Hilde was determined would prove Berlin's social event of the season.

"Anonymity," Frau Kirchmann said, "is a blessed thing."

Nothing mattered, as long as Lukas and I could be together, as long as I became part of the Kirchmann family.

I'd no idea where the silver and crystal came from that graced our dining room table that night, nor indeed, where the long banquet table itself had been found. Despite her weeks of planning, in two frenzied days Fräulein Hilde and Vater transformed rooms in the main floor of our house to rival any diplomat's mansion in Berlin.

The wrinkle in those last few days before the engagement party came shortly after I'd delivered an unexpected package of cutlets stolen from my home larder to a family of four in an area along the outskirts of Berlin — one of the families on Lukas's old route. I loved this family, not only because they were dear, but because they always asked about Lukas. Their genuine well-wishes and prayers for our coming nuptials lightened my heart.

Just as I pedaled from our agreed-upon spot of delivery, I had the oddest sensation that I was watched, though no one was in sight.

Two blocks from my drop-off point I stopped to check the chain on my bicycle, which had the bad habit of jumping its track. I was just wiping the chain's grease from my hands when a black car slowed before passing.

Instinctively, my heart skipped its beat, and I pulled my bicycle onto the curb, against a stone wall, casually turning my face away. The car looked no different from half the cars in Berlin, but something about it, or about the driver who watched me as it passed, made me think *Gestapo.* It was only September, but I couldn't help shivering.

The day of the party, the house buzzed with caterers and florists creating wonders. A truck from the best bakery in Berlin arrived early, and the spry man who jumped out set to work assembling the most beautiful three-tiered cake I'd ever seen. If this was Fräulein Hilde's idea of an intimate engagement dinner with the closest family and friends, what did she intend for a lavish wedding?

Dr. Peterson arrived for a later afternoon

meeting with Vater, but Fräulein Hilde would not hear of it. She pulled Vater upstairs and called for the tailor. I should have gone immediately to my room.

"Lieselotte." Dr. Peterson plucked a rosebud from the dining room table arrangement. I waited while he inserted it in his buttonhole. "I ran into an old friend of Rudy's yesterday. I was just about to tell your father."

"Oh?" *Why does he want to raise sad memories now?* My senses remained alert.

"Fulstrom. Heyden Fulstrom, I believe he said his name was. Do you remember him?"

I shrugged, turning away, and ran my fingers across a fan of linen napkins. "Rudy was very popular with his friends. There were many."

"Herr Fulstrom remembers you. And your fiancé. And your cousin."

My heart hammered against my chest.

"He was quite surprised to learn that you've only recently become engaged. He was certain he remembered you rescuing your lover from the clutches of another woman, oh, nearly a year ago. Your cousin, I believe he said."

"How odd. He was mistaken."

"It was in his report, verified by a colleague on duty with him at the time. A most

323

mysterious affair, wouldn't you agree?"

I didn't know where he was leading, but I thought it worse to entertain him than to leave. "You will excuse me, Herr Doktor. I must get ready for this evening's festivities."

But as I walked past him, he grabbed my arm. "Who is this cousin, named Anna?"

"Please let go of my arm, Dr. Peterson; you're hurting me."

"Herr Fulstrom thought she looked Jewish — was convinced that Lukas Kirchmann protected her, was hiding her, until you appeared and flung yourself at them." He squeezed my upper arm until I knew there would be bruising.

"I don't know what you're talking about. A year ago? A cousin? I'm sure you'll find I have no cousins."

"Then you won't mind if I share this small oddity with your father, or in a toast this evening — good for a laugh, wouldn't you agree?"

"It doesn't seem very amusing to me. But what you do or do not do, what you say or do not say to *mein Vater,* is of no concern to me." I lifted my chin, casting my best bluff upon the waters and praying it carried me through.

He let go of my arm. "You've made quite a show of marrying your Lukas Kirchmann.

I hope he's all you expect him to be, all your father expects him to be. A man of Wolfgang's station —"

"Will be most pleased to have a daughter married to an upstanding citizen of the Reich."

"Members of the Abwehr remain under investigation, as you are no doubt aware. Your father's position will not protect Lukas Kirchmann if he is found guilty."

"And he is not."

"Rest assured, Fräulein Lieselotte, enemies of the Reich will be ferreted out, no matter who they are, no matter who their families are, no matter how long it takes."

"I should hope so. But you've no need to worry about Lukas or me interfering with your work or the work of the Reich, if that is your concern. I could not be less interested, and Lukas is not one to steal the limelight from another. In any case, we'll be out of this house within the week. Then you and Vater and Fräulein Hilde can plot and plan and do whatever it is you do, unhindered by concerns for me."

"And what will you do, while your husband is off and away, fulfilling his mysterious Abwehr duties, my busy bee?" He leaned too near.

"Perform the duties of a good German

Hausfrau, of course."

The party started at seven, less than half an hour after Lukas's train was scheduled to arrive. I prayed he would not be late. I did not wish to enter the lion's den alone.

At ten of seven I was dressed in a rose satin gown with draped back and diamond earrings — an extravagant engagement gift from Fräulein Hilde and *mein Vater.* I sat at my dressing table, drumming my nails against its top.

Just after seven I heard the first guests arrive and the greetings of the Kirchmanns. Barely a moment later Marta pounded at my door. "Are you decent? Let me in, Lieselotte!"

I pulled open the door in great relief and flung myself into Marta's arms. "Is Lukas here? Has he come?"

"*Nein.* But Papa is meeting him at the station. They should be here anytime."

"I-I'm afraid Dr. Peterson will make trouble. Somehow he's discov—"

"Lieselotte!" Fräulein Hilde knocked impatiently on the door. Not waiting for an answer, she burst in. "Are you ready? Your guests are arriving. Come, come! Where is Lukas?"

"He's on the way from the station. He and

326

Papa will be here any moment," Marta offered.

"I hope so! It's not much of an engagement party without the groom!" She ushered us out the door and down the stairs.

I'd only been upstairs an hour, but the house had been further transformed into a bower of late-summer roses and autumn blooms.

Frau Kirchmann welcomed me with a kiss on each cheek. Vater glanced me over and made a slight bow in reserved approval. Dr. Peterson gave a formal nod but a narrow glance, and my stomach turned over.

A moment later, Lukas and Herr Kirchmann walked through the door and everything flew from my head but the startling blue of Lukas's eyes. I'd always admired them — flecks of light shot through the irises, shining on the darkest of days. But that night they shone like beacons — and they shone for me, radiating a joy I'd never seen.

"My Lieselotte," he whispered, kissing my hands, my hair.

"Ah, ah — you must wait for the wedding night, *mein Herr*!" one of the officers laughed good-naturedly.

We laughed in return, and the room erupted in happiness for us. I'd not smiled so since Mutti was alive, I was sure of it. I glimpsed Vater. The wrinkles in his forehead faded. Fräulein Hilde took his arm and he nodded to whatever she whispered in his ear, smiling. Though it hurt that it was not Mutti standing there beside him, alive and well, it was good to see him happy. I dared to think it a time of new beginnings.

The twelve-course dinner was superb, I was certain, though later I could not remember a thing I ate. The wine was beyond description — that I did remember, and wondered how such a vintage could be found, where Vater had procured such luxuries during our age of rationing, or the money to buy them. That he'd gone to such expense for me — for Lukas and me — touched me, warmed my heart. Surely it could not all be Fräulein Hilde's show and doing.

The clock struck ten and the cake was cut, more toasts made. I couldn't imagine our wedding being happier than that night, though I was eager to move the calendar forward. To imagine that in five days I would be Frau Lieselotte Kirchmann, wife and love forever of Lukas Kirchmann. That when I woke each morning he would wake beside me. Those almost iridescent blue eyes would be the first sight I would see.

My heart nearly burst its chamber.

And then the doorbell rang. Dr. Peterson waved away the butler who'd been hired for the evening and answered it himself, as if he expected someone. I felt a flicker of concern but turned away, determined not to let that man rob me of joy.

But when he returned to the room, tucking what looked to be a telegram in his breast pocket, and glanced from Lukas to Frau Kirchmann in triumph, my heart sank. When his eyes found mine, I knew this evening would not end well.

23

Hannah Sterling
February 1973

I took a tray to Grandfather's room in the early afternoon, but he was sitting in his chair, staring out the window, and did not acknowledge me. I took another tray to him at supper, but saw that he'd not eaten, and there was no sign that he noticed me now.

"Grossvater, you must eat."

He kept staring out the window.

"You must keep up your strength."

"For what purpose?"

It was all he'd said since our time in the library. But the question was too hard for me. I pitied my grandfather as I pitied any old and feeble person, as my heart went out to the brokenhearted. But I was quite sure I didn't like him very much, that he had not told me all — even of his own version of the story — and that I should not trust him.

"Do you want Dr. Peterson to stop by?"

It was the last thing I wanted, but I knew Grandfather depended on him.

"*Nein.* They both warned me against . . . What's done is done."

I didn't know what to say. I'd not asked him to leave me anything, and yet I felt caught, trapped in a web of guilt. "Do you need help in getting ready for bed?"

"I am not so feeble as that, Hannah." He nearly spat my name.

I picked up the untouched luncheon tray. "If you need anything, just call for me. I'll come."

He didn't answer.

It was a long night. Every time I closed my eyes I saw my mother as a young woman, furtively throwing things in a bag — clothing, a photograph of her mother, her favorite book — and stealing away in the dark of night in the midst of blackouts, curfews, and frightening uncertainty. *Did she have any money? Where did she go? Did anyone help her? Who was the Jewish boy she ran off with — the one she was "besotted" with since childhood? Could he have been my father? What did Grandfather mean about his mother nursing Grandmother? They must have been longtime friends or servants. And yet they were helping Jews . . . my mother was helping Jews right under Grand-*

father's nose. *My mother, part of the resistance.* I rolled over, punching my pillow. That did not describe the reserved and closed-off woman I knew to be my mother. . . . The young Lieselotte sounded so brave, so passionate, so in love. *What happened to change you, Mama?*

I replayed Carl's words about questioning Grandfather on his activities during the war and the Confessing Church. *"Make him tell you what happened to your mother." So much for that.*

Grandfather had given me his view, his version of the Confessing Church's sins, but he'd skillfully avoided answering questions about Mama, except to accuse her of ruining his life. *What was the tipping point? What was the shame that made him disown her, force her to run away?*

If Carl's parents knew Grandfather during the war, might they also have known Mama? Why hadn't that registered before?

It took me less than ten minutes to dress and reach the phone in the hallway. It rang seven times before being answered. "Carl?"

"*Ja?* Hannah? Isn't it a little early?"

"Is it? I need to ask something."

"Anything, my early-bird American friend."

"I want to meet your parents."

There was silence on the other end of the line. "Carl? Are you there?"

"*Ja, ja,* I am here."

"Well, what do you think?"

"You are very eager and I am flattered — a bit surprised, but no, I do not think that it is too soon." I heard his smile. No one else I'd met in Germany could melt the phone lines with their teasing. "I will phone them in a couple of hours. They will not yet be awake."

I glanced at the grandfather clock in the hallway and realized it was four thirty in the morning. "Oh, I'm sorry. I didn't realize how early it is."

"I will forgive you if you meet me for breakfast. And I will take you to them afterward."

"You're not driving today?"

"This is my day off. You're in luck, Fräulein Sterling."

"I'll see you at the café then — at eight?"

"I count the minutes."

Thank You, God, for Carl. I replaced the receiver and waited, but this time did not hear Grandfather prowling the house, did not catch him listening above stairs.

There was no point going back to bed, so I washed and dressed, curled my hair. I picked up a photograph of Mama from the dresser and stroked her face. A very little like mine. Enough to tell I was her daughter, but I bore other features more prominent — wide brown eyes, a fuller mouth, broader at the cheekbones, a little higher forehead. I was not as small or delicate as my mother had been — more tall and lean, but sturdy. Still, I wondered if I'd have been up to running away in the middle of a war.

I pulled back my hair and wound the sides up into soft rolls, pinning them to look like Mama's picture as a young woman. The oval dressing table mirror reflected some resemblance. Perhaps it would be enough to jog the memories of Carl's parents.

Carl's entrance into the café filled the room like May-morning sunshine on the mountain back home — a breath of fresh air after a long and frigid winter.

We'd drained second cups of coffee by the time I finished telling him about Herr Eberhardt, about Grandfather's making me a co-owner of all his assets, and finally about his tirade against Jews and the Confessing Church. "You said your parents knew of my grandfather. I'm hoping they'll remember Mama."

"*Ja,* they remember her." He set his cup on the table, wiping the ring it left with his finger. "They will tell you all they know."

"Why didn't you tell me before?"

"You weren't ready to hear. You were angry because I questioned Herr Sommer's character, his 'contribution to the war effort.' "

Heat rose from my stomach to my hairline. "Well, I'm ready now. Grandfather was furious over the idea that Mama helped Jews. I've never heard anything like it — the hateful way he talked. It was almost like hearing people in the South talk about blacks when Rosa Parks wouldn't give up her seat on the bus — so denigrating."

"So, you understand. Prejudice does not disappear because laws change. Even losing a war rarely changes the passions of the fallen." He pushed back from the table. "In America there is a saying, I think: 'Does the apple not fall near the tree?' "

"I'm not like Grandfather. I despise prejudice. I marched with Dr. Martin Luther King Jr. for civil rights in 1963. I took the bus to Washington, DC. I was only eighteen years old, but I knew right from wrong."

"Civil disobedience."

"Civil disobedience, but conscientiously required."

"Perhaps the apple does not fall far from

the mother-tree after all."

"For the first time in my life, I hope that's true."

Carl smiled and threw coins to the table. "My parents are ready to receive us."

I don't know what I expected, but Carl's parents looked so much older than Mama and Daddy had. I supposed they must be older — Carl himself had been ten years old when the war ended and he was the youngest of three children. His mother served coffee and cake at the kitchen table.

"Your mother was a brave woman," Herr Schmidt remembered. "She bought and sold on the black market to feed many. It was dangerous, so very dangerous."

I felt Carl sit back.

"For Jews? She was buying for Jews? Did she hide them herself?"

"Nein!" Frau Schmidt intervened. "She was but a girl; where would she hide them, and her Vater a member of the Nazi Party? He —"

Herr Schmidt placed a hand over his wife's. "Remember, Helga, Hannah is the granddaughter of Herr Sommer."

"Please, I understand that my grandfather embraced Nazi political views during the war. I don't know what my mother did."

The older couple exchanged a meaningful glance.

"It wasn't only that he embraced Nazi political views," Herr Schmidt said. "Many did that."

"Vater, perhaps you should begin with the church."

"*Ja, ja,* that is good." Herr Schmidt pulled a pipe from his pocket, tamped the tobacco, and lit it, the ritual helping him step back in time. "Do you know of the Confessing Church?"

"Carl told me a little about it. That's all I know."

"Some saw early that the Reich was trying to replace the church's doctrine with its own, that Herr Hitler was trying to stand in the place of our one true teacher, Jesus Christ. Men and women banded together to confess Jesus Christ as our Lord and Savior. Many — not all — also stood against the maltreatment of our Jewish brethren."

"Especially after Hitler declared that Christian Jews were not really Christian." I remembered what Carl had told me.

"It never mattered to the Reich if Jews were Christians or Communists or Orthodox or atheists. To them they were a people to be eliminated. And so they began."

Frau Schmidt spoke up. "But that's when

some in the Confessing Church stood up and began to help the Jews in a more concerted effort."

"Some more than others," Carl nearly accused. "Not everyone helped."

"Ja," Herr Schmidt replied, "this is true, and to our shame." The prolonged glance and tension between father and son was confusing. "Your mother, God rest her soul, was one who helped."

"She was fearless." Frau Schmidt's eyes watered. "And she was faithful. Do not let anyone tell you otherwise."

"Please, I beg of you, tell me about her."

"When we met your mother, she was already deeply involved. About the time her mother died — your Grossmutter — she began coming to church with the Kirchmann family."

" 'Kirchmann'? Did you say 'Kirchmann'?" Mama and Daddy's wedding certificate flashed through my brain.

"Ja, ja." She nodded. "Frau Kirchmann became, I think in many ways, a second mother for Lieselotte."

Herr Schmidt snorted. "It was not Frau Kirchmann who drew her."

"No." His wife smiled. "It was Lukas. I believe Lieselotte loved Lukas since she was a child. He was her older brother's friend."

"Uncle Rudy." I made the connection, but the name resounding in my ears was *Lukas.* Who was this Lukas Mama loved? And if she loved him, could he . . . ?

"*Ja.* Only the young men divided paths when the Sommer boy joined the Wehrmacht. He never came home. Lukas's father arranged for his son some kind of 'essential war work' with the Abwehr — the intelligence-gathering organization — that kept him out of the army."

"But all the while the Kirchmanns helped Jews — hiding them, moving them across the borders into Belgium and the Netherlands, some even to France and, through others farther south, to Switzerland." Frau Schmidt shook her head. "They were daring, and your mother with them."

"They weren't alone," Carl insisted. "A number of Confessing Church members helped."

"*Ja,* but not many in such direct ways. The Kirchmanns stole ration cards, forged identity cards, siphoned *Benzin* from the trucks of the Gestapo. They were brazen, and fearless," Frau Schmidt repeated.

"Or foolish," Herr Schmidt reproved. "They risked their lives and all those connected with them. In the end they were caught."

The Schmidts exchanged their worried glance once more.

"Tell me, please."

Herr Schmidt began, "Lieselotte and Lukas had just announced their engagement in the church that Sunday."

"It was not a secret." Frau Schmidt poured more tea. "The announcement appeared in the newspaper — such a happy couple. I remember hearing your Grossvater did not approve Lukas's lack of involvement in the Party. Still, he held a grand event to celebrate their engagement, in his home. He invited his Nazi friends — a good chance to show off his newfound wealth, to make his way into their social circle, I always thought. Lieselotte and the Kirchmanns were terribly afraid of such exposure, but determined to carry it off. It was the kind of thing they did, part of their ruse to keep above suspicion."

"Something must have happened that night." Herr Schmidt puffed on his pipe. The air grew thick and Frau Schmidt waved the smoke away. "We never knew what. But the next day — late in the afternoon — Herr Kirchmann came to the door and left a package."

"He left it with me." Carl's color deepened. "My parents were out and he asked me to give it to them — asked that we get it to one of the other church members. He said they were going away — that they must go away very soon. It had all been arranged by Lieselotte's father. I can see Herr Kirchmann standing in the doorway as if it were yesterday."

"It was over twenty-five years ago, Carl," his mother admonished.

"And every day I relive it. We should have done as he asked. It was so little to ask!"

"I don't understand." I glanced from Schmidt to Schmidt.

"Herr Kirchmann had risked his life to gain a dozen passports and new identity papers for Jews in hiding. He said he must go away, that they would no longer be able to help as they had before. So he asked that we get the passports to them."

Herr Schmidt removed his pipe and I saw the lines in his forehead deepen. "I take responsibility. I refused to deliver them, refused to allow Carl to deliver them. It would have put my family in jeopardy. If caught, I would have been sent to prison; my family would have starved. They might have taken us all away." All these years later, Herr Schmidt sounded weak, but defensive.

"It was a choice made daily by the Kirchmanns, by a dozen others, but we broke the circle," Frau Schmidt whispered. "And for that break — for our refusal to help — a dozen Jews were sent to camps."

"A dozen Jews died," Carl insisted.

Herr Schmidt's hands trembled. "I have not forgotten that day, have never forgiven myself."

"It was not your decision alone," Frau Schmidt replied softly. "I, too, was afraid. I was the one who threw them into the fire."

I didn't know what to say, how to comfort or reprieve them . . . if I even had that right, if I believed I should. *"I was afraid . . . a dozen Jews died . . ."*

"That night the Kirchmanns disappeared," Herr Schmidt went on, "they were taken into hiding. Herr Sommer had arranged passage for them — that was all he told Carl. We didn't know where or how. But the Gestapo discovered their hiding place and came early the next morning to arrest them — all of them."

"Except Marta," Frau Schmidt added.

"Yes, except Marta."

"Who is Marta?" I'd not heard that name before.

"The younger Kirchmann child — she and Lieselotte were of an age, fast friends, like sisters. Later she told us she'd snuck out, saying good-bye to a school friend, when the Gestapo came. Because of that, she was saved, and hidden by members of the church until the end of the war."

"And that's when Mama ran away? Did she try to follow them?"

Herr Schmidt shook his head. "We don't know for certain. Only that she disappeared the same night."

Frau Schmidt smoothed her hand over the pinned rolls in my hair. "I think . . ." She hesitated. "Herr Sommer may have been the one to report them."

"Sold them to the Reich." I glanced at Carl, remembering his words, but still did not want to believe. "You can't know that. You have no proof."

Herr Schmidt set his pipe on the table. "When we learned that the Kirchmanns had been taken, I went to the pastor of our church — Pastor Braun. I meant to tell him what I knew, what Carl had heard the day before about them leaving."

"Yes?"

"Frau Braun said that Pastor had been taken earlier that morning. She said she would go to Lieselotte's father and beg his help for his daughter's sake."

"What happened?"

Herr Schmidt would not look at me. "Frau Braun never returned home. Pastor

343

Braun did not survive the camp."

"You're certain Grandfather didn't try to help them — any of them?"

Herr Schmidt set his pipe on the table. "They were uncertain times."

"No one dared ask, or talk to another about such things. No one risked trusting his neighbor. They might denounce you. It was not uncommon for children — brainwashed in the Hitler Youth — and brownshirts to denounce their own parents," Frau Schmidt all but pleaded for me to understand.

My stomach nearly scraped the floor. "What happened to the Kirchmanns?"

"Helmeuth — Herr Kirchmann — and Lukas were sent first to Dachau, and then somewhere else. We lost track. We heard only — months after the war — that Helmeuth and his wife had died in the camps."

"And what about Mama's fiancé? What about Lukas?"

Herr Schmidt shook his head. "He came back — after the war. Marta took him in. But he was a broken man."

After the war . . . Mama and Daddy were married in 1945. Why did she marry Daddy if Lukas was alive? Did she not know that he'd survived? "Is he alive now?"

"I do not know. We never saw him — it's just what we heard. I cannot imagine it, but we have seen neither of them for many years."

"Does Marta live in Berlin?"

"We don't know where she lives now."

"The envelopes." Carl pressed my hand. "The envelopes you showed me. I didn't recognize the address. I meant to ask you, Vater, if you knew it."

"I left them in the car — in my purse. Carl, would you —"

"I'll get them."

Carl's absence left a giant hole in the room, but I couldn't bring myself to fill it. *What do I say to them? How do I even feel about what they did — what they failed to do? Would I have done any better? Mama did.*

Carl was back in thirty seconds and I pulled them from my purse. "Here. The writing is old — faint. The stamped dates look like they're mostly from the early fifties."

"*Ja, ja* — this is it." Herr Schmidt squinted at the envelope. "Danziger Strasse, 143."

"This is what?"

"The Kirchmanns' address — before they were taken away. It is in East Berlin today, beyond the wall. But the name has

345

changed . . . let me think."

"Dimitroffstrasse," Frau Schmidt said.

"*Ja,* that is it."

My heart beat faster. "That means Marta or Lukas wrote to Mama after the war, after I was born. Is there a chance they're still living there, or that relatives or friends are still in the neighborhood?"

"*Nein.* I told you, they moved away — I don't know where. They had no other relatives, though perhaps there are others from the church of those days who would know Marta, and where she moved. Frau Kirchmann came from Austria — long before the war, before Hitler came to power. Perhaps they returned there."

"Mama always claimed she was Austrian."

"Your Mutter? *Nein,* she was German. Only Frau Kirchmann was Austrian." Frau Schmidt sounded positive.

"Could they have married — before the arrest?"

"I do not see how. The engagement celebration came just two days before the Gestapo."

My heart fell.

Carl must have seen my disappointment. "Marta would know. She might be the only one who would know."

"She would at least know if Lukas is still

346

alive," I all but pleaded.

"Why is it important to find Lukas now? After your mother is dead and all these years have gone? If he is alive, this could only bring him sad memories." Herr Schmidt tamped his pipe again.

Frau Schmidt covered his arm with her hand. "Because she wants to better know her Mutter — the girl her Mutter once was. And perhaps —" she glanced sympathetically toward me — "your Vater?"

24

Lieselotte Sommer
September 1944

Just after midnight our party ended. The hours stole the luster from Vater, but Fräulein Hilde still shone like the midday sun as she graciously thanked our guests for coming. Dr. Peterson shadowed the edges of the room and lit a cigarette, making no move to leave.

I had no chance to warn Lukas or his parents — and nothing to say. It was simply a feeling, a sick feeling in my stomach based on Dr. Peterson's innuendos and facial expressions — his very body language. But his presence shook me as though all my anchors had been cut and I was drifting, slowly but perilously, out to sea.

Before I excused myself, I thanked Fräulein Hilde and *mein Vater,* making certain they knew how very much the evening meant to Lukas and me, how we looked forward to sharing our wedding day with them. Still Dr. Peterson stayed.

I bid them all good night and made for the stairs, my ears perked for anything that might be said.

"It was a grand success," Fräulein Hilde gloated.

"Thanks to you, my dear," Vater crowed.

"A grand success and a very long day. I'll bid you good night, Wolfgang. Dr. Peterson, go home and give this poor man rest. He's played the victor's role tonight — and played it well." I heard the satisfaction in her voice as I reached the top stair. I couldn't wait longer without being noticed, so I went to my room. Minutes later I heard Fräulein Hilde's car drive away and the latch close on Vater's library door.

After tonight's social statement before the Nazi Party members Vater and Fräulein Hilde so wanted to impress, I couldn't imagine what Dr. Peterson could complain about. Lukas and I had comported ourselves admirably, and the Kirchmanns had engaged in witty conversation at every level.

But the telegram — what could that be? What more could there be to his Heyden Fulstrom story? Even if Dr. Peterson contacted Heyden again, even if he and his friend on duty swore that I'd kissed Lukas in public and that Lukas had been with another young woman, that would only show my inappropriate expression of passion for him — not worth a fuss now that we were about to marry. They couldn't prove Anna was Jewish — not now. The Levys were well hidden away in the cellar of friends. It had been stupid of me to claim Anna was my cousin, but I could put that down to my foolishness or nervousness at being questioned by guards in the street.

I changed into my nightdress and turned out the light, then crawled into bed and reviewed everything I could imagine. Just before falling asleep I remembered the car that had slowed when I'd checked my bicycle chain earlier in the week. Had it come from behind me or before me? I rolled over, uncertain of my memory. That was days ago. I closed my eyes and tried to sleep.

For all my worry and the previous night's excitement, I slept until seven. Vater had already left the house. Perhaps my fears were unfounded after all. I breakfasted in my room, eager to escape the hustle and bustle downstairs and to plan my day. How soon could I see Lukas? The very thought warmed me through.

I'd promised to meet Fräulein Hilde at

350

the dressmaker's for one final fitting of my going-away suit and luncheon on the terrace of her favorite hotel. It would provide a suitable opportunity for her to glory in the success of last night's dinner and for me to thank her once again for all she'd done.

I'd dressed to go out and was just pulling on my gloves and adjusting my hat in front of the hallway mirror when Vater walked through the front door. I glanced up, smiling, glad to be at last on comfortable terms with him. His barely controlled fury met my eyes.

"What is it? What's the matter?"

He grabbed my elbow and ushered me none too gently into the library, closing the door.

"Vater? What is it? What's happened?" My mind ran through every possible scenario that might produce such anger — none of them good.

" 'What is it? What's happened?' " he mimicked. "Do you take me for a fool, Lieselotte — a fool? Is it your quest to ruin me, to destroy everything I've built?"

"I don't know what you're talking about." But fear sped through my veins.

"How long have you known about Frau Kirchmann?"

"Frau Kirchmann? Known what?"

" 'Known what?' " he mimicked again, then pulled a telegram from inside his breast pocket and threw it on the desk before me. "Known this! Known that she is *Jewish*!" He spat the word.

"She's not," I pled. "Frau Kirchmann is Austrian — they're Austrian! Her parents —"

"The woman who raised her was not her mother. Her mother died in childbirth — her Jewish mother! Or did she forget to tell you this? Did Lukas fail to mention that he is one-quarter Jewish?"

"I don't believe it." I turned the telegram over and read it. It bore the Nazi insignia and was addressed to Dr. Peterson. "Dr. Peterson! He is behind this — a plot to destroy Lukas — the entire Kirchmann family!" I threw the paper back at my father. "This is an out-and-out lie. Dr. Peterson has done everything in his power to stop our wedding, and now this. You can't believe him, Vater. This is ludicrous!"

"Peterson is my most trusted colleague. Were it not for him, I would still be clerking in a lowly government office."

"But why does he — ?"

"My life within the Party is an open book. Peterson knows this. The very link that my own daughter has with that church — that

Confessing Church — is enough to make my membership questionable."

"But Mutti —"

"Is the only reason I tolerated your flagrant disrespect for my wishes. It is because I promised her, and I would not break that promise. But this — this hiding of Jews behind Christian skirts — is criminal. Do you not understand?"

I did understand what that meant in the New Germany, and I feared where his accusations would lead. "I don't believe it — not for a minute. This is more of Dr. Peterson's manipulations if it's anything at all. Even if it's true, you'll soon be rid of me and Lukas. It won't matter. We won't besmirch your good Nazi Party name."

He slapped me across the face — so hard I fell back on the chair. "You will end it. I will give you twenty-four hours to call off the wedding. Say you've reconsidered — say anything, but call it off."

"No — no!" The sting on my cheek felt like nothing compared to the empty chasm looming before me. "Don't ask this, Vater. I love him!"

"They will be arrested the moment this is known. They will all be arrested — Frau Kirchmann, Lukas, and Marta because they are *die Juden,* and Herr Kirchmann because

he has kept this hidden. Lukas — a member
of the Abwehr — he'll be lucky if he's not
shot."

"*Nein,* Vater! Please! No one needs to
know."

He pushed the heels of his hands into his
eyes. "Everything I've built, all I've planned
with Hilde, will be lost if this becomes
known — when it becomes known."

"But it doesn't need —"

"If I don't report it, *I* will be reported —
arrested. Do you think Fräulein Hilde will
marry me then? My reputation, my position, my honor before the Party — I will
lose everything!"

I thought he might slap me again, but he
looked at me with as much defeat as anger.

"Perhaps I can help." I jumped at Dr.
Peterson's voice behind me.

"You." I turned. "You never wanted —"

"What I want is of little importance,
Fräulein. What matters is your father's position — all we've spent years building. We
need for this problem to disappear without
question, without trace."

"You're the one who initiated —"

"*Ja, ja* — and you should be thanking me
that you've not married a criminal!"

Now I desperately wanted to slap him.

"What?" Vater demanded. "What can

make such a thing disappear? It is recorded. It will be no time before this connection is made to the investigation into the Abwehr."

"But the fact that they've not been arrested yet means it has not. There is time to move them."

"Move them?" My head swam.

"Ja." Dr. Peterson glanced at the door behind him, as though he feared someone might be listening, and stepped farther into the room. "What do you think, Wolfgang? Could we get them out?"

Vater's eyes narrowed, then widened. He searched my eyes and turned away. "Perhaps. Perhaps there's a way."

"For a price," Dr. Peterson said. "It will cost dearly to move them — all of them — out of the country."

"Out of the country?" I couldn't believe this.

"They must leave Germany," Dr. Peterson insisted. "Leave any occupied zones. It's their only chance . . . That is, if you care to give them that chance."

My world had fallen apart in minutes. How? I closed my eyes to shut it out.

"What do you think, Wolfgang? Can we get four good passports? What will it cost?"

"Five!" I opened my eyes. "If Lukas goes, I go with him. After the wedding."

"Nein," Dr. Peterson insisted. "That's too long. They must go tonight — tomorrow at the latest. I can have passports made from their identity papers on file. I know someone."

I shook my head, not able to comprehend Dr. Peterson helping the Kirchmanns, and less able to comprehend that he knew about forging passports. The members of our resistance hadn't been able to move anyone out of the country for months. But I wouldn't let them contemplate separating me from Lukas. "Then I'll go without marrying him." I turned to my father. "Vater, I won't stay."

He hesitated, glanced Dr. Peterson's way, and nodded. "Lieselotte, call Lukas and his father. Tell them to come here, that I must see them. Now. There is no time to lose. Do not speak openly on the telephone."

"I'll go to his house. I'll bring him back with me."

"Nein." Dr. Peterson spoke too quickly. "Time is of the essence. They'll need to arrange their affairs."

"But —"

"You're to meet Fräulein Hilde, are you not?"

"Ja." I looked at my watch. "But this is more important. I can explain —"

"*Nein,* Lieselotte! Hilde must not know — under no circumstances. You must promise me. She will not understand. It is our duty to report them." Vater knelt before me. "I am doing this for you, my child. You must understand I am doing this for you. Keep it from Hilde. Speak of this to no one. That is all I ask."

"*Ja,* Vater — I will do as you say." Instinctively I hugged him. But he stiffened and pulled back.

"Make the phone call, then go to your luncheon. Act as if everything is normal. We will talk later."

I nodded. As I passed Dr. Peterson, my stomach roiled. If he had not requested a formal inquiry, if he had not initiated the search, none of this would have become known, none of it necessary. But he had offered to help the Kirchmanns — to help my Lukas and me escape. "*Danke,* Herr Doktor."

He nodded, but his smile was so near a sneer I could not tell the difference.

As I hurried from the house my throat tightened and my stomach gripped. I did not trust him — either of them. But what choice did we have?

25

Hannah Sterling
February 1973

Through Carl's official status as a Berlin driver, we obtained permission to enter the eastern sector the same day. Still, there were questionnaires regarding the purpose and length of our visit and a detailed itinerary to complete. We were required to exchange money at an exorbitant rate after we and our car were thoroughly searched. Carl's magazine and my paperback book were confiscated, as if *Jane Eyre* might corrupt the residents of East Berlin. By the time we crossed Checkpoint Charlie, I felt almost violated. Only my need for answers bolstered my courage.

Carl wasted no time in finding the Kirchmanns' old street. We searched up and down the street, but there was no number 143. We knocked repeatedly on doors in the vicinity. At last a woman cracked her door

— perhaps four inches.

"There's been no number 143 as long as we have lived here — ten years at least." She closed the door in our faces.

We knocked on three other doors, but there was no answer.

"Look." Carl pointed to an old woman carrying her shopping bags from the bus corner.

"She's old enough; she might have lived here then." I could barely restrain my hope and barely contain my anticipated disappointment. It took us five minutes to convince her we meant no harm, that we just wanted to locate Marta Kirchmann for my mother's sake.

Carl translated her German. "Yes, I remember the Kirchmanns very well. A good family — good neighbors. But it turned out the mother was a Jewess and that they'd been helping Jews — hiding them in their own attic! Of course, in those days, they disappeared. So many people here one day and gone the next. We never knew where . . . Marta? *Nein,* I do not know where Marta went. I saw her and her brother after the war. Nothing but a vapor, he was. They moved away after a time . . . too many bad memories, I suppose. The new owners pulled down the old house; the kitchen had

359

been bombed near the end of the war and the building was never sound again. They built this apartment house. All the numbers are mixed up — such a mess."

We thanked her and returned to Carl's car. He opened the door for me, resting his hand on my back. "I'm sorry, Hannah."

But I was too spent to respond, too near tears from hopes built high and dashed to the ground.

On the drive back to Grandfather's, Carl promised, "I'll check the address you found in Herr Sommer's ledger. It will be easier, quicker for me to get through checkpoints again than for you. I'll let you know what I learn. Who knows — perhaps someone there will remember the Kirchmanns."

I nodded and pressed his shoulder in gratitude. We drove in silence until we reached the house.

The kitchen was cold. It didn't look as if Grandfather had stepped inside it. He must be hungry. I didn't know if I could look at him after all I'd learned at the Schmidts'. *I could live with you as a miserable, selfish old man . . . but a conniving murderer? A mercenary who dealt in blood money? That's how you made your wealth — the wealth you intend to pass on to me . . . or to buy my allegiance with.* The realization made me want

360

to vomit.

My head throbbed and my joints ached. I threw my coat and gloves over the chair and set the kettle to boil.

He must be hungry — unless he ate the breakfast I left for him. But that was hours ago. No matter what I think about him, I can't let him starve. I wouldn't let a prisoner starve. I stood at the foot of the stairs, listening. No sounds came from Grandfather's room.

I cut sandwich bread, slathered it with mustard, and draped it with cheese. There was cold roast beef in the icebox and some soup left from the day before. By the time the tea was made and his tray prepared, I'd eaten half my sandwich. I drew a deep breath and headed for Grandfather's room. I had no idea how I'd look him in the eye.

I knocked softly. No answer. I knocked again and called, "Grandfather?" I pushed open the door. "Grossvater?" His bed was empty, the eiderdown still rumpled, as though he'd just risen. But his dressing gown and slippers were thrown across it. He'd apparently eaten the bun and coffee I'd left for him this morning. I listened at the stairs, but there were no sounds from the third floor.

Could he be in the dining room or library? I balanced the tray on my hip to try the

361

library door, expecting it to be locked. But it easily gave way.

The curtains had been drawn closed and the brass lamp on the desk was lit, papers scattered across the desktop. The ledger I'd seen for only a moment lay facedown on the floor — as if thrown. One end of the bookcase had swung away from the wall, a dark and narrow opening behind it.

It was a scene from an Alfred Hitchcock movie. I set the tray on the small table by the door and looked again, half expecting it all to have disappeared. And that's when I saw Grandfather's hand stretched out on the floor.

"Grandfather!" Behind the desk his body lay crumpled, his face contorted, his leg bent at an odd angle. I was sure he was dead.

A soft, barely perceptible moan escaped his lips — lips nearly blue.

"What happened? Grandfather, what happened?" He couldn't answer, didn't open his eyes. *Think! Think! Who should I call? Dr. Peterson.* But I didn't know his number or how to reach him. So I pummeled the telephone cradle for the operator.

"Please, my grandfather has collapsed! I think it might be his heart, and I don't know how to reach his doctor."

Between my lack of German and the operator's feeble English, it took five minutes to communicate the address and need. But help would soon be on the way.

I pulled a pillow from the wingback chair and, lifting his head, tucked it beneath. "Someone will be here soon, Grandfather. They'll get hold of Dr. Peterson. I'm sure he'll come. Hang on."

I sat back on my heels, trying to think what to do next. The room was a shambles — at least compared to its normal state. *If someone sees this, they'll suspect a burglary. They'll take an inventory of all they see. And if they see that ledger, won't they draw the same conclusions Carl has? If they take the ledger, I'll never see it again. I'll never learn the truth.* Before I thought it through, I picked up the ledger and squeezed it between two volumes on the bookshelf. I pushed the desk drawer closed. Everything looked normal, except for the bookshelf and the narrow hole in the wall. *A walk-in safe? A secret room?*

Running my hand round the edge of the hole, I searched for a light switch, finding nothing but a lock on the outer edge. I pushed the bookcase a little wider, hoping the lamplight would reveal more. Shapes — large rectangles and small boxes — sat on shelves or leaned against the one blank wall in a room no more than three feet by nine, cleverly situated between the dining room and library walls. A hidden space no one could detect.

The far-off wail of an ambulance broke the spell.

If I close this door, how will I open it again? It looks as if it needs a key. The wail screamed closer, intensified, then stopped abruptly. I pushed the bookcase, watching it swing easily toward the wall. At the last moment I stopped it. A pounding came on the front door. Slipping a slim book between the wall and the back of the bookcase, I shoved the bookcase as far as it would go. A latch on the back all but caught. The pounding came again, and a voice called out, demanding entrance.

Casting a last quick glance over the room, at Grandfather still askew on the floor, I ran to the door.

The ambulance medics swept in. All I did was point toward the library.

"He has heart trouble. I was out all day, and when I brought in his tray, I found him like this." I babbled in English, not knowing if they understood.

Both medics glanced at the tray and back at me, as if questioning my story. I could only guess how it must appear.

In three minutes they had lifted Grandfather, moaning softly and deathly pale, onto a gurney. I spotted a ring with two brass keys — one small and one heavier — where his body had been. I picked it up with his handkerchief that had fallen and slipped it into my pocket.

"His doctor?" one of the medics demanded. "Have you telephoned his doctor?"

"Oh, thank heaven you speak English!" Flustered, I could barely focus.

"His doctor?"

"Dr. Peterson, but I don't know how to reach him. I have no number. I told the operator."

"You are?"

"Hannah Sterling — he's my grandfather, Wolfgang Sommer. I'm visiting from America."

The other medic grinned. "I believe."

"Your grandfather has prescriptions?" the first medic asked.

"I — I don't know. Probably. Do you want me to check his room?"

"*Ja*. It is best. Where?"

"Up the stairs, first door on the left." I raced after him.

"Medications within the last hour?"

"I don't know. I'm sorry." We searched

Grandfather's bedside table, the top dresser drawer of his walnut bureau, the bookcase by the window, his bathroom medicine cabinet — nothing. If hand-wringing were an occupation, I'd have been well paid.

"Not to worry, Fräulein. The hospital should have his file. His doctor will be telephoned."

"Can I go with you to the hospital? I have no car."

"*Nein,* it is *verboten.* Here is the number of the hospital where we take him. Phone them after one hour." He whipped out a card. In less than another minute they were out the door and the house fell completely silent, except for the pounding of my heart.

26

Lieselotte Sommer
September 1944

I came home to find Lukas and Herr Kirchmann leaving my father's library. The pain
and resignation in Herr Kirchmann's eyes
was palpable. The pain and panic in Lukas's
eyes frightened me. But as long as we could
go together, that was all that mattered.

"My little Lieselotte." Herr Kirchmann
spoke first, drawing me into his arms. "I am
so sorry, so very sorry for this trouble we
have brought to your door."

My head moved from side to side, but it
felt no more attached to my neck than my
feet. "It can't be true. Can it?"

He touched my face. "There is so little
time. I will leave Lukas to explain. But I
swear to you, neither he nor Marta knew —
until today. We'd hoped it would never matter so long that we nearly believed it was
not so." He shook his head, disbelieving the

moment. "Know, dear girl, that we love you — that you are our family forever."

My father cleared his throat. Herr Kirchmann closed his eyes and regained his composure. "There is much to do. I'll go now." He placed my hand in Lukas's. Without turning to speak again to Vater, he left by the back door.

"Lieselotte," my father called. "You saw Fräulein Hilde? You were not gone long."

"She suspects nothing. I told her I had a terrible headache — not enough sleep last night. It was just as well. She had scheduled a dress fitting and forgotten until this morning."

"This is good."

Lukas squeezed my hand. "We must talk."

We'd walked halfway to Lukas's house before he found the words. "It's true — what my father said, that I did not know until today."

"Vater said your grandmother died giving birth to your mother. But how he would know this, I can't —"

"*Ja,* this is true, and she was Jewish — not my grandfather. Grandfather married again within a few months." Lukas shrugged. "He had a baby, and no one to care for her. So he married their housekeeper — a Gentile — who raised my mother as her own. Mutter always thought of her as her mother — the only mother she ever knew."

"And so she claimed her lineage as her own."

"*Ja*. It was not hard to do at the time — not hard to write her name on the birth certificate. But it was a difficult birth and a doctor was called in. Perhaps it was his record that told the name of her true mother, or the record of the church where she was baptized. I don't know."

"Dr. Peterson dug it up. It's his fault. None of this would —"

"God sees everything, knows everything. There must —"

"Lukas, you speak of ideas, ideals — this is our *life*. All our lives. I can't think what made him go looking — what made him suspect."

Lukas snorted. "He has the memory of an elephant, the slyness of a fox." He tucked my hand in his pocket as we walked. "It was something Marta said, years ago. Do you remember the Christmas party — the last Christmas party your mother . . ."

I waited.

"Dr. Peterson brought in those candlesticks — silver, ornate, worth a fortune."

"*Ja,* I suppose. So, what about them?"

"Marta was excited to see them. She said Mutti had a pair like them — with the fruits and flowers engraved just so. She said her grandmother had given them to Mutti, and that one day they would be hers."

"Why does that — ?"

"Apparently it is tradition in a Jewish household for the mother to pass the Shabbat candleholders to her daughter, from generation to generation. Dr. Peterson suspected they were from a Jewish household because he'd 'bought,' or more likely confiscated, the pair he displayed that day from a Jewish house that had just been Aryanized."

"You mean, all these years, he's —"

"Bided his time . . . or forgotten until recently — I don't know. I knew he suspected my lack of enthusiasm from the time I delayed joining the Hitler Youth, that he's tried to prove me part of the assassination conspiracy, that he's despised Father because of his connection with the Confessing Church. But I underestimated the depths of his hatred, not to mention his connections. I can't be certain he is the cause, but my parents' house was searched last year."

"I remember. Your mother believed they put in a listening device."

Lukas sighed. "They found and took the candlesticks. On their own that might mean nothing. They could have been taken by overzealous underlings simply for their value. But with Peterson's memory of them . . . I must wonder."

"He says he's concerned about Vater's reputation, but there's something more — I don't know what."

"He's closely aligned with your father in his work and financial dealings. If your father is ruined through connections to my family, Dr. Peterson, too, will perhaps be ruined. Whatever they're doing, they've become extremely wealthy. War creates strange opportunities for the shrewd — ones they will do anything to protect."

He lifted my hand and kissed my fingers. "To think we've been hiding Jews, moving Jews all this time, and we ourselves are Jews!"

"The apple of God's eye." I squeezed his hand in return. "I'm proud our children will carry Jewish blood."

Lukas froze. "Lieselotte. We must go alone — my parents and Marta and I. That is the only deal they would make."

The chasm that had loomed before me earlier in the day opened at my feet. *"Nein,"* I whispered. "I talked with them. I told Vater

I must go with you — married or not. He understood; he agreed for Dr. Peterson to find five passports — five good passports."

"Just now he told Father and me he could not do it. Four is all he could get — all he would get. Dr. Peterson said that if you do not stay behind, it will seem that your father knew about us all along, that he hid Jews from the Reich, that he allowed his Aryan daughter to marry a Jew. He will be ruined."

I shook my head. "I will not live without you; I will not. We can't trust Dr. Peterson."

"But I trust your father. He's helping in every way he can."

I shook my head again, disbelieving.

"Lieselotte, your father is a hard but honest man — I must believe this. We have no choice. If he was simply going to turn us in, he could have done that by now. We must trust him. And after the war, when this is all over, we'll find each other. We'll marry and —"

I could not stop the shaking of my head. I wouldn't believe there was no other way. I'd plead, I'd beg and grovel — whatever would persuade Vater and Dr. Peterson. There must be something they'd not thought of yet — something we'd not thought of.

What was Lukas saying about valuables?

"I'd hoped to put the stones in a ring for

you one day."

"Stones?"

"The rubies and diamonds my mother had taken from Grandmother's tiara — three she had not yet sold to buy food. She gave them to me to have made into a ring for you. There's been no time yet, but I wanted to surprise you with them on our first anniversary. I'm so sorry, my Lieselotte. They must go now for the passports."

"Of course they must! Your life — our lives — are worth more than anything, as long as we are together."

"I know what you're thinking. I begged him too, offered everything — but he refused."

"And you would go without me?" I stopped walking.

"If I don't, you will be arrested. I won't have that, Lieselotte. You don't know what the camps are like. You would not survive. It would be different if we were married already, if there was no other way, but we're not. You can't legally marry me knowing I'm one-quarter —"

"You know that doesn't matter!"

"But it is the law, and if we break this law, we'll both be arrested. It will do us no good to be thrown into separate prisons — separate concentration camps. This way, at least you will be safe. I must know you're safe."

It was impossible — all of it impossible.

He took me in his arms. "Keep faith, my darling. You must keep faith and, when you can, help those still in hiding. At least we're getting out alive, thanks to your father. He stood against Dr. Peterson — he's risking a great deal to help us."

I was outnumbered.

"Come with me now. It will be best if you carry the payment to your father."

Frau Kirchmann emptied her savings from all the places a good *Hausfrau* might hide them — the cookie jar, the foot of a twisted stocking in her drawer, a cloth bag beneath the mattress of her bed, and a tiny pouch of three precious stones hidden in her sewing basket.

"In plain view," she whispered, dropping the stones one by one into my palm. "These were my mother's. They were to go to Lukas, for your ring."

I refused to cry. Their lives were more valuable than any wish I might make, whether or not I went with them. Though I was far from reconciled to my fate.

"I am so sorry, my daughter. So very, very sorry. If I could turn back time —"

"Shh, Mutti," Lukas whispered. "Lieselotte knows. We'll find each other when this is over. This is not the end."

"When the war is over." I repeated what I'd heard him say, though how could I believe it?

"Ja, ja." Frau Kirchmann nodded, wiping her tears.

Herr Kirchmann had gone to the bank to withdraw all he could without arousing suspicion and to get someone else from the church to deliver forged papers. Others would have to fill in their portion of relief routes for refugees. Marta had gone to see if Pastor Braun knew who might help.

Lukas paced the floor, praying for a miracle, an inspiration. But an hour passed, and neither Marta nor Herr Kirchmann returned. Lukas said we dared wait no longer lest they think we would not pay.

"Tell Dr. Peterson my Helmeuth will bring the rest as soon as he returns," Frau Kirchmann ordered. "At least this much will show him our good faith."

We'd tied handkerchiefs around separate small mounds of precious stones and coins, rings and brooches. Everything small, valuable — what our Jews in hiding called "portable wealth." Lukas helped me into my coat just as Marta burst through the door, coat half buttoned, panting, terror in her eyes.

"They've been arrested! The Eisners were arrested!"

"No!"

"They shot Kurt in the street —" she reached for her mother's arms — "and dragged Frederich from the house, then Miriam and their baby!"

"Did they see you?"

"Mutti! How can you ask — ?"

"Did they see you?" Lukas shook his sister.

"Nein," Marta sobbed. "I stayed hidden. But I saw that man — that Dr. Peterson — with the Gestapo."

"Dr. Peterson!"

Marta looked at me, accusing. *"Ja,* he stood in the street, and showed them where to go — the very house! He watched the raid, then drove away."

I sat down. "In a black car."

"Ja," Marta confirmed.

"How do you know this?" Frau Kirchmann asked.

I moistened my lips. *Could I have been the cause?*

"Lieselotte?"

I looked at Lukas. "Last week . . . after I made a delivery . . ."

"Ja? What then?" Frau Kirchmann prompted.

"There was a car — a black car. I don't know if I was followed, but it slowed."

"It could have been anybody." Lukas wrapped his arms around me.

I pulled away. "I don't know. How would — ?"

"He waited until the Eisners were taken away; then the remaining Gestapo agent paid him," Marta said.

"Sudden wealth," Lukas murmured. "Blood money."

"Blood money," I repeated, and the bile rose in my throat.

27

Hannah Sterling
February 1973
The phone rang and rang, but Carl did not answer. *He must still be in East Berlin.*

At last a woman answered.

"Carl Schmidt, please."

She began rattling something off in German.

"Please, I don't speak German. Do you speak English?"

"Ah." I could hear the pride in her voice. "My English not so good. Herr Schmidt is not here."

I closed my eyes. *Why did I send you off on that wild-goose chase? I need you here — now!* "Please, as soon as he returns, tell him to come to Hannah. He'll know. He'll understand."

"Ja, ja," she replied knowingly, with a bit of a smirk audible. "I tell him."

What? So I'm just one more girl in a long

line? I couldn't think about that now.

I didn't want to open the door behind the bookcase alone, to snoop through whatever Grandfather had hidden there, but this might be my only opportunity. If it was in some way linked to the open ledger, if the ledger was linked to families he'd sold out, I had to know. And I had to know where my mother fit in that picture.

When Grandfather returned home, he would surely change the locks once he suspected I'd seen the ledger or the secret room. Once Dr. Peterson or Herr Eberhardt realized I was alone in the house, they'd appear and take charge, perhaps remove everything. Could they do that? I didn't know.

I grabbed a flashlight from the kitchen and headed for the library. Removing the book, I swung the bookcase outward. It was not as easy as swinging it closed, and I wondered if it was this effort that had set off Grandfather's heart.

The latch for the bookcase was cleverly hidden in the recess of the wall and the keyhole concealed in the bookcase itself — behind heavy volumes. No one could see it unless they knew precisely what to look for.

I turned the small switch just inside. Light flooded the tiny room — a narrow aisle, really. Shelves, floor to ceiling, were lined with an assortment of jewelry displayed and tagged in a sort of pencil-written shorthand I couldn't decipher. Small pieces of sculpture also rested on the shelves — some made of ivory and others heavy, marble and possibly gold. I could not imagine their worth. There were first editions of classics in English and beautifully bound and tooled leather volumes in German, also tagged. There was silver — coffee urns and teapots, trays. Beautiful bowls of intricately cut crystal. Stacked against the wall were oil paintings, some canvases loosely rolled and wrapped in brown paper and others free-standing in their frames.

I've no idea how long I stood in the treasure trove. I was examining the contents of a jewelry display case and had just emptied a velvet bag of cut gems into my palm when I heard a knock that seemed far away. *Was that the front or back door?*

Cupping my palm, I poured the gems back into the small drawstring bag, stowing it on the shelf. The knock came again, louder this time.

I slipped through the wall opening, closed the bookcase, this time letting it latch, and flicked off the flashlight.

An urgent knock on the library window

made me jump, and I drew open the drapes. "Carl!"

He motioned for me to let him in and I ran round to the kitchen door.

"My landlady said you telephoned, that you said to come right away. Are you all right?"

"I am now." My heart would not behave itself — for fear of Grandfather's state and for the wonder of discovery of the hidden room and surely for the pure relief that Carl Schmidt was standing there before me. Propriety to the wind, I fell into his arms.

"Now, now — what's happened?" He held me close, pushing hair from my eyes.

Swiping away tears I hadn't intended, I poured out my discovery of Grandfather sprawled on the floor, told him about the ambulance and the hospital. And then, the ledger. "Grandfather must have been reading it when he had his heart attack. I want to get to the hospital, but there's more. This might be my only chance to show you."

We'd nearly reached the library when the front door opened.

"Dr. Peterson!" I didn't know if I was more unnerved that he'd appeared or that he had his own key to Grandfather's house.

"Fräulein Sterling, I imagined that you would be at the hospital with your Gross-

381

vater." It was an accusation.

"I was just about to leave. My driver has just arrived. The ambulance wouldn't allow me to ride with them."

He conceded. "Do not let me detain you."

"Why aren't you with him? You're his doctor. And how did you know?"

"Herr Eberhardt telephoned me. I came for his medicine, of course. I must make certain the hospital combines nothing to conflict with his current prescriptions." But his eyes wavered.

"The medic said it wasn't needed. That they would have everything on file."

"I must make certain that Wolfgang took nothing more than what I have prescribed. He is an independent sort, as you know," he said, clearly trying to make light. "I will check his medicine cupboard to see for myself. Do not let me detain you," he repeated and stood aside.

"I think it's the other way around." I motioned him free access to the stairs.

The set of his jaw told me he wasn't pleased, but he brushed past us. He paused by the library door and pushed it open. The hesitation in his profile told me that he hadn't expected the room to be unlocked.

"That's where I found him. He'd collapsed on the floor. I think he broke his leg

— it was twisted so strangely. But you would know that if you've seen him."

"He was not conscious when you found him?"

"No, I don't think so."

"He was . . . reading? Doing what?"

"I've no idea. I wasn't here. I don't think that really matters now. Would you like me to help you look for his medicine? Although, I must tell you, the medic and I already searched."

"*Nein.* I know the way." He backed out of the room, closing the door. "It may be best to leave everything as it is, in case there are questions later."

"What sort of questions?" Carl stepped in front of me.

Dr. Peterson's brows rose. "And you? You are the driver?" The doctor's contempt was visible.

I edged around Carl. "May I remind you that this is my grandfather's house, you're his doctor, and you've just walked in — with your own key — claiming that you are looking for medicine that you probably prescribed. And now you proceed to tell me to leave everything as it is."

"Herr Sommer and I have a long-standing arrangement. Forgive me if I did not look at you as proprietary in his home. I understood you are here for only a short visit. Though Herr Eberhardt tells me Wolfgang believes that is not true."

His challenge undermined my confidence. "You seem to know a great deal about my affairs."

"It is my business to —"

"I am not your business, Dr. Peterson. Now, if you would like to complete your *medical* business, I'll wait and lock up."

"There is no need. I have my own key."

"I'll wait and lock up. We will follow you to the hospital. That's where you're going when you leave here, isn't it?"

The fury in his eyes could have smoked a pig, reminding me that despite his age, I'd never want to meet him in a dark alley. "I will be a moment."

While he took the stairs to Grandfather's room, I sank against Carl.

"Steady," he whispered. "You were *wunderbar*. Maintain your ground."

I squeezed his hand — in appreciation, in confidence, in need of his strength.

"Get your coat," he whispered into my hair. "We'll follow right away."

En route to the hospital I told Carl about everything I'd discovered, including the secret room. "So many expensive things —

works of art, some surely priceless."

"Can you match them against the ledger's entries?"

"I don't know. There wasn't time. But I'm very much afraid they will match, and I'm even more afraid that Dr. Peterson knows it — that in some way he's part of it all. Why else would he be there?"

"Whether or not he knows about the ledger, he must know about Herr Sommer's unusual finances. He said they have a long-standing arrangement."

"I'm just not sure what his connection is. Did he expect to inherit from Grandfather and now I've thrown a wrench into those plans? Is that why he hates me so?" I shuddered, cold beyond cold. "You saw the way he looked at me."

"I don't like the idea of you staying in that house alone, Hannah. As long as Herr Sommer was there, it was one thing. He kept Peterson in his place. But now that he is away and so vulnerable . . . if the doctor or Herr Eberhardt have any connection to his money or this . . . this heist, you are not safe."

"I don't know what else I can do."

Carl glanced my way. "Stay with my parents. I am certain they will agree."

"No, Carl — thank you. I don't think I

should do that."

He gripped the wheel, his mouth grim. "Think about it. Please say you'll think about it."

I pressed his shoulder. "I'll think about it. I promise."

We lost Dr. Peterson in the hospital parking area but assumed we'd see him in Grandfather's room. The attending hospital doctor took me aside after I'd viewed Grandfather through the window.

"I assumed the broken leg. But a stroke? Will he recover?"

"It's difficult to tell to what extent. His heart and age are certainly against him, but the next few hours will tell us much more. There is nothing you can do here until he awakens. You should go home, get some rest. If and when your Grossvater is able to return home, your own strength and stamina will be much needed."

"I'm here for now, but I don't know how long I can stay in Germany."

"Oh? Forgive me, but I understood from Heinrich Eberhardt that you are Herr Sommer's primary caregiver. This is not correct?"

"Herr Eberhardt? What has he to do with this?"

"Your grandfather's medical files listed him as immediate contact."

"Not Dr. Peterson?"

"Dr. Peterson?" The doctor picked up Grandfather's chart and flipped through its pages. "There is no Dr. Peterson listed."

Carl waited in the hospital lobby. He flipped his magazine to the waiting room table and met me in three long strides.

"Dr. Peterson is not even on his contact list, let alone listed as his doctor. Eberhardt, his lawyer, is the primary contact." I pulled Carl toward the door. "Why would he do that? Dr. Peterson said he's been treating Grandfather for years."

"Something's not right. Perhaps the relationship between Herr Sommer and Dr. Peterson is not as friendly as they claim."

"But why would he lie? Why would either of them pretend a long-standing trust that doesn't exist?"

"I can't answer that. But if Herr Sommer doesn't trust Peterson enough to list him in his medical records, you must not trust him either."

I tightened the belt of my coat. "I think some changes are in order. Do you know where to find a hardware store?"

"Hardware store? I don't know this word."

"Hardware — nuts, bolts, screws. Locks. We need some new locks and dead bolts."

I hadn't imagined we'd be too late. Grandfather's kitchen door stood wide open. It had been made to look like a burglary. The dining room silver was stolen, the marketing purse pinched, Grandfather's room ransacked, the library nearly overturned, and every lock in the desk broken. But the ledger was still neatly hidden among the volumes on the shelf. Every room had been searched, including mine. Even my lingerie drawer had been turned upside down and its contents thoroughly rifled. That violation was the last straw.

Carl pushed his hands through his hair in frustration. "If it was Peterson, he must not have found what he was looking for. If he'd known where to look, he'd not have bothered with all this. It took time."

"Destruction never takes long. But I won't lay bets on Dr. Peterson alone. Herr Eberhardt seems to have a great deal at stake as well." I unbuttoned my coat, then remembered the keys in my pocket.

Carl's eyes widened as I pulled them out, then met mine.

"Hide those well, Hannah, and then we must call the police. Now."

■ ■ ■ ■

By the time the police had come, taken photographs and fingerprints, and given me no hope at all, it was after seven. Carl brought in pizza. Not Germany's best effort at foreign food, but welcome.

Changing a lock was something Daddy taught me that had come in useful more than once, though I'd never expected to need that skill in Germany. Carl was no novice either.

"That should do it." He gave the last screw of the dead bolt inside the kitchen door one final turn. "I think we should do something about these downstairs windows — possibly all the windows."

Carl looked so serious I wanted to kiss him. He was growing more and more into my knight in shining armor. But I didn't know where acknowledging that might lead and wasn't ready to find out . . . not here, not now. I tweaked his cheek. "Just changing locks will challenge the 'good doctor' and the 'noble lawyer' if they come calling. I'd hear a window breaking, and these dead bolts will keep anyone else away."

"I don't know, Hannah. Are you certain you don't want me to stay the night? I can sleep downstairs."

I closed my eyes and breathed. "That's so tempting, and I appreciate your offer. But it's not a good idea. Peterson and Eberhardt would have a heyday with that in painting my picture for Grandfather. If he doesn't recover, they'd surely try to assassinate my character in the courts."

"The courts?"

"You haven't seen the storeroom. It's got to be worth fortunes. They won't let it go easily. You should have seen Eberhardt's face when Grandfather changed his will — extending the 'house and its contents and all my worldly goods' to include me."

"Worldly goods stolen from Jews."

I nodded. "I'm afraid that's true, but we've got to go through that ledger. I won't fully concede until I do."

"I meant to tell you, I searched for the address in East Berlin. It is there, but rebuilt since the war. I found a neighbor, a Mrs. Gruber, who remembered the family living in number 3 at 39 Rochstrasse. She said they disappeared around the middle of November 1938."

"She can remember that exactly?"

"They were longtime friends — Martin and Roseanne Goldstein. She remembers them well. She saw them last shortly after

Kristallnacht — the Night of Broken Glass. She said Herr Goldstein owned a beautiful bookshop beneath their apartment — that he specialized in rare first editions and did a great deal of business with German and English collectors.

"It was late that November night. All the street woke to the crash of breaking glass. The storefront windows were shattered, broken out . . . dozens of his books scattered through the street and set on fire. Herr Goldstein and his son tried to stop them — the brownshirts — but the older man was dragged through the street and beaten senseless."

"And the son?"

"Shot in front of the store."

My heart stopped.

"She remembered Frau Goldstein screaming and screaming from an upstairs window — said it reminded her of the women keening in the Bible — Rachel weeping for her children because they were not. Frau Gruber said she watched it all from behind the curtain of her upstairs window and has despised herself ever since for not doing something to help."

I squeezed Carl's hand and he clasped mine in return. *His own regrets from her mouth.* "What could she have done?"

"Probably nothing." Carl sighed, the moment not lost. "Not then. But afterward she took the Goldsteins into her home. Her husband planned to help them clean their shop and home and set them to rights. They offered the Goldstein family their grave plot to bury their son."

"I've never known anyone . . . They lost everything."

"The books, *ja* — most of the inventory — but not everything. She remembered a man, a member of the Nazi Party — he'd flashed his Party badge — and his son in Hitler Youth uniform. She said they intervened during the beating, keeping the brownshirts from destroying everything in the shop. For some reason the hooligans listened to them and moved on. Once they'd gone, Herr Goldstein sorted from the pile in the street, plucked a book he held to his chest, then presented it to the man in gratitude."

Rare first editions . . . the inscription in A Christmas Carol? *Yes, November 1938 . . . dear Father in heaven . . . Grandfather.*

"She said that two days later a knock came to her door, and Herr Goldstein stepped outside to talk to a man. Frau Goldstein joined them. Frau Gruber watched through the window again. She couldn't hear every-

392

thing, but she remembers Frau Goldstein crying that they could not risk their only daughter to the Nazis, and that the man offered them help. The Goldsteins refused to divulge his name, determined to protect him for his work in helping Jews escape. Herr Goldstein paid him well to get them out of the country."

"And she never knew his name?"

"*Nein*. But there is this. She said she watched him leave, that there was something familiar about him. He turned once, looking up the street. She was certain it was the same man who'd stopped the looting that night."

"And what happened? Did they get away?"

"The Gestapo came the next night, broke in the door, and dragged them to the street."

"The entire family?"

"*Ja*."

I sat down before I fell down.

"I'm sorry, Hannah." Carl pressed my shoulder. I grabbed his hand like a lifeline.

28

Lieselotte Sommer
September 1944

Saying good-bye to Frau Kirchmann was nearly as hard as saying good-bye, even for a time, to Lukas.

But there was so much to do, so much for them to arrange in the next twenty-four hours. That's all the time Vater had given them. How or where they would go, we didn't know, only that Dr. Peterson was supposed to be working it out. All he lacked was the money needed to make the transaction, and then a few hours to have the documents prepared. We dared not cross him. I no longer doubted his ruthlessness or power, or that of my own Vater.

The only comfort Lukas or I derived was that Vater seemed determined to protect me. Was that because I was useful to them — in that I'd led them to the Eisners? Or was it because we were mistaken, and the arrests had no link to me, to the black car?

I hurried home, my pockets stuffed with the treasures intended to buy the Kirchmanns' papers, to purchase their lives. It was nearly dusk when I arrived — so many of our precious hours already spent.

I'd almost reached Vater's library when I heard Dr. Peterson's voice through the open door.

"Stop worrying. As long as Herr Kirchmann believed you, it will be done. He persuaded Lukas, and Lukas will persuade Lieselotte. You're quite convincing when you want to be, my friend."

I pressed my back against the wall and listened.

"I told you to wait for the arrests of the others until the Kirchmanns are in custody. The moment they learn —"

But Dr. Peterson cut Vater off. "You worry too much. Lukas will be back any moment with the payment. As soon as we have that in our possession, we'll make our move. They'll have no time to learn about the others. Besides, you've sworn them to secrecy!"

The telephone rang and I nearly jumped from my skin. Vater answered from his desk.

"Ah, Hilde — I'm glad it's you." His voice changed to silk in the blink of my eyes. "Lieselotte? No, I'm sorry, my love, she is not here. Out with Lukas, I suppose." He paused. "*Ja, ja,* I will have her telephone you. A meeting tomorrow is good." He cleared his throat. "*Nein,* no need to come here. It is better if Lieselotte comes to you, is busy with you. Peterson and I have more properties to Aryanize, and they must be done tomorrow. Having her out of the house for those transactions is good. *Ja, danke.* I'll see you then. Good-bye, my love." The receiver clicked in its cradle.

"I warn you, Wolfgang, keep Hilde away. Keep her away until this is finished."

"That's not simple. She's invested herself in Lieselotte's wedding as though she's her mother. We must think of a reason to postpone it — for Lieselotte to call it off."

"Hilde is not stupid. One look at Lieselotte and she will know —"

"Then she must not see Lieselotte after the arrests," my father said quietly. "It must all be done at once, tomorrow, while they are out."

"*Nein.* That may be easiest, cleanest, but it is imperative Hilde is convinced that Lieselotte called the wedding off on her own, that she chose Lebensborn over a marriage to Lukas. If Hilde learns that Jews tended Elsa, that you knew Lukas was Jewish and still part of the Abwehr, that you

396

would allow your daughter to marry —"

"All right. All right! You think I don't know this? But you saw her with him last night — today. What would — ?"

"The Jewess, the one called Anna. A story can be made that Lukas was having an affair with her. Lieselotte only learned of it today, after their arrest."

"Perhaps. A ruse, a lie — a good one, but we must convince Lieselotte to make it work. It would take time — proof — to convince her."

"I can have pictures created, faces covered. She can be shown — but only after the arrest is made and they are gone. You, her father, insulted and aggrieved for your daughter — not because Lukas is Jewish, but because he slept with a Jewess."

My father didn't answer right away. "Yes. But it must be convincing. She loves him."

My throat tightened. It was all I could do not to sob aloud.

"Where is he with the money? He should have been here by now." Dr. Peterson's chair squeaked.

"He said it might be tomorrow morning before he could get the full amount from the bank. I told you to wait — what if they hear of the arr— ?"

"You were not there — they will make no

connection to you, Wolfgang. Stop worrying."

I crept into the kitchen, knowing I must get word to the Kirchmanns.

I lifted the latch and gently opened the back door. Before I could close it behind me, Dr. Peterson pulled the door wide. "Lieselotte — you've returned. . . . Where is Lukas?"

"He . . . he's helping his father obtain the payment."

"Is he?" Dr. Peterson looked wary. "Herr Kirchmann promised to send valuables, and cash —"

"*Ja, ja* — he sent some with me. They will bring the cash as soon as possible. It might be tomorrow if he has trouble."

"So —" He held out his hand.

"I must give them to Vater, must place them in his hands myself," I stalled.

Dr. Peterson stepped aside, bowing, and extended his arm to usher me toward the library.

As I walked, I separated the pouches in my pocket between my fingers as best I could, by feeling the little bundles. I'd give the gold coins — they were heavy and cumbersome — and the bundle of brooches. But I'd save the rings and precious stones — valuable trading commodities to send my true family into hiding. Shelter and food were never free.

"Lieselotte." Father said my name without emotion as we entered the library.

I pulled the heavy bundles from my coat pocket and placed them on his desk. "These are from the Kirchmanns. Herr Kirchmann will bring cash as soon as he can."

Father looked up at me. "The price of passports, of ship passage, of forged identity papers, is much higher than this. He mentioned rings . . . stones."

I shook my head as if I knew nothing. "Perhaps they're at the bank too. He said something about a safe, a box — I didn't pay attention. I was much more interested in learning that you told them I would not be going with them — that you could only obtain four sets of papers. I told him he was mistaken — that you'd promised me," I challenged.

"We did the best we could; there is nothing more to be done," Dr. Peterson intervened.

"I'm not talking to you, Dr. Peterson! I'm talking with *mein Vater!*" My voice rose.

"Lieselotte, Dr. Peterson is my guest. You must —"

"Yes, Vater, he is your guest — not mine. As near as I can tell he's the one who's brought all this on our heads."

"You must not accuse him when it is the Kirchmanns who've broken the law."

"Let me marry Lukas. Let me go with them."

"We've been over this, Lieselotte. There is no way —"

"Tell her, Wolfgang," Dr. Peterson broke in. "Do not spare her. She is not a child."

I whirled on him. "Tell me what?" And then back to Vater. "Tell me what, Vater? What more can there be?"

"I did not want to hurt you, Lieselotte, to shame you."

"What are you talking about?"

"Lukas," Dr. Peterson interjected. "Lukas and a Jewess."

"What? What are you saying?"

He shrugged, as though what he said broke his heart. "Perhaps it is the same Anna you found him with last year. Perhaps the affair has been going on all this time."

"Lukas?" I laughed. "An affair? That's crazy — absolutely crazy."

"I'm afraid not, my dear." Vater sounded genuinely sad. "I'd hoped you'd need never know, but . . . there are pictures. Because he's part of the Abwehr under investigation, Lukas's life has been . . . scrutinized. He was found, sleeping with a —"

"I don't believe you. It's a lie — another of Dr. Peterson's lies!"

"I will bring the pictures, so that you may see for yourself," Dr. Peterson offered.

I sat down heavily on the chair opposite Father's desk, as though I might doubt myself, might believe them. As though this new "truth" threatened to destroy me at last.

"It is most generous of your father to send them out of the country, Fräulein. He has every right to have the man arrested, and could do so now. You must simply say the word."

I looked up at him, as if considering what he offered.

He shrugged. "It's a simple thing to call off the wedding, not so simple to get them out of the country. If you do not wish —"

"I never said I believe you. I don't! Lukas loves me — has loved me as I love him . . . for years. It can't be. But . . . he has been away a long time, and . . ." I sat up, letting the clock tick. Then, as if resolved, "I will look at your pictures, and then I will decide."

"I'm sorry, my dear. Hilde and I will do all in our power to help you through this time."

It was not hard to manufacture tears. "I have a headache. I'm going to bed."

401

"Shall I bring the pictures tonight?" Dr. Peterson's voice, slick as oil, slimed over my nerves.

"Tomorrow," I said. "I'm going to take something to make me sleep. Perhaps when I wake this will all be a horrid dream." I dug my nails into my palms and walked out, praying my performance was as convincing as theirs had appeared.

29

Hannah Sterling
February 1973
The next morning I brewed coffee and spent hours going over the ledger. I copied out every name and address, the dates listed at the beginning and the end, and the entire inventory.

As I wrote, I pictured Grandfather, and perhaps Uncle Rudy in his Hitler Youth uniform, approaching frightened people — the Goldstein family first: Martin, Rose-anne, their daughter; and then the Rosen-baums . . . the Kaufmanns . . . the Horo-witzes . . . the Jacobses . . . the Eisners . . . the Levys . . . The list went on and on. I imagined him sympathizing with their circumstances, offering a hand, pitying the damage from *Kristallnacht,* commiserating about the Reich's statutes against Jews, join-ing their disbelief, reinforcing their fear, gaining their trust. And then presenting the idea, the offer, the hope of salvation. I pictured it all — families waiting under cover of darkness for their promised savior. Then the Gestapo bursting through their doors. Searchlights blinding their eyes, cars and vans and trucks gunning their motors, whisking them away in the dead of night while neighbors cowered behind blackout curtains, praying they wouldn't be discovered, praying they wouldn't be next.

My head throbbed, my throat dried, and I held back my vomit.

There were twenty-three families in the ledger, and one hundred ninety-two individual names in all. The last family listed was the Kirchmanns. They numbered four, but there were no first names given.

I spent the next two days taking inventory of the storeroom, matching the items against the ledger. Carl had to work, but he telephoned twice a day to make certain I was all right, as solicitous as an old mother hen. Other times I answered the phone and no one responded. Eventually I'd hear a click. I didn't know if it was Dr. Peterson or Herr Eberhardt or both, toying with me, determined to frighten me, seeing if I was there, hoping I'd fled. But I wouldn't give in and wouldn't give up.

404

When I'd finished at last with the inventory, I pulled open the curtain. Beyond the courtyard outside Grandfather's garden, deepening shades of rose and gold and purple sank behind the rooftops. Dusk settled in quickly, along with a palpable gloom. I closed the book and sat in the gathering darkness.

The desk telephone rang, making me jump.

"Hello?" I hoped it was Carl but felt tentative each time I answered.

"Fräulein Sterling?"

"Yes, this is she."

"Dr. Keitzmann."

"Yes, Doctor."

"Herr Sommer regained consciousness less than an hour ago."

Dread, fear, relief, disappointment warred inside me.

"Fräulein? Are you there?"

"Yes, Doctor. I'm here. I'm just surprised."

"*Ja,* it is good news. I didn't expect it myself. He is not able to talk, not able to feed himself, but that may come in time. We will give him a few more days. I wish to keep him here for observation."

"Thank you. Thank you so much for letting me know."

405

"You may come and see him as you wish."

"Thank you. Perhaps tomorrow." *That's too soon!*

"Good night, then."

"*Danke schön.* Good night."

If he had died, it would have been easier . . . so much easier. They'll want me to bring him home, to care for him. How can I possibly do that, knowing what I know?

The telephone rang again and I nearly jumped out of my skin again.

"Hannah?"

"Carl." Just saying his name was the greatest relief.

"Could you use some dinner? Can I take you out?"

"There's nothing I would like more. But I look a fright. I've not even combed my hair today."

"Then we'll go somewhere dark, and if the waiter questions your appearance, I'll tell him that I dug you up in the archives, that he should be pleased to be graced with such a relic." The smile in his voice was the very best thing I'd heard all day. I didn't even mind being called a relic.

"Then come quickly and whisk me away."

True to his word, the restaurant was dim — candlelight dim. I felt faded and drained, completely washed out, but Carl coddled and doted on me as if I were Miss Universe.

"You finished the inventory?"

I nodded, sick at heart.

"It is as we thought?"

"Most of it's still there. I'm guessing that's what he's been living off all these years — selling small pieces little by little. Probably with the help of Peterson and Eberhardt."

"What will you do now?"

"I don't know. Grandfather will be coming home soon, and everyone expects me to care for him. I've no idea how I can possibly do that, how I could possibly be near him now."

"Everyone?"

"Dr. Keitzmann, Grandfather's doctor at the hospital. Dr. Peterson — though I'm not sure he deserves to be called *doctor*. Herr Eberhardt. Grandfather himself."

"They don't know that you know yet."

"No. And I don't know how I dare stay there and tell them, or how I can stay there and *not* tell them."

"You'll go back to America, then?"

I shook my head. "I . . . I just don't know. I've not accomplished what I came for. I've discovered far more about Grandfather than I'd bargained for, but so little about Mama. What happened to her between the time she

407

became engaged to Lukas Kirchmann and the time she married my . . . my . . . the man I called Daddy? And who was my real father?"

"Perhaps she discovered precisely what you have. That would be enough to make her leave Herr Sommer, if she was trying to help the very people he turned in — and especially if he had her fiancé arrested. It is enough for you to turn against him now, is it not?"

"But where did she go? How did she end up marrying my — an American? I can't help but wonder . . . It's significant that the last entry is for the Kirchmanns. September 1944. Grandfather apparently stopped then. Why?"

"If he'd been instrumental in the arrest of her fiancé — in the destruction of his daughter's life and hopes — you don't think that would have been enough to make him stop?"

"It's not that. I'm just wondering. The Kirchmanns are listed in the ledger as four, but their names are not given — the only entry where first names aren't given. Your parents said that there were four Kirchmanns — Herr and Frau Kirchmann as well as Lukas and Marta."

"And Marta did not go to the camps."

"No, she was not arrested. So who do you suppose was the fourth one?"

He stared at me. I could see the wheels turning. "Now you are the one jumping to conclusions."

"Am I?" I searched his face. "My mother gave Kirchmann as her maiden name on her marriage certificate."

"That might be loyalty — or hiding from her father. The numbers might only mean the number of passports or identity cards Herr Sommer invented, not how many were actually arrested."

"But he listed the arrests and date of arrests in a separate column from the family. In the case of the Goldsteins, he listed only three arrests. The fourth name was crossed out because —"

"Because the boy was killed on *Kristallnacht*."

"Yes," I agreed.

30

Lieselotte Sommer
September 1944

I locked my door and changed my clothes. I knew the importance of layering clothing for warmth and economy, of wearing two sets of underwear, two dresses, a sweater and coat and carrying nothing but a handbag to hold everything I might want in hiding.

The only memento I tucked into the lining of my purse was Mutti's photograph — one of the two of us together when I was but six. Laughing, smiling, cuddled together on a swing one summer holiday. It was the way I remembered her, before the cancer, before the world turned upside down. A toothbrush and powder, a hairbrush, aspirin, and the nightgown intended for my wedding night filled the little bag. I bunched up my pillow and eiderdown to resemble a sleeping form in the bed.

Finally, night came in earnest. When I heard Dr. Peterson's car drive away, I listened for Vater's feet upon the stairs. He paused by my doorway.

"Lieselotte?" he called softly, trying my door. But I'd locked it.

"Please, Vater. Go away and leave me alone. I'm going to sleep. I can't talk about this any more tonight." My voice broke.

"All right, my child. Sleep well."

"Tell Sophia not to call me for breakfast. If I can sleep, I must."

"I will leave word. Good night."

I didn't answer. How could he expect me to?

I heard his door close and waited until the clock in the hall struck nine. He would listen to the radio until he fell asleep. Silently, I unlatched my window, climbed onto its wide sill, and let myself down by the thick wisteria vine that clung to the back side of the house. A dog barked three houses beyond. I froze, crouching behind an evergreen, until his owner opened the door, cursing, and dragged the dog inside.

Frost had already settled, making the cobblestones slippery. I ran on the balls of my feet, lightly, soundlessly, keeping to the shadows of stone walls and foliage. It seemed hours before I reached the Kirch-

411

manns' back door. Three short taps, and then three again — so soft I feared they might not hear.

But the door opened and I slipped in.

"Lieselotte!" It was Lukas, and before I could speak he pulled me into his arms, my lips to his. It was as though we'd both been starved, and here, at last, grew luscious fruit.

But there was no time. I pulled away. "Where are your parents?"

He led me into the living room — already disheveled from packing books and table linens and family photographs. As if they were really leaving Germany, embarking on a new life with treasures from the old.

Herr Kirchmann looked up in surprise. "Lieselotte. I have the money. I was coming first thing in the morning."

"*Nein.* It's a lie, all a lie." I pulled the bundles of stones from my pocket. "They're planning, as soon as you bring the rest, to have you arrested — all of you."

Frau Kirchmann came from the bedroom. "What is this? Wolfgang promised. He told Helmeuth —"

I shook my head, exhausted. "He's tricked us. He's used us — me most of all. Father and Dr. Peterson are behind the arrests. That's how they make their money — they and Fräulein Hilde. Sudden wealth, they

412

call it, and laugh."

"No —"

"Yes — you'll be next. They've only waited this long because of Fräulein Hilde. Father wants me to publicly call off the wedding so there will be no connection between our family and —" I couldn't say it.

"*Die Juden,*" Frau Kirchmann finished, sinking down onto the sofa.

"*Ja,*" I whispered. "They believe Fräulein Hilde would not marry Vater if she knew, would expose him to the Party — that they would both be ruined if . . ." I pulled my beret from my head, the room suddenly too warm, and looked up at Lukas. "They're going to say you were found sleeping with Anna — a Jewess — and that I called off the wedding."

"How could — ?"

"Dr. Peterson is creating pictures from pieces. I don't know how it's done, but they will make them look convincing. You will all disappear as soon as you pay the money."

"And you — what will happen to you if you do not marry Lukas? What about Herr Sommer's wedding? They wanted you married before then, or sent to . . ." Marta did not finish.

"Lebensborn," I said. "Vater's already made arrangements. He'll convince Fräulein

Hilde that I chose to go there of a broken heart. Chose to do my duty for the Reich after all."

"*Nein,*" Lukas swore. "I will not let him —"

"You can't stop him," Marta insisted. "But you can marry Lieselotte. Marry her now — tonight."

Chills of hope ran the length of my legs, my torso.

"If she is married to you, what will he do?"

"Whatever he wants." Herr Kirchmann sat down heavily beside his wife. "He has the upper hand and can do whatever he wants."

I held out the bundle of precious stones from my pocket. "When I realized what they were planning, I gave them only the coins and brooches to make them think I knew nothing. These can help you go into hiding — tonight. You must go quickly."

"And you will come with us," Lukas insisted. "You can't go back."

I squeezed his hand and smiled into his eyes. "I thought you'd never ask."

"Who has room? Where can we all go on such short notice?" Frau Kirchmann asked her husband.

"I don't know. I'll talk with Pastor Braun. We might need to split up — five is too many to take into one home."

"Lieselotte and I will stay together," Lukas insisted.

"You're not married," Frau Kirchmann whispered. "You can't —"

"Then we must change that," Lukas vowed.

One hour later we'd all stolen away from the house, with nothing but the clothes on our backs and a small satchel each to carry whatever was most precious, to take into hiding and the hope of life ahead.

It was agreed that we'd hide in the church until a family — or two or three families — could be found to take us in.

As we waited, not knowing what the next day or hour might bring, Lukas and I stood before Pastor Braun. Herr Kirchmann — Vater Kirchmann — stood for Lukas, and Marta for me — just as we'd planned all along. Frau Kirchmann — Mutter Kirchmann — and Frau Braun sat on the front pew, looking on as our witnesses.

Lukas took my hands in his, and we pledged our hearts and our lives — however long they might be, whatever they might be — to one another. Blessed of God, and by his family and the church, no wedding could have meant more to me.

When it came time for the ring, Lukas's mouth straightened in regret. Pastor Braun nearly shrugged it off — and it wasn't important, not in the wretched scheme of things. But my mother — my dear mother-in-law and mother-in-love — stepped between us and pulled her wedding ring from her finger.

"I've worn this since the day I married your father."

"*Nein,* Mutti. It is yours," Lukas whispered.

"It is the future." And she slipped it on my finger.

I gasped, my heart spilling over — the evidence in tears streaming down my cheeks.

I thanked God for my husband, and for his family, and whispered the memory of Ruth's story: "Your people will be my people. Your God my God. Wherever you go, I will go."

Mutter Kirchmann took my face in her hands and kissed me on both cheeks. And then Lukas pulled me to him. Our lips met, and we kissed, the longest, warmest kiss of our lives so far, until the pastor coughed and, smiling, we pulled apart. Whatever happened next, at least we belonged to one another.

■ ■ ■ ■

Pastor Braun hid us in the cellar of the church. Just before dawn we stole through back streets to attic rooms above a private library — an alcove for Marta and her parents on one end, and on the other an alcove for Lukas and me — a bridal suite beneath the eaves.

Throughout the day we maintained absolute silence, wound in one another's arms, sleeping from sheer exhaustion, then waking, stirring silently, sleeping again, and listening to the sounds of library patrons, visitors, and workers coming and going in the hallways below. That night we whispered all the things we'd never said, the words we'd kept pent up in our hearts. And then we stopped talking, stopped remembering. There was no point in planning — not now. Others planned for us — what they could do, who they could find to feed us, move us, help us. Who knew what tomorrow might bring to two newlyweds hiding in a library attic? There was only this night, this moment. We lived and breathed and loved as though it was our last.

And in the morning, just before dawn, the raids began.

31

Hannah Sterling
March 1973

I visited Grandfather once in the hospital, but he was sleeping and I did not wake him. I left word with the nurse, asking her to let him know I'd been there. That was the best I could do, the most I could bring myself to do for him.

It was over two weeks before Grandfather regained enough strength to return home. By then he could hold a fork, albeit shakily, with his right hand, though he couldn't always bring the food to his mouth. He was unable to speak and needed help dressing and bathing. Dr. Keitzmann's nurse connected me with a male nurse to help with the more intimate details of his care for the first month. After that Dr. Keitzmann promised to reevaluate him.

I imagined staying another month — cooking, cleaning, overseeing Grandfather's finances and bills. I didn't want to stay, to be in the same house with him and under Dr. Peterson's possible scrutiny, and yet I didn't see how I could leave Grandfather as he was. Another month would give me a better picture of his health, and with Geoffrey, his nurse, in the house to look after him, I could spend more time working on a new plan with Carl.

Dr. Peterson had not visited Grandfather in the hospital to my knowledge and hadn't phoned — at least hadn't identified himself as the caller — or come to the house. But Herr Eberhardt stopped by the day after Grandfather returned home to make certain his client was well cared for.

"This nurse is competent, is adequate?" he asked.

"Yes, I think so. I prepare Grandfather's food and check with Geoffrey several times a day. So far Geoffrey seems very attentive. We just don't know how much recovery to expect."

"Perhaps it is an act of Providence after all that you are here," Herr Eberhardt conceded. "At least you are family."

"Thank you. I didn't imagine you'd approve." Nor did I know what Providence thought of it all.

"I did not approve of Wolfgang's rash

419

behavior in trusting someone with his entire fortune whom he'd never met or known existed until two months before. I was concerned for him."

"As was Dr. Peterson."

"Yes, they have lived as confidants for many years. I believe Dr. Peterson would have preferred to carry this role himself."

"I'm sure he did."

"*Ja,* but now I agree with Wolfgang. He was wise. I think family is a better option. You would become his heir at any rate, now that your existence is known."

"Was Dr. Peterson to inherit before I appeared?"

"Ah, that is not for me to divulge. But your presence certainly changed his prospects. You understand that the documents your Grossvater signed were not only his will, but made you co-owner of his assets now."

"Yes. I'll keep his bills paid up to date. But I must ask you, does this mean that I am free to conduct his affairs as I see fit?"

"Well, yes — within reason, I suppose — as long as he is unable to do so. The house is to remain his residence as long as he lives or is able to stay here, as well as the use of a sizable trust for his needs and expenses, but even what remains of those pass to you at his death. From that time forward, you are free to sell if you wish. In fact, Dr. Peterson has expressed a strong desire to buy the house, should it come to market."

"Has he? How very interesting."

"I suppose there is some sentimental value from a long-standing friendship."

"Hmm." It was hard to read Herr Eberhardt, to know if he was as innocent as he appeared or simply very good at hiding the truth. "There's one thing I'm curious about. Dr. Peterson has insisted that Grossvater is his patient, but Dr. Keitzmann had no record of that. You were listed as his only contact."

Herr Eberhardt nodded, bemused. "Dr. Peterson no longer practices. To my knowledge he hasn't practiced since the war, but Wolfgang has remained his one loyal 'patient.'"

"Is he still able to prescribe medicine?"

"I . . . do not know the answer to that."

"Grandfather said he takes heart medication that Dr. Peterson claimed to have prescribed. But Dr. Keitzmann has also prescribed medicine."

Herr Eberhardt frowned. "I am not a physician, Fräulein Sterling, and you are not my client. I cannot directly advise you . . . but Dr. Keitzmann is Wolfgang's most recent attending doctor and is currently overseeing his care."

"My thought exactly."

Late that afternoon I took Grandfather coffee. He searched my face as he did each time I came into the room. I could not look at him long. He was such a paradox, this feeble man who depended entirely on me at the moment, who'd willed me everything — given me everything he owned — and yet had perpetrated unthinkable opportunistic evil. Evil so great that at the very least he had alienated his daughter and betrayed the man she'd loved — the man and his family. *And what about Mama? Was she also on the receiving end of that betrayal?*

Daddy had always warned me that Mama couldn't talk about the war, about what had happened to her. But had she talked to him? And even if she had, there was no one to explain to me what actually happened except Grandfather.

I needed to confront him, to ask him about the families, the unbelievable cache of collectibles. *But he can't even talk now. Even if he recovers his speech, how can I do that with him teetering on the precipice? One stress more and he's likely to fall off the edge, and that would be the end of him.*

Ironically, it was Dr. Peterson who settled the question for me. Just after Grandfather's nurse had retired for the night, the doorbell rang.

"Dr. Peterson?" I didn't invite him in, but stood in the doorway. "Isn't it rather late for a social call?"

"This is not a social call. I've come because I am concerned about my patient."

"Your patient?"

Dr. Peterson squared his shoulders and pushed past me. "Herr Sommer has been my patient for many years."

"But you've not visited him in the hospital, and haven't actually practiced since the war, I understand." It was all I could do to control my temper and keep the fear from my voice at the same time.

"I cared for his wife, Elsa, until her death; for his family; and have cared for Wolfgang all these years. You will appreciate that I am most concerned with his current state of affairs. I believe he would be better served in a medical institution than here."

"He has a private nurse — around the clock — and he has me."

"Were he to suffer a second stroke, it could be fatal." He stepped too close.

"I'm sure you're right. We'll just have to do our best to see that doesn't happen."

423

"I suggest, for the sake of Wolfgang's life and well-being, he be admitted to an excellent medical facility outside Berlin — state-of-the-art equipment, the best doctors in their field, in addition to my care. They specialize in physical therapy for stroke patients. No expense must be spared in his recovery."

"No expense?"

"Nein." It was the first sign of hesitancy he'd exhibited. "He is, of course, my friend as well as my patient."

"And he's my grandfather," I insisted. "I believe he's getting the best of care here and that he takes comfort in being in his own home. Familiar surroundings and all that. Dr. Keitzmann will reevaluate him before long and we can ask his opinion as well. But I doubt Grandfather could afford a state-of-the-art facility, or anything beyond the care the state provides."

"Which is why I wished to speak with you privately. I am willing to make an excellent offer on this house — enough that Wolfgang will have everything he requires for the rest of his life and you will be able to stay near him, if you wish. Or return to America, if that is your preference."

"That's very generous of you, Dr. Peterson."

"For the sake of my friend, Fräulein, you will find me more than generous."

"I see. I don't know what to say. When do you propose making this transaction? I suppose it wouldn't matter if I stayed in the house longer, as long as Grandfather moves to the medical facility, since that is your primary concern."

Dr. Peterson shifted. "Actually, Fräulein, to make this offer as generous as possible, I am required to sell my own home. I would need to take possession immediately."

"Immediately?"

"That would be most convenient."

"As I said, I need to think about it. It would mean selling everything, and Grandfather has expressly stated — in writing — his wish and right to live in this house to the end of his days."

"It is true that he wishes to live here as long as possible. Wolfgang has so many memories here. But perhaps those memories would best be set aside in the interest of his return to health. A bit of new scenery —" he shrugged — "new faces, an advanced therapeutic program, might work wonders."

"Wonders." I smiled. "Like I said, I'll think about it and let you know."

Dr. Peterson shifted his hat to his head. "Do not think about it too long, Fräulein

Sterling. Each day counts in a stroke victim's recovery. I am certain you do not wish to prevent his recovery, nor be deemed responsible for his decline."

On Monday morning I telephoned Carl and told him of Dr. Peterson's visit. "It felt more like a threat than an offer."

"*Ja,* as it surely is. He must know of Herr Sommer's 'procurements.' Perhaps he is even a partner. He doesn't know that you've found the secret room, and you must not let him know — certainly not until you decide what to do. If he forces you from the house, he buys everything."

"I'm worried that even if I don't sell — and I really don't think I can as long as Grandfather's alive — he'll find a way to force me out. It almost felt as though he'd accuse me of not taking proper care of Grandfather — that he'd hold me responsible if Grandfather doesn't recover."

Carl sighed heavily into the phone. "I don't like you living there, Hannah. Men have murdered for fortunes, and these men have done as much. As long as the valuables are there, you are not safe."

"As long as they're here . . . That's the answer."

"What are you saying? That we move them?"

"I'm saying it's time to give it back — all of it. A means of redemption."

"Hannah —"

"Will you help me?"

With Dr. Peterson on the prowl, I dared not leave the house. But Carl used every spare minute from his job to inquire after Marta and Lukas Kirchmann and track down the names and addresses of Grandfather's victims from the list I'd made. He knew of government and civilian organizations that had formed detailed lists of survivors over the years — including names and addresses of Jews who'd been relocated and their property Aryanized, the dates and locations of individual arrests. There were even records of the camps people had been sent to, if they were transferred to other camps or released, as well as those who did not survive. And then there were records of where they went after the war — at least for some of them. It was the first time I truly appreciated the Germans' penchant for meticulous record keeping.

"They were generally termed 'displaced persons.' Every story is different," Carl confided quietly over coffee in Grandfather's kitchen. "Some eventually emigrated to Palestine, some to the United States, some to other countries across the globe. Some returned to Berlin or to other places in Germany; often families combined their survivors to create a new family. Many waited for months in camps until family members came looking for them or until they could find a family member to take them in. Of course, many never returned from the camps."

"It's what we call looking for needles in haystacks."

"So far, I've located two individuals who returned and reclaimed their original homes."

"Only two?" I couldn't hide my disappointment. He'd been looking for nearly three weeks.

"Jews were not sent home again in the way they disappeared. They either perished or survived. In many cases whole families perished. Some survived but the families never reunited. Even today I read stories in the newspaper about family members who find each other for the first time — all these years later."

"But relatives? Are there no relatives?"

"There is a limit even to German records. But I have more ideas, just lack of time and resources to pursue this full-time. It is one thing to track down what happened to the victims. It will be quite another thing to find heirs and present them with long-lost possessions."

"I'm sorry. I just thought I could return everything — or nearly everything — right away. Maybe I should take the list and work on some."

"I'm not certain how much success you would have."

"Well, my German's pretty lousy, and I might not know the organizations to contact, but you could tell —"

"You are American."

"Yes?"

"Many Germans, especially those who were alive at the end of the war, are still bitter for America's bombing of Berlin when the war was already lost to us. Hundreds upon hundreds of civilian deaths and destruction of property for no good purpose. The chances of Germans gladly opening their doors to you, even if they speak English . . ." He shrugged.

"Whoa. I hadn't imagined that." Never had I felt such frustration — or at least not since Mama lay dying.

"Have you thought of telling Herr Sommer about this? Of telling him what you want to do? When a man comes close to death, he sometimes seeks forgiveness for his past."

"I can't — just can't bring it up. I don't know if Grandfather will regain his ability to speak. I'm not even certain of his ability to reason yet." Though I knew I didn't want to confront him, either. "Even if I did, what if it brings on another stroke? What if he forbids me?"

"Would that stop you?"

"He's made me co-owner, so I think I can legitimately do what I want, as long as he's not able to take care of his own affairs, and as long as he doesn't convince Herr Eberhardt to change his deed or will again."

Carl set his knife and fork aside. "Are you not tempted to keep it — to keep something for yourself? It is a fortune, after all — perhaps many fortunes. You may not be able to locate the original owners of the property in every instance. What will you do then?"

"I can't believe you said that. Not after what Grandfather did. How can I keep it — any of it?" I shook my head, then quipped, "Not that it couldn't supplement a teacher's salary."

"No matter what you do, you must be ready for that question, that accusation. Do you realize that by making you co-owner, and now that you know about his crime, he has effectively made you his accomplice?"

"What?"

"You know about the valuables. You know what he did to get them. By not coming forward to the authorities immediately, are you not concealing evidence? Are you not a benefiting party?"

"That's not how it is at all. You know that."

"My concern is that Dr. Peterson may misconstrue it in just such a manner. Herr Sommer may even have designed it this way — to keep you, how do you say, 'on a hook with a carrot dangling.' "

"Bait. Bait dangling."

"If Peterson cannot convince you to sell him the house, he may try to bribe you, or failing that, accuse you, perhaps have you arrested."

"Is that possible? I mean, I know the laws in Germany are different than in America, but that's so wrong."

"The premise is wrong. Everything about this is wrong. It didn't stop it from happening. Do not give Peterson an answer about the house. Keep stringing him along for as long as possible. Buy time. But, Hannah, consider letting the organizations that search for families find them. Let Germans handle this."

"I can't. I want to do this myself — give back everything into the hands of those it was stolen from. I want to redeem my family for what we've done."

Carl shook his head. "You can't re—"

"Please, Carl. I'm going to do this my way."

Time was running out. Whether Grandfather survived and thwarted my efforts or died and I found myself facing accusations or court trials initiated by Dr. Peterson, I felt greater urgency to locate the families of victims and return their valuables. It was the only means of penance for Grandfather's horrific deeds, or of seeking forgiveness for the way I'd long felt about Mama. This was my opportunity to carry on her real work and make some peace with her memory — a peace in death that I never found in life. And it was the right thing to do.

I needed Carl's help and he needed to work, so I hired him as my driver, praying Grandfather's funds I used were not ill-gotten. I duly sat in the backseat, careful not to put Carl's job at risk, as we drove to the first address Carl had tracked down in West Berlin.

"You may be right about Germans — Jewish or not — not trusting Americans, but I can't sit at home and do nothing," I told him.

"By leaving the house, you leave it open to Dr. Peterson."

"We changed the locks. Geoffrey's under strict instructions not to open the door to anybody except Dr. Keitzmann."

"You are opening a can of bugs you cannot close, Hannah."

" 'Can of worms.' You really do need to work on your fishing lingo," I teased, but Carl still frowned into the rearview mirror. "Stop worrying so much. This is why you located our first survivor."

"What if this woman does not wish to be found?"

"She'll wish it when I give her what's owed her. Whether it's sentimental or she sells the jewelry for cash, she'll be glad. Especially if the neighborhood is as poor as you say."

Carl looked away, but I could tell by the tightened cords in his neck that he'd not said all he thought.

Dusk was falling when we turned into the narrow *Strasse*. Brown block buildings lined up like gloomy inner-city apartment housing. Painted black window boxes awaited spring flowers. I imagined red geraniums and green ivy spilling over the boxes and sills in summer, vastly improving the landscape.

"I think you should be prepared for —"

"For heaven's sake, Carl, stop worrying — stop talking! Nothing ventured, nothing gained." My nerves had reached the breaking point.

We pulled to a stop before number 238. "This is it. Her maiden name was Kaufmann. Julia Kaufmann. Her married name is Gordon."

"Doesn't sound too Jewish, does it?"

"*Nein.* You may need to consider —"

"Stop. Just let me do this." I admired so many things about Carl, but he was cautious beyond reason — a thing unnervingly common to Germans and one that drove me crazy. They couldn't just get on with it. I marched up the steps and knocked on the door, Carl's disapproval trailing me. "Translate only if she doesn't speak English," I told him. "If she does, let me do the talking."

He sighed, obviously frustrated, and pushed his fingers through his hair before donning his chauffeur's cap again. I turned to the door and ignored him.

It took three knocks, but a woman came to the door. *"Ja?"*

"Frau Gordon?"

"*Ja?*" Suspicion sprang to her eyes.

"*Sprechen Sie Englisch?*"

"A little. What do you want?"

"Was your birth name Kaufmann?"

"Who are you? What do you want?" This time she whispered and there was no mistaking her fright.

"My name is Hannah Sterling. I . . . I've come to return something to you, something I believe belonged to your family. May we come in?"

"*Nein,* please." Worry pulled at the corners of her wide eyes. "We have guests."

Undeterred, I pulled a slim case from my purse and opened it. The golden chain, holding a delicately etched Star of David in a wreathed circle, lay beautifully against the deep-blue velvet.

The woman's gasp told me all I needed to know, but I asked anyway. "Do you recognize it?"

Color drained from her face, and rather than reach for the case, she glanced over her shoulder and pulled the door closed behind her, forcing us down a step and herself into the bitter March cold. "You must leave. I beg you to leave and not come back."

"This is yours, isn't it? It belonged to your

family — perhaps to your mother or grandmother?"

"*Nein, nein.* You musn't say that. Please . . . I don't know you. I don't know who you are or what you want. I don't want to know."

"I want only to return this — no strings attached. Truly."

She frowned, and I realized my colloquialism was lost on her.

The door opened suddenly behind her. *"Was ist passiert?"*

Carl pulled the case from my hand, closing it.

"Amerikaner." The woman paled, then said in English, "They were looking for directions. That is all."

"Where are you going? Do you know your way?"

"Yes, *danke schön.* You have been most helpful, Frau." Carl tipped his hat and pulled me by the arm down the stairs.

"But —" I began.

"We can find our way now. *Danke schön!*" Carl called, nearly pushing me into the car.

The woman turned, encouraging her husband through the door and into the house before we pulled from the curb.

"What on earth are you doing? Why didn't you let me finish? She has no idea how I came by it. Even if she didn't remember the

436

necklace, I have three other rings — all probably more valuable than the pendant!"

"Did you see how frightened she was? She doesn't want to talk with you."

"But —"

"Did it ever occur to you why her married name is not Jewish? That perhaps she doesn't want her husband or guests to know she is Jewish? That she may never have told them?"

"This isn't the 1930s or '40s. There's nothing to be afraid —"

Carl's color rose and he let loose an angry and frustrated tirade in German, which I could not understand . . . perhaps for the best.

By the time we reached Grandfather's it was after seven. The silence in the car rang just as loud as Carl's tirade had done.

"Would you like to come in? I could put something together for dinner."

"*Nein. Danke.* I must go."

"All right." I opened the door to get out, then stopped. "I just don't understand why she would still be afraid, or why you came so unglued."

"That is right, Hannah. You do not understand. And what you do not understand can be frightening, even dangerous for others. Let me think. Let me think how we can best proceed. Above all, do not contact anyone else. There is a better way. There must be a better way."

32

Lieselotte Kirchmann
September 1944

I dreamed of a picnic beneath spreading linden trees, a lovely summer's day on the banks of the Spree — a spot just outside Berlin that I'd visited once as a child, with Mutti and Vater and Rudy, where we ate plum cakes and watched the boats go up and down the river.

But in my dream, Lukas and I were the grown-ups and we fed one another Kuchen — our intended wedding cake, rich with raisins and sugar icing. Lukas took the last bite and licked my fingers. I licked his, and then he kissed my wrists, my arms, my neck.

A child — a toddler — called out, dancing too near the river, and Lukas left me to pull the little one back.

She reached up, laughing, and called, "Vati!"

The little boy beside her turned and ran,

squealing, to me. The two children were our own. Lukas pulled us all into a circle on the picnic blanket, rolling, tumbling. The children, delighted, giggled with glee.

"Lieselotte," Lukas whispered in my ear. I reached for his face, but he shook me — gently, urgently. "Wake up."

"No." I smiled. I wanted to dream this dream forever.

"We must get dressed. There are dogs in the street — raids."

I opened my eyes. Barely dawn. The light through the attic transom streaked gray.

"No," I whispered, closing my eyes again. "They will not come for us. They don't know we're here."

I heard Lukas pull on his trousers, tuck his shirt, fasten his belt. "Come," he whispered.

But I turned over, determined to shut out the world. *They'll never find us. Please, God, they can't find us.*

Lukas pulled me to a sitting position, tugged my dress over my head. "When they come," he whispered, "you must have your shoes on. Don't go without your shoes and coat."

And then I, too, heard the barking dogs. As surely as I knew I would love Lukas until I died, I knew they would come. Every

440

remnant of my dream gone, I pushed him away. I could dress myself. "Tell your parents," I whispered.

With the library not yet open, our need for quiet evaporated. There was no one to hear our footsteps, our frantic scramble for clothing.

Mutter and Vater Kirchmann must have heard the approaching raid long before I did, for they appeared, dressed with coats and cases, just as I slipped into my coat.

"Marta's gone," Mutter Kirchmann whimpered. "We don't know where."

"Gone? Where could she have gone?"

Vater Kirchmann pushed his hands through his hair in fear. "She said nothing. She's left everything here."

"Which means she plans to come back," Lukas assured them.

"If she can," I whispered, as much to myself as to them.

Mutter Kirchmann sobbed, but clasped a hand to her mouth to stop the sound.

"We must hide her things," I pleaded to Lukas, "so they'll not think there's another, so they won't come back —"

That's when the pounding began on the library door, three floors below — the *bang, bang, bang* of rifle butts striking wood, and then the thunder of boots upon the steep

441

stairs, as if they knew exactly where to search.

"Say nothing of Marta," Vater Kirchmann ordered.

The attic door burst open. How pitiful we must have looked, the four of us huddled, ready and waiting.

"Kirchmann!" the officer in charge barked, glancing at his orders. "Four. Convenient. You make our job easier." Lukas and Vater Kirchmann straightened, each holding tight to his wife. "You're under arrest."

"On what charge?" Vater Kirchmann did his best to maintain dignity, but the men with guns, the snarling dog barely held at bay, made my heart race.

"Enemies of the Reich — aiding and abetting Jews." He jerked his head toward those awaiting orders, and they sprang toward us. "Move!" The officer stepped back. His henchmen shoved us forward, all but throwing us down the dark and narrow winding stairs.

Through the front door we stumbled, into the deserted early-morning street, where a truck waited. Herded at gunpoint, we grabbed a suspended strap and climbed into the back of the open truck, its bed lined with rough plank seats. Our cases, so important at first, already became cumbersome. But we clung to them, as if they'd save us, as if they held the key to our identities — our past lives and our future beyond this burning time.

A guard slammed the tailgate closed. The motor gunned. We all jerked forward, then back. I glanced up, appealing to the windows of the street for help. The blackout curtain of a curious neighbor fell quickly into place.

Mutter Kirchmann scanned the streets through the cracks in the truck's plank walls, searching, I knew, for any sign of Marta. Where could she have gone? What would become of her?

Lukas wrapped his arm around me, gluing us together for whatever lay ahead. I closed my eyes, wanting so much to shut out the nightmare, terrified that it was only beginning.

Vater Kirchmann leaned forward and whispered, "Lieselotte, when they realize who you are, they must let you go."

"Shut up!" the guard who'd loaded prisoners aboard shouted. "No talking!"

I was glad for the order. I didn't want them — anyone — to realize who I was other than the wife of Lukas Kirchmann. Anything else might separate us and I could not, would never, let that happen.

Through the streets the truck jerked, screeching to a stop before what looked to be an abandoned ruin. Soldiers jumped from the truck and stormed the building. Mutter Kirchmann gasped as they dragged Anna and Jacob, even their baby, from their hiding place in the cellar. *Who could have told? Who even knew?*

Lukas reached for Anna, pulling her up into the truck bed. Her husband handed up their child, and Mutter Kirchmann pulled Anna and baby into her embrace as her husband climbed in behind.

Two more stops — one known to me and one not. But I could tell Vater Kirchmann knew them. So they were all from our routes. Someone had infiltrated, someone had followed or bribed or tortured for our secrets.

I knew Mutter Kirchmann worried for Marta, was thankful she'd not been found. I couldn't help but wonder if she'd been caught — beaten or tortured and . . . No. I must not think that. She would never tell.

But if we'd been arrested, and these from our routes, then did that mean everyone? Everyone in our church who helped? Everyone hidden by members of our church? Frau Ziegler and Herr Klietsman, both from church, were arrested next, dragged from their early-morning beds. Our church family — so strong — now crumpled like a house of cards. And yet from those familiar faces, pale and drawn, shone stalwart eyes. I was frightened and comforted to know others in our plight.

"Pastor Braun?" Vater Kirchmann whispered to Frau Ziegler.

Sadly, she shook her head. "Arrested earlier this morning."

I closed my eyes and buried my head beneath Lukas's strong arm.

Chaos reigned in the train yard. Gray-clad guards barking orders, shoving men, women, and children at gunpoint. Babies crying, children screaming for their fathers and mothers, for older siblings. Hollow-eyed women and pasty, gaunt-faced men — the ghosts of those hidden away for months — round-shouldered in defeat. Wide-eyed little girls clasping dolls made of rags and skinny-legged little boys in short pants — long since too short.

I clung the harder to Lukas, and Vater Kirchmann herded us close together.

Sharp whistle blasts pierced the air, and the dogs — large German shepherds — lunged against heavy chains, circling the crowd as if we were breakfast.

Ahead stretched a long row of railcars — cattle cars — their doors standing wide. With no attempt made to separate us into families or by gender, gun barrels prodded us forward, forcing us to climb aboard as quickly as possible. Stragglers, punched and kicked, all but fell headfirst into the cars, pushed up by those behind.

The car we neared was full, the occupants calling that there was no more room. But the guard paid no attention and shoved us forward, shouting obscenities. Lukas helped me up and scrambled in behind me, pulling up his mother. Vater Kirchmann made to climb aboard, but the guard pushed him back hard onto the platform.

"Helmeuth!" Mutter Kirchmann screamed. "Helmeuth!"

But her pleas only seemed to inspire the guard to evil, and he goaded the fallen older man, prodding him with the end of his rifle barrel. "What is it, Jew lover? Fallen on hard times, have we? Somebody reported your misdeeds, did they? What can we do to shorten your incarceration, eh?" He laughed, lifted his rifle, and pointed at Vater Kirchmann's face.

Before I could stop him, Lukas jumped from the train and placed himself between

446

his father and the rifle barrel, lifting his father from the platform.

"You! Get back in the car!" the guard shouted, shoving his rifle into Lukas's chest. "Move!"

"Don't shoot that man!" a higher-ranking officer barked, making his way down the platform. "We need every able-bodied man for digging ditches."

"There's no more room, sir."

"Then make room! But don't shoot workers. Is that understood?"

"Heil Hitler!" Then the guard barked, "Wait here," and jerked two old people — a man and a woman — by their arms from the edge of the car, no matter that they cried out in pain as they hit the platform.

"Get in!" he shouted to Lukas and Vater Kirchmann.

"We can make room for —" Lukas pleaded.

"We can! We can make room!" Mutter Kirchmann called, barely able to stand for those jostling behind her, craning their necks to see.

"Get in, I said!" The guard raised his rifle and Lukas obeyed, pushing his father up before him.

Both men turned, ready to reach for the older couple, but the door was slammed and bolted. And then gunfire — two bullets, a pause, and one more.

A hush swept through the cattle car. A child whimpered. Lukas groaned, shuddering beneath his heavy coat.

The long whistle blast came again and the train jerked forward. Everyone fell sideways. Caught in a scramble to keep our feet beneath us, we groped and jostled one another until we stood like shoots of *Spargel* tied with twine.

"Dear God in heaven," Vater Kirchmann prayed as his wife pulled his head — nearly a foot above hers — to her shoulder to comfort him. "I had no idea. I would never have —"

"Shh, shh," Mutter Kirchmann crooned so softly I barely heard her. "God in heaven knows this. He knows and sees all."

I wrapped my arms around Lukas's waist, pulling him as close as possible, and looked up. Tears streamed down his face; his mouth set grim. *Please, please,* I begged in silence. But the nightmare kept on.

We rumbled down the tracks, seeing no more than our hands and the faces before us, for there was only one high and narrow window near one end of the car. Daylight streamed through it . . . first the morning sun, then bright white light.

At times the train swerved and lurched to a stop. Usually that meant we'd pulled to the side, and in time — perhaps minutes or half an hour — another train rumbled past. With all our stopping we couldn't have gone far. At last we slowed to a stop and the sounds of the engine changed.

"Where are we?" The question passed from mouth to mouth.

A man lifted a child to his shoulders to peer out the high window. "What do you see?"

"Oranienburg!" the child cried. "The sign says Oranienburg."

"Sachsenhausen." The dreaded word came down the line. "That camp."

I gripped Lukas's hand and he held me up. "That camp" was known far and wide for its cruelties, its horrors, its tortures.

"They'll separate us," Mutter Kirchmann whispered.

Nein! I nearly screamed. "I will not leave you. Lukas, I will not leave you!"

"Stay together. Hold hands," Lukas ordered our little group. "When the door opens it will be a madhouse. Hold tight to one another."

But Vater Kirchmann's eyes told a different story. "No matter what happens, it is our duty to remain strong — for each other,

449

for ourselves, for Marta. Even if we are separated. Do you understand?"

I shook my head. "No, we can't — we can't be —"

Lukas gripped my hand tighter. "You can." He lifted my face with his hands, forcing me to meet his eyes. "You can do all things through Christ who strengthens you, Lieselotte — remember this! Say this over and over to yourself. Your strength is greater than your own."

But I couldn't say it.

"People come out of prison. The war has already turned. It won't be long now. We'll all come out and we'll begin again. Do you hear me?" He shook me. "Do you hear me, Lieselotte?"

I wanted to be strong, to be all that Lukas wanted and needed in that hour. But I was afraid, so very afraid.

And then the doors slid open with as much vengeance as they'd closed. The sudden light felt blinding, though it was late afternoon and a steady drizzle had begun. We'd traveled but forty kilometers, but with all the stops and starts it had taken hours.

"Out! Out!" the guards shouted, pulling and shoving, not waiting for us to climb down. "Men to the left. Women to the right."

"No, please, no," I begged as we staggered to the platform.

Lukas took my face in his hands again and kissed me, tender and deep, but I could not stop crying. "Wait for me, and I will find you. I swear I will find you when this is over."

And then a cry as a rifle butt slammed against his ribs. "Move on!"

"Stay together!" Vater Kirchmann called to Mutter Kirchmann and me as he pulled Lukas with him.

Weeping, wailing — a din of anguish rose from the growing line of women until rifle fire split the air.

An officer spoke from a megaphone. "Women, return to your cars."

Gasps and cries — more rifle fire — and silence . . . all except for the sound of soft rain hitting the pavement.

Mutter Kirchmann grabbed my hand and pulled me toward the train. I looked for Lukas, strained my eyes for him and craned my neck above the crowd of women. I scrambled back into the cattle car and pulled Mutter Kirchmann up, then swept the crowd, holding on to the door of the car to keep from being pushed back by the women climbing aboard. Look as I might, search as I did, I caught not one more glimpse of my husband.

The rain drove harder, in sheets and torrents, as though the sky and all the angels wept for us. The door slammed shut.

33

Hannah Sterling
March–April 1973

A long night passed, a long day, and another long night. Carl did not phone and Grandfather did not improve. Geoffrey did everything needful except cook, and that took little of my time, given my limited skills and Grandfather's limited ability to chew.

Daily — the highlight of each day — I bicycled to the outdoor market and strolled the stalls. March was nearly over, but vendors still wrapped in layers against the cold.

German diets focused on root vegetables and meats, especially pork products. I longed for more chicken and green and yellow vegetables in my diet. *An occasional mountain-stream fish would be nice. But I might as well wish for the moon.*

I'd just splurged on a jar of honey and turned from the stall when a woman in a brown woolen coat matched my stride. "Will you walk with me, *meine Dame?*"

I could have jumped out of my skin. "You — you're the — yes, yes, I'll walk with you."

She steered me to a side street, and into a small café. The warmth rushed into my face, nearly knocking me over, making my head go light.

I followed her to a small table near the back. She ordered two hot chocolates. *"Amerikaner* like *Schokolade, ja?"*

"Yes. Oh yes. I'm sorry if I embarrassed you the other day, or if I made things awkward in any way. I just wanted to return . . . what belongs to you."

"How did you find me? Where did you get that necklace?"

Carl had told me to expect such questions from anyone I approached. I should have prepared myself from the beginning. But I'd never been able to formulate an answer that didn't implicate my family or me. "It came into my possession recently, and I knew I needed to return it to its rightful owner. I had reason to believe that might be you."

"You are not German."

"No. But tell me, is it yours?"

"It was my mother's. I have not seen it since . . . since I was a very young girl."

I nodded, hoping she'd go on.

"My family — my husband and his family, even our children — do not know." The pain in her eyes, some mixture of fear and despair and betrayal, pierced my heart.

"Are you afraid? The war's been over so lo—"

She sat back as the waiter delivered cups of hot chocolate to our table, nervously nodded her thanks, and warmed her hands round her cup. "The war is over, yes. That does not mean that the enemies of the Jews have gone, or that they will not come for us again."

"There are no more Nazis." It was all I could do not to reach for her arm.

She shook her head, looking at me so patiently, as if I were a child who didn't know better. I recognized the expression from Carl's face.

"Help me understand." I leaned forward.

She pulled back, lifted her cup to her lips, but reconsidered and set it down again. "The Nazis began by making great speeches and announcements that life would be better for everyone, that Adolf Hitler possessed great plans to rebuild Germany. They insisted that everyone must be listed in one category or another. We registered — as soon as the order came. We believed the

Führer meant for everyone, all of us, to benefit. We were all Germans, after all. We registered because we were Germans, and we registered as Jews, because we were Jews as well. Practicing Jews, some not, some baptized as Christians."

I nodded.

"*Mein Vater* was a respected banker in the city. *Meine Mutter,* a Jewess — from a wealthy family, a family who'd lost their estate during the Depression. One night, in the middle of the night, long after we'd all gone to bed, the Gestapo came to our door. Before *mein Vater* could rise from his bed they burst into the house, the beams from their torches shining in our eyes, running over our beds. *Meine Schwester* and I cowered beneath the covers until I heard them screaming at our parents. I crept to the doorway and saw them drag our Mutter from her bed. They barely let her grab her coat or shoes. They made *mein Vater* kneel on the floor, his hands behind his head, held him at gunpoint, spat on him, called him names — vile names.

"I followed them into the hallway, shivering in my bare feet and thin nightgown, watching, not saying a word, too terrified to speak. They shoved her in a car and sped away. *Mein Vater* ran into the street after them. They shot at him. *Meine Schwester* and I screamed and screamed." She'd begun breathing faster as she spoke.

"That had to be so frightening." I didn't know what else to say, and I meant it. Such horror for two young girls!

"Frightening? It was only the beginning. We waited — for days and weeks. *Mein Vater* walked every day to the prison to ask about our Mutter, but they would tell him nothing, only call him names and spit on him and send him away humiliated for having married a Jewess. He lost his position —" she snapped her fingers — "just like that.

"One night he said they had asked about *meine Schwester* and me — half Jews. We must go into hiding, he said. Ever since *meine Mutter* had been arrested and *mein Vater* lost his job, he'd been selling off her jewelry to buy food on the black market from a girl — a Gentile girl, but with a good heart. *Mein Vater* had full rations, you know, because he was Aryan. But *meine Schwester* and I, we were half Jews. Our rations were . . . not enough."

"Your father sold the necklace I showed you to the girl for food?" My heart leapt to my throat.

"*Nein,* not that one. He sold it, and the last of her jewelry, to the girl's Vater, for our freedom — for new identity cards and passports for us to go to England. *Mein Vater* said he would come later, as himself, once he divorced our Mutter. My parents had long agreed that if she was ever taken, divorce and sending us away was their only way to save *meine Schwester* and me."

"And the papers? Did the man bring them?" But I knew the answer before she gave it.

"*Nein.* We thought they must have been arrested and their underground work exposed. The man never came again, but the Gestapo came. When they pounded on the door, *mein Vater* slipped with us out through the attic and across the roofs of the building next door.

"We ran first to our neighbors three houses down, hoping they would hide us. But the man — we'd known him all our lives — ran into the street, shouting to the Nazi pigs that we were there, to come and get us."

The drums began rumbling in my stomach, pounding toward my heart.

"*Mein Vater* was quick, and so smart. He pulled us through the alley and across stone walls and back gardens. We ran and ran, all the while we heard the commotion in the street. We hid beneath a little bridge until we heard the cars drive away."

"And then? You went home?"

Her face registered incredulity at my words. "We could never return home. We'd have been arrested. The Jews in our neighborhood were rounded up and sent for relocation. We walked all night, out of the town and into the country. When daylight came we hid in a ditch, and Vater covered us with grass.

"When nighttime came again, we walked — nothing to eat, nothing to drink. We reached farms; if there was a dog to bark, we walked on. If no dog, we stopped and Vater hid us in a ditch or in their barn, then knocked on the door, begging food. This is how I learned to milk a cow — because we were hungry, because we were thirsty. The cow did not care that we were Jews."

"How long did you live like this?"

"For the duration of the war. We hid in ruins, in empty buildings, in barns. Sometimes, someone would take us in for a day, a night. Vater could find day work — sometimes. But it was dangerous. He should have been conscripted when they started taking older men. He pretended to be a cripple, but who would hire a cripple? Such men, if found out, were arrested and often shot. Whatever someone gave us came directly from their own rations. Many days we ate nothing — we grew thin, like scarecrows, which also marked us from far away."

A tear trickled down her cheek. I wanted to wipe it away, but I dared not move, dared not break her chain of remembrance.

"Finally, Vater did the unthinkable. He separated us, saying he had no choice. No one could take us all — no one would. *Meine Schwester* went to a farmer near Cologne. Vater returned to Berlin and enlisted. He believed he had a better chance of surviving the war that way and finding us again afterward than if he continued to hide. He gave me to a businessman who promised to smuggle me into Switzerland in crates of his product."

"Did he?"

She closed her eyes, suppressing a groan. "I survived the war, in my way. I was fed, and had regained most of my strength by the end. But I paid a different price to that businessman, and to his 'colleagues.' *Meine Schwester,* Miriam, was denounced by the farmer's neighbor. The farmer was hanged and Miriam was sent to Sachsenhausen, where she was experimented upon — because she had brown eyes. They tried to make them blue. They blinded her, and then they killed her."

I swallowed. "And your Vater?"

"Dead, in the war. I don't know where except that he was sent east."

"Did you ever hear from your mother?"

"A neighbor, after the war, told me that my mother was killed in Dachau. But the woman's sister told me later that Mutti had escaped near the end of the war and returned to Berlin, searching for us. She said that when the Soviets came, Mutti was raped . . . by an entire raiding party."

"I'm sorry . . . so very sorry."

"I don't know which told me the truth — or if either did. If they only wanted to be more cruel to a dirty Jew. I do not think of them — I try not to remember. But when you opened the jewelry case, it was as if Mutti stood on my doorstep."

"I would like to return it to you — if you want it. And there are other things. Two rings — one a ruby and one with sapphires."

She bit her lip. "My grandmother's. They were to go to Miriam and me when we married." She searched my face. "Who are you? How did you come by them?"

"I'm sorry. I can't tell you that. But I can assure you that there is no risk in your accepting them. I just ask that you forgive those who held them so long."

"Forgive? Who do I forgive? *Meine Mutter*

461

and *mein Vater, meine Schwester,* are long dead. Can rings and a necklace bring them back?"

"No." I swallowed. "They can't. But perhaps they can bring you something — some connection to them. Some peace?"

"They will not bring me peace . . . only sad remembrance. But I will take them, if only to remember their names on this earth. I would love for my children to know of them. I would love for them to know of Mutti's stout heart, of Miriam's sweet laughter. But do I dare tell them they are one-quarter Jewish? Will I sign for them a death warrant in the future?"

"I hope not. Dear God, I hope not."

Carl met me for dinner. It was good to sit down in a restaurant, to look out into the dark street and know I was safe and warm and fed, that nearly thirty years had passed since the last bombs fell on the city.

"You went there again?"

"No, she saw me in the marketplace and asked me to walk with her to a café." I toyed with my soup spoon. "She's afraid, after all these years, to tell her children — even her husband — that she's Jewish. She's afraid it will all happen again."

"Can you blame her?"

"I don't blame her at all. It just makes me so very sad. I wish the world were a different place."

Carl reached for my hand and I clung to his, no words to fill the space.

"What will you do now?" he asked finally.

"I'll visit the next person on the list and try to return what I can."

"Even if they do not want to be found?"

What can I say? That I'll give up the search because one person is afraid? "I don't know how to answer that. Maybe I should write them instead?"

"And have it opened by someone like this woman's husband — someone who doesn't yet know? Or traced back to you — to Herr Sommer's home?"

I sighed. "I don't know, Carl. I'll think about it. It's all so complicated. I didn't expect it to be so complicated."

" 'Oh, what a tangled web we weave . . .' "

" '. . . when first we practice to deceive.' But I never meant to deceive anyone. I just want to do the right thing, to do the thing my mother would have done."

"Ah, Hannah . . . I am sorry you didn't know her — the person she was as a young woman. Perhaps knowing her actions — whatever they were — would have left you a very different legacy."

"I'm sorry too. You have no idea how sorry."

34

Lieselotte Kirchmann
September 1944

Our train headed north — that's all we knew, all that those nearest the small window could surmise. Whispers ran through the car. Women sat where their husbands had stood and clung to those they knew, those they trusted. Twice our train pulled to the side and waited — once for an hour, perhaps, and another time for what seemed like several hours. The door did not open.

It must have been after midnight when we started again. The September night, already cold, penetrated the cattle car. Damp chill set into my bones. I needed to use the toilet, but there was only one bucket in the corner — already filled and overflowing with urine and feces from earlier in the day. I could smell that others suffered the same plight.

We rattled on. Mutter Kirchmann and I leaned against each other's shoulders, dozing, waking, starting with the jostle of the train.

Finally, we pulled to a stop. Doors slid open on their metal grooves in the cars ahead, orders were barked, dogs growled, alert.

Our door slammed open. *"Schnell! Mach schnell! Raus!"* guards shouted.

We pulled feet beneath us, but they'd gone numb, and we groped for the woman before or behind to steady ourselves. Moving forward, women jumped from the train, reaching back for others. Guards grabbed and shoved. One woman, having fallen from the train, cried out that she'd twisted her ankle. The guard shouted obscenities, tried to raise her, but she stumbled again. He swore at her once more. A single shot rang out.

Mutter Kirchmann grabbed my arm, pulling me forward, weaving our way into the midst of the throng. A blinding light shone in our faces through the graying dawn. In that bizarre light they divided us into groups to march five abreast.

"Schnell! Schnell!" The order was shouted again and again, as if we could walk any faster.

Over uneven ground, roughened by stones and exposed forest tree roots, we marched

466

— stumbled — able to see only the five women in front, doing our best not to trample them or be trampled by those behind. Uphill we climbed, and climbed, finally reaching a narrow plateau that opened the vista before us.

Searchlights lit rows of gray buildings, long and narrow — bunkers or barracks of a sort, penned by high fences heaped with roll upon roll of barbed wire. Guard towers surrounded the camp. A towering square building belched a line of steel-gray smoke against an already-smoldering sky.

"Ravensbrück!" The single word passed from woman to woman.

Mutter Kirchmann and I clasped hands.

"Work camp," said one woman.

"Death camp," said another.

I knew the name, as did every German on the street. *This can't be happening — can't be real!*

We marched downhill, trudging through a quagmire of black mud, so deep it oozed over the tops of our shoes, sucking them from our feet. Steadying and pulling one another free only broke momentum and tripped us over one another. I remembered Lukas's admonition about keeping shoes on our feet and stopped to pull them from the mud, caking my hands in sludge. Finally, we labored uphill again, our feet leaden weights and slipping in the squish of our shoes, until we reached looming iron gates. Across the top, huge iron letters read, *Arbeit Macht Frei* — "work makes you free."

"Schnell! Schnell!" the angry order came again.

We stumbled through. Posts with signs of skulls and crossbones stood as sentinels, indicating the deadly electric wiring that ran round the tops of high concrete walls.

Someone spied outdoor spigots and shouted, "Water!" Groups of women in threes and fives broke ranks and surged forward, but they were cut off by the guards and beaten back with truncheons.

Herded to a large, open area — like a giant flock of geese — we trudged; then the order came: *"Halt!"*

Guards surrounded our perimeter. An hour went by as we stood, frightened, exhausted from lack of sleep and worry, uncertain what might come next. Another hour passed, and tentatively, we sat down on the cindered ground, unbuttoning our coats and pulling off hats as the sun rose higher.

For the first time Mutter Kirchmann and I dared whisper, fairly certain no one else would hear. "You must tell them a mistake

468

has been made, that you're the daughter of an important Nazi Party member. Your father will get you out. I'm sure he will."

"I won't go without you."

"There is nothing you can do for me here. As long as I know you and Marta are safe, I will be all right."

I squeezed her hand. I would not leave the only woman who'd mothered me for years, who loved me as her daughter. And how could I face Lukas if I left his mother? What kind of person would that make me? Surely they couldn't keep us penned like this forever.

Another hour and another, until the sun rose white-hot above us — welcome and warming us through. But the dust in the area, the cinders that fell like snow from the great smokestack, dried our throats and thickened our tongues — and all the time those spigots in the distance. How easy it would be to fill a pail of water and pass it through the crowd of women!

"Achtung! Achtung!" A deep voice blared over loudspeakers. We were roused and ordered into a line for a thin turnip soup and a roll, our first food or liquid in more than thirty hours. I gulped the soup down without looking, but the woman beside me

vomited, swearing that hers was filled with worms.

Mutter Kirchmann closed her eyes, and I knew she was praying. I saw her murmur, "Helmeuth" and "Lukas" and "Marta." Then she whispered, "Lord, keep Lieselotte and me in the hollow of Your hand, in the center of Your will. Spread Your wings over us. Let us see Your presence and the evidence of Your love even here."

I could not say amen. If they did this to women, what was happening to Lukas, and to Vater Kirchmann? If God was watching over them as He watched over us, perhaps we'd best change our prayer. But I could not utter such blasphemy aloud.

Mutter Kirchmann whispered to me, "Our circumstances don't dictate our reality."

I squeezed her hand, assuring her that I loved her and wanted to believe, wanted to understand.

From that moment we stood at ramrod attention in formation, in complete silence. Not a whisper allowed, and not a trip to the toilet — which beckoned, though it was nothing more than a ditch in the open.

Night fell. My feet had long since gone numb with standing. I thought that if we could only sit down — lie down — sleeping right there on the ground in the open air would not be so very bad.

But an hour after dark the order came to form ranks again and follow. We marched into a long, low building. Sprawling open, like a warehouse, the room divided into sections. Groups of male guards with rifles stood at the entrance to the next room division. Women — clerks, with boards and paper lists — sat at long tables. Female guards marched the length of each formation, shouting orders to throw our hats and coats in separate heaps and return to our lines.

"Give your names — last name first!"

If our line moved too slowly to match names against the seated clerk's clipboard, a gunpoint pushed us forward.

"Mmm, such a pretty Fräulein to lighten our days." One of the male guards stepped into line behind me, lifted my hair from my neck, drawing it to his nose.

I didn't answer but, terrified, moved forward in line as quickly as possible.

"Does the cat have your tongue, little girl?" he teased, rubbing my hair against his cheek, his lips.

"Name!" the clerk at the table barked.

I stepped forward, flustered, and said, "Sommer . . . Li—" I coughed.

"Again!" The clerk looked up.

"Excuse me. I'm Kirchmann — Marta."

"What is this? You don't know your name?" the clerk bellowed.

The guard behind me smiled. "Do I make you nervous, pretty Fräulein?"

"*Ja,* check. Kirchmann, Marta. Next!" the seated woman shouted.

I turned to follow the line but glanced back at the flirting guard, who'd stepped away and winked.

Two women guards stood at the top of the next line, one with a clipboard and one with a long pair of scissors. Without explanation, the woman with the shears began chopping off the hair of the first woman in line — one, two, three snips and a long sawing — leaving tufts and spikes of hair on one side, and nothing much more than her victim's scalp on the other. The hank of rich, dark hair was thrown to the floor, and the woman with the clipboard announced, "Brunette."

Down the ranks they walked, desecrating the head of each woman, dividing the hair spoils by color into separate heaps on the floor.

Tears of pity welled in my eyes as they sawed Mutter Kirchmann's rich auburn bun from her head, but some dread mixture of anger and fear and a desire for revenge filled me as they cut my hair — thick, golden hair that Lukas had run his hands through two nights before, hair that had caressed his face, his lips.

Women could not, dared not, look one another in the eyes. What could such a thing mean? Why had we been made to look so hideous — not a haircut, but a rabid shearing?

Orders bled from one section into the next, so that it was hard to hear from the back what was said in each formation. But when the women in front of us began unbuttoning and pulling off their dresses, their shoes, their undergarments, their faces registering shame, my heart sank in horror and disbelief.

It wasn't that I'd never changed clothes in front of other girls — that had been routine in my gymnasium classes at school and even in the BDM when we changed into our uniforms. But not this. I'd just given my body to Lukas in our marriage bed, just two nights before shared the intimate uniting of our lives, our very souls — all that made us "one flesh." I belonged to him and he to me. I never again expected to so much as change my blouse before another human being.

"I can't." I shook my head. "I can't. Lukas —"

Mutter Kirchmann pulled my hands from before my heart. "Lukas wants you to live — would insist that you live."

The female guard prodded a hesitant young woman two rows ahead with her truncheon. *"Schnell!"*

"Hurry!" Mutter Kirchmann whispered. "It's a shower. They're sending us to a shower."

I unzipped my skirt and let it fall to the floor, unbuttoned my blouse, and stepped out of my shoes. Following the other women's examples I folded everything into a neat bundle.

"Everything!" the guard shouted, staring at me.

"Tochter!" Mutter Kirchmann whispered.

"I can't."

"*Ja,* you can, and you must. We're not the first ones and we won't be the last. But we will live!"

I set down my bundle and pulled off my undergarments. Bent over, I grouped everything in a pile and stood, holding them before me, covering myself.

The female guard sneered, pointing to the floor. I looked around and realized the other women had set their entire bundles on the floor. I set mine down too. The way she looked at me — how I hated her!

We were savagely shaved, then herded by the group of leering male guards toward the shower room. Three minutes of icy water poured from spigots in the ceiling, but I was too numb, too shaken, to appreciate anything. When the shower stopped, Mutter Kirchmann led me toward the entrance.

Back in the open room, dresses had been thrust into a pile on the floor. In that mad scramble I woke, desperate to find my skirt and blouse — the last shred of my identity. But they were not our own clothes, and not dresses that fit our bodies or even the weather — simply whatever we could grab from the heap or the hands of another, just as starving animals rip the food from the mouth of their opponent. I'd never fought like a tiger, but in that moment I learned and fought for Mutter Kirchmann and me, shivering in anger and desperation to cover ourselves.

Mutter Kirchmann must have pulled the dress over my head, or else I did it without thinking. Each dress had a large *X* sewn on the front and back. Only later did I realize how grateful I was to have grabbed thick woolen dresses — the difference between freezing or not in the months ahead.

We were herded yet again through the line of SS guards, and they ran their hands over us — up and down, front and back and on the sides, searching our bodies, lingering on and fingering some women more than others. What they thought we could have hidden was impossible to imagine. That they wanted to violate and humiliate us, to demean us, was clear. In that moment something of my nature returned, and I wanted desperately to kick them, to bite them, to spit in their faces.

Before I could form a plan, I was shoved forward and the moment passed. Marched through yet another line of female guards, we stopped before a table spread with colorful cloth triangles.

"Charge?" The clerk didn't even look up.

"Criminal," Mutter Kirchmann whispered, and I after her. We were, after all, "dangerous enemies of the state."

"Sew it on. See the chart for placement." The clerk handed us green triangles, and the next clerk doled out needles and thread.

How they expected us to sit on the cold, damp floor and sew with steady fingers after all we'd been through, I didn't know. But sewing a patch on my right sleeve was the most normal thing I'd done in so many hours I could no longer count them.

Needles collected and counted, we were ordered to the exit door and found ourselves standing once again in the cold night air.

The long, sweeping arc of the searchlight continually scraped high walls, and the barbed wire, three rolls thick, that ran along their tops, reminded us of the futility of any hope for escape.

Marched down the wide avenue between buildings, we filed into Barracks 28 and were assigned to beds already packed with women. They must have expected new recruits, for many grumbled and some swore, but all shifted sideways, and we lay like spoons in a drawer until morning.

Mutter Kirchmann tucked me on the inside and took the colder outside shift on the bunk first, the thin blanket not even covering her. I should not have let her do this. I should have been the one to protect her, but I didn't.

I lay awake until the sirens wailed long before dawn.

It was still pitch black when the guard threw open the door, shouting, blowing a whistle, ordering everyone outside for roll call. With barely enough time to shake the sloth from our limbs we hurried to the parade ground to stand in new formations — ten wide and ten deep.

Roll call began at four thirty. We no longer bore names, but were assigned numbers by the woman guard bellowing over the list on her clipboard — numbers we quickly memorized, numbers called over and over again in roll calls. That morning, someone — a number — was missing. The guard made us run through roll call three times before she determined the person was indeed not there.

Ten minutes later we heard a gunshot from the direction of our barracks. Mutter Kirchmann looked at me and I at her. We would never sleep late. We would never be too sick to stand in formation.

35

Hannah Sterling
April 1973

Carl traced the next two families on the ledger's list to America — one now living in Brooklyn, New York, and the son of another on the list living in a little town called Woodbine, New Jersey. He traced a third name to a daughter living in a kibbutz in Israel. I wrote to Ward Beecham, asking him to follow any lines of inquiry at his disposal in order to locate the US émigrés. I didn't explain the situation fully, only said in general terms that I needed to talk to them about something I'd discovered from WWII. I warned him that I wasn't sure how I'd proceed if he found them; I could only follow the trail as it unfolded.

The fourth and sixth and seventh and eighth had perished in concentration camps across Germany and Poland. There was no one to contact — no one I could trace. But the fifth name on the list lived in an institution for older men in Hamburg. And he was still using the name listed in the ledger — a name that sounded distinctly Jewish, so I knew he was not hiding that fact from anyone.

Carl's employer hesitated to send a car all the way to Hamburg, but I paid handsomely, as long as Carl drove. I couldn't imagine making the trip without him.

Beyond the reception desk of the institution in Hamburg, we faced sterile white walls and floors polished to a sheen so high I feared slipping and skidding to the end of the hallway. Rooms, sealed off from one another, seemed more like a series of apartments than those of a nursing home.

We waited for Mr. Horowitz in a large common dining room, empty in the early afternoon. An orderly wheeled him in and promised to return after his late lunch break. He wished us all a good visit.

"Mr. Horowitz, thank you for seeing us." I stood and extended my hand but he didn't take it. I thought perhaps he didn't speak English, so I turned to Carl.

"Herr Horowitz, danke schön —"

"I understood the American. But I do not know why you are here."

"Oh, I'm glad you speak English. It makes everything so much easier," I bubbled, smiling, desperate to brighten the mood, desperate to make him like me.

He didn't smile in return.

"My name is Hannah Sterling." I moistened my lips. "I'm visiting from America. I wanted to talk to you about something that happened during the war."

I reached for the chair across from him, but Mr. Horowitz's eyes glazed abruptly — as if hoarfrost suddenly settled over a summer field. "Orderly! Orderly!" he called after the man who'd wheeled him in. But the young man was long gone.

"What is it? Can I help you?" Carl asked. "I will go for the orderly if you like, but he said he would return after luncheon."

Herr Horowitz's stubbled chin trembled in indecision and frustration. Finally he spat, "He will not come until he has finished eating."

"Herr Horowitz, we don't wish to upset you, but we —"

"Then why do you come? Why do you torment me?" he demanded. "Can you not leave an old man in peace?"

"You've misunderstood; we're not here to torment you at all, but to help you. In fact, we —"

"Journalists — American journalists digging up the horrors of the past. Again and again you come, writing stories and making your movies. You think the Shoah was an amusement ride for your readers."

"*Nein,* Herr Horowitz," Carl assured him. "Fräulein Sterling is nothing of the sort. I swear it. She wants to return something to you — something of great value that she believes once belonged to you."

The old man's wary eyes searched my frame.

On Carl's cue, I rushed in. "Long ago, in the early years of the war, you lived on Wilhelmstrasse, in Berlin; isn't that right?"

He glanced away. He didn't nod, but his jaw muscles tightened, a shadow of remembrance sweeping his face.

"There came a day, I believe, when you tried to get new identity papers, or perhaps you tried to leave the country."

His breathing changed, grew more shallow, but I pressed on.

"A man offered to provide those papers — or promised you something — for these." I pulled a small velvet pouch from my purse and opened its drawstring. I lifted his hand and, before his widening eyes, poured into his palm three gold rings, two filigreed and encrusted with diamonds and the third a perfect circle of emeralds. "Are they yours?"

His breathing labored, he fingered the rings in wonder. "Where did you find them? Where did you get them?"

"You recognize them, then?"

"My Rebecca's wedding ring . . . her mother's emerald anniversary . . . Where did you get them?" he gasped.

I glanced at Carl for support. "I found them among the possessions of someone whom I think you might have known — the person you gave them to. I want to return them, to say I'm so very sorry that he took them, and that —"

"He sold us out!" Any spirit of dread or defeat died away, and Herr Horowitz's eyes blazed in a sudden fury. "He promised me freedom — papers, new identities, for all of us!"

"Can you tell me what happened? How did you find this man? How did he find you?"

Herr Horowitz slumped back in his chair, stone-faced. A full minute passed before he spoke. "Wolfgang Sommer." The name sounded vile in his mouth and horrific in my ears. "A clerk in the municipal office, a nobody. I was his superior until all Jews were 'relieved of their duties for the greater good of the Fatherland.' Civil service positions closed to the children of Abraham. Consequently, those Aryans already on staff . . . some moved up the ladder, prematurely promoted. Not always in the best interests of the work at hand."

"He took over your position?"

"The one below mine. I barely knew the man. But I learned, months after dismissal — from our rabbi — that Sommer's daughter was active in the black market. When authorities cut the rations of Jews so severely — too severely to survive, especially for the children — we approached her."

"You met . . . Fräulein Sommer?"

"My wife met her. All their transactions were carried out behind the butcher's shop."

"Was she fair in her dealings?" I held my breath. Carl nudged me, but I needed to know this.

Herr Horowitz shrugged. "We believed her at the time. As fair as anybody. More than most, even generous — at first. This is why I trusted her Vater, why I believed him. It was, perhaps, a long ruse they developed, a way to build trust."

"No, please. I don't believe that. Perhaps Fräulein Sommer's father followed her or tricked her. Maybe she — did you ever meet her?"

"Only my wife. Why do you care? How

did you come — ?"

"Please. Please tell me what happened. What did you mean that he sold you out? I'll explain everything as best I can, but it's very important that you tell me."

"What difference it makes now — to you — I do not understand."

"Please."

He stared beyond me. "After the letter came . . ."

"The letter?"

"Ordering us to report to the collection point. We knew what it would mean, that we would be held and then deported — sent away in the railcars to the camps. Everyone knew that much by then." He grunted. "Early on we didn't understand so much about the camps . . . mostly that no one came back."

"How did you make contact with . . . with the man who promised to help you?"

"Wolfgang Sommer came to me. He said he was the father of . . . I do not remember her given name. The girl who supplied my wife with food. He claimed that he knew people, people who could get us out of Germany — all of us. My wife, my two sons, my daughter — so little." Herr Horowitz's voice caught.

"And you paid him with these?"

He nodded, hatred in his eyes. "With these and the lives of my family."

I held my breath.

"The night we were to meet him . . . beneath the bridge beside the Spree nearest our home, at ten — after the curfew. We waited there from seven o'clock to make certain we were there, and ready, no delay."

"He never came?"

"The Gestapo came, driving us into their trucks. My wife tripped, tearing her stockings, cutting her leg badly. But they did not care. They shouted at my wife — my gentle Rebecca who spoke all her life just above a whisper — and threatened to shoot her if she did not hurry."

"So you all got into the truck?"

"*Ja,* but Wilhelm, my youngest son . . . so spry . . . such a runner." Memories filled his eyes. "Always a thing of beauty to see him throw back his head and run like the wind — run for the joy of being alive and in the day, in that one moment." Herr Horowitz stopped.

"And then?"

He sighed. "Wilhelm climbed into the truck last, after his older brother. We were driven to the outskirts of Berlin. Already we knew we were betrayed but had no idea where they were taking us. And then the truck stopped at a roadblock — too dark to see more than your hand in front of your face. The guard jumped from the back and was gone — only a moment.

"Wilhelm slipped from the truck and ran. He ran so quickly I imagined for a moment that he would be free — at least one of us would go free. But the guard at the roadblock lifted his machine gun and opened fire into the night. So many rounds! Such noise — and Rebecca screaming, screaming as I never heard her."

"Did he get away?"

"They shot him like a dog in the dirt."

My heart stopped. In my mind I saw the child running, running, stop short, hang motionless, suspended in midair, and fall, blood trickling from his neck in the moonlight. I was convinced we all saw him again in that moment. "I'm so sorry. So very, very sorry."

A minute may have passed while Herr Horowitz worked his jaw, trying to control the emotion that spilled from the corners of his eyes.

"Dachau. Two years. Rebecca was herded — like cattle — with the women, and Benjamin with me. Our daughter taken away with other small children and those too old to work. We never saw either of them again.

I do not know how long my wife lived, what happened to her, if she was shot and buried in a mass grave or burned in the ovens." He closed his eyes. "The little children and elderly — killed right away."

"I'm so very sorry."

"You said that. What difference does it make — you coming here, you being sorry?" He pushed the wheels of his chair and came close to me, close enough to spit in my face if he'd wanted. "They shaved us and examined us, laughing at any infirmity, shooting or gassing immediately those who were weak. We worked as slaves, our tormentors standing over us with whips and riding crops and clubs, nine hours each day. At noon we stopped for half an hour — no food, only a brief rest in the hot sun. At night we were given a cup of rutabaga soup. A dirty broth with barely a vegetable.

"Eighteen months Benjamin lived. He was taller than me and heavier when we walked through those gates of hell. When he died in my arms, he weighed nothing — almost nothing."

I looked away. I couldn't listen to any more.

"Do you see the color of my skin, eh?" He pushed his arm beneath my nose and pinched his skin, pulling it from the bone.

"For three years after liberation it was the color of ash. Stained from the grime. It took so long to grow new skin. For those two years in Dachau I never washed — not but once was there a shower in all that time. One and a half seconds we had for the toilet and to wash, if we'd been able. Hundreds of men in four minutes. That was it.

"Covered with lice, we slept huddled together, desperate to keep warm. And if you slept near a broken window, too bad — you were frozen dead in the morning and piled in stacks, like wood, outside the door, waiting for the burial detail."

"Please, I don't want to hear any more." I couldn't stop my tears.

"You don't want to hear any more? You say you don't want to hear any more? Do you see the snow outside — the snow that is beginning to fall?"

"Herr Horowitz," Carl cautioned, "please calm yourself. Lower your voice."

"Yes," I breathed, relieved for a new turn of conversation, relieved for the late snow in April. "I see it."

"I thought for the first month that it snowed every day in Dachau — even in summer. But it was the crematorium, running day and night, seven days a week. The ashes of the dead so thick it looked like snow on the trucks that drove in, like snow against the windows of the barracks, like snow on our faces as we turned out and stood for hours in roll call. It could have been the ashes of my wife! Do not tell me, Fräulein, that you do not want to hear any more. You have heard nothing! You have endured nothing!"

I bent over, holding my sides. I could not stop the tears streaming down my face.

"You cry like a child, as if your sorrow, your pity, will bring back my Rebecca or Sarah, my Benjamin or little Wilhelm. As if you have lost someone! You bring me these trinkets now, when I am an old man and have no son and no daughter to give them as a remembrance or even an inheritance from their family. What do you expect me to do with these? Eh, what do you expect?"

"I . . . I don't know. I thought only to offer them as a — a peace offering, a kind of atonement."

"These baubles? Atonement for the lives of my wife, my children?" Herr Horowitz nearly stood from his wheeled chair. He flung the rings across the room. *Ping! Ping!* They bounced off the radiator. "Blood money! You offer me blood money. Such cruelty I have not seen, not even in the SS!"

I covered my ears with my hands, shutting

out his anger while his voice rose.

"Orderly! Orderly!" he screamed. "Come! Come now, before I kill them with my bare hands!"

"The orderly is not back yet, Herr Horowitz." Carl stood between us. "Calm yourself; please calm yourself. Fräulein Sterling meant only to honor you. She could not know what you have endured."

"*Dummkopf!* The young are always foolish."

"You may be right. But foolish is not the same as cruel — at least it is not intended."

The old man's fury wavered until he sat back, exhausted. Carl crossed the room and fished beneath the radiator for the rings. He held them in his palm, waiting. I pulled my hands from my ears.

Herr Horowitz held out his hand. "Give them to me." He spoke softly, as a child whispers.

Carl placed them in the old man's hand and sat beside me, wrapping his arm around me, holding me up. The silence stretched long. I knew we should go. We'd done what we'd come to do. But I could not move.

"I apologize to you, Fräulein. I have never screamed at a young woman before. I do not wish to come to the end of my long life doing so."

I sat back, swiped away the last of my tears, shaking my head. "It's all right. It's nothing."

"*Nein.* It is something."

We sat in silence, except for the jerked movement of the wall clock's minute hand.

"May I ask — ?" But Carl pressed my fingers, urging me to stop.

"Ask what you will," Herr Horowitz answered.

I pulled my hand from Carl's. "How did you get out of the camp alive? Were you there to the end of the war?"

"Till the end of the war. And then —" he shrugged — "there was nowhere to go. All our property had been Aryanized. German Gentiles living in our homes, using our things — those they had not thrown away or sold. So we lived in the camps for months. The same camps we'd been living in as prisoners, we lived in as free men."

I'd heard that before, but it seemed too cruel to be true.

"They said the food was better and the labor less under our 'liberators.' But I wouldn't know. I lay naked like the dead for three months in a camp hospital ward. So many sick and dying. There were not enough blankets or clothing for all. Many continued wearing the prison rags they'd worn during their internment. Clothing was given to those who would most likely survive, or those able to clamor for it."

"But you recovered."

"I did not want to. I wanted only to die."

"What made you live?"

Tears glazed his eyes. "*Meine Schwester. Meine ältere Schwester* came looking for me. She knew I'd been sent to Dachau. She never stopped, never gave up." He swallowed. "I remember her that day, as yesterday. I saw her walk in, a lady in her dress and high-heeled shoes and handbag. She began at one end of the ward and looked into the face of each patient. Sometimes she read the name on the chart at the foot of the bed. No one looked as they had once looked. We were men only in our thirties and forties, but we looked ancient — unrecognizable with our sunken cheeks and hollowed eyes.

"I can still see her standing in the middle of my ward. She called my name, but I did not answer, was too weak yet to answer. She looked just like an angel, a vision that would surely vanish, as all my family had vanished.

"When she found my bed she searched my face. She nearly passed by. It was the first time I had cried since Wilhelm died. I cried and I cried. I could not stop. I'd thought all my family was dead, and here was my angel Schwester.

"She turned and saw me . . . knew me . . . cradled my head against her chest, like a baby, then laid me down. My skin peeled off in her hands, so thin it was. I was ashamed. I knew I must have disgusted her. Never had I allowed myself to be dirty before the camp. Tears poured down her face, but she did not turn away from me.

"And then she did the thing I will never forget, the thing that spoke of her great love for me. She pulled her panties from beneath her dress and gently pulled them up my legs — the first covering I'd had in months. She gave me my dignity again — the first dignity anyone had given me since the day Herr Sommer stole these." He fingered the rings in his palm.

36

Lieselotte Kirchmann
October 1944

By the second week we understood the established routine — a routine broken daily, hourly, according to the whim of the guards on duty.

Whistles blew at 4 a.m., followed by a mad dash through flying straw and dust to the center of the room to grab what at least looked the color of ersatz coffee and our morning ration of bread. By four thirty, regardless of the weather — rain or sun or early snow — we slogged to the *Lagerstrasse,* the wide, open ground before the hospital, to join thousands of prisoners from other barracks.

We stood at attention in our ten-wide, ten-deep formations for an hour, or it might be four hours. Finally released to our barracks, the whistle might blow again, and we would rush back to the cinder avenue and begin roll call once more — calling out our numbers, over and over again.

Workers inside Ravensbrück lined up for two "meals" per day. The thousands that marched to the local factory, Siemens — a mile and a half from camp — received three. Eleven grueling hours each day we loaded heavy metal plates from railway cars into a handcart, then pushed the handcart to a receiving gate within that factory.

Only the morning and evening marches to and from camp made the work bearable. Looking up, the mile and a half through the forest, beneath the changing autumn leaves framed by a blue sky, reminded us that life went on somewhere — at least in the realm of birds and clouds and scuttling squirrels. Were we not starving and filthy, with torn dresses and broken shoes, it might have been a stroll through Berlin's Tiergarten — at least that's what Mutter Kirchmann said each morning. Birdsong kept me from utter despair. If that one little bird could live — like the sparrow whose life Mutter Kirchmann said was important to the Lord — then perhaps so could I. If that one little bird could live and breathe and sing and fly away — even to see my Lukas, wherever he was — then perhaps I, too, might one day see him.

During the march to and from the factory, women whispered to one another — as long as we weren't caught. Making acquaintance, asking for information about husbands or sons or daughters or news of the war. How close were the Allies? Were the Russians near?

We grilled new recruits for outside information. After the first week I understood that urgency — every bit of news was a slice of heaven from home.

In our second week Mutter Kirchmann met the Dutch Sisters. Forbidden the use of names, we rarely asked, but we knew they were sisters — women Mutter Kirchmann's age who bunked across the narrow aisle from us in Barracks 28. They were a blessing to her that I could not be. "Very religious," I called them, and often closed my eyes at night, pretending to rest from my exhaustion, while they sang hymns and read, eyes and voices aflame, from books of a New Testament one of them had smuggled into the barracks.

I rarely joined in. My fledgling faith in the God of my Confessing Church wavered. How could He allow Ravensbrück? And if He didn't, then He was either not God or not there. Perhaps, as some said, He was on leave.

"Lieselotte," Mutter Kirchmann whispered night after night in my ear. "We musn't lose faith. We don't know why things happen, but —"

I am ashamed to say I shut her out. I couldn't listen. I couldn't comprehend.

At the end of the second week, as dusk fell during our return from the factory, the guard blocked our entrance to Ravensbrück — just beyond the heavy iron gates. A number was shouted. Weary after a grueling day at Siemens, my brain didn't register the number. All I could think about was crawling onto our hard wooden bunk.

The woman beside me whispered, "That's you — that's you she's calling!"

The guard shouted the number again. Uncertain, I glanced at Mutter Kirchmann. It was not a good sign, being noticed. I stepped forward from the lines. The *Kapo,* a prisoner in charge of prisoners — often more cruel than the guards — motioned me to follow her. The columns of workers, including Mutter Kirchmann, marched silently into camp, while I, quickly as possible, followed the *Kapo* down an alley.

She stopped, then came behind me, impatiently pushing me along. "*Schnell!* Do you think I have all night?"

We turned a corner, nearly running into

another guard — a man, who slipped her a roll of bills, then pulled me roughly by the arm. I couldn't see his face, but the very fact that it was a man terrified me. "No," I whimpered. "Please."

"Shut up! I'm not going to hurt you — not if you do as I say. Not if you become the meal ticket I've wagered." It was the SS officer who'd goaded me the day Mutter Kirchmann and I were first processed, the one who'd flirted and run his hands and eyes over me with vigor. My heart beat so fast against my ribs it nearly burst its cage.

He pulled me along, then pushed me through the door of a whitewashed building. The bright lights, the row of sewing machines, the women still bent over their needles surprised me.

"I — I don't know how to operate a —"

But he wasn't interested and pushed me through the doorway at the far end of the room. Three other women stood in the center of the narrow room — each looking as frightened as I felt, and each about my size — height and shape and hair color. I glimpsed two men in suits and fedoras standing in the shadows against the back wall. I narrowed my eyes to better see but was immediately shoved to turn the opposite direction.

"Spread your arms!" The order surprised all of us, but we obediently spread our arms.

"Close your eyes and turn around — keep them closed!"

My heart beat all the faster. My mind ran through every scenario I could imagine — none of them good.

I wanted to open my eyes, to glimpse the men observing us, perceive their intention, but was afraid.

"Face the wall! Hands on the wall!"

We obeyed. And then I heard the officer's heels walk to the back of the room, heard the men murmur, heard the voices become more intense, grow demanding, then falter. Something familiar in the cadence, even though I couldn't hear the words, made me tilt my head to listen. I lifted my head, certain I recognized a voice — a voice I'd known all my life.

"Vater?" I whispered.

"Keep your eyes closed! Face the wall!" the officer barked, new anger in his voice. Footsteps quickly crossed the room. The door opened, then closed with a decided latch. My heart wouldn't stop beating. Had Vater come to release me — to free us?

The officer walked behind us, slapping one woman after another on the backside. "You, you, and you — return to your barracks. Now!"

But he hadn't slapped me. And that made my heart stop. Freedom? For me, and if for me, then surely for Mutter Kirchmann! Vater must have realized what happened, must have come looking for me!

"Not a word." He grabbed my arm and pushed me forward, opposite the doorway where the man with the familiar voice had gone. *This can't be right! The other way! They left the other way!*

"Mein Vater," I whispered hoarsely.

"Apparently not." He jerked me into a long, dimly lit hallway, blocks of cells on either side.

"But . . . I heard —"

"What you heard —" he pushed me into a cell and slammed the door behind him — "is a man who claims not to know you, who claims that his daughter is dead." He pulled his gun. "I expected to be rewarded for my trouble and expense in finding the missing Fräulein Lieselotte Sommer, beloved daughter of the great and rising Party member. But it doesn't seem he really wants to find you — and my discovery has only led to my superior's fury."

"No. Please, let me talk to him. There is a mistake, a misunderstanding."

" 'Mistake' — an understatement. Well, I

501

say if Herr Sommer believes his daughter is dead, we have nothing to lose. We might even prove him right."

"No! No!"

"On the other hand, there are things more profitable to me than your death." He smiled slowly and holstered his gun. "Yes, more pleasurable and profitable, indeed."

My heart stopped. My legs barely held me up.

He unbuckled his holster and his belt and tossed them aside.

I cowered to the farthest corner of the cell, but it did no good. I screamed and screamed, but he came on, ripping open my filthy prison dress. And when I continued to scream he slapped me, again and again, hard across the face.

37

Hannah Sterling
April 1973

Night had fallen by the time Carl unlocked Grandfather's kitchen door. He turned the electric switch. I winced in the sudden light as he led me to the table and a straight-back chair.

Carl lit the stove and placed the kettle on the burner. He swirled warm water round the china pot, emptied it, and spooned in tea leaves. He set cups to warm but did not speak. What words could follow Herr Horowitz's story?

When the kettle whistled, Carl poured boiling water into the pot and covered it to steep. He sliced bread, slathering it with butter and honey.

"I can't eat. Please don't fix me anything."

"You will eat and you will drink your tea and we will talk this through."

"There's nothing to say. I don't want any

503

part of this; no more."

"But you said —"

"I know what I said. I know it was my idea to track him down, but I had no idea he would hate me — they would all hate me. It's as if I called the Gestapo, as if I slammed the door of the camp on them." I wrapped my arms around myself. "I feel dirty . . . like I can never get clean. As if I shouldn't have lived, as if my family should not have survived." The tears I'd pushed down for hours came very near the surface.

"But your mother did survive, and you were born . . . if for no other reason than to tell them you are sorry your grandfather did this. If for no other reason than to listen to their stories and remember, to promise that you will never forget."

"Remembering doesn't redeem anything!"

"No. Who are we to redeem anything? We're not redeemers, after all. We're not saviors! That's what Hitler claimed for Germany — and look what he did!"

I covered my face with my hands. If only I could shut out the world, shut out the blinding light.

"Fräulein Sterling?" Geoffrey stood at the door.

It took me a moment to remember who he was or why he was here. *Grandfather.*

"I wanted to let you know that Herr Sommer has asked for you."

"Asked for me?"

"*Ja,* he started to speak yesterday — moans, really. But today he asked for you by name."

Carl pressed my hand.

"He is sleeping now, but perhaps tomorrow — in the morning?"

I didn't know what to say.

"Perhaps you can let Fräulein Sterling know in the morning how he's doing," Carl suggested quietly.

Geoffrey hesitated. "*Ja,* I will do that." He turned to go, but stopped and turned again. "There is a man who has come twice to the door, asking for Herr Sommer. The first time I did not answer — as you instructed. But the second, he beat on the door, demanding."

"Dr. Peterson?"

"*Ja,* that is his name."

"You let him in?"

"*Nein.* Your instructions were clear. But I thought you should know I opened the upstairs window and told him to go away. The neighbor across the street had come out onto her walk to watch. I thought she might telephone the *Polizei.*"

"Thank you, Geoffrey. Thank you for telling me."

"*Ja,* well, *gute Nacht,* then."

"*Gute Nacht.*"

I pulled my hand from Carl's. "If he's able to say my name, that means he'll regain his speech."

"He can't hurt you. You must remember that."

I leaned my head back. "He's hurt so many." I pushed the heels of my palms into my eyes. "I don't think I can do this."

"You've already met with two survivors, and you've set in motion contact with those in the US. Your attorney has written them."

Nausea washed over me. "Ward Beecham can handle that. He doesn't need me."

"Then perhaps it is time to do what you came for, to discover what you need to know. If Herr Sommer remembers your name, he most likely remembers where he was and what he was doing when he collapsed. He must realize you've put the pieces together. You hold the cards. That gives you leverage."

"He's dying. Anything I ask him could bring on —"

"*Ja,* he's dying, so there may not be much time. How important is the truth to you?"

I considered that. Could I go home knowing only what I knew? I pulled my hands away from my face. "I must know what happened to Mama and what made her the mother I knew."

"Then ask, Hannah. Before it is too late, ask!"

When I reached Grandfather's door the next morning, my fledgling confidence wavered. Carl had made it sound so simple the night before. His urgings reminded me of a Scripture I'd learned in Sunday school as a child: "Ask, and it shall be given you; seek, and ye shall find; knock, and it shall be opened unto you."

I needed to ask now, before Grandfather died, or before he regained strength enough to refuse me. I wanted to follow the trail — to seek and find my mother. I wanted to be courageous, to knock on the doors of the past and have them opened to me, to reveal the truth. But what I most wanted was a happy ending to it all — a happy ending I could in no way imagine. And if the ending should not be happy, what then?

It was the memory of those he'd used and abused — those whose lives he'd betrayed and thrown to their deaths — and the need to understand my mother and what happened to her that carried me through that door.

507

The minute I entered, his eyes found me. I couldn't keep the heat from my face or disguise my fury.

He blinked, and I knew he knew.

"G-Geoffrey," he whispered. "L-leave us." His words were deliberate, with a slight slur, but clear enough.

Geoffrey looked to me for confirmation. I nodded, and he slipped from the room.

"You f-found . . ."

"Everything. The ledger, in all its detail, and your treasure room."

I couldn't read his face. Anger? Defiance? Humiliation? Defeat?

"I want to know about my mother. What happened to her, and who is my father? What did you do to them?"

He closed his eyes.

"You do n-not understand."

"No, I don't. So explain to me why you sold human beings to a death machine."

"We did not kn-know."

"I don't believe that. You were a member of the Nazi Party. How could you of all people not know?"

"Beginning —" He shook his head.

"You're saying that in the beginning, you didn't know that they would be tortured and starved and killed?"

"We did n-not know."

508

"But later — the dates in the ledger kept on until 1944. By then you must have known."

He didn't answer.

"There's no way to justify what you did, no way to reconcile your conniving, your complicity in murder, with human decency."

He lay in bed, his eyes watching me as if he stood on trial in the middle of a courtroom — like a replay of the Nuremberg trials. I felt powerful in a way I'd never felt, as if I could rake him over the coals and pronounce judgment on his evil heart — judge and jury rolled into one. But even that did not feel clean. *Who am I to judge?* "Why? Why did you do it?"

He turned his head away.

"My mother was part of the resistance. I know now that you preyed upon people she'd been helping. And she discovered that, didn't she?"

He didn't speak for the longest time and it was all I could do not to shake him, to thrash him. At last he whispered, "Jew lovers."

"What 'Jew lovers'? The Confessing Church members? The Kirchmanns?"

"Pretending they we-were n-not."

"You said Frau Kirchmann nursed Grossmutter. And Mama loved Lukas

509

Kirchmann — they were engaged. You gave them a party, gave them your blessing. What happened that you sold them out? Why?"

"Jews! She was part Je-Je—"

"You sold your daughter's fiancé and his family away because they were partly Jewish?"

He closed his eyes, acquiescing.

"Mama must have hated you for that. Is that why she left you — why she ran away? Or did she run away? Was she arrested with them? What happened to Mama? I need to know!" I wanted to shake him.

But Grandfather turned his face to the wall and did not speak.

"She did not run away — not exactly."

I whipped around to find Dr. Peterson standing in Grandfather's bedroom doorway. "What are you doing here?"

"Your good friend Geoffrey stepped out for a cigarette. He failed to lock the door. In any case, you've no right to keep me from my client. We have a great deal to discuss, do we not, Wolfgang?"

Grandfather's eyes widened in vulnerability. I hated Dr. Peterson and his smug, nearly licentious stare, but I would not back down now. "What do you mean she didn't run away?"

"Ah, Wolfgang, you have not told her?"

Grandfather looked like a squirrel in a sharp-fanged steel trap.

Dr. Peterson wagged his finger at Grandfather, as if scolding a small child. "I warned you not to alter our arrangement, my friend. Bringing Fräulein Sterling into our partnership . . ." He shook his head. "Not a wise plan. Though it does increase our leverage with her."

He glared at me in a proprietary way. My skin crawled.

"Under the circumstances, I believe it will do her good to know the truth."

Grandfather attempted to reach out for Dr. Peterson. He nearly fell out of bed, but I caught his arm and helped him back.

"Your mother was quite the advocate for the downtrodden, Fräulein Sterling. But you would learn that on your own, eventually. So I'm not telling anything out of school, am I, Wolfgang?" He smiled unpleasantly. "Unfortunately, her sympathies were misguided by her infatuation — for at that age, we can hardly call it love — with the Kirchmann boy. You must not blame your Grossvater, Fräulein. We were all taken in by them."

Dr. Peterson laid his hat aside and pulled the scarf from his throat. "We all believed the Kirchmanns Aryans of the finest order.

But Frau Kirchmann was the daughter of a Jewess, which meant she was a *Mischling,* a half-breed. I believe I was first to suspect." He shrugged. "A coincidence that the truth came to light the night of Lukas and Lieselotte's engagement party. Is that not correct, Wolfgang?"

"You denounced the family at Mama's engagement party?"

"*Nein, nein* — not I, and not then. I simply brought my suspicions to the attention of your Grossvater. He set in motion all the rest."

"Grandfather?"

"Sh-she b-broke the law."

"Because she was in love?"

"You musn't simplify this, Fräulein Sterling," Peterson interrupted. "Your mother stole food and ration books, dealt shrewdly in the black market — for quite some time. Because she was complicit in forging documents and helping Jews steal funds from the Reich, she deserved detainment, at the very least. It would have been illegal not to report her."

"My mother stole funds from the Reich?"

"You may know that Jews were allowed to leave the country possessing a certain amount of funds — anything more drained crucial assets belonging to the Reich. Helping them to leave with more than the law allowed was tantamount to stealing. It *was* stealing."

"Their own money."

"We simply made sure the Reich received its due — and we didn't do badly ourselves. Wolfgang and I were quite a team in those days, weren't we, my friend?"

Grandfather paled.

"You mean you followed my mother and used her kindness to trick people into trusting you."

Peterson removed his coat. "That is not exactly how I would describe it, but yes, in essence. Your mother . . ." He smiled again, that oily smile. "Quite a pretty girl, young, naive. Her infatuation with Lukas Kirchmann blinded her. As long as she led us to criminals thwarting the Reich, she was quite useful."

"You mean as long as you could use her relationships to exploit innocent people."

"The Jews were not innocent, Fräulein. You speak as if they were human! They were vermin and lawbreakers. Jews brought on the degradation of Germany — our betrayal and loss of the Great War, that hateful, spiteful, humiliating Treaty of Versailles! They caused our economic and moral downfall! It is something you Americans cannot grasp.

Though I daresay if the shoe were placed on the other foot — if America could rid herself of those races who've become a burden on your society, then . . . well, you would see that we are not the only ones with vision. We were simply the only ones with a Führer made of steel."

His prejudices sickened me. "What happened in 1944 to Mama? What happened that you stopped selling Jews?"

"Selling Jews?" Dr. Peterson winced. "How mercenary you make it sound. It was Wolfgang who stopped the process. Shall I tell her how?"

Grandfather's breathing labored. "I f-forbade the marriage," he stuttered. "It was illegal!"

"However, that did not stop her, did it, my friend?"

"They married? Lukas Kirchmann and Mama married?"

"*Verboten!* It was f-forbidden!" Grandfather's eyes flamed.

"But they married anyway; is that what you're telling me?" It was the missing piece in my puzzle. *Mama didn't just pretend she was a Kirchmann — she was a Kirchmann. Then that may mean . . .*

"You must understand, Fräulein, that such a marriage was not only illegal, it was ruinous — to Wolfgang's reputation, to his status within the Reich, even to his own prospects of marriage at the time."

The images played through my mind like a film. "You denounced her. You denounced your own daughter?"

"Nein!" Grandfather barked. "The K-Kirchmanns — not Lieselotte. I never in-in-t-tended . . ." His words grew indecipherable.

"Tell her the truth, Wolfgang. She is now our 'partner in crime.' It is on her head as well as ours."

But Grandfather closed his eyes, turning away.

"Then allow me," Peterson continued. "For her own good, your Grossvater did all he could to prevent the marriage. But Lieselotte was headstrong, a willful girl. She ran away to the Kirchmanns. One of those so-called pastors of their Confessing Church married them." He spat the words, then shrugged. "The only logical solution: have the family disappear in the way others had gone."

"You had them arrested? You tricked them out of their money and had them arrested?" I had to say the words, needed Grandfather's confirmation to be certain. "And Mama — she was the fourth Kirchmann."

515

"I d-didn't know," Grandfather gasped. "N-not then."

"The youngest Kirchmann — Marta — was not there that day. Mama was taken in her place. Taken where?" I stared at Grandfather in horror, in wonder that a man could do such a thing. "Where was she taken?"

"One of the camps, of course." Peterson all but smirked.

"But when you realized, you got her out of prison — away from the camps. Didn't you? Grandfather?" Grandfather didn't answer. I shook him, but he was limp, simply staring at me. "Tell me you got Mama out!"

"Such difficult times," Peterson continued. "Such negative publicity . . . To carry the shame of such a daughter . . . What could he do? What could any of us do?"

I pulled away, sat down on the chair by the bed, unable to think, trying only to format the onslaught of information to my brain. Trying to picture my mother as a young woman, torn from her new husband, from the only family who loved her, and taken to a camp, a concentration camp. *Mama . . . oh, Mama.*

"Better to forget her."

"Where? Where did they take her?"

"I believe the women were eventually

taken to Ravensbrück — at least for a time. Isn't that right, Wolfgang? Or was it Dachau? I really can't remember — so long ago. Prisoners moved here and there as required."

What did they do to you, Mama? "The Kirchmanns?"

Dr. Peterson shrugged, stepping closer. "As you might imagine, we did not follow their 'career.' What you need to understand — what is important now — is that we work together to close the circle on this past. It is a sad story, of course, but a story that is finished. We must think of the present, and our future.

"It would be best to give me the ledger. Once we divide the remainder of the assets, there will be no need to recall this unpleasantness again."

"You're insane."

"There is no need for melodrama, Fräulein. Now that you know, now that you have been made by your Grossvater a legal partner, you, too, are responsible for the information you carry. Do not forget that. Do not forget that in the eyes of the world you, too, are accountable."

"No, Dr. Peterson, I will never forget — and I will act accordingly."

"That is good." He spoke with reservation. "Until now, things have been safe in Wolfgang's possession. But with his health . . . precarious, you will both agree that —"

"Get out," I began quietly. "Get out, or I'll call the police this instant."

"Do not be foolish, Fräulein." Dr. Peterson stepped closer — too close. "The *Polizei* will find you just as embroiled as we. An accomplice to the retention of such valuables is —"

"No, I'd suggest you not be foolish." Carl stepped through the doorway brandishing a tire iron, followed by a wide-eyed Geoffrey. "I believe you heard the lady. It is time to go, Herr Doktor."

Dr. Peterson glanced from person to person. "Wolfgang, tell her. Tell her that half is mine. Tell her or —"

"Or what?" Carl asked. "You will have Herr Sommer and Fräulein Sterling arrested? If I do not miss my guess, Herr Sommer has your own complicity well documented, and I will bear witness to all you have said this day. Quite a testimony for the papers and the courtroom. Now get out."

"Half is mine, I tell you. It has always —"

"Fräulein Sterling has already contacted some of your victims. They, too, are ready to testify against you and Herr Sommer. You were evidently not as discreet as you imagined."

Dr. Peterson paled. "That is absurd. I don't believe it. Besides, we broke no laws."

"You heard him." I felt my courage returning, though Carl's improvisation about the willingness of the victims to testify, or their ability to identify the doctor, made me wince.

"Testimony regarding the ledger — its discovery and contents, and the contents of your hoard — is already on file with an eminent attorney. If anything untoward — anything at all — happens to Fräulein Sterling or her Grossvater, it will be turned over to the *Polizei* and to an organization with which you are already most familiar, Dr. Peterson. I have no doubt they will expedite prosecution."

"Such fools! Nazi hunters do not frighten me."

Carl tapped the tire iron against his opposite palm. "Ach, but they should, Herr Doktor. Truly, they should."

Dr. Peterson's bluff crumbled. The rage in his face could not hide the fear in his eyes. "You will be sorry. Wolfgang, you have betrayed me with this Jew lover. You will —"

But Grandfather's stare was without emotion.

"Herr Sommer? Herr Sommer!" Geoffrey was at his side in a moment, taking the pulse in Grandfather's neck, pulling the stethoscope from the bedside table.

Dr. Peterson grabbed his coat and hat, heading for the door. "This be on your heads!"

"Grandfather?" I searched Geoffrey's face, but he listened intently to Grandfather's chest through the stethoscope.

Grandfather didn't move; his chest never rose or fell. The front door downstairs slammed.

Geoffrey pulled the stethoscope from his ears. "I'm sorry."

"He — he's dead?" I couldn't comprehend that. None of us could, if the prolonged silence was any sign.

Geoffrey noted the time of death and wrote it down. He moved about the bed, doing other things, removing medical equipment, folding Grandfather's hands. All the while I stood there, not believing. Carl wrapped his arm around me.

At length Geoffrey stood back, making room for me, offering to give me a moment alone with Grandfather.

But I couldn't. I turned into Carl's outstretched arms as Geoffrey lifted the sheet over Grandfather's face.

As if Mama's death is replaying itself. I trembled, as I'd done in mourning. But how could I mourn after what I'd just learned? *You can't be gone. You haven't told me everything. You never told me about Mama! Did you ever see her again? Did you get her out? Is Lukas my father — or was there someone else?* I wanted to scream in agony and despair and frustration.

Carl cradled me in his arms, rocking me from side to side.

"Shall I telephone the mortuary?" Geoffrey quietly asked. "I pronounced the cause and time of death, but you'll need someone to pick up the body."

I couldn't do this alone. I looked to Carl. *Please, please take over for me.*

"*Ja,* that is good. *Danke schön,* Geoffrey."

"He received good care, Fräulein. You have no need to worry about that man — that Dr. Peterson. Herr Sommer's heart gave out, as we knew in time it would. I will vouch for that."

I couldn't turn, couldn't stop shaking.

"Come." Carl pulled me toward the door. "You must go to bed. I'll bring you some hot tea."

"No — no, I don't want to be alone. Please."

He pulled me toward the door. I glanced one last time at the sheet-covered form, not knowing what I felt, understanding only that this moment would not come again, and that every connection to my mother was severed.

38

Lieselotte Kirchmann
November 1944–April 1945

It had been more than a month since I'd crept back to Barracks 28 in the middle of the night, my dress torn and blood running down my legs. Mutter Kirchmann had cried over me and the Sisters had washed me as best they could, cleaning the bruises on my face and arms.

But they could do nothing about the terrible knot in my throat and the ache in my stomach. My heart had been ripped from my body — the body I'd saved so carefully, all of my life, for Lukas.

Over and over at night I woke, screaming from my nightmares or memories. Mutter Kirchmann held me in her arms and whispered, "Though a mother — or a father — forget their little child, I will not forget thee. God loves you, my Lieselotte. He loves you with His everlasting love, with the love of

His life."

I wanted to believe her. I knew she believed, and the Sisters so close to her believed. They radiated light — some life inside I could not see. But all the light had gone out of me. All I could see was Ravensbrück, the brutality, the cruelty of men and women, and the hatred.

It was not unusual for women worked to the bone and within an inch of life to miss their monthlies. No one thought anything of it as the days melted into one another. With no sanitation, it was better for all of us to be free of that curse. But when the morning sickness began, Mutter Kirchmann realized first what it meant.

"You must let me do the heavier pulling from now on. You must take special care — for you and your baby."

"This is not my baby! This is not —"

"New life — a life created by God in your womb, Lieselotte. A child to be brought into this world."

"How can you say that? How can you forget Lukas?"

"I never forget Lukas. How do you know the child does not belong to Lukas?"

I gasped and groaned. *Would that this is our baby! That I carry part of him in me!* "It can't be."

"How do you know? The time was so close together."

Sobs of uncertainty, of hope against hope, fought with disbelief and despair, racking my body. Light as I was, my heaving shifted the straw on our hard wooden pallet and must have awakened the woman who slept on the platform beneath us, a Dutch woman who worked in the dispensary.

"Shh," she whispered, reaching round the bunk for my arm. "You musn't let them know."

"If they knew, perhaps they'd grant lighter work —" Mutter Kirchmann began.

"*Nein. Nein!* All pregnancies are terminated or experimented upon. If you value your life, or the life of your baby, never let them know," she whispered.

If I value my life? If I value this life inside me? How can I live without Lukas, or live with the knowledge that this child might not be his, is probably not his?

"Let me see what I can do — something for the sickness, and some vitamins, maybe."

"*Ja, ja,*" Mutter Kirchmann enthused. "And she will need more to eat."

They meant well, but they were out of their minds. The only way to get more food was to steal it from the mouths of the women around me. I wouldn't do that. I

525

would die before I did that.

There were those willing to help me die, willing to end my nightmare quickly — without ever telling the guards. And there were those willing to help me kill my baby. I was not the only woman raped by guards — before or after incarceration at Ravensbrück. Some chose not to go on, or not to carry their child. I considered this.

But when it came to it, I wanted to live and wanted my baby to live. Mutter Kirchmann was right — I didn't know for certain that the baby was not Lukas's. Even if it wasn't, I could not take its life.

Though it hardly seemed possible, I didn't need to steal to survive. The Dutch woman slipped me vitamins, and the food, others offered freely. Not because Mutter Kirchmann asked them. As the days passed, one and then another realized I was pregnant with that sixth sense women have about such things. And strange as it may seem, in that dark and evil place, the child growing within me became a source of light and hope for them.

Often I'd find a crust of bread pressed into my pocket or a cup of the thin turnip gruel passed across bunks to me. At night, women, exhausted from their day's labor, sometimes touched my arm, sometimes reached shyly to rub my abdomen, smiling at their own memories.

In the factory, women, without a word, suddenly appeared on either side of me, helping to push the heavy cart, lightening my load. I hadn't the strength to thank them, but I wondered that they used their energy for me — for the child growing inside me.

"New life!" The more feeble of the Sisters often squeezed my hand in passing as smile lines wreathed her face. And I wondered that it was true. Could there be new life in Ravensbrück?

I cherished their care, but sometimes I felt such a fraud. Finally, I confided to the Sister, "But I don't even know if this is my husband's baby — if —"

"But God knows this is His child, just as you or I or anyone here."

"What if . . . what if that trash of a Nazi is the fa— ?"

"My dear," she laughed softly. "We're all trash. It's only His love and grace, His forgiveness, that make us clean." She wrapped her thin arm around me. "And it's only by forgiving that we can be free of that poison that would steal our life." She held my face in her hands. "Don't hate, my child. That's a prison worse than Ravensbrück."

■ ■ ■ ■

In early November a coat was issued to each prisoner, and we stopped going to the Siemens factory. Word spread that perhaps the factory had been bombed. Daily we wondered if the camp itself might be bombed. We never knew if the explosions we heard by night came from Allied bombs or if the Germans themselves destroyed bridges and land structures to keep their enemy at bay.

Guards grew more sadistic in their beatings as the weather turned colder — as if they didn't have enough to do, as if our suffering entertained them.

The Bible readings, the recitations of poems in different languages, the hymns sung by small groups and occasionally in a solo continued in the barracks at night. Sometimes I prayed, giving the outcome of our lives to God. And then I'd take it back and worry until I fell asleep, exhausted.

Mutter Kirchmann urged me to trust that God would provide all things needful. She reminded me of the Scripture Lukas gave me at our parting: "I can do all things through Christ Jesus who strengthens me."

"But can I do them in Ravensbrück?" I

asked, sarcastic.

"You can do them anywhere," she admonished. "Because He does it in you."

In late November the frail one of the Sisters weakened. The stronger Sister rubbed her pencil-thin legs by night and cradled her head to drink when she grew too weak to lift it after a long day's work. But even when she could no longer read her Bible aloud to the women at night, still, as she listened, her face shone as if she'd been to the top of the mountain and seen God Himself.

In December, the weak one was delivered to the infirmary, and the hole in our society gaped, a great chasm. The stronger Sister stole away every chance she found to glimpse her suffering sister through the hospital window — to offer smiles of encouragement and to reassure herself that her dearest one, through weak and in terrible pain, was still alive.

One day in mid-December, the stronger Sister came back too soon, a mixture of sorrow and grief in the stoop of her rounded shoulders. We knew without asking, and our hearts ached for this faithful Sister, and for ourselves. But we also breathed relief that our special light suffered no more, and even envy at the hope of what lay beyond the confines of Ravensbrück, of all this weary life.

The Dutch woman who worked in the dispensary snuck the Sister in to see her dear one before her body was sent to the crematorium.

"You should have seen her face," the Sister whispered to us later — her own face a study in contradictions. "So beautiful! A picture of peace, as it was when she was a young girl, so long before the war."

"Heaven!" Mutter Kirchmann whispered, the awe and wonder, the hope of our future, in one word. I wanted to believe.

The stronger Sister was released — called from the ranks of roll call one morning near the end of December — so unexpectedly that we didn't understand our terrible loss until nightfall. It was as if grandaunts had left our family circle, and their sweet voices — singing hymns in Dutch and sometimes in German — left a great void.

That night, Mutter Kirchmann insisted that I join them. I could not deny her, though my heart wasn't in it. And yet, the doing of the thing — the singing aloud, the praying, the listening to Scripture as it was translated into German from the Dutch Testament left behind by the Sisters —

made a difference. Something grew inside me — more slowly, more feebly than the child, but just as sure.

Sometime in what might have been the fourth month I felt the baby move — what Mutter Kirchmann called the quickening. It was in that moment that the baby first seemed real to me — as if it might actually grow and thrive. And what then? If the baby lived, how would I care for it? It was one thing to hide my pregnancy; quite another to hide a baby. And for the first time I knew I wanted to hide it, to protect it. But I could not do that alone.

A woman two bunks down and one across had once been a fine seamstress for wealthy patrons of the arts. She unraveled the hem of my uniform and, pulling away threads, found a way to gusset slim pieces in each side so that the seams didn't show. It was enough to accommodate the slight bump in my figure and to allow me to stuff extra newspapers up my coat as the temperatures dropped.

Roll call continued, despite the deep freeze and falling snow. Some mornings we stood for two hours as inches of snow covered us, stamping our feet to keep them from giving way beneath us. Mutter Kirchmann's hair had turned white in the few months we'd been here. By February, it was falling out in clumps.

"It's the poor nutrition. Not enough vitamins," the Dutch nurse lamented. "I see it every day."

"Take mine," I insisted to Mutter Kirchmann. "Your life means more to me than my own. I cannot live here without you."

"But you can, my dear, and you must."

"Nein." I would have sobbed if I'd had the energy.

"You must bring my grandchild into the world, and —"

"It may not be Lukas's child," I protested, but feebly.

"But our Lukas will love this child as his own, so of course it is my grandchild."

"How can he?" Though I desperately wanted him to. No matter the father, this child was mine — bone of my bone and flesh of my flesh.

"Because he loves you, because he —"

"What if he's not alive?" It was the question I asked each day, the one I feared to voice, the question that kept me from abandoning my heart to my baby.

"Then you must live for him, and raise this child for him. Never, never give up."

I couldn't imagine raising my child without Lukas and Mutter Kirchmann beside me. I couldn't imagine living — or my child living — beyond this pit of Ravensbrück.

"Remember what the Sister said. 'There is no pit so deep that He is not there.' " Mutter Kirchmann squeezed my hands, and I knew she'd read my thoughts. "Jesus loves you, my darling girl, and He is with you always, even when I cannot be, even if Lukas cannot be."

The bombing came still nearer. Rumors spread that the Russians had broken through German lines in the east, that prisoners must be moved west. Each morning at roll call new numbers were shouted and pulled from the ranks. Those prisoners were transported from camp — no one knew where. I prayed — more fiercely than I'd prayed for Lukas — that Mutter Kirchmann and I would not be separated.

It might have been late March when Mutter Kirchmann's number was called. Snow still lay on the ground, but morning light came earlier. She hesitated, waiting, I know, for my number to be called too. The numbers droned on — mine not among them. *No, dear God! No!*

The numbers finished. The women in line were counted and their numbers called off.

533

Mutter Kirchmann's number was shouted again, and the guard began walking down the ranks. She could not wait. Squeezing my hand, she mouthed, *"I love you, my Lieselotte. God be with you and the baby!"* She walked forward and followed the line inching through the door of the processing center.

How long we stood for roll call that morning, I don't know. It might have been forever. I grasped no sense of time.

Of all the things that had happened in Ravensbrück, being separated from Mutter Kirchmann was the worst, the most final, the thing that could not be undone or scabbed over or rationalized or prayed away or replaced in my heart.

That night, as I lay in my bunk, the space empty beside me, I could not cry. The shock was too deep, too great, to cry. I cradled my baby, willing it to move inside me, to reassure me that this life would not desert me. But how could I protect him or her? How could I protect a life so fragile?

Mutter Kirchmann's words trickled back to me — the same words Lukas had left me with: *"I can do all things through Christ Jesus who strengthens me."* And the Sister's words: *"There is no pit so deep He is not there."*

I was not sure.

A week later the Swedish Red Cross came and took hundreds of women away. I was not one of them.

Still another week passed. Sometimes I prayed that the bombs we heard in the east might come and blow us all away.

Finally, in what must have been early April, at predawn roll call, my number was read from the list. It took half a minute for me to realize, to understand that I must walk forward.

I passed through the processing center in a daze. There were no more checks, no inspections — just a herding of us through the forest to a spot beside the railroad on the outskirts of town, far from fields or townspeople.

Surely they mean to shoot us in this deserted place, so no one will hear — my first thought. My second was to wrap my arms around my middle, sorry that my baby, still barely a bump protruding from my abdomen, would know no life outside my womb, sorry that I would never know if my child was a boy or a girl, sorry that I'd never look in its face and hopefully see Lukas's eyes or mouth or nose.

But then the train came, stopping right

there, in the middle of the forest. A long metal ramp was shoved to the ground.

"*Schnell!* Get aboard!"

We fumbled and climbed into the cattle cars, pushing one another forward, too weak to pull ourselves up.

No checking of numbers from endless lists — just more shouting and shoving. The only counting came when a guard barked, "One hundred!" and pushed the heavy door through its metal groove until it slammed, sealing us in the dark.

39

Hannah Sterling
April-May 1973

A week later, Carl stood beside me as I collected the urn with Grandfather's ashes. Long ago, Grandfather had made arrangements for cremation. That, too, was a first for me. The whole idea of burning bodies brought horrific images to my imagination.

"It's not the same thing as what they did in the camps," Carl counseled quietly.

"I know. I just . . . just wish I could undo all of it. His whole life. What he did to my mother, to everyone he touched."

"You cannot cancel another man's sins. We cannot even cancel our own."

I closed my eyes.

"But you can continue what you started."

"I . . . I don't know if I can. No, I can't. I can't."

"You will keep the remainder, then?"

"No, of course not. There must be someone — those organizations that you mentioned that find people . . . perhaps they can return the items."

"As long as it is not you; is that what you mean?"

"I didn't steal them, Carl. I didn't send people to their deaths. You know as well as I do that nothing I've returned has made anyone happy."

"Happy," Carl repeated. "Did you expect them to be happy?"

Maybe I did. Maybe I expected them to be glad to have their things returned. I thought, at least — I don't know . . . that they would know I was trying. But that didn't even sound right. It wasn't about me. Why was I making it about me?

"Perhaps," Carl said softly, "there is more of the journey important for you, if not for them. You still don't know about your mother — what happened to her after the camp — or about your father."

"Grandfather's dead. Your parents didn't know. Who is there left to ask other than Dr. Peterson, who seems to have conveniently disappeared? I can't see him being helpful, and I don't know that I'd believe anything he told me."

"Then we need to find someone who knew your mother or Frau Kirchmann in the camp."

I nearly dropped Grandfather's urn. "Is that possible? Can we find such a person?"

"A prisoner of Ravensbrück? That should not be impossible — there are lists. But there is someone else we must find as well. And perhaps that person can lead us to the first."

"You mean Lukas — or Marta, the youngest Kirchmann."

Carl smiled, nodding.

"But your parents said they'd gone — moved away. All our searching has turned up nothing. We don't even know if they're still alive, or still living in Germany."

"This is true." He took the urn from me before I dropped it. "All it means is that we haven't searched in the right place."

It took three weeks of letter writing and phone calls, of Carl translating endless pages of questions and then translating my answers, of reassuring the powers that be that our motives were pure, that I was only trying to locate someone who remembered my mother.

Finally, Carl tracked down the barracks my mother and Frau Kirchmann had been assigned to, and in the process found the name of a woman who'd been incarcerated in Ravensbrück at the same time and assigned to the same barracks. He telephoned her and she agreed to see us on Saturday.

With a stop for luncheon, the drive to the outskirts of Cologne took just over five hours. "Helga Brunner . . . she's seventy-seven now? Do you think she'll remember my mother?"

"She's likely to remember one of the Kirchmann women. Frau Kirchmann was more her age."

"Yes, of course." I drummed my nails against my knee. I felt like I was going to meet my mother for the first time — which was silly. *Please, God, please let me see her as she was. Help me understand the woman she was before life and Grandfather changed her.*

We stood before the painted black door and rang the bell. It took a few minutes — minutes in which I almost despaired of anyone answering — before we heard the slow but rhythmic tapping of a cane and the shuffling of slippered feet.

The door opened to reveal a woman who looked more than ninety.

"Frau Brunner?" Carl asked.

"*Ja?* I am Helga Brunner. You are . . . ?"

"Carl Schmidt, a friend and driver of Hannah Sterling, the daughter of the woman we wanted to talk with you about. Do you remember my telephone call?"

"I am old, young man, and a bit decrepit, not senile."

"Forgive me, Frau Brunner, I —"

"Never mind. You are young, as if that is an excuse. Come in, come in."

"*Danke schön,* Frau Brunner." I stepped through the door. "I can't tell you how much this means to me. There's so much I want to know about my mother." I followed her into her sitting room and bit my lip to stop my babbling.

She motioned us toward her settee while she sat down heavily in a straight-back chair and pushed her three-pronged cane aside, staring at me through thick glasses. "You don't look much like your Mutter."

"You remember her? Lieselotte Kirchmann?"

"Lieselotte? *Nein, nein!* I mean, I did not know her name, but she was the young one. There were two women together — like mother and daughter, but not by birth." She smiled softly. "So, our little mama finally got her answer."

"Her answer? Anything you can tell me about my mother I would truly appreciate."

"You say that now, but you may not appreciate all I have to tell, what I remember.

541

Horrendous days. Truth is often hard to understand, sometimes harder to believe."

"I'm not afraid to hear whatever you might say."

She nodded, and her rheumy eye took my measure. "Perhaps. It is difficult — very difficult — to learn of violations to your mother, your grandmother."

"My grandmother?" My throat constricted; I was certain she did not mean Elsa Sommer. "My mother never told me the name of my real father. She married someone after the war — an American, who raised me as his own. I've only learned, since Mama's death, that he could not have been my birth father. She didn't know him then." *The math wasn't right. Oh, Aunt Lavinia, if you could see me now.*

Frau Brunner's eyes rose and she nodded slowly. "That war produced a great many orphans, and stories to explain their existence."

I wasn't sure I understood. "Please tell me anything you know, anything you even suspect from that time."

Frau Brunner shifted in her seat, straightening her back. She closed her eyes and remembered aloud, "We told each other our stories — a half-dozen times, a dozen. We rehearsed lines of plays. We shared the

542

tedious details of recipes, how to turn a collar, how to smock a dress, how to knit a particularly difficult pattern. We recited Scripture and poems and sang songs until our vocal cords could not contribute anything more. Starving and thirsty and beaten, but we talked on — whenever we could get away with it."

"You were a community of women." I understood how important that could be, at least in theory.

"We did all to survive, to keep our sanity. The Nazis did everything to dehumanize us — to steal our dignity. Talking about daily life, the life we'd left behind, reminded us of who we were."

I remembered Herr Horowitz and bit my lip. "You were already there when my mother came?"

She nodded. "Such a pretty girl — so frightened. She stuck like glue to her mother-in-law. But the older woman could not keep the guards away."

"The guards?" I felt the sickening rumble of snares in my stomach.

"You are certain you want to hear?"

"Yes, please." I held my breath.

"She'd been married such a short time."

"Two days, when they arrested her, I think."

"*Ja,* two days with her husband and his family. I did not know the full story, but I gathered that her father did not approve the marriage, that he denounced them, turned them in — the entire family of her husband — to the Gestapo."

I nodded, swallowing.

"The older woman was rumored to be half-Jewish, but some mistake in the lists occurred and she was not sent to the Jew barracks — which assuredly saved her life. She and the young one, both convicted of harboring Jews — a criminal offense — were assigned to our barracks.

"The older woman encouraged the younger to tell the guard that there had been a great mistake, to contact her father — an important Nazi who would surely reward him handsomely. But the girl refused to leave her — like a daughter to her, and the older woman a mother. A Ruth and Naomi pairing, if I ever saw such. I think of them so."

Thank You, God, that Mama had such a woman in her life as Frau Kirchmann. What would it be like to have a mother love me like that?

"When they had taken our clothes and shoes and shaved our hair, they stole even our names, that remnant of our identity.

Numbers replaced them."

"Did you know Frau Kirchmann's name — the older Frau Kirchmann?"

Frau Brunner opened her eyes and smiled sadly. "I remember all the numbers of the women in that barracks, shouted out in roll call day after day. The ones who walked out at the end and the ones who never walked out. But I did not know their names — at least not most of their names."

"I understand."

"As I said . . ." Frau Brunner closed her eyes as if it helped her remember. "The young woman, so very beautiful — I still see her golden hair. There was one guard in particular, very soon after the two women arrived . . . Something to do with a mix-up in the names of the older woman's daughter and a search for the missing daughter of a Nazi Party member — I don't know how it happened that he knew."

"Yes, Carl's parents said that the day they were arrested, the youngest girl was away. They must have thought my mother was that girl, her sister-in-law — at least that's what we think."

"Possibly. The older woman worried over her daughter but was careful not to speak of it much. Informants in the barracks — always. Information was exchanged for a slice of bread, a bit of potato, a needle and thread, old newspaper to line our clothes against the cold. If word got out that there was a family member not arrested, they would surely go after her. If not, she might be safe."

"The women turned on one another?"

Frau Brunner shrugged. "*Ja,* for favors. But not all. You must understand this. We were shouted at day and night, called bad names . . . no longer treated as human, and in time, we stopped thinking of ourselves as human. That is what they wanted, what they worked toward — to dehumanize us, to make us compliant so we responded submissively, without thinking, without reasoning. Under such circumstances, it does not take long to behave as a mangy dog begging a bone — to fight one another over bones."

"Someone reported my mother?"

Frau Brunner shook her head. "This I do not know, but a guard learned that her father was a Nazi. One night, as we returned from work at the factory, the guard pulled the younger woman from our ranks. I don't know all that happened, but I think she believed her father appeared — that he rejected her."

"Her father saw her there, and left?" Carl broke in.

"*Ja*, this is true — so she thought. She believed she heard his voice." Frau Brunner shrugged. "At any rate, she was not released." She sighed as if the story had sapped her energy. "None of us chose Ravensbrück. We all suffered, some more than others."

"Grandfather actually left her there. He was there, and he walked away, leaving his daughter." I said the words, still trying to comprehend.

"*Ja*. But the guard was not through. He'd expected reward for his discovery and evidently received reprimand. He wanted revenge."

"Revenge?" I wasn't sure I wanted to hear this.

Frau Brunner stared at me so long I thought she might have forgotten my question. "He raped her. And then he brought two others to rape her."

The world dropped from beneath my feet. *Mama! Oh, Mama!*

"She missed her monthly. But that was not unusual. So little food and we were worked so hard that most women dried up. It didn't take long."

"She was preg—"

"*Ja*, she was pregnant, and she kept the baby, though she risked her life to do so."

Frau Brunner smiled. "When were you born, Hannah?"

"June 5, 1945."

"A miracle from Ravensbrück."

I pulled away. "You've just told me my father was a Nazi — a criminal guard."

"Nein," she retorted. "This I did not say. I say only that your mother did not know the father of her baby, that she risked everything to carry her baby. Pregnant women were eliminated or experimented upon — and yet here you are, alive.

"Two sisters — Dutch women, I think . . . Such preachers they were. They and the older woman and perhaps a half dozen of us women in the barracks worked to help your mother carry you. We shared our food — a crust of bread here and there, only — but that was our ration, our thread to life. We kept the little mama warm at night and took turns doing what we could to make her load lighter in the day while we all worked, nearly to death.

"One of the sisters died — I don't know her name. But I remember her as a bright light. That is all I can say — she radiated light among us. And then the other sister — the one who has written the book about it all — was released not so very long after."

"And the baby lived." But she ignored me.

"Finally, the two women — the older first, and later the younger, your Mutter — were sent away. I don't know where. Many women were shipped or marched elsewhere near the end of the war."

She sat back, taking me in. "Until Herr Schmidt telephoned me, I thought perhaps they had perished. Now, I see they live on in you." She smiled. "The promise of a baby brought life and hope to our barracks, no matter that we all risked our lives to see you live. She could have aborted you — there were ways. But she didn't. She chose to give you life."

"But my father —"

"*Nein,* I say again, she didn't know the father — how could she tell? Her husband? One of those wicked guards? But seeing you now, I believe . . . yes, I believe you must have been her husband's child. How else could you have the eyes of her Naomi?"

We drove back to Berlin, stopping only for dinner in a lovely old hotel. But the restaurant's mesmerizing music — Frank Sinatra in English — the warmth of the snapping wood fire, the sweet white dessert wine, and the yellow table roses served only to mellow me to the point of sleepiness, and numbness.

"It's been an exhausting day for you." Carl kneaded my palm with his fingers.

"I just keep thinking about my mother. Wondering how she endured any of it. Everything Frau Brunner told me about her — I never knew. And I can't help but wonder if her memories are reliable."

"She mentioned two sisters. Have you heard of them?"

"No."

"I remember a few women with the same name from the lists I saw. One was Cornelia ten Boom and her sister — very much in the news these days. She's written a book — her story of her time in Ravensbrück. *The Hiding Place,* they call it."

"So they really were there at the same time, or else Frau Brunner has read the book and incorporated their story into her memories."

"I do not doubt her mental capacity. The thing that I could not comprehend was how Herr Sommer saw his daughter in that vile place and did nothing to help her, to save her."

"She wouldn't bend to his will." It was the thing I knew most about Grandfather, the thing I could also understand about my mother.

"*Nein,* but how could he abandon and

condemn his own child? This I cannot understand."

I pressed his hand in return. "That's
because you're a good man. Not all men
are good."

Carl shook his head. "He spent an entire
life scheming and stealing and condemning
others to fates worse than death . . . and for
what? What did he gain? A closet full of
treasures he could not enjoy, did not dare
to show to the world? And no one to share
them with. A pitiable, wasted life."

"I can't pity him. And I can't forgive him.
I'll never forgive him, and yet I'm so very
sad."

"No, Hannah. Such bitterness will eat you
away. Do not let him rob your life as well."

"I'll take that risk. He's dead and ashes,
but I still want to shake him."

"Shake him? Is that an American cure?"
He smiled.

"Maybe a Southern one — a good old
North Carolina mountain-man cure."

"And you are now a mountain woman? I
thought you were the 'miracle of
Ravensbrück.' " He smiled broader, but not
in a teasing way.

"It's a miracle that I lived — that my
mother kept me. But I don't know why. I
can't help but think Frau Brunner was

romanticizing about Frau Kirchmann being my grandmother. How can she remember her eyes after all these years?

"And although I hate to say it, I don't think my mother especially loved me. She kept me at arm's length. If anything, I think that would be proof that she didn't believe I was Lukas's daughter, that I was . . . the child of . . ." I couldn't say it.

"And for you, this is hard?"

"Well, of course it's hard! To think I might have been the product of my mother's multiple raping? I'm sick. I'm absolutely sick."

"Then we must learn the identity of your father — if we can."

"I don't see how that's possible. Frau Brunner said Mama and her mother-in-law were sent away. Even she didn't know where. We don't know what happened to them. I don't even know how Mama met my fa— Joe Sterling."

"You're forgetting Lukas and Marta."

"Finding them might explain what happened to them, but they won't be able to tell me who my father is — not if Mama didn't know."

"Frau Brunner only said your Mutter didn't know in Ravensbrück. Perhaps she knew later."

"I can't change the past. But, oh, I wish Lukas could be my father. I would so prefer that to — to —"

"We must find him — and Marta."

"That will certainly require a miracle."

"Another miracle." Carl squeezed my hand. "I believe they follow you, Hannah Sterling."

When we returned to Berlin, we found the police surrounding Grandfather's house, tramping the snow in and out of the front and back doors. The neighbor across the street, the same one Geoffrey had observed spying on Dr. Peterson's tirade, had reported the burglary.

Carl spoke at length with the policeman in German, as well as Frau Huber, the neighbor. I waited as patiently as I could.

When they'd finished, Carl turned to me, eyebrows raised. "Thanks to the inquisitive Frau Huber, the illustrious Dr. Peterson is now in custody."

"You're kidding. He tried to break in?"

"Ach, he broke in, for certain. Frau Huber saw us leave this morning, knew the house was empty."

"I'll bet she did." I smiled, and Carl winked.

"So, when she saw the curtains suddenly

drawn closed and no car in the drive, she suspected someone was in the house and telephoned the *Polizei*. By the time they arrived, Dr. Peterson was on his way out the door with fifty thousand marks."

"Fifty thou—"

"Shh." Carl pulled me aside. "Evidently there was a safe built into the floor in the library. That is what was robbed."

"I didn't know one existed."

"Peterson evidently knew."

"That's why he wanted the house and the ledger. Do you think that means he doesn't know about —"

"I suspect Herr Sommer never showed it to him, though perhaps he knows about it in theory and intended to find it. This safe must contain all Herr Sommer had converted to cash."

"Then Dr. Peterson has no idea how much —"

"Probably not."

"Excuse me, Carl; I must thank Frau Huber personally — and profusely."

40

Lieselotte Kirchmann
April 1945

I lost track of the days spent on the floor of the stationary cattle car. Day passed into night and night into day, and the cycle repeated. Surely we'd been forgotten. Then, without warning, the door would slide open and a basket of turnips might be thrown in, or a pail of water set just inside before the door slammed shut again. Those nearest the door got the water. The rest of us had fallen too weak to fight for it. One by one, each day, another closed her eyes forever.

When the train finally moved, it rattled our bones so hard we could not bear to lean against the sides of the car, could not bear to lean against one another. We'd grown so thin, our bones protruding, that we sat on our hands to protect our buttocks and tailbones from the jostling of the train. I did my best to protect the little bump at my waist, but could not imagine how my little one survived, certain — dreading — that one day I would no longer feel movement.

Bombing continued day and night. We gave up cowering at the explosions, waiting for the hit. *Let it be a merciful death,* became my prayer.

Guards called for the dead each morning. What they did with the corpses — if they were buried by the side of the tracks or thrown to wild animals or simply left to rot in the sun — I did not know. I knew only it was a relief to have the door slide open, to breathe fresh air for a moment, and to see daylight.

It gave me an opportunity to peek into a world from beyond time. I couldn't separate my sleeping from waking, though I no longer dreamed. None of us dreamed any-more. Days and nights became one. If I could have slipped into oblivion, I would thankfully have done so.

Finally, the doors were pushed wide. *"Schnell! Raus!"*

But we were so very weak — those of us left — that we could barely stumble from the car to the ground. The sun blinded. I blinked against the sudden pain and stag-gered forward, following the woman in front of me, allowing those behind to push me along.

More orders, more shouting as we marched through new gates. We were assigned to low bunkers — holes in the ground — and the bombing continued.

Between bombing raids we walked outside, talked with other prisoners — something we'd not been allowed to do at Ravensbrück. Prisoners asked newcomers for names, towns, news of relatives and of the war. They called out names of loved ones — real names, not numbers.

And so, I began begging, "Kirchmann, Kirchmann," wherever I went. The name tasted good in my mouth. No energy to talk, to ask more, but they understood, and shook their heads.

Guards called for work details, but those too emaciated were not sent. Day after day, I wandered from bunker to bunker under the watchful eye of guards toting machine guns as they stood sentinel in high towers. I wandered as far as allowed, searching for Mutter Kirchmann. And then, one day, there were no guards in the towers — they'd simply vanished.

I couldn't think what new horror that might mean, but I wandered farther than I ever had before, pleading, "Kirchmann,

Kirchmann," expecting no answer.

A woman stopped me. "You're from Ravensbrück — I remember you there." That she recognized me when I couldn't have recognized myself was a miracle. But the faded number on her coat looked vaguely familiar.

"Ja."

"I was in Barracks 28 with you — and the Sisters. Do you remember?"

"Ja, the Sisters, and my mother-in-law, Frau Kirchmann."

"Frau Kirchmann? She's here — with me. She led our hymn singing until — she's very weak. I don't think she'll ma—"

"Where? Where is she?" Life surged through my veins for the first time since Mutter Kirchmann had been taken away.

"Come."

I followed her into a bunker several buildings beyond, praying the discovery would be real and worth the terrible effort to walk so far. The smell ranked awful — even worse than in my own barracks. Sickly sweet and rotting — like meat gone to maggots.

"There, by the wall. It's good you've come. I don't think she'll live the night."

Lies! I won't listen to lies. "Mutter Kirchmann . . . Mutter Kirchmann!" I knelt beside the sleeping form — gaunt cheeks and sunken eyes, matted hair so thin and white. No rise or fall came to her chest. I feared I'd come too late. *No!* I laid my head on her bunk beside her arm and would have cried if I could have mustered tears.

I closed my eyes. Moments passed, minutes, perhaps hours.

"Lieselotte." The whisper came like angel's breath.

A precious dream. I would not open my eyes lest it fade.

"My Lieselotte."

I lifted my head to see the supreme effort speech cost her. "Mutti Kirchmann."

She closed her eyes again and smiled. "Thank You, Father. Thank You." Her breathing grew labored, and then so peaceful I thought she'd passed, but she hadn't. "Baby?"

"The baby lives." My throat caught. *Barely.* I pulled her hand to my stomach. As if on cue, the little one kicked.

"And so must you," she whispered.

"We'll all live. The guards are gone — only a few officers remain. The bombing's almost stopped. The Allies must be very near; it won't be long now."

But even as I talked, rattling on, I felt her fading. *No! Hold on! Please, hold on!*

When she stopped breathing, I couldn't

be sure. I crawled in the bunk beside her, gently lifting her head to my shoulder, cradling it against my chest. More mother than my own mother, I could not let her go.

Night fell and the woman from Ravensbrück urged me to return to my barracks, to get my ration. I couldn't — wouldn't — move.

"They'll take her away in the morning. We're to stack the bodies of the dead outside the building. She can't stay here — not now."

But I rolled over, stretching my arm across Mutter Kirchmann, determined to protect her, to keep them from taking her away.

"Until morning, then, but then you'll both have to go. If they come back, catch you here . . ."

I didn't listen. I closed my eyes and thought of Lukas, of all the Kirchmanns, blessed and loved, on my wedding day. Now there would be one less . . . and perhaps one more.

Morning came, but no rations. Two of the women pulled me from the bunk and carried Mutter Kirchmann to the yard, laying her stiffened body on top of a heap of rotting corpses awaiting pickup outside the bunker.

I stood beside her for the longest time, the early-morning chill seeping through my coat. I couldn't leave her. If the Allies were truly coming, they could help me get her home to Berlin, where Vater Kirchmann could bury her, where Lukas and I could lay flowers on her grave and light candles in the night, where we could tell our precious child about her — or his — beloved grand-mother all the years of our lives. If I could be the mother to my baby that Mutter Kirchmann was to me, life might come full circle.

I waited until the women from the bunker moved away before crawling on top of the heap of corpses, wound my fingers through Mutter Kirchmann's stiff ones, and closed my eyes.

41

Hannah Sterling
May 1973

I woke the next morning, relieved beyond words that Dr. Peterson was locked behind bars, that I no longer needed to wonder if he might appear brandishing a pistol over my bed in the night.

But a robbery is a violation, even when the perpetrator's caught and put away. *I've had enough of Berlin. I must talk with Carl about dispensing the rest of the cache. I need to get out of this house, to go home . . . but where is home? Not Berlin. And not the mountain — not anymore. Winston-Salem? What will it be like to return to teaching after leading a life out of an Agatha Christie novel?*

The telephone rang as I poured coffee in the kitchen. I jumped — something I did too often now — sighed, and headed for the hall phone, balancing my cup and saucer in one hand, sure my coffee would grow cold by the time I took my first sip.

"Hello?"

"Fräulein Sterling? Fräulein Hannah Sterling?" The German accent came thick.

"Yes, this is Hannah Sterling."

"My name is Frau Goldfarb. I believe you are looking for me."

"Goldfarb? I'm sorry, I don't think so." *Who in the world?*

"You may know me better as Marta Kirchmann."

I nearly dropped the phone. I did drop my coffee — all over my favorite robe. "Marta Kirchmann? Marta Kirchmann?" I couldn't stop saying her name.

"*Ja,* Hannah. I knew your mother, Lieselotte, and I loved her very much."

I gasped upon hearing my mother's name. Tears sprang from somewhere deep inside. I couldn't speak, couldn't control the shaking of my hands.

"Are you there?"

"Yes, yes, I'm here. I'm just so — so surprised." *And I can barely breathe! Thank You, God! Oh, thank You!*

"Would you like to meet me? For I would like very much to meet you."

"Yes, oh yes, I would like that. I would love that."

"I've spoken with your young man. He

563

knows where I live."

"My young man?" I repeated, realizing she meant Carl. *Is Carl my "young man"?*

"*Ja,* he sounds very nice." I heard the smile in her voice. "He knows where to come. Tomorrow — shall we say at two?"

"*Ja* — yes. Oh, thank you, Frau — Frau —"

"Goldfarb. But you may call me Marta."

"Thank you . . . Marta. I'm looking forward — very much — to meeting you."

"We have much to talk about. And I have photographs you may wish to see."

"Of Mama? Of my mother?"

"*Ja* . . . and more. Come and see."

"I will. I surely will. Thank you so much! *Danke schön!*"

"*Bitte schön.* I will see you tomorrow."

"Yes, yes." I hung the phone in the cradle. *Thank You, Father in heaven. Thank you, Carl.*

Carl picked me up at noon and drove me to the café for lunch.

"I'm sorry, I'm just too excited to eat. She sounded so . . . sweet and happy. Do you realize she's the first happy-sounding person I've met in Germany?"

"Well, I don't like the sound of that," Carl huffed.

"Oh, I don't mean you — I mean all the

people connected with the Holocaust."

He shrugged. "You expected something different?"

"No, of course not. But you know how they always say that something good comes out of something bad? Can't there be in this?"

"A silver lining to the Holocaust? It is a question beyond my comprehension. Over six million Jews died, and many millions more besides — other targets of Hitler and countless civilians, soldiers. The cost in human life . . . staggering, unbelievable. I think it is not a question that any of those we've met would appreciate."

"I know, that's not the right question. Maybe the question is, what can I do to redeem this? What good can I bring out of the horror?"

"Perhaps it is not our job to bring redemption — not that we shouldn't do all we can to reduce suffering, but we can't change what happened; we can't make it right."

"I just so want it to be right, to change things," I pleaded.

Carl lifted my hand and kissed my fingers.

We reached Frau Goldfarb's just before two. I wanted to run to the door. I wanted to run away from it. *Will Lukas be here too?*

Has he come? Marta would know, if anyone would, about my father. She'd know what happened to Mama, to Lukas, to them all. *And she wants to meet me.* The wonder of that stole my breath.

"Knock on the door, Hannah." Carl stepped aside. "Knock, so it will be opened for you."

The knot in my throat and drums in my stomach snapped to attention. I'd barely raised my fist to knock when the door flung open.

"Hannah! Hannah!" The joyous woman — tall and thin — across the threshold drew me into her arms as if I were her long-lost prodigal child. "Lieselotte's daughter — let me look at you."

She pushed me gently away and ran her eyes over me, from head to toe and back again. Tears spilled from her eyes and mine. I couldn't speak. I couldn't articulate anything.

"Come in, come in!" She grabbed my hand and pulled me inside, Carl on my heels. "Let me take your coats. Here, now, run ahead into the sitting room. I hope you're famished, because I've been cooking and baking — ach, this is like Christmas!"

I walked into a medium-size room painted a soft yellow. The furniture was covered in a

566

raised rose fabric — welcoming and pretty over heavy dark wood. Globed table lamps glowed pink and yellow, making everything warm and lovely. The mantel over a blazing fire shone, crowded with old black-and-white and sepia-toned photographs. I'd never seen the people pictured there, but somehow they looked familiar.

Marta pulled me to the settee, never taking her eyes from me. "You're so like her."

"Like Mama? Like *meine Mutter*?" I said doubtfully.

"Hmm." She considered, then smiled. "*Nein.* More like mine."

"Yours?"

"Wait here." She squeezed my hands and hopped up, years falling from her stride. She pulled a framed portrait from the mantel. "Do you see the resemblance?" She pointed to a dark-haired woman, slim, tall, younger than me, laughing and happy on her wedding day.

"This could almost be me. This *could* be me!"

"*Ja, ja,*" Marta laughed. "This is *meine Mutter,* and Lukas's *Mutter.* This is Hannah Kirchmann."

"Hannah? Her name is Hannah?"

"*Ja,* my dear, dear girl. It was. And you look like your father. I look into your eyes and I see *mein Bruder,* Lukas, and *meine Mutter."*

Lukas is my father. My father! But where is he? Please, God. "Carl's parents said they think Lukas survived the war?" I couldn't keep the hope from my voice.

"*Ja,* he did, but he was never the same. He had been a strong man. They broke his bones — his fingers and toes. They starved and beat him to tell them names of others who helped smuggle Jews across the borders, but he did not tell — not one name. You come from strong stock."

"I don't understand. Why did Mama marry again if Lukas — if my father — was still alive?"

"Ach, but she did not know he was alive." A veil fell over Marta's features. "Carl told me that neither of you know what happened after Ravensbrück." She breathed deeply. "I will tell you all I have learned.

"Near the end, we knew Germany would lose the war. The Allies were all but at the door, and the Nazis began covering their tracks — erasing whatever evidence they could of the horrors they had committed. They knew that the world would hold them accountable. They consolidated prisoners. Death marches and gassings and shootings increased."

"We met a woman — Frau Brunner — who said Mama and . . . and Grandmother . . . left Ravensbrück." *I have a grandmother — had a grandmother. I bear her name. This is my family.*

"*Ja,* this is true. Trainloads of women were sent to Dachau. For days the trains sat on the tracks — locked — while the administration of the camp ran away and new crews replaced them. By the time the Americans came, many — most — in the cars had died. Even in the camp, corpses were stacked high."

"But what about — ?"

"A few weeks — not long — after the liberation, an American soldier came to find Lukas."

"My fa— Sterling. Joe Sterling."

"*Ja.*" Marta nodded and hesitated, looking away. "He told me about Lieselotte, that he had found her in a heap of corpses at Dachau — a heap the Nazis had not had time to bury. He said her fingers were intertwined with those of an older woman — a woman who was dead." She turned to me once more. "I wanted to believe him, believe that the woman was *meine Mutter,* that Lieselotte had been with her when she closed her eyes on this world. Lieselotte was a daughter to her, as much as I — more

569

than I, at the end." Marta picked up her mother's portrait. "He said Lieselotte was in the hospital and very ill. He did not tell me that she carried a child. But he said that he could get medical help for her to save her life if he could marry her."

"What?"

"American GI medical benefits, he said. He knew there was not enough medicine — not enough German doctors or hospitals — for all the needs of those suffering after the war, but he said that Americans take care of their own. He said she would die if she didn't get treatment."

"But what about Lukas?"

Marta shrugged, as if helpless. "Neither he nor Father had returned from the camp, though others had. I feared he was dead. I believed all my family dead." Marta's eyes pleaded with me to understand. "Lieselotte was my only family member left alive — so I thought. She had taken my place in the camp. Because she was arrested, because she gave my name as her own, they never came looking for me. She saved my life." She hesitated. "I believed Joe Sterling. I believed him when he said that Lieselotte was dying and that marrying her was the only way she could receive the treatment that might save her life."

"But she was already married!" I wanted to turn back time. I wanted them all — Marta, Mama, Joe — to make different choices. "You had no verification that Lukas was dead."

Tears fell from Marta's eyes. "No, I did not. Records were destroyed in the bombing. I told Joe they could pretend that she'd never married. He said that the marriage need only be for a little while — long enough for her to get the treatment she needed — and he would return her to me before he was sent stateside. He promised. He seemed so kind . . . sincere."

"I don't understand. Joe Sterling raised me as his own child. He never brought Mama or me to Germany."

"No."

"And Lukas came back."

"Two months later — a wreck of a man, very weak and broken. He weighed less than a ten-year-old child. Nothing like the man the Gestapo arrested. Nothing like the man Lieselotte married."

Marta stood and walked to the mantel, retrieving another photograph, and handed it to me. My heart nearly stopped. *Mama — and Lukas, my father.*

"Their wedding day — evening. It was a simple affair — a secret affair to keep it from Lieselotte's father. This picture I snapped is the only evidence that remains.

"I thought Lieselotte would come back the moment she recovered. I explained to Lukas what happened. And though it broke his heart that she might marry another — even if it was only on paper — he got a little better with the hope of seeing her. But another month passed and she did not come. Eventually I went to the American base and asked for Joe Sterling, but was told that he and his wife had gone to America. My heart was sick. How could I tell Lukas?"

"Did you tell him?"

"I waited the year, hoping he would recover more, and if he recovered — when he recovered — we could find her, go to her."

"But he didn't."

"Perhaps, if Lieselotte had been here . . . I wrote to the American base in Oklahoma where Lieutenant Sterling was stationed, but the letters were returned, with scribbles across them: *Moved — Left No Forwarding Address.*"

"You must have found her — sometime."

"*Ja.* Three, maybe four years later I spoke to an American soldier stationed in Berlin. I told him I was trying to reach an old friend — Lieutenant Sterling and his wife, Lieselotte. He pitied me. He said it was hard for German brides in America and knew she'd be comforted to have a friend write from home."

"By then Mama and Daddy'd moved to the mountains of North Carolina." *Joe wasn't my father. Why didn't he return Mama to Lukas and Marta, like he promised?*

"*Ja,* I do not think Joe wanted me to find her. I know he did not."

I pulled the banded group of envelopes from my purse — the envelopes I'd carried with me ever since Ward Beecham had given me the key to Mama's safe-deposit box. "These came from you?"

Marta turned the envelopes around, adjusted her glasses, and read the return address. "Where did you find these? Lieselotte kept my letters?"

"No. I don't know. Maybe she didn't want Daddy — Joe — to see them, or maybe she kept them hidden somewhere else. I found these envelopes in her safe-deposit box after she died, but no letters. It was part of the trail that led me to you. But Carl's parents said that you and Lukas had moved. Is he . . . is my father still alive?" I'd been desperate to know, afraid to ask. Once the answer came it could not be undone.

"I am sorry, Hannah. In the camp, Lukas

contracted tuberculosis. So many developed diseases — no sanitation, no medicine. After the war there was not enough help. He struggled to get home. He fought to recover, and lived a few years . . . but what shall I say?" Marta wiped the moisture from her eyes. "I am not surprised Lieselotte never told you about your father, but I am sorry she did not. He was a very brave man, a good man. He saved many lives, but he could not save his own."

My father . . . my own father — a good man, a generous and loving man. If only I'd known you. If only there was time for us. But you're gone. Oh, Mama, why didn't you tell me? Why didn't you come back? What made you stay away? You hated Joe — I know you did! "Did she write back to you?"

"*Ja,* at first. She was astonished to learn that Lukas lived. Lieutenant Sterling had told her that he'd gone in search of Lukas and his family, but that we had all perished in the war. Because Lieselotte believed that, she believed the rest. Lieutenant Sterling convinced her that the child she carried could only be born alive if she received treatment and that the treatment she needed could only be found in America. He promised to return her to Germany if she ever wanted to come."

"But he didn't return her."

"Because it was not true. It was a lie to make her marry him." Marta set the photographs on the coffee table. "Lieutenant Sterling spoke some German, but Lieselotte spoke so little English before she left Germany. How was she to know? She trusted him. Anyway, who could she ask for help?

"Of all the things he was guilty of — lying and stealing another man's wife and child — I think Joe Sterling did love you. Lieselotte wrote me that."

"I don't understand why he wanted to marry her. Mama couldn't have been that beautiful after so many months in concentration camps. Why did he concoct such a story?"

"War makes men mad. Mad men do mad things." Marta shook her head. "I only know what Lieselotte wrote — that he was injured in the war and could not have children of his own. Somehow, he believed that if he married this pitiful, pregnant woman he'd rescued, he could not only become a father to her child, but in some way he could redeem his part in the horrors of that war, redeem the lives he'd stolen by saving this one — these two."

"Mama hated him. I never understood, but now I see why. Why didn't she leave him? Why didn't she return to Lukas?"

"Don't you know?" Marta smiled sadly. "Perhaps that is because you are not yet a mother." She leaned back against the settee. "She wanted to leave. She begged him for a divorce and to help her return to Germany. She wanted to take you, bring you to Lukas, even knowing he was ill and not likely to recover. She wanted to be with him, her first love and her husband. But Joe Sterling refused. He said he would keep you, that she would never be allowed to leave the country with you." She shrugged. "His name was listed as the father on your birth certificate. He had every legal right to keep you."

"They fought. They fought nearly all the time. Or they were silent."

"He went for you, for your mother, you know."

"What?"

"Once Lukas knew your mother lived, that you existed, nothing could stop him. He recovered enough to work — a full year — before he saved sufficient money to go to America. He told me only that he saw Lieselotte and that he spoke with Joe Sterling. He never said what happened, only that she could not return to Germany, that it was right she did not come."

Marta sighed. "Whatever happened between them, or with Joe, it broke his heart. The letters from Lieselotte stopped. I wrote again and again, but my letters were returned, unopened, marked *Refused.* I knew Lieselotte would not have done this. It was not her handwriting. And she'd said my words and news of Lukas were lifelines for her. Eventually I gave up. I stopped writing."

"I must have been five or six by then." What tickled the back of my memory? *The tramp. The tramp in the mountain grocer's. The man Mama bought food for, the one who lifted my chin . . . the man she cried over for hours. Could that have been Lukas . . . my father? Did he see me? Did he see his mother in me? Did he know who I was?* "She stayed for me."

"*Ja,* she stayed for her precious daughter."

"No wonder she hated me. She must have wished over and over that she'd aborted me." *I kept you from the man you loved — Mama, I'm so sorry!*

"What? *Nein, nein!* Lieselotte loved you with all her heart. She said it was you that kept her alive through the hell of Ravensbrück, the hope of you that kept her going to the end at Dachau. She wrote this to me!" Marta grabbed my hands and shook

577

them. "You gave her the will to live, Hannah. That is the greatest gift there is in the face of despair. It is love!"

42

Dear Hannah,

When your letter first arrived I was angry. I could not believe my brother would do such a thing. Joe loved you, and I think in his way he loved your mother. I knew all along that Lieselotte was pregnant when she and Joe married, and that she married him so she could come to America. I thought she was a gold digger, but even I know that's not fair. Your mother never cared anything about money. It was people and their needs, though she had a mighty stiff way about her.

Joe told me he'd checked, and that Lieselotte's first husband had died in the war. He said he never wanted you to know and that I was not to talk with

579

Lieselotte about any of it — the war had been so hard on her and she'd lost all her family.

In the end, all I can say is that I don't really know why he lied, except the war changed him. I could never get close to him after that like we'd been before. Joe was a good man in so many ways. You know that. You know he loved you.

I'm so sorry for the part I've played in this, Hannah. I'm so sorry that I didn't treat Lieselotte better. If you will forgive me I promise I'll do better, at least by you. I'll be a kinder, gentler person — less ready to judge things and people I don't understand.

I understand that you're this Marta woman's last living relative. But you're mine, too. Please come home, honey. I miss you so.

Lovingly,
Aunt Lavinia

I set Aunt Lavinia's letter down. I needed to separate Aunt Lavinia from Daddy Joe and all he did. I believed that she was sorry for the part she unwittingly played. I knew how easy it was to judge people based on bias and incomplete pieces of information. I'd done exactly that to Mama. Such mixed emotions and so many memories to sort through, to try to separate Daddy Joe's interpretation from what I really saw in Mama.

But it was time to go home. I'd done nearly all I'd come to do. I'd found my grandfather, though that had turned into something far different than I'd hoped or imagined, something I could not — would never — forgive him for. I'd found my true parents — as much as a person could — through Aunt Marta. And I'd grown fiercely proud of them both.

Aunt Marta gave me all of Mama's letters to read — she'd saved and pressed each one, hoping that one day Mama might return or bring me to see her. But that never happened. I pored over them, trying to absorb each word, to finally hear my mother's true voice. Her last letter had been written just before Lukas came to find us in North Carolina. I read the final paragraphs again and again:

All the years of our separation I have prayed for this, imagined this, dreamed this — that Lukas would be found alive and together we would one day hold our precious daughter, that he would see his mother's eyes in her small face, even as

I do, that we would rock our Hannah to sleep between us.

And now that Lukas himself might make my dream come true, I must stop him.

Marta, Joe will never let us go. If I ever tell Hannah about Lukas, Joe said he will leave me and take her where I will never find her. If I tell Hannah what Joe did to make me marry him, he will deny it and turn her against me. Already he coddles her and turns her head, telling her he loves her more than I do, that there is something wrong with me — that I cannot love, that I am closed off, that the war did bad things to me. How I hate him. How I hate the person I have become with him.

I am glad Mutti Kirchmann cannot see me now. She would grieve the darkness of my heart.

I am sick as I write this, Marta, and I am afraid. Every day I am afraid I will do something to lose my daughter. I dare not draw her close for fear of Joe's taking her away. I would run and find a means to return to Germany and to Lukas — my only love — in a moment, except for Hannah. I cannot leave or risk my precious daughter — our precious daughter. So many secrets . . . secrets I must carry to my grave.

This will be my last letter to you, dear sister. Joe has forbidden me to write again.

Tell Lukas not to come. Tell him I am sorry beyond measure, and that I love him with all my heart. I will love him forever.

Your sister,
Lieselotte

"Our precious daughter . . ." Mama — my poor, dear Mama. How I misjudged you! But why didn't you return to Germany after Daddy died? Was fear so braided into your being by then that you couldn't? Was it because we had no money? Did you know Lukas had died and couldn't face returning? Did you try and not know how to find Marta? I had a thousand questions that could never be answered, not this side of heaven.

But I know now that you loved me, Mama. That you put me first — even before Lukas. That you kept all these secrets because you loved me is more than I can comprehend. I'm so sorry I didn't know you better, that I didn't love you more.

Aunt Marta promised to visit me in America. I'd introduce her to Aunt Lavinia. My two aunts, my last living relatives. Carl promised to visit too, and to go with me to New York and Woodbine to meet with the remaining men and women my grandfather and Dr. Peterson had so terribly abused — a promise and plan we finalized during a walk through the Tiergarten.

"Herr Eberhardt's promised to investigate further the families we couldn't locate," I told him. "He'll return what he can, place a few pieces with museums, then handle the sale of those things not returnable, as well as the sale of the house. He's going to help me send the proceeds to Israel for Holocaust victims."

"This is good, Hannah. It is a relief that Herr Eberhardt is a good man."

I shook my head. "Grandfather was so cunning. He hired an honest man to handle day-to-day matters and create a facade of normalcy. Donating the money seems the best solution. But there's still that family to visit in Israel. Are you game?"

"It is not a game."

"That's an American expression."

"Ah, another one."

Sweet Carl. Funny Carl. How I would miss him. "I want to visit Yad Vashem while we're there. There's not enough documentary evidence to have Mama declared one of the Righteous Among the Nations — not officially. But I want to write her name, Lieselotte Kirchmann, on a stone and leave it there, in the garden. It might mean nothing to others, but I'll know it's there. And maybe Mama knows."

Carl squeezed my hand in understanding. "I am honored to go with you. And I am glad — relieved — you will allow someone else to help you carry this burden."

"I'm willing to let Herr Eberhardt do this mostly because I don't know what else to do, and I think returning all we can would have pleased Mama. I think Herr Eberhardt hopes it will bring some sort of redemption for his part too. I guess that's what we all want — some sort of redemption." I closed my eyes and turned away. *Even Joe thought he could redeem his part in the war by marrying Mama, by playing his idea of Daddy Warbucks to me. In some twisted version of the universe I understand that . . . but, oh, how I hate it. How I hate that he kept Mama and me from Lukas! The consequences of so many things can never be undone. And then there was Grandfather . . .*

"I'm still so ashamed, so angry with Grandfather," I confessed to Carl. "I feel that for all the strong Kirchmann blood I carry, and for all the good my mother did,

I'll never get rid of the grime of my grand-father. I can never do enough to make up for what he did."

"No, you cannot. There is no way you can fix what he did, or all that came afterward. You will not get rid of the grime you feel until you forgive him. For your own sake."

"I can't forgive him. I can't even think of him without having nightmares. I'll be glad to get out of that house. I'd just as soon burn it and his memory to the ground."

"Hannah —"

"Look, Carl, I appreciate all that you've done. I never would have gotten so far without your help. I care about you — I do. But please don't tell me I should forgive him or that I should quit trying to —"

"To earn your mother's love? To be as strong and brave as she? Will that in some way make up for Herr Sommer's crimes?"

I pulled my hand from Carl's arm. "No. But all my life I've wanted to do something my mother would be proud of. This is the closest I've come. Until I met Aunt Marta, I'd no idea that I was what kept Mama in America. Because of me she stayed with a man she never loved, a man who, for all his outward kindness, had lied to and tricked her, then cut her off from those who loved her — whom she loved. She was never able to be with her real husband — my own father. How do you think that makes me feel?

"Nothing I can do — not in my whole life — will be enough to make up for that. And nothing Grandfather could do — even if he'd lived another hundred years — could make up for the horrible crimes he committed. I hate him. I absolutely hate him!"

"Hannah, Hannah, you must —"

"Carl — stop. I don't want to argue with you. We must agree to disagree on this."

"For your own sake, Hannah, you need —"

"I need for you to back off, Carl. Please, please don't fight with me about this."

"I'm not fighting, I —"

"No more. I'm going back to the house to pack."

"Let me drive you."

"Space, Carl," I warned, backing up. "I just need a little space."

I threw my coat across the bed, pummeling it with my gloves and scarf. I kicked my shoes across the room so hard they bounced off the wall. I'd been hard on Carl. I didn't want to hurt him, didn't mean to hurt him. I cared for him. But his insistence that I forgive Grandfather rang insane. The man had committed — willfully — the unforgivable. I couldn't comprehend the magnitude of the wickedness he'd done to my family, to Herr Horowitz and his family, to so many others. *How many lives are destroyed when we do one wicked thing? And he never repented, never tried to undo any of it!*

If I don't stay angry, I'll crumple, and that I refuse to do.

I spent my last week going through Grandfather's desk and personal papers and met twice with Herr Eberhardt to deliver the last of the valuables I found in the house. He apologized, so very sorry for the way he'd been duped by Grandfather and Dr. Peterson and for his suspicion of my motives. He would make certain Dr. Peterson never succeeded in making a claim against the property. I left a humble lawyer and a good friend when I shook his hand goodbye.

The last morning I spent packing. My plane wouldn't leave Berlin until seven thirty that night. Carl had promised to drive me to the airport, though I'd not heard from him since our argument. We'd planned an early dinner together beforehand, but I didn't want to end on a strained or sour note, certainly not with another disagreement. I left a message with his landlady to cancel. I hoped he understood.

By noon on the day of my departure I set my bags by the front door. I'd walk out the way I came in.

At twelve thirty the phone rang.

"Hannah!" Carl sounded way too excited for a man who'd been turned down for a dinner date.

"Carl, I didn't expect to hear from you this early." The frost in my voice made me wince, but he seemed not to have heard.

"There is someone I want you to meet before you leave — someone you've got to meet."

"Thank you, but I don't want to meet anyone else. I'm tired and ready to go home. I'll see you in time for our trip to the airport." The receiver was halfway to its cradle when I heard him call again through the line.

"Hannah — please. I promise I won't badger you about anything. But this is a woman who knew your mother — a woman from Ravensbrück. I've talked with her. She's one of the sisters Frau Brunner talked about — the one who's written a book about her experiences — and she's amazing. She's very busy but she's agreed to see you this afternoon before you leave — she wants to

589

see you."

"I don't know, Carl."

"Do this for yourself, Hannah."

I didn't know what to say. I had nothing left.

"Then do it for me. Please."

43

Hannah Sterling
May 1973

Carl loaded my suitcases into his car and drove me to a late lunch at the small café where we'd stopped for luncheon and coffee so many times. All the waiters knew me — the American woman with the funny accent.

We toasted to the future, to seeing one another in New York and Woodbine, and gave wide berth to any discussion having to do with Grandfather or forgiveness or the war. But finally, my curiosity won.

"You said this woman we're going to meet has written a book about her experiences in Ravensbrück."

"*Ja*, I'm glad you asked." Carl grinned, pulling a slim volume from his coat pocket. "A bon voyage gift for you." He slid it across the table.

The Hiding Place, by Corrie ten Boom

with John and Elizabeth Sherrill. The back made it clear that the story played out during WWII. I looked up at him. "Thank you. You've read it?"

"*Nein,* not yet. But I will. In German —" he smiled — "for ease."

I couldn't help smiling in response. "I'm going to miss you."

"I hope so." His grin widened. He threaded my fingers through his own and pulled me closer, across the table. But any romantic notion stopped short when the café's clock cuckooed the time. "Two o'clock! We must go."

Out the door in five minutes, we marked record time for ending a German meal.

Carl wove through steadily growing traffic just outside the city to a large church. In America I'd have called it a cathedral. "We're going to church? I thought we were going to talk with Miss Ten Boom in her home."

"*Nein,* not her home. First we hear her speak; then we go backstage to talk with her — a rare privilege."

"She's a celebrity?"

"I think she is. But that doesn't matter. It matters only what she says, what she can tell you of your mother."

"Aunt Marta told us that."

"But she was not in Ravensbrück. Miss Ten Boom was in the camp with your mother and was friends with your grandmother. She knew them even better than Frau Brunner. And her English is *wunderbar.*"

We slipped into a pew about a third of the way from the front and on the far side. After a hymn and some introductions, which I really couldn't understand, an older lady — maybe in her seventies — walked to the pulpit. Because we were off to the side, Carl summarized and whispered translations for me.

Miss Ten Boom began with the way in which her parents had raised her, and her family's belief that the Jewish people were the apple of God's eye, His chosen people. She told how, once the Nazis occupied the Netherlands, her family helped Jews get ration books and helped them find hiding places — in their own home and among others willing to help.

"They bought food on the black market, and some in the network forged passports and identity papers. The Ten Boom family built a secret room in Corrie's bedroom and hid Jews there when the Gestapo came to raid them," Carl explained.

"They sound like Mama and the Kirchmanns," I whispered.

"*Ja,* I think so too. Very brave, like your mama."

I squeezed Carl's hand. He squeezed mine in return.

"And then one day the Gestapo came to arrest the family — the old father, Corrie, and her sister Betsie. Other family members who had helped too. Most of the Ten Boom family were taken away. Most never returned, but Corrie survived.

"She told about the family's arrest. How the father — over eighty years old — was taken to one side and told that if he agreed to behave himself he could stay and die an old man in his bed."

"Yes?"

Carl shook his head. "He told them, 'If I stay, I will open my door to anyone who needs help.' He died in prison ten days later."

I felt the stab in my heart.

"And her sister died in the camp — but not before she'd brought the light of Jesus to Barracks 28."

"Mama's barracks," I whispered. "She's the one Frau Brunner talked about."

"Shh. Let me listen."

I waited, in agony. Corrie ten Boom's expressive face, alternately smoldering and shining, told her story, even though I couldn't understand her words. Her eyes mesmerized — sometimes cold and hard, and then wide in surprise. Sometimes indignant, then warm and growing soft . . . caring, loving, kind. *Who is this woman?*

Carl stopped translating, riveted to the speaker. His face told a story too — a transformation from curious to astonished to concerned, almost angry, and then to some kind of revelation. At one point tears filled his eyes. A sacred hush swept the room before Miss Ten Boom reached some kind of climax in her talk, for a collective gasp and then a sigh ran through the tensed crowd.

While a hymn was sung Carl whispered the rest of the story into my ear — as much as he could in the time. And then he hesitated.

"What is it? What else did she say?"

"I think she should tell you — when you meet her."

"*You* tell me. She just told hundreds of people!"

But the hymn finished, and Carl shushed me. "We can go backstage now. She will see us."

Carl took my hand and I followed. My knees trembled like Jell-O. To meet another person who'd been in Ravensbrück with my mother, someone who'd been close to Grandmother Kirchmann and had done all she could to help Mama so she could carry me . . . She might know things Frau Brunner or even Aunt Marta never knew.

Carl knocked on the door of the room being used for Miss Ten Boom's dressing room.

"Come!" the voice, cheerful and warm, called us.

I'd barely entered the room when Corrie ten Boom rose, her large eyes narrowed, as if trying to see something in me that wasn't quite visible.

Her hands reached for mine. "The miracle of Ravensbrück . . . life from the depths of hell. The image of your grandmother." Twin tears teased the corners of her eyes.

I couldn't stop my own tears. "I'm sorry — I don't know why I'm crying."

"For the miracle of grace — for the realization that you are so deeply, dearly loved that God brought you to this world for a purpose, despite the demons of hell doing their best to cast you out."

That made me cry all the harder.

"Carl — that is your name, isn't it?"

Carl nodded.

"Your dear friend, Carl, told me your

story — that you have been searching for the truth of your mother and of your father, of your birth and family."

"Yes." I nodded, swiping my tears with the back of my hand.

She smiled, handing me her handkerchief.

"Oh no, I couldn't. I don't want to soil it."

She pushed it into my hand, shaking her head that it was no matter. "Your mother — so young and beautiful, so brave to have helped those she did. And your grandmother — how she loved Jesus! Light shone from her as it did from my sister, Betsie."

I breathed, trying to take in this moment, this woman who knew my mother and grandmother.

"You have a godly heritage." She smiled again. "I see your mother found her answer. God is so good!"

"Her answer?"

"She didn't know; she worried so who your father was. You could not look like his mother if you were not his child."

I gulped, so grateful for this new reassurance for me, for my mother.

"The question is, Hannah, do you bear the stamp — the resemblance — of your heavenly Father?"

"I . . . don't know. I hope so." But I did

know. I couldn't feel such turmoil and be like Him.

She nodded, considering, her brow slightly furrowed. "Then you've forgiven your mother for hiding her past? Forgiven the man who raised you for not telling you the truth? Forgiven your grandfather his cruelty?"

My nerves tightened. I glanced accusingly at Carl. He'd certainly spilled every bean. He met my gaze and never looked away. I was the one left standing . . . condemned in my own truth.

"I don't know how to answer that," I lied.

She smiled, tilting her head, as if she peered inside my brain.

I moistened my lips. There was no way to frame the truth attractively. "No . . . no." I lifted my shoulders, helpless to explain. "I forgive my mother. I wish — so much — that I could turn back the clock and talk with her, make her tell me all that happened, talk to her about my real father . . . and thank her for carrying me, for loving me enough to keep and raise me. But I don't understand why, after my father — the man who raised me — died, she didn't tell me."

Miss Ten Boom shrugged too. "Perhaps she thought it was too late, or that you wouldn't believe her. It seems she left you the clues to go in search of others who could tell you, others you might better receive this truth from."

Not believe her? Not believe such a story from Mama? That's possible. I always believed everything Daddy Joe told me. It's true; I wouldn't have believed her in a million years — not a bit of it, not if I hadn't made the journey myself. Did you know this about me, Mama? Did you know me so well?

"And the man who raised you? He loved you, provided for you?"

"Yes, but he lied and kept me from my real father — kept Mama from going to her true husband." I couldn't help the rise in my voice.

Miss Ten Boom nodded. "He has much to account for. But you — do you have peace in your anger toward him?"

I swallowed. I'd always loved Daddy, thought he was my hero, my champion against Mama. How crazy and mixed up my world was! *So, who am I to know right from wrong, truth from lies? But peace?* I shook my head. I felt no peace.

"And your grandfather."

I closed my eyes. "There is no way to forgive him — no way to comprehend what he did, what he'd do a thousand times over if given the same chance. I don't understand him at all — not what he did to Mama and my real father and his family, nor what he tried to do to me to draw me into his web."

"Selfishness is sin — ugly and dirty. You see where it leads — where it led your family. There is no way to understand the depths, the depravity, of sin."

I nodded.

"Neither is there a way to understand forgiveness from sin. We cannot do it. It is beyond our comprehension — beyond our human ability."

But she was speaking in the abstract. My face must have revealed my thoughts, my doubts, for she pulled me forward to a chair beside her own.

"Did you understand what I said tonight, from the platform, about when my family was arrested?"

Carl leaned forward. "I translated as best I could, but I did not translate that part of your story."

Corrie nodded. "When my father and Betsie and I were arrested, I did not know who had reported us. But I was certain I could not forgive that person. Because of his willful actions, my father died, my sister died, so many of my family died in the camps. But when we learned who it was, do you know what my sister said?"

I waited, then shook my head.

"She said, 'Oh, how he must be suffering! We must pray for him, Corrie.' That was my sister. It was her first thought — to pray for the wrongdoer." She leaned forward conspiratorially. "It was not my first thought."

I smiled, understanding.

"Once, when I was speaking in a church in Munich, in Germany — a place I'd begged the Lord not to send me — I saw a man, a former SS. It was the first time since Ravensbrück that I'd seen any of those who'd jailed us. I remembered him as if it were yesterday — the order to strip our clothes from our bodies, to stand naked before the leering guards . . . my poor Betsie's face.

"After the service he came up to me, bowing, smiling from ear to ear, telling me how grateful he was that he'd been forgiven — that Jesus had washed his sins away!"

My breath caught, appalled at the man's audacity and horrified that this dear woman had been made to relive that awful moment from her past, from her beloved dead sister's past.

"Do you know what he did?" she asked.

I could not imagine.

"He reached his hand for mine. He wanted to shake my hand, this guard from Ravensbrück! I could not take his hand. I did not want to take his hand."

I nodded.

"But I had traveled Europe, preaching forgiveness. I understood the need to forgive as Christ forgave us — and there I stood, unable to forgive this man who'd wronged me and my sister."

I held my breath, imagining myself turning on my heel, walking away in such a moment, vowing I could do no such thing.

"And that is when I saw my sin, my angry, vengeful thoughts, roiling and boiling in all their ugliness. *Lord Jesus,* I prayed, *forgive me! Help me to forgive this man!*"

I could never do that.

"But I felt nothing and couldn't lift my hand to take his. It would not move from my side. I prayed again — a silent prayer. *Lord Jesus, I cannot forgive this man. Give me Your forgiveness.*"

I swallowed.

"Do you know what happened? The most amazing thing — the most incredible. It began in my shoulder and traveled the length of my arm right into my hand — a current, like electricity. It passed from me to him, and with it a love in my heart for this stranger — this man who had been my enemy — that I cannot explain."

She leaned toward me. Part of me wanted to pull away.

"Do you know what this showed me? What this means, Hannah? This is proof that Jesus does not expect us to forgive in our own strength — that the hurts in this world are not healed by us, not forgiven by us, but by His great love. Jesus said to love our enemies . . . and with that command He gives us the love to do it."

We left Miss Ten Boom twenty minutes after meeting her. A car waited to take her to the next city on her tour, where she would again preach that evening about her experiences and God's extraordinary power to forgive and to heal.

The question she'd asked me . . . *"Do you want that healing?"*

Yes, of course.

"Are you willing to surrender your anger, your desire for revenge, in order to get it?"

I'd replayed Miss Ten Boom's question twenty times in my brain. If Daddy's and Grandfather's sins had been paid for by the lifeblood of Jesus, how could I ask for more? That was the question Miss Ten Boom had asked when the former guard from Ravensbrück assumed her forgiveness.

But that man had repented, had already asked forgiveness. Neither Daddy Joe nor Grandfather ever asked forgiveness — not even on their deathbeds. Didn't that make it different?

As Carl and I drove to the airport, I knew I was leaving Berlin with a new set of hatreds and angers — no longer directed toward my mother but toward her persecutors, and mine.

It must have been the same conclusion Mama came to — that she could not forgive them, that they did not deserve it, that they'd never repented, never tried to make amends. But what had that led her to but a life of bitterness?

Miss Ten Boom had said in parting that it was one thing to believe in Jesus and another to accept the abundant life He freely offered. "The only cost to you, to me," she'd said, "is complete surrender of our own notion of our rights and leadership — total abandonment into His love and grace."

Mama had never surrendered that. I knew from her letters — the ones Aunt Marta gave me. I knew from the grim line of her mouth each time I pictured her — that prison cell that held her . . . the one others built. But did she hold the key and refuse to use it? Did she understand that freedom could have been hers — in her heart if not in her circumstances?

I didn't want that bound-up, angry, agonized life. But the cost of surrender . . . what would that leave me? If I didn't keep the injustice close to my heart, who would I be? It had defined my life so long . . . toward Mama, and now toward Daddy and Grandfather. I understood Mama better in that moment than I ever had. I could not — would not — risk such vulnerability. And still, there was no peace in my soul.

I checked my ticket and luggage while Carl parked the car; then we hurried through the terminal together. I kissed Carl good-bye at the gate, but was reminded of Miss Ten Boom's inability to raise her own arm to greet the man from Ravensbrück. Carl had been my friend and confidant, the one who'd walked with me every step of this journey. I wanted to love him, did love him . . . and yet something was missing. He read the confusion, the lack of response to his passion in my face. I saw the flicker of disappointment in his eyes.

"For you, for later," he whispered and slipped a package from his coat pocket into mine.

"What?"

"*Nein* — don't open now. On the plane . . . after you leave Frankfurt."

I hugged him one last time. "I'll see you in a month for the meetings in Brooklyn and Woodbine."

"I wouldn't miss it." He smiled.

I wanted to tell him not to read more into that than I intended, but he took me in his arms and tenderly kissed me again. I tried to push him away, but he lingered, and when he finally stepped back, I didn't want him to.

The plane taxied to the end of the runway. I'd waved to Carl, standing in the terminal, as long as I could.

It had been one thing to keep him at arm's length, quite another to walk on without him.

Is this how you felt, Mama? Alone? Always alone with your secrets?

I didn't want that life sentence, didn't want to be held in a prison of my own making. I couldn't compare it to Mama's or to Miss Ten Boom's, whose enemies arrested them, tortured them. My enemies were all dead, and still they haunted me, threatened to ruin my life. And there stood Carl, ready and willing to love me with all my faults and failings. He asked only that I choose

freedom by choosing surrender to Christ —
what we both knew would make me truly
happy. *Why is it so hard?*

I leaned back against the headrest as the
plane gathered speed down the runway and
lifted into the twilight. Dutifully, I didn't
open Carl's box until I'd changed planes in
Frankfurt and was bound for London.

Once we were airborne, I pulled the small
box he'd given me from my coat pocket. I
couldn't imagine its contents. Unlocking
the tray table from the seat in front of me, I
pulled it down and untied the string around
the white box. Inside was nestled another
package wrapped in string, but I knew from
its fragrance exactly what it was. I opened
the envelope and Carl's note.

Enjoy this for me, Sweet Hannah. I'll
take just a bite . . . mmm . . . delicious.
Thank you for sharing!

God's love is like your favorite apple
strudel, Hannah. We can see it, view it
from a distance, know it is there, and,
clutching our hands, still deny ourselves.
Or we can let go of the things that bind
us so tightly and reach for this great
pleasure. We can taste it — feast on its
richness. Choose freedom and forgive-

ness. Choose life, my dear one.

All my love,

Carl

Carl. Dear Carl. Sweet and funny Carl. Always making jokes to get a point across.

Choose — as if choosing forgiveness is so easy.

My layover in London took hours, and then a cancellation and another long delay — long enough for me to think carefully through Corrie ten Boom's words and Carl's message. By the time we finally taxied down the runway and headed west, I was exhausted. I sat, still thinking, until shades went down and most of the lights went out. Passengers snored softly. I wanted the strudel. . . . I wanted life and joy in Christ, but . . .

Dear God, I can't do this alone. I can't forgive alone. I'm not even able to love alone. I'm always looking for some sign of deceit, some indication of failure or ulterior motive. First it was Mama's, then Grandfather's, now Carl's — even mine.

What is that but guilt and misery? I'm so afraid! I don't know any other way to respond but to be on my guard. I don't want to be hurt. I can't trust.

I couldn't sleep. I couldn't return to my

608

old life as my old self. A lifetime of me — angry as I was with drums always rumbling — was impossible. Throughout the long night I argued with God, begged and pleaded, then did my best to turn off my brain. But it was no use.

I couldn't move forward. I couldn't control anything or anyone. The only fragment of justice I controlled fell under the heading of mercy — returning what I could to the families wronged. But even that changed nothing. It redeemed not one solitary life, and it couldn't bring me the peace and freedom I'd hoped for, that I so desperately needed.

I lifted the window shade near dawn, just as the first streaks of pink slit the horizon. A new day . . .

Tears slipped down my cheeks. *I can't do this, Lord. The sins of my parents and grandparents are not mine to forgive. Their wrongs are not mine to redeem. Miss Ten Boom was right. Only You can forgive.*

So please, Father — Heavenly Father — forgive me my fear of . . . everything. Of not knowing who I am without my anger. Forgive my bitterness, my loneliness. I surrender my hatreds, my longings, to You.

Empty me of me, and fill me with Your Spirit. I don't know who I will be without this load of guilt and fear and anger. I can't imagine what it will be like to not be in control, always trying to win favor, to earn love — Yours, or that of the people in my life. I might slip up from time to time — might have to surrender again. But I want to know You. Not just believe in You, not just believe You exist and have redeemed me. Let me walk with You; show me this abundant life. I won't — please help me — I won't waste one more day trying to earn what You've already given me!

I closed my eyes and slept, perhaps only moments. When I opened them, morning dawned — a full sunrise — outside my window, and in my heart. Peace I'd not known flooded the recesses of my brain, my soul.

Other window shades lifted. Passengers around me stretched, visited the lavatory, picked up newspapers.

My heart was still singing, warm and full, when the stewardess stopped with her cart and asked if I wanted coffee.

"Yes, *danke schön.*" Something hot would be wonderful. It had been a long, a hard, a perfect night.

"And for breakfast, the choices are —"

I shook my head, smiling. "*Nein, danke schön.* I think I'll just have a bit of this apple strudel — the richest and sweetest in the world. . . . A gift from my love."

NOTE TO READERS

In 2009 I walked the paths of Ravensbrück — the largest WWII women's concentration camp in Germany, where approximately 132,000 women and children were incarcerated, and surviving records estimate that between 50,000 and 92,000 women died of starvation, disease, experimentation, gassing, overwork, and despair. What I learned and saw in that concentration camp museum setting would fill a book. What I came away with were questions: *How did survivors reclaim their lives? How did they or their families come to terms with what happened here? Did they ever forgive their captors? How?*

As I stood at the memorial, I grasped the cold and lifeless hand of one of the Two Women Standing sculpture and made a vow that I would never forget, and that I would one day tell her story.

Something else I learned while in Germany was that the war bred secrets in families — secrets of good deeds unrewarded and secrets of evil deeds never discovered.

There's something about keeping secrets that changes us at our core. The need to protect our families or ourselves, and consequently to keep knowledge from or deceive others, perpetuates a twisted trail.

Sometimes secrets die with their holder or fade away barely noticed. But sometimes secrets carry grievous weights and pass their consequences, directly or indirectly, into future generations — lies, betrayals, affairs, abuse, fortunes made or lost, addiction, abandonment, divorce, abortion, debt, treason, disease, murder, theft . . . the possibilities are endless. And sometimes, secrets are not so secret as we believe.

In *Secrets She Kept,* Hannah Sterling is propelled by a longing for a relationship with her mother that never existed in life. After her mother's death, Hannah determines to peel back the layers of time and unravel her mother's mysterious past in hope of understanding her.

What Hannah discovers shocks her, undermining her confidence in herself and her family, and in her ability to discern truth and goodness in others. She learns that she's not viewed either of her parents or their world objectively. She learns that she, too, has contributed to the dysfunction in her family by her own choices and by her reactions to her parents' choices. Unwittingly, she bears the consequences of her parents' sins.

It's the story of our fallen human nature. Numbers 14:18 (ESV) reminds us, "The LORD is slow to anger and abounding in steadfast love, forgiving iniquity and transgression, but he will by no means clear the guilty, visiting the iniquity of the fathers on the children, to the third and the fourth generation."

Like Hannah, we learn that in seeking redemption for the sins of our families or ourselves, we cannot redeem ourselves or change the past; we can't even release ourselves from the weight of our own guilt. Our earnest work or most noble actions do not provide restitution to others. Like Hannah, we find our families — and ourselves — perpetuating sin and in desperate need of forgiveness.

Like Hannah, we're also faced with the need to forgive others. But forgiveness goes against our grain, against our sense of personal justice and entitlement. Forgiveness requires letting go of wrongs done to us, requires surrender of tension, anger, even hatred, and a surrender of our right to collect debts or exact justice.

Holding on to guilt or grievances, no matter how justified they seem, eats away at our heart and life like cancer. Withholding forgiveness is tantamount to carrying a load of boulders on our back, or shackling our feet with balls and chains. Every day is exhausting, every breath a chore. Forgiveness, received and given from the Lord, frees us for abundant life in ways nothing else can. But how do we get there?

Release — forgiving or being forgiven — can't be exacted or even bought. It's beyond human ability or comprehension. It's divine. That's what I learned from Corrie ten Boom (*The Hiding Place*) as she forgave the guard from Ravensbrück. She didn't do it — couldn't do it — alone. She surrendered her own sin and inabilities to Christ and asked that He do it through her. Jesus was her real, her true hiding place. He is ours, too.

This is Hannah's story, and it's yours and mine. Forgiveness requires our confession that we can't perfect or fix things, our repentance for our own sins and shortcomings, our belief in the saving sacrifice of Jesus Christ to pay our debts, and our daily walk in the newness of life only He can provide.

It's a lesson we learn and live, then repeat again and again. Praise God!

I love hearing from you, learning your stories, and sharing your walk. Visit me anytime at my website, www.cathygohlke .com, or on Facebook at CathyGohlke-Books.

God's blessings and grace for you,
Cathy

DISCUSSION QUESTIONS

1. Have you ever wished for a better relationship with a parent or family member but not known how to achieve one? Did you find a new path to further your relationship? How did you go about it?

2. Hannah grew up thinking of Joe Sterling as "my hero, my champion against Mama." Why do you think she accepted what Joe told her about her mother at face value? Has anyone ever influenced your view of someone else in a similar way?

3. Why do you think Joe manipulated Lieselotte into marrying him, and into staying with him despite his promise to release her once she regained her health? How did this information change your view of Joe?

4. Do you agree or disagree with Lieselotte's

decision not to confide in her daughter about her past and the identity of her biological father? Did Lieselotte do the right thing in staying with Joe? Please explain.

5. What do you think about Hannah's decision to investigate her mother's past? Would you have followed such a trail?

6. Do Lieselotte's feelings about her father and brother change as the war progresses and their involvement with the Nazi Party intensifies? Do you think Lukas continues to consider Rudy a friend? Why or why not?

7. Were you surprised to learn that Herr Sommer disowned Lieselotte and abandoned her in Ravensbrück? Why do you think he makes this decision? Do you see evidence that he regrets this course of action later in his life?

8. What do you think motivates Dr. Peterson to manipulate Herr Sommer and his family? How does Herr Sommer, in turn, manipulate Dr. Peterson?

9. Hannah hesitates to accept what she

learns about her grandfather's role during the war and struggles to know how to interact with him once she knows the truth. If you discovered that a relative had committed a heinous crime, how would that information change your relationship?

10. When Lieselotte says she wants to assist the Kirchmanns in their work to help Jewish people in hiding, Lukas challenges her, asking if she feels the Lord has called her to this. She thinks, "If I said yes, I would be lying. If I said no, would they let me help? I could not lie to Lukas or his parents . . . nor could I tell him — explain to him — that if I did nothing, I would die inside. I would burst and die of loneliness, of anger, of frustration, of helplessness." Finally she tells Lukas, "I only know I must do something that helps someone. Everything I see frightens me nearly to death. If I am caught, I would rather die for something than live for nothing." Have you ever felt this way? What did it propel you to do?

11. Our regrets often come from mistakes we've made, but Carl is haunted more by the family's inaction — as are his parents, to some degree. Have you ever regretted

your own failure to take action?

12. Have you read Corrie ten Boom's *The Hiding Place* or seen the film? If so, how did her story impact you? Do you think you would help others as the Ten Boom family did? What do you think of her forgiveness of the guard from Ravens-brück? How would you have responded in the same situation?

13. Hannah learns that it is one thing to believe in the forgiveness, redemption, and saving power of Jesus Christ and another thing to fully surrender and walk in newness of life. Discuss the difference and how each one is achieved. Why is it so difficult to surrender our rights in order to forgive or be forgiven?

ABOUT THE AUTHOR

Cathy Gohlke is the two-time Christy Award–winning author of the critically acclaimed novels *Saving Amelie, Band of Sisters, Promise Me This* (listed by *Library Journal* as one of the best books of 2012), *William Henry Is a Fine Name,* and *I Have Seen Him in the Watchfires,* which also won the American Christian Fiction Writers' Book of the Year Award and was listed by *Library Journal* as one of the best books of 2008.

Cathy has worked as a school librarian, drama director, and director of children's and education ministries. When not traipsing the hills and dales of historic sites, she, her husband, and their dog, Reilly, make their home in northern Virginia and the Jersey Shore, enjoying time with their grown children and granddaughter. Visit her website at www.cathygohlke.com.